R.J. Ellory is the author of nineteen novels published by Orion UK, and his work has been translated into twenty-six languages. He has won the Quebec Booksellers' Prize, the Livre De Poche Award, the Strand Magazine Novel of The Year, the Mystery Booksellers of America Award, the Inaugural Nouvel Observateur Prize, the Quebec Laureat, the Prix Du Roman Noir, the Plume d'Or for Thriller Internationale 2016, the Theakston's Crime Novel of the Year, both the St. Maur and Villeneuve Readers' Prizes, the Balai d'Or 2016, and has twice won the Grand Prix des Lecteurs. He has been shortlisted for two Barrys, the 813 Trophy, the European Du Point, and two Crime Writers' Association UK awards.

Among other projects, he is the guitarist and vocalist of The Whiskey Poets, and has recently completed the band's third album. His musical compositions have been featured in films and television programs in more than forty countries. He has two television series and two films in pre-production, and has recently premiered his first short film, 'The Road to Gehenna'.

Also by R.J. Ellory

Candlemoth
Ghostheart
A Quiet Vendetta
City of Lies
A Quiet Belief in Angels
A Simple Act of Violence
The Anniversary Man
Saints of New York
Bad Signs
A Dark and Broken Heart
The Devil and the River
Carnival of Shadows
Mockingbird Songs
Kings of America
Three Bullets
Proof of Life
The Darkest Season
The Last Highway

NOVELLAS

Three Days in Chicagoland:
1. The Sister
2. The Cop
3. The Killer

THE BELL TOWER

R.J.ELLORY

ORION

An Orion paperback

First published in Great Britain in 2024
by Orion Fiction,
This paperback edition published in 2024
by Orion Fiction,
an imprint of The Orion Publishing Group Ltd.,
Carmelite House, 50 Victoria Embankment
London EC4Y 0DZ

An Hachette UK Company

1 3 5 7 9 10 8 6 4 2

A CIP catalogue record for this book is
available from the British Library.

ISBN (Paperback) 978 1 39871 0399

Typeset at The Spartan Press Ltd,
Lymington, Hants

Printed and bound in Great Britain by Clays Ltd,
Elcograf S.p.A.

www.orionbooks.co.uk

Acknowledgements

As always, I would like to express my profound gratitude to Orion, Sonatine, De Fontein and the many publishers around the world who continue to support my literary endeavours with such enthusiasm and passion.

Endless thanks to my readers for their continued loyalty and generosity, without whom I would not be able to spend my life doing something that I love.

To my family – tolerant, forgiving and patient – because living with a writer is like living with several different people, each of whom is just a little crazy.

I

August 1976

The night before the shooting, Garrett Nelson slept like a man awaiting his own execution.

Varnished with sweat, the damp sheets a tourniquet around his awkward limbs, he twisted in and out of wakefulness. Jolting upright with a start, he was sure of sounds that then proved to be nothing. Actuality and imagination, each of them reflected in a strange funhouse of mirrors, became seamless. In one moment, he believed himself to be elsewhere; in another he was younger; in yet another he was walking through a darkened house looking for someone whose name he didn't know. Shadows moved with him, but he could not see who cast them.

Later, he would think those fractured and half-forgotten dreams were a premonition of what lay ahead, both in the following days and subsequent months.

When light at last separated the sky from the land, Nelson rose and showered. He tried to remember what he had seen, the sounds he'd heard, but they evaporated like mist from the surface of a river.

Nelson had been Deputy Sheriff of De Soto County, Florida, for a little more than eight months. His predecessor, Walt Barrow, had served only one four-year term, and then – his wife pregnant with their third child – he'd been persuaded by his in-laws to pursue a less demanding and potentially dangerous career. As far as Nelson knew, Barrow now worked in sanitation and was as miserable as a man could be.

At the end of that same term, Sheriff Eugene Bigsby had been re-elected for a second. He was a fair and honest man. When he asked Nelson if he would step up to the plate as deputy, Nelson had no difficulty in accepting.

Nelson possessed no yearning for the post of Sheriff. It seemed to him an administrative function, each action and re-action answerable to some faceless politician. The duty of law was both public and personal, and no distant bureaucrat could profess to understand how the world worked when their own world was so divorced. The decisions a man made when faced with the worst that humanity had to offer were his and his alone. Ultimately, a man answered only to himself and the law. Only he would ever know if he did right or wrong.

A little after eight on the morning of Wednesday 4th, Nelson left his house on the outskirts of Fort Haines for Arcadia and the Sheriff's Department.

The sky promised nothing but more humidity and heat. Here in Florida, storms did not clear the air but served only to thicken it.

As was his routine, Nelson stopped at a diner on Lakes Avenue to get coffee and a bear claw. Timing was everything. Too early and the coffee was a brackish stew that had simmered through the early hours. Too late and it was strong enough to strip the rust from highway signs.

April Sherman was at the counter. She and Nelson had dated a couple of times in high school. She was no longer a Sherman, having married into the Griffin family. April's husband – an auto mechanic someplace down off of North East Roan – was a drunk. Living with someone like that left you with a strange kind of hopelessness. April had that on her like a shadow. With two little ones to fend for, she was tied into that deal for keeps.

Nelson took a bar stool at the counter.

'Hey, April. How's tricks?'

April managed a tired smile as she bagged his pastry. 'Keepin' the train on the tracks. You know how it is, Garrett.'

Glancing back from the door as he left, Nelson saw she was still watching him. He remembered her as a teenager. She was a firework in a bottle. Whatever had lit that girl's spirit had long-since been dulled by the blunt reality of living.

Fort Haines sat northeast of Arcadia. Much the same as any other town in the Florida Heartland, it had little to recommend it. Looking something like the abandoned back lot of a once-grand film studio, it featured buildings started and left incomplete. With time, those buildings took on the appearance of things going to ruin rather than things unfinished. With its fair share of juvenile delinquency, drug dealers, liquor store robberies, domestic violence, abandoned children and auto theft, the task of policing it was a matter of predictable routine. Just like Haines City, a good seventy miles north by crow, it had been named after Confederate Colonel Henry Haines. Haines City itself was a different animal. Back a couple of years, they'd opened Circus World, some Ringling Brothers enterprise that generated huge sums from tourist revenue. Nelson didn't doubt that such an investment had brought with it that usual roll-call of crooks and thieves. The brighter the lights, the darker the shadows. As of now and for the foreseeable future, he was just fine where he was.

Arriving at the office, Sheriff Bigsby was standing in the doorway behind reception.

'Come on back, Garrett,' he said soberly.

Nelson followed him, glancing at the receptionist, Marla Cooper. Marla, now in her early fifties, had been holding the fort for more than two decades.

'Maybe you're gettin' yourself fired,' she said. 'Maybe he heard about your gamblin' and drinkin' and womanisin'.'

'Yeah, an' maybe we'll add a murder to that list just before I leave.'

'My boys'd come for you. They'll be fishin' your guts out of Lake Placid.'

'Garrett!' Bigsby hollered from his office.

'Run along now, sonny,' Marla said.

'How any man could love you, I do not know,' Nelson replied.

Bigsby was standing by the window. He turned as Nelson entered.

'We got ourselves a mess over in Highlands County,' he said. 'Sheriff there, you know him?'

'Sam Cox. Know of him, sure.'

'He's a man down. Asked for our help with somethin'.'

Nelson took a seat.

'What's goin' on?'

'Don't have all the details, but it's drugs. Truckstop off 27 near Venus. Seems to be a switching point for cargo. Shipments coming up from Naples. Sam thinks they're getting stuff in across the Gulf by boat, unloading it, then by road to Orlando. Changing vehicles en route. He's got DEA involved, Feds more an' likely, but he wants his own presence. Asked if I could send you over to pitch in.'

'If they've got DEA and Feds, why does he need Sheriff's Department?'

'Hell, I don't know, Garrett. It's Sam's bust, I guess. You know how folks are. They get territorial about this stuff. Anyway, he's an old friend, and he asked me for help. I ain't gonna tell him no.'

'Sure, no problem. You want me to head over there now?'

'Yeah, soon as. Go to the office in Sebring. If they need you to stay over a day or two, they'll get you a place. Keep Marla up to speed.'

Nelson got up.

'I know you'll do a good job, Garrett, but keep your wits about you. Drugs is bad business and it's bad people who do it.'

2

Nelson took 70 east, then headed north on 27 once past Lake Placid.

Arriving at the Highlands County Sheriff's Office a little after ten, he was ushered into a briefing room.

Sam Cox was holding court.

'Sheriff Bigsby send you over, son?' Cox asked.

'Yes, sir. Deputy Nelson.'

'Welcome to the party. Take a seat.'

Nelson did as instructed. He surveyed the room. Eight uniformed men sat around the table, a further two suits stood with their backs to the window. Nelson guessed they were federal.

'Now, this is a DEA operation,' Cox said. 'We ain't here to give anything but support. Last thing we need is heroics and drama.' Cox nodded toward the suits. 'Florida Bureau is here in an advisory capacity, but the Drug people take the lead on this, no matter what happens, okay?'

There was a murmur of consent from the gathering.

Cox turned to a map of the area around Venus. Beside it were photos of the truckstop in question.

'We got four trucks,' Cox explained. 'Two men per cab, a third in the trailer. There are three ways out of there. North and south on 27, then west maybe three or four miles to the junction of 17.

From there, 731 is a straight run south into Glades County. That's wild country, as you know. There's cars all around that truckstop, couple o' bikes too. We know there's keys in them and they're fuelled up. You're gonna have a dozen men doin' everythin' possible to evade capture. We got ourselves a bottleneck here, so there's a hope we can corral 'em up, but that could also work against us. These ain't the sort of fellers who are gonna give it up easy for a quiet life in Southern State.'

Cox paused and looked around the room.

'Any questions?'

There were none.

'Okay, so you all know who you're riding with 'cept for you, Deputy Nelson.'

Cox indicated a man across the table.

'That there's Travis Faulkner. He's one o' mine. You're goin' out to where 17 and 731 meet west of Venus. The likelihood of you seein' anythin' but countryside is slim, but you never know. Keep your wits about you. We're all on the same radio channel. Anyone gets out of there, it's gonna be your job to stop 'em.'

Nelson nodded at Faulkner. Faulkner raised his hand in acknowledgement.

'Those trucks're comin' in around three,' Cox added. 'That's the schedule they work on. Everyone needs to be established by noon at the latest.'

Out behind the office, Nelson waited for Faulkner to appear. The other men dispersed in twos and threes. The Feds hung back and had words with Cox.

'So what did you do to get dragged into this mess?' Faulkner asked as soon as he came out of the door.

'Dumb luck, I guess,' Nelson replied.

'Well, I reckon we got ourselves a few hours of nothin'

followed by a few more of the same.' He smiled, extended his hand. 'Travis,' he said.

'Garrett,' Nelson replied, and shook the man's hand.

'Let's get your gear and head out. We can stop by a place I know and get some coffee and sandwiches.'

Travis Faulkner was personable and talkative. He was a handful of years younger than Nelson, and had been in the Department just shy of a decade.

'Never wanted to do nothin' else,' he said, 'save get drunk and fool around. But hell, you can only do that for so long before you wind up in too much trouble to get out of. Now I got myself a nice girl, a place to live, and we's set on havin' ourselves a family. You got yourself a girl?'

'No,' Nelson said. 'I'm still workin' on that one.'

'You don't want a family?'

'I've thought about it, sure.'

'Well, maybe you need to think about it some more. Only thing a man can't beat is the passage of time.'

Nelson didn't reply. He looked out of the window.

'Hell, it ain't none of my damned business,' Faulkner said. 'We ain't known each other but a minute. I don't mean to get all up in your face.'

'It's not a problem,' Nelson said. 'And you're right. Maybe I should think about it some more.'

The car slowed, started to turn.

'Well, all we need to think about right now is those sandwiches. This here's the best place in the county for pulled pork an' slaw.'

Faulkner and Nelson arrived at their assigned station off of 17 and 731 well before noon.

Faulkner radioed in to confirm their arrival.

The day was humid, the temperature in the high eighties. It was a choice between sitting in the car with the fan circulating steam or remaining outside and at the mercy of mosquitoes, midges and chiggers.

An hour passed, and then a second. Every thirty minutes or so, Faulkner would radio in to report that nothing was happening.

Their car was off beneath an overhang of trees, visible solely for the few seconds it would take to pass it. Aside from two pickups and a motorcycle, the only other movement on the road was a child on a bright yellow bicycle. Moving like molasses, that bicycle appeared to their left and made its slow-motion way across their field of vision. The boy riding it couldn't have been more than eight or ten. Where he'd come from and where he was going was anyone's guess. It was an incongruous sight, and both Nelson and Faulkner followed his laborious progress for a good three or four minutes without saying a word.

When the boy spotted the patrol car he came to a halt. He stayed motionless, straddling the bike and looking at them intently, as surprised to see them as they were to see him. He just stared for a good thirty seconds, and then he slowly raised his hand and waved.

Without thinking, both Nelson and Faulkner raised their hands and waved back.

The boy started off again, moving even more slowly than before.

'What the hell?' Faulkner said.

'Maybe that was their point man,' Nelson said.

'Then I'm guessin' that'd be the outlaw, Babyface Redneck.'

Nelson laughed. Faulkner too. They spent the next fifteen minutes making up names for a notorious mob of four-foot gangsters.

3

The first indication that things had gone awry came over the radio just before three-thirty.

The sound of muffled gunfire was unmistakable between the frantic and urgent calls for back-up.

Faulkner tried to reach Sheriff Cox but to no avail. He suggested they head back towards the truckstop to give assistance.

'We stay here,' Nelson said.

'You hear that?' Faulkner asked. 'Sounds like they need all the help they can get.'

'I hear it, Travis, but we need to stay put in case anyone makes it out of there.'

They went back and forth on it and finally reached a compromise. They would head towards the truckstop, maintaining no more than ten or fifteen miles an hour. The road was narrow, and if something was coming their way they could turn and block the escape route.

They started moving a little after three forty-five. Nelson drove. Faulkner kept trying to reach Cox.

At 3.51, a message came through to them directly from Cox's deputy, Scott Helm.

'Travis? Travis, you there?'

Faulkner fumbled with the radio, dropped it. Nelson came to a stop.

'That you, Scott?'

'Got a car coming your way,' Helm said. 'All hell broke loose. Got a bunch of men down. I think Sheriff Cox got hit.'

'What car?' Nelson asked.

Faulkner relayed the question.

'Christ, I don't know, Travis. It's dark. Black, maybe. It's gonna come right at you, and it's gonna be fast.'

There was more gunfire – short bursts, and then a single crack. The radio went dead.

'Scott? Scott, you still there?'

Faulkner released the call button. He looked at Nelson.

'I'm backing up,' Nelson said.

Reversing the car and then turning sideways to block the road, Nelson switched off the engine. Exiting the vehicle, he told Faulkner to get both shotguns.

Moments later, the pair of them crouching at either end of the car – Nelson taking cover behind the hood, Faulkner behind the trunk – they waited.

Nelson felt his heart in his chest. His mouth was dry, his hands slick. He wiped them on his pants, held the gun steady, looking back along the road in the direction they'd come.

He looked at Faulkner. Faulkner's face was bleached of color.

'Stay with it, Travis,' he said. 'They ain't gettin' past us.'

Faulkner nodded involuntarily. Everything about the man exuded blind panic.

More than ten years in the Sheriff's Department, Nelson could count on one hand the number of times he'd had to draw his sidearm. Only once had he fired it, and then it had been nothing but a warning shot. This was now gearing itself up to be a stand-off, and the man to his right seemed even less assured than himself about how this would play out.

The air was heavy and hard to breathe; perhaps nothing more than the tension of the situation, but Nelson felt his chest rising and falling far faster than normal. Crouching there, he was aware of every muscle, every sinew, every nerve. He was wound tighter than a clock spring.

When the sound of the engine became audible, something changed.

'Here we go,' Faulkner said.

'Easy now,' Nelson replied. He pulled the stock of the shotgun tighter into his shoulder.

They saw the dust before they saw the vehicle. Helm had been right. It was coming at speed.

Nelson leaned into the car and switched on the cherry bars.

The sound of the approaching engine grew louder. It would crest a rise in the road just a couple of hundred yards away, and – once the police car was sighted – they would need another twenty or thirty yards to come to a stop. And that was if they chose to stop. Each side of the road gave onto rough scrubland, much of it waterlogged and thick with underbrush. An evasive maneuver to skirt the patrol car and make it back onto the road would not be wise, but desperate people rarely made rational decisions. The sole intention of the occupants would be to evade capture. If officers had been killed back at the truckstop, then this was already a capital offence. A chance of escape, even if they risked their own lives in the process, was a far better option than the inevitable consequence of arrest.

'Don't fire unless they try to get past,' Nelson said.

Faulkner didn't respond.

'Travis!'

Faulkner snapped to.

'You hear me?'

'Yes, yes, I hear you,' Faulkner said.

The car came into view through a tornado of dust. Almost

without hesitation, the brakes were applied and the car started to turn.

'They're heading off the road!' Nelson shouted.

The sound of the oncoming vehicle was a roar in Nelson's ears. He heard nothing else. He rolled sideways and away from the hood of the patrol car. He was up on his knees, the shotgun levelled. He was unaware of Faulkner, seeing nothing but what was directly ahead of him. Steadying himself against the fender, he aimed for a point beyond the edge of the road across which the car would pass.

The thunder of the suspension as the car headed into the scrubland was punctuated by the sudden retort of a pistol. A bullet shattered the rear passenger window of the patrol car.

Nelson glanced back. Faulkner was flat to the ground.

'The other side!' Nelson shouted.

Faulkner hesitated before moving, but then he was on his feet, ducking low and moving around the trunk of the patrol car.

Nelson aimed for the rear wheels of the car. He fired, fired again. The second shot took out the taillight and part of the wheel arch, but the car didn't slow.

The engine screamed, the wheels fighting to gain traction on the wet ground.

Nelson got to his feet but stayed low, using the hood to support his gun, releasing another shot that hit the trunk. He aimed higher, took out the rear window, and then dropped to the ground as another volley of pistol shots erupted from the back seat.

The car was almost past them, rapidly gaining speed and set to make it back onto the road.

Nelson moved quickly, Faulkner in lockstep behind him, and just as the car came back out of the scrub, the front tires once again meeting the road and gaining purchase, they fired in unison. The rear driver's side wheel blew out, the rubber spiralling off the hub. The metal hit the hard surface. A Catherine wheel of sparks erupted.

Faulkner fired again, hitting the rear door broadside. The car slewed, out of control now, and spun twice before hitting the opposite edge of the road and flipping onto its side.

The engine still running, the wheels still spinning, a wide cloud of dust obscuring their view, both Nelson and Faulkner hung back, shotguns shouldered, awaiting any sign of movement.

Nelson indicated that Faulkner should approach from the rear. Faulkner moved cautiously.

Moving to the left and just as tentatively as Faulkner, Nelson made his way along the road until he stood parallel to the front of the car. If anyone was alive in there, they would have to come up and out of the side of the car. Such a thing was unlikely considering the force with which the thing had overturned, but there was also the possibility that an occupant could have been thrown clear. Barely six feet from the edge of the road, Nelson slowed down.

Still there was no sound beyond the engine, now a faint rumble, and the still-revolving wheels, the spiral of rubber from the blown tire slapping against the wheel arch.

Nelson reached the front of the vehicle. The windscreen was cracked, but within he could make out the slumped form of the driver. The pistol shots had come from the back seat. Whoever had fired them could still be in there, still conscious, all set to let loose again in some futile attempt to evade the law.

'If someone is back there, show yourself!' Nelson shouted. 'Ain't no way out of this! You got a weapon, you better set it down and show your hands!'

Still, there was nothing. The wheels had stopped moving. The sound of the engine was a faint growl.

Faulkner had come full circle and was facing the roof of the car.

'I'm guessin' they're dead or out cold,' he said.

'I can see the driver,' Nelson replied. 'Can't see anyone else right now.'

'Gonna push the car back over,' Faulkner said. 'Give me a hand.'

Setting down their shotguns, Nelson and Faulkner leant their weight against the upper edge of the roof and the car fell back onto its wheels. Even as it toppled, they stepped back, picked up their guns, and levelled them at the rear window.

Whoever had been in the back seat was not visible.

'Behind the front seats, more likely,' Faulkner said.

'Open the back door,' Nelson said. 'Slowly. And stay down.'

Nelson moved forward, the barrel of his gun pointing into the well behind the seats as Faulkner grasped the door handle.

'After three,' Nelson said.

Faulkner lost his footing. The door swung wide. Nelson's attention was caught by the glint of sunlight off the wing mirror. It was a split-second distraction, but that second threw off his concentration.

Even as he saw the movement near the floor of the car, even as his finger tightened on the trigger, the flash and snap of the pistol came fractionally ahead of his own weapon.

A round of double-aught buck from a Mossberg 590A1 riot gun tore into the head and upper body of the man in the rear of the vehicle. At such close range, the damage was both devastating and immediately fatal. In that moment, reeling back from the door, Nelson thought it was the shotgun's recoil that had thrown him. Only when he was on the ground did he understand that he'd been hit.

The gunman's last act, firing low and no more than four feet from Nelson, had been to shatter Nelson's right-side femoral shaft and dislocate the femur from the pelvis. The pain, searing through his entire body like a ragged blade, meant that consciousness lasted a mere thirty seconds.

The last thing he heard was Faulkner's voice – 'Stay with me, Garrett... stay with me for God's sake...' – echoing ever more faintly as he was swallowed by an abyss of blackness and silence.

4

'You are a very lucky man,' the surgeon said.

His name was Elliott Gardner. He wore a suit beneath his white lab coat. With his fine-rimmed spectacles and his thin grey beard, he possessed the demeanor of a retired schoolteacher.

Withdrawing a pen from his jacket pocket, he held it vertically.

'This is the femur,' he said. 'It's your thigh bone, basically. At the top there's a ball and socket connection to the pelvis. At the bottom, it's connected by cartilage to the tibia and fibula. The shaft of thigh bone is the strongest bone in the human body. It can withstand a huge amount of pressure and force.'

Gardner paused and smiled. 'However, a .44-caliber bullet at such close range was forceful enough to fracture it. Which is what has happened to you.'

Nelson, his mind clouded with painkillers, frowned.

'And how exactly does this make me lucky?' he asked.

'Because of the femoral artery,' Gardner said. He traced a line down and around the length of his pen. 'Had the bullet cut this artery, even nicked it, the blood loss would have been catastrophic. Compromise the integrity of that artery, and people go unconscious and die within minutes.'

'I am thinking that not getting shot at all would have made me the lucky one,' Nelson said.

'Yes, of course, but I understand that some of your colleagues lost their lives.'

'Yes,' Nelson said. 'That's what I was told.'

'Then you are indeed lucky, Deputy Nelson.'

Nelson didn't respond. He'd been in the St. Petersburg hospital close to a week, much of that time so submerged beneath anaesthetic after-effects and morphine that he'd lost track of time. He knew that Travis Faulkner had come to see him. He'd been the one who'd told him that Sam Cox had died of his injuries. One of the DEA agents and another Highland County Officer had also been killed in the truckstop gun battle.

'You know Hemingway?' Gardner asked. 'He said, "The world breaks everyone and afterward many are strong at the broken places." Bones are like that. They heal, but it takes time, of course. And then, in some cases, they are indeed stronger. You now have a metal pin running through your femur. You won't be able to put your weight on it for six weeks or more. You'll need a wheelchair, and then you'll walk with crutches. You'll need physiotherapy, and it will be demanding. It can take as much as six months for full recovery, but we need to maintain regular check-ups to ensure there is no permanent nerve or muscle damage.'

'How long do I have to lie here?' Nelson asked.

'A few more days,' Gardner said, 'and then we'll transfer you to an open ward. After a week or so, and as long as everything is in order, you'll be able to go home.'

'So, I'm looking at six months before I can go back to work?'

Nelson knew what was coming before Gardner uttered the words.

'This injury has permanent consequences. Even if there are no complications, you'll more than likely walk with a pronounced limp. For a long time, vigorous exercise, running, other such things will be out of the question. The simple truth, Deputy, is that it's highly unlikely that you'll be considered medically fit to resume your previous line of work.'

'That's all I know.'

Gardner reached for Nelson's notes at the foot of the bed. Scanning them, he said, 'You're thirty-nine years old. Your general health is good. How long you have been in the Sheriff's Department?'

'Eleven, close to twelve years.'

'And before that?'

'A whole bunch of things. Drove a truck, worked in factories, a couple of years on a car production line.'

'So law enforcement isn't all you know.'

A wave of nausea rose from Nelson's gut and filled his chest. He wanted to sleep. He wanted to disappear. He wanted to go back in time and tell Eugene Bigsby that someone else should be sent to Sebring.

'You'll need to make decisions,' Gardner said, 'but they don't need to be made now. The only thing we need to focus on is your recovery and rehabilitation.'

Nelson felt like he was drowning. Flashes of sound and color interrupted any sequitur train of thought.

He could smell cordite, gasoline and sweat. He could feel the spray of blood as it erupted within the confines of the vehicle. He remembered the way in which the man's head had almost evaporated in a hail of buckshot in the back of the car.

In that moment, the face of the perpetrator became the face of his own father.

The faint white ghost of Elliott Gardner grew smaller as he walked away. The sound of voices became a wash of unintelligible noise, an overlapping series of whispers, and somewhere within that, he could hear the faint echo of gunshots.

There was the beginning of things and the end of things. Everything in between was pain and shadows.

*

On the 12th of August, Nelson was moved out of post-op to intensive care. On the 14th, he was moved to a general ward.

Gardner told him they would be reducing his painkillers over the next week to ten days.

'These things are highly addictive,' Gardner explained. 'The consequences of prescription medication dependency are just as debilitating and life-threatening as any other narcotic, legal or illegal. You will recover your strength if you do what's asked of you, but you have to appreciate that this cannot be rushed. In my experience, those who recover most rapidly are those who have a reason to recover. That reason has to be your own. Only you can decide that.'

'I just want to go home,' Nelson said. 'Right now, that's all I want to do.'

'You live alone?'

'Yes.'

'No wife, no family, no girlfriend?'

'No.'

'And you have interests, other activities besides work?'

'Like what?'

'Oh, I don't know. Reading, hiking, restoring vintage automobiles. The things that people do.'

'I don't have anything like that.'

'Then you should find something,' Gardner said. 'It will be some months before you are fully mobile again, and you need to occupy your hands and your mind with something constructive.'

'I'll give it some thought.'

Gardner nodded understandingly. 'Do you feel depressed?'

'No. Frustrated, sure. Not depressed.'

'Are you worried about the future? About what will happen, where you'll find work?'

'I have some money saved,' Nelson said. 'And I guess I'll get some kind of medical pension from the Sheriff's Department. I have time to figure it out.'

'You do, yes, but you won't make it through this on your own. No matter how resilient and determined you are, your life needs to be something more than drinking beer and watching TV.'

'Why does it matter to you what I do?' Nelson asked.

'Because your mental and emotional welfare has a great deal to do with your physical welfare. They are very much connected. The more reasons a person has to get well, the more rapidly they'll get well. It's not complicated. There are endless studies on the subject.'

Nelson didn't respond.

'The day after tomorrow you'll start work with your physiotherapist. A week, maybe ten days of that, and if you're doing well we'll release you. You'll need to be back for sessions twice, maybe three times a week. You have someone who can bring you here?'

Nelson shook his head.

'Then we'll get some transport arranged. There'll be a provision for that in your medical cover.'

'Okay.'

'You have any questions for me?'

'No, but I guess you'll be around if I think of any.'

Later, in the vague separation between wakefulness and sleep, Nelson's mind was crowded with images. For the most part, they made no sense, but there were moments of seeming lucidity that possessed as much substance as reality. He saw himself standing in a field, his arms extended, a complex, slow-motion cloud of ever-shifting colors around him. The colors broke up into fragments, and then it was like some vast murmuration of starlings that swept back and forth across his field of view. The sound – like wind, like heartbeats, like distant voices – ebbed and flowed ceaselessly. He felt small, insignificant, meaningless. He believed himself hollow, transparent, a shell. There was a sense of waiting for something, of anticipation, but there was no anxiety or disturbance. He was calm, patient, listening closely to the sounds as if here he would somehow find a reason for what was happening to him.

In the early hours of the morning, he asked for water. His throat was parched. He told a nurse that he was dreaming with greater frequency and clarity than he'd ever experienced.

'They'll do that,' she said. 'The painkillers.'

He acknowledged her, but he did not believe it. Something was happening to him, something important, and yet he had no sense of what it was.

5

It was mid-morning on Monday, the 16th. The nurse who'd brought his breakfast had told him that his physiotherapist would be arriving before lunch.

'Can you think of someone you hate?' the nurse asked. 'I don't mean just dislike, but someone you really hate.'

'I don't have anyone I hate,' Nelson said.

'Well, you will soon.'

When the physio arrived, she was not at all who Nelson had expected, though what he'd expected he wouldn't have been able to say. Petite, dark-haired, intense, she spoke to him like he was being scolded for something unknown.

'My name is Hannah Montgomery,' she said, 'and I grew up with four brothers. I am more than capable of taking care of myself. I am also immune to emotional blackmail, reasons why things can't be done, and any kind of idea that you know my job better than I do. There are no rationalizations or excuses that you can think of that will get you out of doing what I tell you to do.'

'Well, I'm glad to know where I stand from the get-go.'

Hannah sat on the edge of Nelson's bed.

'I am thirty-seven years old. I am single. I am not interested in establishing anything beyond a purely professional relationship with you or anyone else. If you give me any shit at all, I will assign you to a different physio. Are we clear so far?'

'As daylight.'

'Okay, good. So, tell me what happened.'

'You don't have a file?'

'I want to hear it from you.'

'I got shot,' Nelson said. 'In the leg.'

'And how was that?'

'How was it? It fucking hurt. That's how it was.'

'You spoke to Dr Gardner?'

'Yes, I did.'

'And what did he tell you?'

'That I have to stop taking painkillers. That I better find another job.'

'And that you have to do physio, and lots of it. You should have started already, and the longer you leave it, the more muscle strength you'll lose. That we can handle, but it will be more of a challenge at the start. We'll see how it goes. If there's no major issues, we'll let you go home. Then you get to come back in for sessions several times a week until you're all fixed up.'

'Sure.'

'You have any questions about what's happened to your body?' Hannah asked.

Nelson shook his head.

'You have any questions for me before we begin?'

'I was wondering if maybe you were free for dinner on Friday.'

Hannah looked at him. Her expression didn't change. 'That one you can have. That's the only one you get.'

Nelson raised his hands in conciliation. 'I surrender,' he said.

'Always the best way,' Hannah replied. 'Okay, so now I'm gonna go get you a wheelchair.'

*

'We're gonna run through a program of seven exercises,' Hannah explained to Nelson in the Physiotherapy Center. 'Straight leg raises, something called bridges that strengthen the glute muscles and help stabilize your leg for standing, walking and climbing stairs. We do clamshells. You lie on the ground, knees bent. I put a resistance band around them and then you move the knees slowly apart. Hip extensions next. Then there's something called abductions to rebuild muscle strength on the sides of the hips. Then sitting-to-standing and step-up routines. We take it slow. We run them until you feel the burn. We do more than you're comfortable with, but not so many as to strain or tear anything.'

'I do have one question,' Nelson said. 'If I should have started this earlier, then why didn't I?'

'Because I am one of very few physiotherapists who work with these kinds of injuries. I cover this hospital, also some others in Tampa and Orlando. I was completing programs out there.'

'For other people who got shot?'

Hannah shook her head. 'No, there was no one dumb enough to get shot.'

'And they're doing okay?'

'No, they all died. That cleared my diary. Now, enough questions. We have work to do.'

If Nelson had believed his injury had given him the greatest pain he'd ever experienced, then his belief was misguided.

He knew little of the subject, save that pain was so multifaceted and subjective that it could not be measured. What became very real very quickly was that his own tolerance of pain was nothing close to what he'd imagined.

Though the first session lasted little more than thirty minutes, he ended it in agony, drenched with sweat and utterly exhausted. Once Hannah was done, she had him lie on his back on the floor. As soon as he closed his eyes, she nudged him in the shoulder with her foot.

'Stay awake,' she said. 'No sleeping.'

'Can I get some painkillers?'

'No. Not yet. And I need you off the floor in less than a minute. You're taking a cold shower.'

'What the fuck, Hannah?'

'What the fuck you, Garrett. Come on, get up. You need to keep the blood moving. Blood will rush to the areas of pain. It helps to heal them faster.'

'I don't want a cold shower.'

'That will constrict blood vessels. It will hurt less.'

'But I thought—'

'What you think isn't important. I know what I'm doing. Alternate heat and cold is good for circulation. Now get up.'

'Can I get a hand, at least?'

Hannah stood over him. 'Don't be such a fucking baby, Garrett. Get off the floor or we're doing all those reps again.'

Garrett turned onto his side, leaned up on his elbow, pushed himself up into a sitting position.

'There we go,' Hannah said.

'Does this get any easier?' Nelson asked.

'Not for a while, no. And tomorrow you're gonna feel like you got run over by an interstate hauler carrying bridge parts.'

'Well, that's something to look forward to, isn't it?'

'Pain reminds you that you're alive, Garrett.'

'What's that, your life mantra?'

Hannah smiled. 'One of them, yes.'

'I think that's the first time I've seen you smile.'

'On your feet and into the shower or it'll be the last.'

'What about the cast?'

'We'll get it covered with a waterproof sleeve. We do know what we're doing here, you know?'

Nelson shook his head. 'Christ, you really are edgy, aren't you?'

'Oh, you ain't seen nothin' yet. You've got me on a good day.'

As if to confirm Gardner's observation that Nelson led a very solitary life, he did not receive a single visitor in the subsequent week.

Considering the physical demands of the therapy sessions with Hannah and the fact that he slept a good ten or twelve hours each day, he would not have been good company anyway. It wasn't only his leg that hurt, but also his lower back, his shoulders and his neck. The gradual reduction of painkillers highlighted the ease with which he could have become dependent. He knew he had to steel himself against the urge to plead for them, and he did so. He understood enough of his own nature to appreciate that falling into such a habit would be effortless. Climbing out of it again would be nigh impossible.

At the end of his session on Sunday, 22nd, the day after his cast was removed, Hannah came to the ward. With her she brought crutches and a walking frame. She showed him how to use both, asked which he preferred.

'Crutches, definitely,' Nelson said.

'You're going home tomorrow,' she explained. 'You need to keep yourself moving. You can't spend the day in bed or sat in front of the TV. You take it slowly. It hurts too much, you stop. You use the walls and doorframes to support your upper body. Don't fall over. Don't forget that it'll be another six or eight weeks before the bone knits properly. You've got sessions here with me three times weekly. Someone will come get you and bring you here. You refuse to come, I'll fetch you myself. If I have to do that, you won't like what I'll make you do.'

'I don't like what you make me do already.'

Hannah paused for a moment. The stern schoolma'am softened.

'You've done real well, Garrett. You're gonna be fine. You're healing just as expected. There's no complications. You should be proud of yourself. You haven't given me half as much crap about this as most.'

'Hey, maybe you could write me a letter of recommendation. Doesn't give out as much crap as other people do.'

'Have you thought about it? What you're gonna do?'

Nelson shook his head. 'Not really, no.'

'How long were you a cop?'

'More than ten years.'

'It's a way of life, right?'

'It can seem that way, yes.'

'And you can't go back.'

'Seems not,' Nelson said. 'As you know, I have a limp. Gardner says my right leg is now one inch shorter than my left.'

'You want to stay in the same field of work?'

'How d'you mean?'

Hannah shrugged. 'Well, I got a father and brother in the prison service. They work out at Southern State. Maybe you wanna have a talk to them. See if that's a possibility.'

'They take cripples?'

Hannah reached out and took his hand, squeezed it reassuringly.

Nelson withdrew his hand sharply. 'Hey there, no fraternizing with the clientele, lady.'

She laughed. 'You are such a jerk,' she said. 'A likeable one, but a jerk all the same.'

Hannah stood up. 'I'll be back before lunch tomorrow. I'll be coming to your place with a couple of orderlies. We'll move things around so you've got easy access to different rooms. We'll need to get your bed downstairs, sort out how you can get groceries, take out your trash. The usual stuff. You really don't have anyone who can come over and help you for a few weeks?'

'No.'

'Your folks?'

'My father's dead. My mother lives over in Murdock. You don't want to get her involved.'

'She doesn't know you're here, what happened to you?'

'No, she doesn't, and I don't want her to know.'

'Because?'

'Because she's a special kind of crazy, Hannah, and it's not what I need in my life.'

'And you've got no siblings.'

'No.'

'What about close friends, people in the Sheriff's Department, a neighbor maybe?'

Nelson shook his head.

'So you're not only a physical cripple, you're an emotional one, too.'

Nelson looked at her. Hannah looked back.

'Does that disqualify me for the prison service?' Nelson asked.

She started laughing. 'Oh, I think it's a prerequisite for that job.'

'So that's it, I guess.'

'Sure is. Back to your desperately lonely existence. No family, no friends, no job. I mean, for Christ's sake, is there no one you actually like?'

Nelson shrugged. 'Well, I guess I hate you a little bit less than I did a week ago.'

6

On the morning of Wednesday, 25th, Sheriff Bigsby came over to the house.

'I should have come to see you in the hospital, Garrett, but hell, that situation out there was a clusterfuck of epic proportions.'

'Come in, Sheriff,' Nelson said. He inched backwards on his crutches, let Bigsby close the front door.

'You need any help there, son?'

'I'm good,' Nelson said. 'The more I do this, the easier it's supposed to get.'

'And is it? Getting easier?'

'It hurts bad. There are times it seems to ease up, but then it gets tough again. But...' Nelson shook his head. 'We lost three guys, right?'

They made their way into the kitchen. Nelson asked if Bigsby wanted coffee.

'I'm good. I just wanted to come over and have a talk with you.'

Bigsby took a seat at the kitchen table. Nelson leaned his crutches against the wall and sat facing him.

'I know I'm out, Sheriff. The doc already told me.'

'And you appreciate how I feel about that, right?'

'How you feel and how I feel is kinda irrelevant now. It is what it is. I have to find a different job.'

'You'll get benefit.'

'I know, but it ain't gonna be the same as a working wage. An' I ain't the kinda person who's gonna spend the rest of my life doin' nothin'.'

'You know we got 'em all, right? Eleven of them, all told. Five dead, six in custody. With the possession, intent to supply, evading arrest, and then the three killings, it'll be life without parole or the chair.'

'Justice was served.'

'Some, I guess. DEA and Feds want them to roll over on whoever's at the top of the food chain, but I don't see that happening. Maybe the DA'll get some traction on commuting death sentences, but these people are powerful. A guy takes a deal and winds up in Southern State, he knows someone'll stick a shiv in his heart first time he's in the yard.'

'As you said, drugs is bad business and it's bad people who do it.'

Bigsby nodded slowly. 'An' I wanted to say sorry, you know?'

'For what?'

'I'm the one sent you over there, Garrett. I mean, hell, I coulda said no to Sam Cox, couldn't I? I coulda found out some more about what was happenin'. If I'd known he had a crowd of DEA and Federal people, maybe I would've—'

'There ain't no purpose in any of that, Sheriff,' Nelson said. 'You can't think like that. Ain't gonna change what happened, and it sure as hell ain't gonna get me back in the Department.'

'Well, maybe there's something that can be done, you know? Maybe some kind of administrative function...'

Nelson smiled. 'I ain't a desk jockey, and you know it. That wouldn't be no different from working in an insurance company or somethin'. No, I'm done. Needs to be a clean break. I got time to figure things. I got options. Thinkin' maybe I'll take a job at the Pen.'

'Well, that ain't the worst idea I've heard. It's a tough place, mind. Talkin' about bad folks, you got the worst of the worst out there, all jammed in together like a fuckin' zoo.'

'I'm gonna check it out. Maybe it won't be right. And if I do it an' don't care for it, I don't have to stay.'

'Sure, sure.'

'Sam Cox was a friend of yours, wasn't he?'

Bigsby sighed resignedly. 'Friend is a stretch. We weren't like drinkin' buddies or whatever, but I knew enough to know he was a good man. Dependable, straight as an arrow. Sad fuckin' state of affairs to lose a man like that.'

'And you're okay?'

Bigsby looked up, as if surprised to be asked. 'Me? Sure, I'm okay. I ain't got time to wallow, Garrett. I got two daughters, five grandkids, a son about to get himself married, a whole department to run. Most days I don't got time to smoke a cigarette in peace without someone hollerin' at me for somethin' or other.'

'That's good.'

'And you? You never spoke of family, far as I remember. You got anyone comin' over here? You got yourself a girl, maybe?'

Nelson shook his head. 'Never really got to it,' he said. 'Never saw myself with a family of my own. Guess some people are built for it and some ain't.'

Bigsby hesitated for a moment.

'What?'

'Was gonna ask about your pa, but it ain't none of my business, is it?'

'What about my pa?'

Bigsby shrugged. 'Rumors.'

'That he was a sheriff? That he was bad?'

'Somethin' like that.'

'It's more than rumors. He was bad. As corrupt as they come. Carried enough guilt to open a store. You heard how he died?'

'Took his own life, didn't he?'

'Put his service revolver in his mouth and blew a hole through the back of his head.'

There was an awkward silence between them. Bigsby looked down, then away, as if he regretted having raised the subject.

'Well, like I said, I'm going off six ways to Sunday. Better get myself back.'

Bigsby stood up, picked up his hat. 'You stay right there, Garrett. I'll see myself out.'

He extended his hand. Nelson took it and they shook.

'You need anythin', you know where I am,' Bigsby said. 'You were a damned good deputy. Hell of a hole I've got to fill.'

Nelson should've said nothing about the suicide. He wore the burden of that final act of irrational defiance like a heavy, ill-fitting coat. Now thirty-nine, his mother a widow for two decades, he'd once been asked whether he'd pursued a career in the department as an effort to make amends for the sins of his father. That could not have been further from the truth. He'd gone into the law for different reasons, some of which he was still struggling to understand.

Nelson made his way across the kitchen and switched on the radio. Hoping to distract himself from the dark thoughts that crowded his mind, he turned it up loud. It didn't work. Even over the music, he could still hear the furious clamor of the past.

7

By the end of September, Nelson was off his crutches and walking with a cane.

'You'll lose that by Christmas,' Hannah told him.

It was Tuesday, 28th, and he lay on his back looking up at her as she flexed and twisted his leg like she was hoping to wrench it free of his pelvis.

'You enjoy this, don't you?' he said. 'Hurting people.'

'Sure I do,' she replied. 'Especially you.'

The exercise done, Nelson sat up. 'You know, I've been thinkin' about Southern State. I'm goin' half-crazy sat in that house. I really need to get back to work.'

'So come talk to my dad.'

'He'd be okay with that?'

'Sure he would.'

'You'd be there, too?'

'Why, you scared to go talk to someone on your own?'

'Not at all, no. I just want to pretend that it's a date.'

Hannah smiled. 'You go on and pretend all you like, Garrett Nelson.'

'So you gonna invite me or what?'

'I'll speak to him.'

'I'm not driving yet, you know?'

'I'll take you.'

'So it will be a date then?'

Hannah leaned forward and shoved Nelson in the shoulder. He fell backwards.

'Other leg now,' she said, and started in again with the twisting and flexing.

Hannah pulled up outside of Nelson's house just before five on the afternoon of Saturday, October 9.

Nelson had ironed a shirt for the occasion, had on a sport jacket too. His hair was longer than it had ever been. He'd meant to get out to a barber, but hadn't organized it in time.

For some reason he was nervous, not only because he liked this girl, but because he wanted to make a good impression on her family. Whatever was going on as far as a potential relationship was concerned, he knew it was one-sided. She had never been anything but professional with him, and though there had been the odd jibe, she had always cut him off before it became anything more. His belief in his own ability to read people had been undermined. Whatever he knew, it had been founded in police work. He could see a liar from the other side of the county, but this was altogether different. He wanted Hannah to like him. Maybe he needed her to like him. How she felt was a mystery to him, and he didn't care much for being in the dark.

'You made an effort,' she said when he opened the door to her. 'You needn't have, you know?'

Nelson stepped back and she entered the house. She walked on through to the living room, then into the kitchen.

'You lookin' for somethin'?' Nelson asked.

'Making sure you're keeping the place clean and tidy,' she said. 'You're not sleeping down here anymore?'

'No,' Nelson said. 'The guy who brings me to the hospital helped me get the mattress back upstairs a coupla weeks ago.'

'Up and down the stairs is good for you,' she said. 'So, you ready, or do you need a haircut first?'

Nelson smiled. 'Leave me alone.'

The drive from Fort Haines to Hendry County was little more than seventy miles. Hannah let the passenger seat of her Ford Falcon back as far as it would go so Nelson could stretch his legs. She drove like she was on the way to a fire.

Nelson had never been to Clewiston. It sat about eighty miles northwest of Fort Lauderdale.

Crossing the city limits, Nelson noticed a sign. 'America's Sweetest Town', it read.

'Sugar plantations,' Hannah said. 'That sure as hell ain't a comment about the inhabitants.'

'Your family's always been here?'

'Three generations. But you'll get all the history you need from my dad. By the time you leave, you'll know more about Florida than you could ever wish for.'

'And you live with your folks?'

'No, I have my own place up in Lakeport. But we're close, you know? I'm over here several times a week.'

Pulling up outside the Montgomery place, a sizeable Spanish-style building characteristic of the coastal regions, Nelson saw a young man exit from a low, flat-roofed terracotta extension to the right and make his way to greet them.

'That's my brother, Danny,' Hannah said. 'He's the youngest of us.'

Danny opened the passenger door and extended his hand to help Nelson out.

'Hey,' he said. 'Pleased to meet you. Garrett, right?'

'That's right, yes. And you're Danny.'

'That'd be me.'

Nelson got to his feet. He was unsteady for a moment, conscious of a deep ache in his lower back. He reached in for his cane.

Danny came forward to give him support.

'He's all right,' Hannah said to her brother. 'Don't fuss.'

Danny raised his hands in surrender and stepped away. 'She's been the usual nightmare, I guess.'

Nelson gave a resigned smile.

'Don't take it personal,' Danny said. 'She's like that with everyone.'

The Montgomerys seemed set to confound Nelson's expectations. Hannah's mother, Miriam, came out to greet him with such warmth it took him aback.

'I really appreciate your invite,' Nelson told her. 'And you have a beautiful home, Mrs Montgomery.'

'Miriam,' she said. 'And yes, we been here long enough to have it how we want it. Let me take your jacket.'

Hannah showed Nelson through to the kitchen. Through the wide windows, Nelson could see into a sizeable, well-tended yard. There were two men out there – Hannah's father and another brother, Nelson guessed – seated at a wooden bench alongside a large table. Each had a beer and cigar, and when they saw Hannah, the older man beckoned them through.

'That's Frank, my dad,' Hannah said. 'And the other one is my brother, Ray. He's the one who works at Southern State. Come say hi.'

Frank got up as Nelson came through the back door. He didn't wait for Nelson to reach him, but came forward with a smile and a handshake. Nelson put him in his mid- to late-fifties. He had a tough, weathered face. His hair, once sandy brown, had grayed at the temples. Ray, on the other hand, was dark-haired like his mother. He possessed a wound-up intensity, like he was expecting bad news.

'The walking wounded,' Frank said.

'Garrett Nelson. A pleasure to meet you, sir.'

'I'm Ray,' Hannah's brother said. 'Take a seat. Let me get you a beer.'

'Bring me one, too,' Hannah said.

Nelson sat down on the other side of the table. Hannah sat beside him.

'You wanna smoke?' Frank asked. 'These are good.'

'I'll give it a miss, thank you,' Nelson said.

'So, I hear you're a local hero,' Frank said.

'More like a local target,' Nelson replied.

'Hell of a thing you folks broke up, right? That drug thing.'

'It was a DEA operation. Feds, too. We were just pitchin' in as back-up.'

'But they got 'em, didn't they?' Frank asked. 'From what I understand, it was quite an operation. Stuff coming in from the coast and all the way up to Miami.'

Ray returned with beers. They raised bottles, toasted Nelson with a welcome.

'Seems that way,' Nelson said. 'I don't have all the details. I'm De Soto County. Sheriff there asked me to go over to Highlands as they were a man down.'

'And from what Hannah tells me, you're no longer able to work in the Sheriff's Department.'

'That's right, yes.'

'And you're lookin' at maybe comin' over to Southern State.'

'It's a possibility, yes,' Nelson said. 'It's the reason Hannah asked me to come over and talk with you about it.'

'It's a good job,' Ray said. 'Government jobs like this are solid. Healthcare, pension, the works.'

'I've been there more than thirty years,' Frank said. 'Never planned on stayin', but stay I have.' Frank looked at his son. 'Ray here's been there – how long now? – twelve years?'

'Comin' up thirteen,' Ray said. 'Ain't no plans to change it. Got myself a wife, and hope to have kids before too long. Man gets himself a family, he needs a reliable job, right?'

'You ain't married, are you?' Frank asked.

Nelson shook his head.

'Never cared for the idea?'

'Sure, yes. Came close one time, but she was a wild one.'

'They're all wild,' Ray said, 'so you gotta tame 'em.'

Hannah laughed dryly. 'Hell, if I ever seen a man wrapped around a girl's finger, that'd be you, Ray Montgomery. That wife of yours could lock you in the basement without a pot to piss in and you'd still call her sweetheart.'

Ray shrugged resignedly. The bait was taken in good humor.

'You Florida-born?' Frank asked.

'Charlotte County,' Nelson said. 'My ma's still out there.'

'And your pa?'

'Died when I was eighteen,' Nelson said. 'He was in the Department, like me, but he went bad.' He looked at Frank, then at Hannah. For some reason he felt the need to talk. 'Ain't no mystery what happened. Look up his name and you'll find it. Whatever the hell he got into, and I don't know the half of it, it was enough to scare him crazy. He killed himself in the end. I guess that was preferable to spending the rest of his life in jail.'

'That's a hell of a thing. Sorry to hear that, son.'

'It's history,' Nelson said. 'Don't change no matter how many times you tell it.'

'Well, that's your business, Garrett, and I don't mean to pry.'

'You never told me this,' Hannah said.

'Guess it doesn't make for polite conversation,' Nelson replied.

Hannah reached out her hand, placed it gently over Nelson's. It was nothing but a gesture of empathy. It lasted no more than a second or two. Nelson figured not to read anything into it, so he didn't.

'Southern State is its own self-contained world,' Frank said. 'You know much of the history of this state?'

Hannah smiled at Nelson. 'Told you you'd get a lecture, didn't I?'

'That's enough from you, young lady. I'm the boss here.'

'The history of Florida?' Nelson asked. 'I know some, I guess. I know it was Spanish, then British, then went back to Spain again after the Civil War.'

'And then we bought it back off of the Spaniards in the early 1800s,' Frank said. 'But before all that it was Indian territory. Calusa, Maiyama, whoever else. Europeans first came here in the sixteenth century, all set to convert the natives, you know? Built a lot of missions, most of which were destroyed by Carolina and Creek raiders right at the start of the 1700s. Sixty years later, Britain took control again. It was part of the agreement that ended the Seven Years War. Most of the Spaniards went to Cuba. Then, like you said, it was Spanish again just twenty years later. Anyway, the point of telling you this is that Southern State Pen is built near one of those old Spanish missions. It has a long and bloody history. Them same Province of Carolina soldiers killed hundreds, maybe thousands, of the Indians. The rest of them went into slavery. That site, right where the Pen is now, was a holding camp.'

'Surely there can't be much of it left,' Nelson said.

'No, there isn't. Pretty much all of it gone—'

'Except the bell tower,' Ray interjected. 'And that's where we do our killin'.'

'We don't kill people, Ray. We execute them. And since the death penalty was reinstated back in July, we've executed just one person. First one since 1964.'

'How the hell did we get from the history of Florida to Death

Row?' Hannah asked. 'If this is how it's gonna be, I ain't bringin' anyone else for lunch.'

'Because Garrett here needs to understand what he's gonna be dealin' with,' Frank said. 'He takes a job up there, there's every chance he ain't just gonna be in General Population. On Death Row, you're dealin' with people who know their life is gonna end. Not just that, they know when and how. That does something to the mind of a man. All the things he wants to do, he can't. I've seen it. I've been there when men go to the chair, and it ain't pretty.'

'Are you askin' me if I have a problem with the death penalty?' Nelson asked.

'I guess I am,' Frank said.

Nelson reached for the bottle of beer and leaned back in the chair. 'I was more than ten years in the Sheriff's Department,' he said. 'In all that time I drew my gun maybe four, five times. That was enough to settle the situation. Two months ago I blew a man's head off with a shotgun. If I hadn't, I'd be dead. I have no doubt about that. So, seems to me what we're talking about is the law. "To Protect and Serve", right? If the United States Supreme Court has seen fit to reinstate the death penalty, then that means it's now the law. A man commits a crime, he is subject to the legal penalty for that crime. A judge and jury sees fit to end his life, that's because they reckon he's still a threat to innocent people. You undermine that, you undermine the justice system. You have no justice system, you soon have no society.'

No one at the table spoke for a moment, and then Frank slowly nodded his head and smiled.

'Hell son, screw Southern State. Maybe you should run for Governor.'

8

The wild girl Nelson had mentioned was called Diane Warren. Nelson had figured, once married, that she'd settle, so he set his mind to proposing. Folks who knew her warned him, folks whose word he trusted, but it had always been his nature to ignore sage advice and cut his own road. He bought a ring he could ill afford, and took her out to dinner at the fanciest place in Arcadia.

Diane turned him down flat. She even laughed at the notion.

'Is that what you thought was happenin' here, Garrett?' she asked. 'That you an' me was gonna get a little house and have some babies and whatnot?'

He hadn't answered her. He was still drowning in the bitterness of her rejection.

'Jeez, Garrett, you are a dreamer.'

With that, she stood up from the table, reached for the glass of wine, downed it in one, and then told him she was leaving. She proceeded to do so, never once looking back at him. Nelson had sat there in silence until the waiter arrived with two plates.

There was no way forward or back for them after that. They spoke two, maybe three times, and then nothing. Last he'd heard, merely by chance, was that she'd gone north, was now living somewhere near Jacksonville. He could've found out easily enough, but it would've been like hitting his head against a wall to see how much it hurt.

The confusion and uncertainty the incident had engendered – done and over with in a handful of seconds – had stayed with him for a long time. Eight years had passed, and he could still summon that sense of awkwardness and shame. He knew then that he understood nothing of women, and nothing had happened in the subsequent years to change that conclusion.

The drive back from Clewiston to Fort Haines with Hannah seemed so much longer than the journey out.

Nelson was tense, even uncomfortable. Hannah seemed completely at ease, trying her best to engage him in conversation. She asked him what he thought of her father, her brothers, and if he'd come any closer to a decision about Southern State.

Nelson's answers were close to monosyllabic. So much so that she asked him if he was all right.

'Tired,' he lied. 'And my leg aches something dreadful.'

'Is that your go-to answer for when you don't know what to say?'

Nelson turned and looked at her. She was nothing but direct.

'You're about as transparent as they come, Garrett Nelson,' she said. 'You're all wound up about what's going on between us.'

'There ain't nothin' goin' on between us,' he replied.

'Sure there is,' Hannah replied. 'You think I take every cripple to my folks' house?'

'So tell me what's goin' on, then.'

'I'm figurin' you out,' she said. 'At least I'm tryin'.'

'How far you got?'

'A ways, but not far enough.'

'Do you know what you're looking for?'

'Same thing everyone's lookin' for.'

'And what would that be?' Nelson asked.

'Everyone needs someone to see the best in them, and then they need someone to take a gamble on it.'

'Is that how it works?'

'Not often, no,' Hannah said. 'But that's only because people don't really take the time to get past the faces we all wear for the world.'

'You think I'm not being straight with you? Is that it?'

'I don't think you're being straight with yourself.'

'Meaning what?'

'Exactly as it sounds. What are you? Forty?'

'Thirty-nine.'

'Same difference. You live alone, no girlfriend, never been married, no wife. Your pa killed himself, you don't talk to your mom. You've got no brothers or sisters, don't seem to have much of a social life. As far as I can tell, you've got no passion.'

'Passion?' Nelson asked.

'Sure. Passion. Like something that means everything to you.'

'Such as?'

'Hell, I don't know. What do people get passionate about?'

'You mean like a hobby?'

'No, I mean something that drives you,' Hannah replied. 'Hell, maybe it was being a deputy. Doesn't seem that way to me, though. Seems like you've spent your life treading water. Lot of people live their lives that way, all the while trying to convince themselves that someone's gonna come and save 'em.'

'Have you come to save me?'

Hannah didn't respond for a moment or two. 'I ain't decided,' she said.

'And you don't need saving? I mean, you haven't got a husband or kids or whatever.'

They pulled up at lights. They weren't far from Nelson's house.

'Far as I can see, there are three basic human frailties,' she said. 'Endlessly seeking approval, even from people we don't know.

Forever wanting things we can't have. Trusting those we know will finally abandon us.'

'Okay.'

'I think we all suffer from those to one degree or another. We tell ourselves that we get wiser with age. That's bullshit. We've just had more time to convince ourselves that we were right to give up on what we really wanted.'

The lights changed. Hannah pulled away.

'You still haven't answered the question,' Nelson said.

'That's because I don't have an answer for you. Or maybe I don't know you well enough to say it.'

Nelson frowned. 'I don't even understand what kind of conversation we're having here.'

Hannah laughed. She turned right. Nelson's house was up on the left a hundred yards or so. She didn't speak until she'd come to a halt outside.

Turning off the car, she sat for a while. There was silence but for the ticking of the cooling motor.

Hannah turned in the seat. She looked at Nelson unflinchingly.

'What?' he asked.

'Are you plannin' on being a victim?' she asked.

'A victim? What do you mean?'

'You know exactly what I mean, Garrett.'

'I do?'

'You got to make a decision. A real important decision. This is like a turning point in your life. You got shot. Okay, it happened. No one can take that back. Your leg got busted. You can't be a deputy anymore. There's two ways this can go. You can use this as an explanation and an excuse for everything. All the things you don't want to do, everything that goes wrong, you can tell yourself that it's because you're traumatised or because you lost your job or whatever the hell you like. The consequence of that is that you wind up with nothing. Or you can tough it out, you know? Get out of your damned house, go do things, speak to people. Fetch your own damned groceries, start driving again, go to the movies. Hell, I don't care what you do, but it's been two months now and I can pretty much guarantee that this afternoon was the first time you've had a real conversation with anyone since it happened.'

'What do you want from me, Hannah?'

'I want you to get better.'

'Is that all?'

'I want you to prove to me that it's worth taking a gamble on you.'

Nelson looked at her. She didn't smile at him, but there was warmth in her eyes.

'I'm thirty-seven,' she said. 'No, I don't have kids and I ain't never been married. It's too late for a family, I know that. But it ain't too late to make a life with someone. But it's gotta be the right person. I've had too many shitty relationships to waste any more years, Garrett.'

'You make it sound like a business proposal.'

'Sure it is,' Hannah replied. 'It's an investment of yourself in something. I know nothing is certain. I'm not that naïve. And sure, we all got demons at the foot of the bed. But how much power you give those things is entirely up to you.'

'You're assuming that I want to make an investment in you…'

Hannah frowned. It was fleeting, but it was a clear message. 'See, that's exactly the kind of crap I can do without, Garrett. We ain't teenagers. This is what it is. You don't think I see how you look at me? You don't think that all your front and bravado has just about as much substance as giftwrap? You deal straight with me, or take your chips off the table and stay out of the game.'

'Okay,' Nelson said. 'Okay, I get it.'

'I hope so. I really do.'

Nelson was quiet for a time. He looked right ahead. When he spoke, he wanted to look at her but he couldn't.

'I feel like I'm all busted up,' he said. 'Not my body. Me. I feel like I'm all busted up inside. I feel like there's pieces of me scattered all over and I'm just fighting to pull them back together again. Like that thing, you know? How most people got to leave home to realize they had one. Then they spend their whole lives trying to get back. Well, I don't feel like I ever had a home. My father was crazy. I understand why now, but back then he was just mad all the time. Folks think they understand fury. They don't. Sure, they get riled and they holler up a whirlwind sometimes, but that's not fury. Fury comes from another deeper place. It's in your guts. Like a man betrayed, a woman getting cheated on, a child told just too many times that he ain't never gonna amount to anything. That kind of fury puts a gun in someone's hand. That was my father. He did it to himself. He did everything that people said he did and more.'

Nelson turned and looked at Hannah then.

'I've spent my whole life feeling like I'm stained by someone else's sins. That's something that doesn't wash out – not with time, not with other people telling you that it wasn't your fault. I'm haunted by it. I feel guilty about something I didn't do, something I didn't even know was happening.'

Hannah reached out and took Nelson's hand.

'We're all broken,' she said. 'Not in the same places, sure. But we're all still broken.'

'I used to drink,' Nelson said. 'To steady my nerve for something I didn't want to face. Then I'd drink after to settle down. I got out of that. Hell of a thing.'

'People get so afraid of fucking up, they think it's better not to try.'

Nelson closed his eyes and lowered his head. He breathed deeply.

'Why are you doing this?' he asked.

'Doing what?'

'I mean, you never gave me any indication that I was anything but your patient.'

'Even if I had, you wouldn't have seen it.'

Nelson laughed quietly. He opened his eyes, looked up. 'True.'

'So now you can ask me out on a date.'

'Hey, Hannah. You wanna go on a date?'

Hannah didn't reply. She looked straight ahead.

'What?' Nelson asked.

'I'm thinkin' about it.'

Nelson reached for the door handle. 'Well, you let me know when you've decided.'

'I've decided.'

Nelson looked back at her.

Hannah gave him a brief smile. 'Sure, Garrett. Why the hell not?'

9

By the time the Southern State meeting came around in the first week of November, Nelson was off his cane. He limped, but it was less severe than he'd expected. He was off meds, and though he was still doing physio with Hannah, it was now just once a week. They'd been on four dates, one of them ending with Nelson staying over at Hannah's apartment in Lakeport. They'd shared her bed, but they'd been too drunk to do anything but sleep. It seemed both of them were more than content to let their relationship take its own time. They were finding their bearings, each intent on becoming friends before they became lovers.

Frank Montgomery had organized the job interview. Even though Nelson was driving again, Frank insisted that he take him out there.

The journey from Clewiston to the penitentiary was only twenty miles, but winding their way out through the everglades took more than an hour.

'This here's the best way to keep a feller from escaping,' Frank said. 'Nature'll give you a tougher challenge than anything man-made. Sure, we got more than enough fences and wire and gates, but you put a man out here on his own and he ain't gonna make it half a mile before a 'gator takes him. And if the 'gators or crocs don't get him, you got diamondbacks, cottonmouths, copperheads, water moccasins, and rattlers aplenty.'

'How long did you say you'd been there?'

'More than thirty years.'

'You had escapes?'

'Attempts, sure. Back in the thirties, they had a few that got away, but they got sprung from chain gangs. No one has actually made it out of the facility itself since the cellblocks got rebuilt after the war.'

'How many inmates?'

'Right now, about eight hundred or so. But you got different blocks depending on the reason for incarceration. Most federal institutions you got maximum, close, medium and minimum. Here we got just two categories. Minimum, which is somewhere between medium and close. We call it General Population. Gen Pop for short. That holds about six hundred. And then there's High Security that can take up to two hundred, and each in a different building. Cellblock staff to inmate ratio runs at about one to ten. Then you got the watchtower guys and administrative staff, and you're looking at about a hundred people altogether.'

'And then there's Death Row.'

'Right, but that's in another building again. That's its own thing altogether.'

'How many are on Death Row?' Nelson asked.

'Ten, maybe twelve, and they're pretty much the angriest people you're ever likely to meet.'

'I guess I'd feel the same.'

'Oh hell, it's not because they got the death sentence. You know about Furman v. Georgia, right?'

'I know it ended the death penalty, and then it was overturned.'

'These guys all got commuted to life without parole, you see? You tell a man he's gonna die, then you tell him he ain't, and then you tell him you changed your mind and he's gonna fry anyway… well, that's enough to fuck anyone up.'

'And someone was executed already.'

'Back in September, yes.'

'Who was it?'

Frank took a cigarette from the packet in his breast pocket and lit it. He cranked the window open a couple of inches.

'His name was Marcus Boyd.'

'What did he do?'

'There's something called aggravating factors when it comes to capital crimes,' Frank said. 'In Florida we got sixteen of them. They go all the way from crimes committed when someone's already on felony probation to hindering the lawful exercise of a government function. Basically, killing someone doesn't necessarily warrant the death penalty, but you throw in one of these aggravating factors and it's a different thing altogether. The DA can try it as a capital case, sure. But a jury can petition for it and a judge can order it, even when it hasn't been tried as a capital case. One of those aggravating factors is when the crime committed was especially heinous, atrocious or cruel.'

'So what did he do?'

Frank smiled. 'You want the gory details?'

'Sure.'

'Marcus Boyd was a junkie. He'd been in and out of foster homes and juvenile detention for most of his childhood and teens. He did time for a couple of things in his early twenties. All of it was drug-related. Theft, burglary, paperhanging. Things to get money for junk. Anyways, he gets in with some bad characters, real whackjobs into some Satanic shit or other. Now Marcus is pretty dumb. He's the kind of feller who'll piss upstream and then fill his kettle down. He gets involved with a junkie stripper. She's another patsy for these crazies. Can't recall her actual name now, but her stage name, if you can call it that, was "Misty Meanor"'. You believe that?'

Nelson laughed. 'Misty Meanor?'

'Clever, huh? Anyway, Misty gets pregnant, and there's this one guy, some self-styled Manson wannabe, and he convinces Marcus that Marcus is the father. Marcus, being the gullible character that he is, buys into this. Then they tell him that the child is possessed by some fucking otherworld demon or some shit, and that Marcus has to kill it before it's born or the world will come to an end. They get him so cranked on acid that he's not even on the same planet. He believes he can kill the child without killing the girl. When it comes down to it, he basically chops her in half. Kills her, kills the baby, then comes down out of the clouds, realizes what he's done, and tries to kill himself. He can't even do that right. He sets his own trailer on fire, like he's gonna burn the girl's body, himself, and somehow cleanse the world of what's happened. He actually winds up killing the Manson guy and two other people in the process, and he walks away with no injury at all.'

'Jesus.'

'They tried the whole "not responsible for his actions" thing, but it didn't fly. And maybe, just maybe, if he'd only killed the junkies, he would have got life. But he killed an unborn baby. The girl was seven months pregnant, for fuck's sake.'

'You were there for his execution?'

'I was, yes.'

'Well, his plan worked in the end. He did wind up getting burned.'

'He did indeed.'

Frank took a right, and after a hundred yards or so, Southern State came into view. At first, Nelson saw nothing but an endless double-wire fence that ran both left and right as far as he could see. As they drew closer, he saw the watchtowers, the outline of the blocks below, and beyond that – surrounded by yet another barbed-wire fence – the steeple of the bell tower, beside it a one-storey stone building with a flat roof.

Frank slowed down as they neared the other perimeter.

'Welcome to Hell,' he said under his breath, and came to a stop at the gate.

10

Florida Southern State Correctional Facility was first established as a federal detention unit in the early 1900s. Originally nothing more than a compound with a single wall, Southern was then extended to more than eight times its original size. The wall became a fence, and then a second fence was built beyond it. Additional cellblocks were constructed in the 1920s and 30s, the work done by the inmates themselves in the most gruelling of conditions. Its history as a transit camp for Native Americans – ousted from their land and their homes, bound for slavery or deportation – was buried in the very earth on which it stood. Southern had always been a killing place, both isolated and desolate, somehow imbued with a sense of hopelessness and despair.

Passing through the first gate, Nelson felt as if he was disconnecting from the world and entering some dark and forbidding alternate reality. On through the second, and it was as if the air itself changed, now subdued, heavy, and harder to breathe. The light within the compound seemed different, colored a thin gray-yellow like a fading bruise.

Out to his right, Nelson saw a line of men in blue shirts and denims, on their backs the initials FSSCF in bold white letters. There must have been a dozen or more, ahead of them three armed guards overseeing the digging of a trench. Watchtowers loomed tall at each corner and midway along the fence, eight in all, and within each tower was another armed guard.

'Work details,' Frank said. 'They're putting in new sewage lines.'

Frank drove in silence. No one turned to see them pass. Not a single man looked up from his labors. The sense of oppression was tangible, claustrophobic, and by the time the car drew to a halt ahead of a central building, Nelson was already asking himself whether he could work in such a place.

'This here's Central Admin,' Frank explained. 'Warden's office is up top. Lower floor is inmate processing, commissary, armory, communications center. Second floor is doctor's office, infirmary, quarantine and morgue.'

'Morgue?'

'Man gets killed, that's where he goes for the coroner's examination.'

'The ones who are executed.'

'Not only those, but those who are killed by other inmates. And the suicides, of course. A place like this? Some folks look at the twenty, thirty years ahead of them and they figure it's better to quit.'

'There's a lot of them?'

'Enough.'

'Even with all the security and cell checks?'

'Oh, you have no idea how inventive people can become when they want to kill themselves.'

'And the inquests are handled internally?' Nelson asked.

'The coroner is sent in by the county, but the body stays here. We got our own burial ground.'

Frank got out of the car. Nelson followed suit.

Looking back beyond the central building, Frank indicated an area of land beyond the fence that was bordered by high trees.

'That's the penitentiary cemetery. It's known as God's Acre,' he said. 'Ironic, seein' as how it's the last resting place for some of the most godless people on Earth, but that's the name the Spanish missionaries gave it and it's stayed.'

Frank turned to his right and indicated the mission itself.

'And that there's the death house,' he said. 'That's the bell tower I told you about.'

Nelson was struck by the incongruity of a Spanish adobe chapel in the middle of this bleak and unforgiving landscape. Beside it stood a low building in keeping with the main prison blocks. Nelson presumed that this was where those sentenced to execution were housed.

'You'll get to see it later,' Frank said. 'But right now, the boss is waiting for you.'

Warden Emery Young came out from behind an acre of desk to greet Nelson.

No more than five seven or eight, he was heavily built, his dirty-blond hair thinning on top. His features were blunt, his smile that of a man unfamiliar with such things. Nelson's initial impression was one of severity and discipline. Everything about him was tough.

'Sit, please,' Young said.

Nelson did as he was asked.

Young returned to the other side of the desk.

'It's unusual,' he said, 'for us to even consider someone who hasn't gone through standard channels. Most of our people come from other facilities. They have experience. They know how things work. But you come from law enforcement, I understand.'

'The Sheriff's Department over in De Soto County,' Nelson said.

'And you know Officer Montgomery how?'

'Through his daughter. She was my physiotherapist after I was shot.'

'Yes, yes of course. Montgomery told me about this. Wounded in the line of duty.'

'That's right.'

'And now medically unfit to continue.'

'It seems so, yes,' Nelson replied.

'It either is or it isn't, Mr Nelson.'

'Yes, sir. I am medically unfit to continue in that Department.'

Young leaned back in his chair. He rested his elbows on the arms and steepled his fingers. He looked at Nelson for a good twenty seconds, and then he gave that awkward smile again.

'And what makes you think you'd be a good fit at Southern State, Mr Nelson?'

'My understanding of the law. My experience with criminals—'

'Catching them and detaining them are two very different games, let me assure you,' Young said. 'When your work is done, ours is only just beginning.'

'I appreciate that, of course, but I just meant to say that I have some familiarity with—'

Young raised his hand. Nelson stopped talking.

'Southern State is a federal institution, Mr Nelson. The men here are being punished for what they have done. They have committed crimes that make them unacceptable to society, and thus they have to be separated out from that same society for the good of all. In most cases, no matter how long they are here, they will return to the life they knew before they arrived. In some very rare cases, a man might see the error of his ways and decide to no longer be a burden to state and nation. Recidivism levels are high, very high indeed, and that is for no other reason than the nature of the man himself. Do you believe that some people are born bad, Mr Nelson?'

Nelson hesitated. 'Well, I guess that there could be such a thing, yes.'

'No guessing, Mr Young. We cannot afford to deal in guesswork. The only thing that works with such people is absolute certainty. They are not here to be forgiven, nor are they here to be rehabilitated. Their incarceration is a penalty. They eat when we tell them. They sleep when we tell them. They work hard. The rules are simple to understand and even simpler to follow. If they violate those rules, they lose privileges. There are eight hundred men here, Mr Nelson, and I am served by no more than seventy or eighty officers. But it is not the officers alone who maintain the equilibrium of this facility. That is accomplished by routine, authority, discipline, and, ultimately, the possibility that conditions may become a great deal worse if compliance is not forthcoming.'

'I understand,' Nelson said.

'I have been here for more than two decades,' Young said. 'Never once has a man successfully escaped, and no man ever will. If he gets beyond the wire, he will drown or fall victim to the abundance of predators out there in the glades. Nature, it seems, lends itself to our cause.'

'And if I applied for a position here, what would my duties encompass?'

'Initially you would serve an apprenticeship under an experienced officer. I imagine that Mr Montgomery or his son might be willing to undertake that task. They are both proven, trustworthy members of the Southern State family. We have different blocks for different types of offenders. General Population is the least restrictive community. Here we find thieves, fraudsters, conmen and the like. That is where we have the greatest numbers. Those who have committed robberies with violence and those who have killed are found in Maximum Security. Those who are awaiting execution are housed in their own unit beside the bell tower. Currently we have nine.'

'Frank… Mr Montgomery, he told me that an execution took place here back in September.'

Young frowned. 'I am sure he felt it was within his right to discuss this with you, Mr Nelson, but you need to understand that what goes on within these walls is not to be shared with anyone, and I mean *anyone*.'

'I don't think he meant to—'

'That will be a matter for me to take up with Mr Montgomery personally.'

Young's manner was formidable, even intimidating. Nelson guessed he had already blown any hope of being considered for the job, and in some small way he was relieved.

'And so,' Young said, 'do you have any questions?'

'I don't think so. Not right now, at least.'

'You seem like a level-headed man, Mr Nelson. You also have experience working with your colleagues in law enforcement, and that is an important attribute. The business of Southern State is all about teamwork. We work together and things run as they should.'

Young got up from his chair and walked around the desk.

'I will have Mr Montgomery show you around, and then you can take some time to consider whether this is something you wish to pursue.'

Nelson extended his hand and they shook.

'Thank you for your time, Warden Young. It's very much appreciated.'

Unexpectedly, Young then gave him a genuine smile. He gripped Nelson's shoulder.

'I think you'll find that the sense of order we have established here may very well suit you,' Young said. 'A man needs structure and stability. You do well here, you have a job for life.'

11

The first thing that struck Nelson as he stood in the bell tower was the seeming absence of any sound.

Entering through a heavy wooden door, Frank showed him into a room dominated by a spiral staircase to the left.

'That goes up to the tower itself,' Frank said. 'From there you can see right across the whole compound and out into the glades.'

Ahead of them was another door, just as heavy, that gave access to the chapel. No more than thirty feet wide and fifty feet long, the room had been divided in two by a solid wall, in the center of which was a large curtained window. Separated by an aisle, banks of chairs – a good fifteen or twenty on each side – were positioned so that the execution could be witnessed.

'It's back there,' Nelson said. 'The chair?'

'It is,' Frank replied. 'I'll show you.'

Even the sound of their footsteps seemed insubstantial as they walked the length of the room. Up above them a circular window permitted minimal illumination, as if the light itself was cautious of entry.

Frank unlocked the door. He stepped back, waited for Nelson to go first, followed him in, and then closed the door behind them.

'They call it the black widow,' Frank said.

Centering the room, standing a good five feet tall and four feet wide, was a solid wooden chair with a high back. It was aged, blackened in places, and bolted to the floor at each leg. At the front of the chair and beneath the seat, a block of wood sat close to the ground. Spaced a foot apart, two semi-circles had been cut into the block. Nelson assumed that here the condemned man's ankles were secured. Heavy leather straps hung from the arms of the chair, and a wider, longer strap – fixed at the back – came through a gap to secure the chest. To the right on a small table, sat a metal cap. Beside it were two metal plates. Both the cap and the plates had conductors to which wires could be attached.

'Invented by a dentist,' Frank said.

'A dentist?'

'You know how this thing came about?'

Nelson shook his head. He was finding it hard to concentrate. There was something pulling at him, something that urged him to sit in that chair. The feeling was not unlike the inexplicable need to inch ever closer to the edge of a precipice. With it came a sensation of nausea and vertigo.

'Arc lighting,' Frank said. 'Outdoor street lighting. They started installing it back in the late 1800s. Three, four, even six thousand volts were used to power those things. People died, usually linemen and maintenance workers. The actual death that brought it to the attention of this dentist was a dockworker in Buffalo. For whatever reason, this character figured it would be a kick to get into an electric plant and see what it was all about. He wound up touching the ground and brush connections of a dynamo at the same time. Killed him instantly. Anyway, the coroner mentioned it in passing at some lecture, and a dentist, man by the name of Alfred Southwick, was there. He got together with some other guy, a veterinarian I think, whose job it was to euthanize stray dogs. Between them they figured that electrocuting an animal was more humane than poisoning it. They electrocuted hundreds of the things. All their research was published, and on it went from there. The first electric chair was basically a modified dentist's chair. First person to die in one was a guy called William Kemmler in 1890. There was a lot of noise about whether or not it was cruel and unusual punishment, but there'd been so many botched hangings that they figured this couldn't be worse. That first one took eight minutes. They used a Westinghouse generator, and Westinghouse himself was actually there as a witness. First shock just knocked Kemmler unconscious. They had to wait to recharge the generator. They hit him with it again, double the voltage. Ruptured blood vessels, burned his skin something awful, but it stopped his heart.'

Nelson wanted to leave the room, but he knew he couldn't.

'Go on,' Frank said.

'What?'

'You have to. You can't help yourself. Everyone does, you know?'

Nelson looked at Frank. Frank smiled. He nodded towards the chair.

'Take a seat in the black widow.'

Nelson moved slowly, almost involuntarily. The chair was less than eight feet from where he stood. Everything told him not to do it, but there was no way to stop himself. Each step seemed further than the last. In reality, it was a handful of seconds, but, by the time he reached it, it seemed that hours had passed.

He turned to face Frank. Frank's expression was that of a man amused, perhaps taking some morbid pleasure from the unease and disturbance that Nelson was experiencing.

'You got to do it, Garrett,' Frank said.

Nelson reached back until he felt the arms of the chair in his hands. He lowered himself down in slow motion, the hairs raised to attention on the nape of his neck, a thin varnish of sweat covering his entire body. He could feel his heart, his pulse, the blood in his temples. The nausea grew steadily worse until he believed he would retch. He didn't. He couldn't. Not in front of Frank Montgomery.

The cold hard wood beneath him, his ankles against the block, his fingers grasping the arms of the chair, his head now touching the back, Nelson closed his eyes. His breathing was shallow and weak. Everything was weightless and insubstantial.

'You want me to strap you in?' Frank asked.

Nelson opened his eyes. He got up suddenly, almost lost his balance.

Frank grabbed him before he stumbled and fell.

'Okay, I got you,' Frank said.

Without assistance, Nelson knew that his legs would give out beneath him.

'Easy, easy,' Frank said. 'Take a breath, son. It's gonna pass.'

'I'm s-sorry,' Nelson said.

'Hell, don't be sorry. I've seen people lose their breakfast after sitting in that thing. Hell, my first time in here the two fellers I was with actually buckled me in, said they were gonna give me a jolt just so I knew what it felt like.'

'Seriously?'

Frank smiled. 'Serious as cancer.'

'Fuck,' Nelson said. 'What the hell?'

'It needs to be done. You need to get a notion of what happens. Ain't no doubt that you'll wind up in here some day or other.'

'Later rather than sooner, I hope.'

'You plan on workin' here, you gotta come to terms with it. Spend a week or two on Death Row, get to know what some of these fellers did to end up here, and I guarantee you'll start thinking that this is way better than they deserve.'

'How many people are here when someone gets executed?' Nelson asked.

'Executioner, of course, then three duty officers, the prison doctor, a representative from the State Attorney General's office, and then the Warden. Prison chaplain, if the guy wants him, and usually the defense counsel.'

Frank turned to his right and drew back the curtain.

'Out there you're gonna get family of both the victim and the condemned man, also a half dozen or so reporters. Can get awful crowded.'

'And can regular people just come and watch?'

'No,' Frank said. 'Stipulations on who can witness are very specific. Can't have any old Joe wandering in.'

'Can we go back outside?'

'Sure we can.' Frank opened the door, let Nelson leave first.

Walking back towards the outer door, Frank said, 'Don't worry. Next time it won't feel anywhere near as bad.'

'I'm guessing next time there'll actually be someone in that chair, someone who's going to die.'

'Sure, but after a while it's no different from putting down a sick animal. For a guy to wind up here, he's got to be bad. And I mean bad through and through. There ain't no rehabilitation for these people, Garrett. Some people are just wicked, you know? The things they do to one another you wouldn't believe. And they ain't crazy. They know what they did, and more often than not they'd do it again given half a chance. Not an ounce of remorse amongst them.'

They reached the Death Row block and Frank came to a stop.

'In there,' he said, 'you're gonna meet people who should never have been born. That's the simple truth of it. The pain and heartbreak that these people have caused is beyond measure.

And you can't rationalize it, either. They don't think like us, and that makes it impossible for people like us to even comprehend how they could do what they did. Like all them Nazis who killed the Jews in the camps, right? They hanged those fuckers, and as far as I'm concerned, that was too merciful by half. People like that should suffer the way their victims suffered. An eye for an eye, right?'

'Right.'

'That's in the Bible. I ain't a religious man, but that's been around for as long as we have. A man commits a crime, he's got to understand that the penalty has gotta fit that crime. It's like some kind of universal balance. Karma or something, right? Seems that God, Mother Nature, or whatever else you happen to believe in, intended it that way.'

Wanting to change the subject, Nelson said, 'Warden told me that I'd need to do an apprenticeship. Said either you or Ray might help me out with that.'

'Sure thing, son. Either one of us'd be fine. Ray's a good man. Tough but fair. He don't take no shit off these people. He'll show you the ropes. An' if he can't do it for some reason, be a pleasure to get you settled in.'

'I guess I need a little time to think about it,' Nelson said. 'An' maybe talk to Hannah.'

'Hell, Hannah's a Montgomery, son. She's as much a part of Southern as me an' Ray. This place has put a roof over our heads and food on the table for as long as I can recall. It ain't a job, it's a vocation. I guess doin' what you were doin' before is pretty much the same. You ain't doin' it just for a wage, are you? You're doin' it because there's a rule of law and a justice system, and if you don't have these then you got anarchy or whatever and everyone's life goes to Hell in a handbasket.'

'I guess so, yes.'

Frank started walking again. Nelson followed him.

'You take whatever time you need, sure, but I get the idea you've already made the decision. This is a way to give something back. This is a way to protect and serve. These assholes are wild animals and someone's gotta stand on the wall and defend the innocents. These fuckers have caused way too much hurt already.'

12

'He really said that? That I was as much a part of Southern State as him and Ray?'

'His exact words,' Nelson replied.

It was the following day – Wednesday the 3rd – and Nelson was staying over at the Lakeport apartment.

'I ain't never been up there but once,' Hannah said. 'Christmas, maybe three, four years back. Some old guy was retiring and they threw a party for him.'

'It's a hell of a place,' Nelson said. 'Your dad took me in the bell tower. I sat in the chair.'

'Really? What the hell would you want to do that for?'

Nelson laughed awkwardly. 'You can't help yourself. Believe me, it's the strangest thing. You see it and your first instinct is to sit in it.'

Hannah paused in middle of making coffee and looked at Nelson intently.

'What?' Nelson asked.

She frowned, shrugged her shoulders. 'I don't know, Garrett. It just seems creepy.'

'Creepy is an understatement.'

'So are you going to take the job?'

'Undecided. More yes than no. It's kinda fallen in my lap. I get the idea that it's what your father expects of me, and I don't want to disappoint him.'

Hannah poured coffee for them both, brought cups to the kitchen table.

'And why would you be concerned about that?' she asked as she sat down.

'Because ... you know ...'

'Because of us?'

'Yes,' Nelson said. 'Because of us.'

'Hell, you don't have to please anyone but me. Don't take the job because you think it'll influence what my family thinks about you.'

'My options are limited,' Nelson said. 'I don't know anything but police. I don't have some other trade. It's not like there's some burning unfulfilled purpose gettin' me out of bed every day.'

'No, I get that, but this is a job that you don't get to leave when your shift ends.'

'Meaning?'

'I see it with both my dad and Ray. It's a tough gig, Garrett. You're out there dealing with bad people. You do that day in and day out and it's gonna get under your skin.'

'Well, the Sheriff's Department was the same.'

Hannah smiled and shook her head. 'Oh, I don't think traffic violations and drunks is anything even close to what you're dealing with out there.'

'Last day of active duty I blew a man's head off with a shotgun.'

Hannah didn't respond for a moment. 'Yes. Yes, of course. I wasn't trying to make light of it, Garrett.'

'I can do the job, Hannah,' Nelson said.

'I don't doubt that. The only thing you have to decide is whether you want to.'

'Would you have an issue with me taking it?'

'In principle, no.'

'In principle?'

'I like you the way you are,' Hannah said. 'I've seen Ray change. It's subtle, sure, but he's changed.'

'In what way?'

'Moodier, I guess. He doesn't trust people the way he used to. He doesn't laugh as much.'

'Same thing can have different effects on different people.'

'Sure, sure. I know that. I guess I just don't want to lose what you are to me.'

Nelson smiled. 'And what am I to you, Miss Montgomery?'

'I'm thinking that maybe you're the man I want to spend the rest of my life with.'

Later, lying beside her in the bed, the warmth of Hannah's body somehow the realest thing he'd experienced in a long time, Nelson was nevertheless troubled.

Two lives had ended – one in the back of that car when he pulled the trigger, the other the life he himself had known for more than a decade. Violence had marked that event, and violence had a way of never leaving. A shadow had been cast across Nelson's thoughts, and no matter which way he turned, no matter how bright his future might have looked, that shadow would always be there. It was part of him, a second set of fingerprints, and with the slightest contact he could transfer what he remembered and experienced to another. If a single moment could have such a profound effect on him, then what would happen if he spent each and every day at Southern, shoulder to shoulder with those who cast the darkest of shadows?

The sensation he'd experienced sitting in the black widow defied description. There was fear, horror, dismay, disbelief, a profound well of emotions that did not belong to any normal life. And that well was deep, perhaps without end: an abyss out of which no one could ever be rescued.

What he felt for Hannah was love. There was no denying it. It was unlike anything he'd known before, so much so that he wondered whether this was the first time he'd truly loved another person. And the time he'd spent with her family had been good. They were real people, honest and hardworking, and they seemed to have welcomed him without expectation or reservation. This was something it would be so easy to become part of, and yet there was something inside him that gave him cause for concern. Southern State was a world all its own, much the same as the Sheriff's Department. The people you knew, the people you spent time with, even out of uniform, were people who spoke the same language, possessed a similar view towards life, and, most importantly of all, unconsciously excluded anything or anyone that did not adhere or subscribe to that view. He hadn't known what it would mean to work in law enforcement until he'd done it, and even then it had taken years. This would be the same, perhaps even more drastic, but there was a sense that once he'd made the decision it could not be undone.

Most people imagined a life, and then spent their whole life waiting for it to start.

There were others who chose a life only to realize that it wasn't what they'd imagined, but by then it was too late to change it.

Nelson stood on a ledge. Below him was the unknown. He knew he could not stand on that ledge forever. He had to step off, and yet until he did, he had no idea where he would land or what might be broken in the fall.

13

Nelson's in-house Southern State training began on Monday, November 22. The program encompassed orientation, security, basic self-defense, first aid, inmate restraint, the use of chemical Mace, when an inmate should be cuffed, the use of a baton, leg shackles, the endless minor and major infractions that warranted loss of privileges, visitation rights, cell transfers and solitary confinement. Ray Montgomery was assigned as his Training Officer, and Nelson found the man to be so very similar to his father in attitude and behavior.

They began in General Population, a three-storey unit that held close to six hundred men. Cells were double-bunked, four men to each, mealtimes in three groups of two hundred, yard time the same.

As was the case with so many institutional environments, there was a camaraderie evident amongst the men with whom Nelson would work. Alongside that, there was an unspoken obligation for Nelson to prove himself before he would be accepted into their ranks. It had been the same in the Sheriff's Department. Nelson was also aware – much the same as a construction site where the uninitiated newcomers would be despatched to stores for 'skyhooks', cans of 'elbow grease' and left-handed hammers – that there may very well be similar instances of in-jokes and pranks. On edge, ever-aware that he was in a totally unfamiliar environment and dealing with people who were fundamentally opposed to his presence, he was conscious not to make a fool of himself.

That first day served to demonstrate how little he knew of what he was doing, and how much he had to learn.

Beginning with the breakfast sitting, Nelson was charged with the responsibility of ensuring that the food line was maintained, that no one jumped the queue, that each man was swiftly served, seated, and that all trays and utensils were accounted for as men finished their meal.

Viewed with curiosity by the inmates, Nelson couldn't help but feel self-conscious. Two hundred men and the kitchen crew, all of them supervised by a handful of officers, made it clear that the balance between calm and chaos was tenuous. Should something occur, the staff of Southern would be dramatically outnumbered.

Immediately, it became obvious that there were cliques and cabals inherent within the ranks of prisoners. Divided by race, age, term-length and reasons for incarceration, there were invisible divisions across the dining hall. Those that did not belong were well advised to respect those divisions. Appreciation of this was particularly difficult for new arrivals, and that morning there were two.

Nelson spotted them immediately – young, wide-eyed, perhaps still in shock, more than likely having managed no sleep the night before – they left the end of the line with their food and stood motionless. Surveying the room, trying to establish where they should go, one of them caught Nelson's eye. The expression on the young man's face was deer-in-headlights confusion.

Approaching the pair, Nelson asked their names.

'Ballantyne,' the first said.

'And you?'

'Mason,' the second replied, and then as an afterthought, added, 'Mason, sir.'

'Follow me,' Nelson instructed, and he started walking.

The two men followed Nelson. Selecting a table with half a dozen available chairs, Nelson indicated that they should sit.

Four men, already seated, looked up. Each of them stopped eating, stopped talking, and it was immediately evident that Nelson had made a mistake.

The man at the head of the table, his neck embellished with crude tattoos, one of which read 'Lawless', just shook his head. Without a word, that gesture said all that needed to be said. The newcomers were not to sit. They were not welcome. They should sit elsewhere.

Ballantyne and Mason hesitated. Ballantyne put his tray on the table.

'No,' Lawless said.

Ballantyne looked at Nelson. Mason backed up a step.

'These seats are not taken,' Nelson said.

'But they will be,' Lawless replied.

'But until they are, these men can sit and eat here.'

Lawless shook his head. 'These men can fuck off.'

Challenged, Nelson paused for a moment before he responded. Opening his mouth to speak, he felt a hand on his arm. Ray Montgomery was beside him.

'It's okay,' Montgomery said. He turned to Ballantyne and Mason. 'You men come with me,' he said. He started to walk away. Ballantyne and Mason didn't move, perhaps waiting for Nelson to say something.

'Now!' Ray stated emphatically.

'Go,' Nelson added, and the two men followed Ray to a different table.

Nelson maintained his position, looking back at Lawless.

After a handful of seconds, Lawless smiled and said, 'You can fuck off as well… sir.'

There was a smattering of laughter from the other men.

Nelson took a step backwards.

'There,' Lawless said. 'You got it. You just keep on going an' everythin' will be just fine.'

The urge to say something, to assert control, was countered by Nelson's absolute uncertainty. He felt both enraged and impotent. To stand was to incite further tension; to leave was to admit defeat.

Thankfully, Ray returned.

'Hey, dipshit,' he said to Lawless. 'Stop being a fuckin' asshole, okay? You got three months left. Keep your hands in your pockets and your tongue in your fucking mouth, all right? Personally, I'd have absolutely no problem dropping you in solitary for an extra month.'

Lawless smiled, and then he nodded. 'You have a good day there, Mr Montgomery.'

The men at the table went back to their eating and talking.

Walking away, Nelson beside him, Ray said, 'We'll talk about newcomers later, okay? And don't fuck with that guy. Bad news. Bad fuckin' news all round.'

Through November and right up to Christmas, Nelson was Ray's shadow. He followed him everywhere, watching, listening, asking questions, and many were the nights they would sit together to go through schedules, management of ex-facility work details, even the slang terms employed by inmates in an effort to maintain some sort of secrecy about their activities.

Aside from a few brief scuffles over who got to use a makeshift basketball court, the initial month was without further incident. No one got beaten, no one got stabbed, no one took a dive off the gantry.

For Nelson, there was the ever-present sense that establishing authority was a fine balance between toughness and tolerance. He was new – he knew that, as did the inmates – and even as he learned the ropes, he had to give the impression that each action, each word, was considered and certain.

Late one evening, somewhere around the end of his fifth week, Nelson was on gantry walk on an upper landing. Pausing ahead of an open cell, he sensed something was awry. The occupant, a middle-aged man by the name of John Hammett, stood stock-still in the middle of the cell, hands down by his sides, his fists clenched. The expression on his face was one of controlled fury.

Nelson stepped into the doorway.

'Where's your cellmate?' Nelson asked.

Hammett looked back at Nelson but didn't speak.

'I asked you a question, Hammett.'

'How the fuck would I know?'

'Sir,' Nelson said. 'How the fuck would I know, sir.'

Hammett sneered condescendingly.

'Something happening between you two?' Nelson asked.

'You show me where it's written that my business is your business.'

'Everything that happens in here is my business,' Nelson replied, at once feeling both a sense of tension and intense unease.

Hammett didn't speak.

Nelson put the palm of his hand on his billy club. He took another step forward.

'What you plannin' on doin',' Hammett asked. He smiled, then added, 'Sir,' in a sarcastic tone.

'Depends on what you do next.'

'You pull that club, you're gonna find out.'

'Is that so?'

'Maybe I bust your other leg, eh? Maybe I cripple you for good this time.'

'That threat alone is a week in solitary,' Nelson said.

'Do it,' Hammett said. 'Fuckin' do it.'

'Hell, if you know what happened to me, then you also know that the man who did it is dead.'

'Now you're threatenin' me, sir?'

'I'm just sayin' that there ain't no way you can win this, Hammett. You know that well enough. You cut this shit out or you an' me's gonna have a dance.'

Hammett glared, and then suddenly, unexpectedly, he relaxed his clenched fists and stepped back.

Nelson said nothing for some seconds. The expression on his face was an invitation for Hammett to talk.

Hammett shook his head resignedly. 'I gotta move,' he said, glancing at the upper bunk. 'I gotta get away from this guy.'

'You want a cell transfer? Is that it?'

'I don't give a fuck how, but you gotta get this guy away from me or I'm gonna kill him.'

'What happened?'

'Bustin' my fuckin' balls. Hour after hour, day after fuckin' day. Never lets up.'

''Bout what?'

Hammett looked at Nelson square and straight. 'You know why I'm here?'

Nelson shook his head.

Hammett relaxed, the potential stand-off now diffused. He sat on the edge of the lower bunk, leaned forward, his head down.

'I got involved with a girl,' he said. 'It was a genuine thing, you know? I thought it was real. She was younger than me, sure, but she wasn't as old as she said she was.'

Hammett looked up at Nelson. Perhaps he was waiting for

something judgemental in Nelson's expression. Nelson gave nothing away.

'And it went bad,' Hammett went on. 'As bad as it could get.'

'She lied to you,' Nelson said.

Hammett shrugged. 'Lied to everyone, I guess.'

'Who's your cellmate?'

'His name is Bernard Mason.'

'And why's he here?'

'Fraud. Counterfeit checks. Financial shit, you know?'

'He a big guy?'

Hammett laughed. 'No man, he's a skinny little fuck.'

'And you can't deal with him?'

'What, you mean give him a beating? I ain't that kind of person, Mr Nelson. That's not how I deal with things.'

'So, you're just gonna let him wind you and wind you until you snap? What happens then? You lose it and kill him?'

Hammett didn't speak for a moment. He wore the expression of a man defeated. Maybe he was lying, maybe he was telling the truth, but the impression Nelson got in that moment was of a man utterly lost and broken.

'I get you a different cellmate, who's to say they're gonna be any better?'

'I got seven months,' Hammett said.

'If you keep it together, you have. If you do something to Mason, then you got a good deal more.'

Hammett's expression changed suddenly.

Nelson turned. Mason stood in the doorway.

'So what we got here?' Mason asked.

Nelson, thinking on his feet, said, 'You got yourself a reprieve.'

Mason frowned. 'What?'

'Your buddy here just vouched for you.'

'What the fuck're you talking about?'

'Got a report you were someplace you shouldn't have been.

Hammett here says you were here in the cell with him all morning.'

'And where the fuck was I supposed to be, then?' Mason asked.

'That don't matter now, does it? Just be grateful I ain't hauling you into solitary for a month.'

Nelson turned back to Hammett. 'I find out you're bullshittin' me, then you both get a month, you understand?'

Hammett nodded. 'Sir.'

Nelson backed up, let Mason pass.

Standing in the doorway, Nelson looked at both men in turn.

'You assholes are as bad as one another,' he said. Stepping back onto the gantry, he closed the cell door.

The last thing he heard before he was out of earshot was Mason's voice.

'I have no fucking idea what that was about, but I appreciate you coverin' for me, man.'

Nelson walked away, the disquiet still in his gut, and as he reached for his keys at the end of the walkway, he realized that his hands were shaking.

'It's a game,' Ray told Nelson after dinner one evening. They were sitting out on the porch with a beer at the Montgomery house. Hannah had gone on ahead to Lakeport, and Nelson said he'd meet her there later.

'A high stakes game in some cases, but a game nevertheless. Sure, you're not really in any great danger in Gen Pop, but in a couple of weeks you'll be over in High Security. There you've got the lifers, and a lifer is a different animal altogether. Either they did something real bad, or they did a whole number of things and got three strikes, you know? Some of them'll get paroled, but they'll be old men by that time. They know they ain't gonna get drunk or laid or drive a car or have a barbecue or go to a game.

That twists up a man's guts something awful. He's fighting to hang onto some sort of self-respect, some sense that he's still in control of his life, but he knows that he's living a lie. There are gangs, crews, little fraternities. There are people who've robbed banks together, people who know people from other prisons. They're like folks who speak different languages. Even though they're all in the same place, they stick with their own kind.'

'And there's trouble between them?'

'Sometimes, sure. Shit gets smuggled in. Not often, but it happens. Men have been stabbed over a packet of smokes or a bottle of something or other. They have these little feuds and vendettas, and sometimes it ain't nothin' more than a way to relieve the boredom.'

'Ever have riots?'

Ray smiled. 'Oh, for sure. Full lockdown. Tear-gas the crap out of them. Seen that a few times.'

'Officers ever get hurt?'

'That, too. Broken teeth – one guy pushed off a stairwell a couple of years back. You learn to sense these things. You keep your wits about you, have eyes in the back of your head. And there's telltale signs that a storm is brewing somewhere and you shut it down before it happens.'

Nelson thought of the incident with Hammett.

Ray leaned back, took a swig of his beer.

'Warden Young is a hardnose, no doubt about it, but the way he thinks things are, and the way they actually are, are somewhat different.'

'How so?'

'If Young had his way, everything would be absolutely by the book. Schedules, shifts, privileges, penalties, every damned thing would be timed and tracked. However, in reality, you can't run a prison like that. You gotta give a man a few seconds of hope every once in a while. Sure, he's locked up twenty plus hours a day. The food ain't great, the yard is overcrowded, it ain't ever quiet enough to get a good night's sleep, and oftentimes you're sharing a cell with some asshole who snores like a pig and smells worse. It's a hard fucking life. Hell, it ain't even a life to speak of. Sure, most of them deserve exactly what they got, but you still gotta understand that you can only put so much pressure on a man before he snaps. Then you got a whole whirlwind of trouble on your hands. You make allowances every once in a while. Little things, right? You see a feller eatin' some other feller's dinner, you let it slide. You see a guy give some other guy a kick or two, you look the other way. You can't know everything that's going on all the time. It's not possible. These people have their own codes. They have a way of doing things that actually helps to keep order.'

'So how do you know the difference between the situation you ignore and the one you do something about?'

'Sixth sense, I guess. That's all I can tell you. You get a feel for it. Sometimes you go see the guy that got a beating and you find out he's an asshole of the first order and got exactly what was coming to him. That beating put him in his place, stopped him from starting a war. Other times, you know the guy's being put upon, that he's being harassed for no particular reason, and then you sort it out. And then there are the ones that everyone hates. The pedophiles, the rapists, you know? They are outcasts, even in a place like this. They get treated bad. People don't talk to them, fuck with their food, throw cups of piss over them.'

'In High Security, right?'

'And on the block. Death Row. There's a bunch of them waitin' their turn for the black widow.'

'I'm guessin' I'll be on there sometime or other.'

'Sure you will. We'll do a couple of weeks in High Security after Christmas, and then we'll do the block.'

'What's it like down there?'

Ray smiled. He reached for a cigarette and lit it.

'What's it like? Hell, I don't know, Garrett. Where else on earth can you find a place where men are just waiting to die? Even in war, a man has the notion that he might make it out of there alive.'

'People can get reprieved, right?'

'We ain't had the death sentence for four years. Before that, all the executions that got done, there wasn't a single reprieve. Stays, sure, but they all got fried in the end. Governor of Florida ain't what you'd call the lenient and forgiving type.'

'How many executions have you seen?'

'I guess ten, maybe eleven.'

'You get sick after?'

'First coupla times, sure. Everyone does. Ain't nothin' to feel bad about. They say the same about being a surgeon, cuttin' folks open and whatnot. It's pretty grim at first, and then you just get used to it. Besides, it ain't like there's anythin' you can do to stop it happening, and if you're in the employ of Southern State then you can't refuse to do it. It's part of the job, man.'

'You believe in the death penalty?'

'You mean that whole gig about "What is it about killing a man that makes it wrong to kill a man?" Sure, I get that, but I also get that killing that man is gonna sure as hell stop him from killing someone else. Some of these characters are so fuckin' crazy that they'll kill anyone. Another inmate, a guard, a visitor. It's in their blood, in their bones. It's who they are.'

'The ones that are born bad.'

'Yeah, the ones that are born bad.'

Ray leaned forward and dropped the butt of his cigarette into an empty beer bottle.

'Right,' he said. 'Time for us to get on home.'

Nelson got up.

'You hear what they're callin' you?' Ray asked.

Nelson smiled. 'I heard it, sure. Hopalong Cassidy, Pegleg, all that crap. I just ignore it.'

'Which is the right thing to do,' Ray said. 'They see they're winding you they'll wind you all the more. Give 'em nothing and they'll soon quit.'

'Hell, I got thicker skin than that. It doesn't bother me.'

'Good to hear. And you're gonna do fine, you know? You've already got the swing of things. You just need a little more experience and we'll have you managing shifts all on your lonesome.'

'I appreciate your help, Ray. I really do.'

'Oh, think nothin' of it, Garrett. You're family now, and we Montgomerys always look after our own.'

14

If Southern State was a world of its own, then High Security was a world within a world.

There was no comparison – physically or otherwise – between where Nelson was stationed in the last few days before Christmas and the previous weeks he'd spent in General Population. Believing he'd got to grips with how things ran, that grip was tested and challenged almost immediately.

General Population housed six hundred men on three floors; High Security had only two floors, seventy-five men to each floor, behind it the caged yard where access to fresh air and exercise was limited to a far greater extent. Here were found the armed robbers, blackmailers, kidnappers and rapists. Serving sentences ranging from fifteen years to life, there were those guilty of assault, attempted murder and extortion, and thus the rigors and disciplines were far stricter than his previous assignment. The average duration of sentence was sufficient to encourage the gang mentality of which Ray had spoken. Those with similar crimes and similar terms gravitated one to another. Separated not only by race, there was also a clear pecking order, and at the top of each clique was a single individual. For the most part, an uneasy peace existed in the block, but – as with any institution where there was too little time and too little activity to engage the mind and hands – the advent of a minor disagreement could easily escalate into a harbored grudge. Given enough time and the failure of the officers to identify the escalating tension, that grudge could become a vendetta that required resolution by the only means known to the majority of the inmates. Violence was in their blood. There was no denying it. The only time violence didn't solve a problem was when you didn't use enough.

The vast majority of cells held two inmates, but there was ample provision for those who required single berthing. Here were housed the rapists and pedophiles, eating and exercising at different times from the rest of the population. Communal time on the lower floor – a couple of hours in the afternoon when men could play cards, write letters and speak to someone other than their cellmate – were not shared with these people. Even within the confines of a penitentiary there were outcasts.

The yard at the rear of the building was not so much a yard as a fenced compound, and within that fence there were numerous cages – fifteen feet long, eight feet wide – wherein the inmates got to see the sky for an hour a day. Twenty cages, two or four to a cage, and they talked, smoked, either pacing back and forth like animals or standing stock-still, their hands high, fingers grasping the wire, their faces skyward as if drawing every ounce of light and energy possible from the atmosphere.

Watchtowers stood in each corner, lower in height than those on the outer perimeter. Within each tower was an armed sentry. Radio links were on a different wavelength from those in General Population. The tension and sense of claustrophobic containment was palpable, even outside the walls of the unit itself. Whatever degree of focus and concentration had been required in Gen Pop, it was needed five-fold in HS.

Through the first week, Nelson was shadowed by a long-serving officer called Max Sheehan. Though Sheehan had years at Southern under his belt, he treated Nelson as an equal.

'You got two landings,' Sheehan explained. 'For now, and until you get your bearings, there's only two or three people you'd need to know about. Lower landing you got William Cain. He's the big boss of the hot sauce. He's got a sidekick, name of Jimmy Christiansen. Upper landing you got David Garvey. Any which way you look at it, Cain and Garvey are bad news. If there ain't trouble, they'll make it. If there is trouble, they'll make it worse. Just like any other place, you got a hierarchy. That's just the way of things. People with twenty or thirty years to look forward to have to establish a position and maintain it. There's always someone ready to take it off of them if they don't defend it.'

'And what's their position?' Nelson asked. 'I mean, they're in here, right?'

Sheehan smiled. 'We think we're in control. We are, I guess, at least in one way. But the only thing that holds these people in line is an agreement.'

'An agreement?'

'They want out. At least those who have a chance of getting out. If they stay inside the lines, they have a hope. Slim, sure, but hope is everything, right? They fuck with us too much, we can drop another five or ten years on them. That's the fear right there. That's the thing that holds this entire thing together. And so there's an unspoken agreement. You give people like Cain and Garvey enough leeway to feel like they have some control over their own lives, and in return they actually kind of work with you to keep the machinery running.'

'So what does being boss of a landing mean, then?'

'Better food, respect from other inmates, preferential visitation allowances, choice of work assignments. More than anything, it means that we turn a blind eye every once in a while.'

'And how does that help us?'

'Oh, it helps us plenty,' Sheehan said. 'You have no idea the whirlwind of shit that would go down in this place if there wasn't some sort of internal hierarchy. Hell, it really ain't so different from the gang mentality that you see on the outside. Cain and Garvey might run different landings, and even though there might be all manner of beefs between the blacks, the Hispanics, the Aryan Brotherhood crazies or whoever, those things very rarely become anything other than chatter because Cain and Garvey keep it buttoned down.'

If Nelson needed some subjective understanding of what Sheehan meant, it came in his third week.

Garvey occupied a double-man cell but had no cellmate. Inmates were in and out constantly, usually for a few minutes at a time. If each landing was its own city, Garvey and Cain were their respective mayors.

Nelson took the time to look up Garvey's record. A lifer with no possibility of parole, his career had begun as a juvenile with breaking and entering, assault, mail fraud, counterfeit checks, and a whole host of misdemeanors that had seen him spend more time incarcerated than free. By the time he reached adult prison, he'd already served over ten years inside. It was not a single act that had resulted in his life term, but rather the three strikes policy. Rehabilitation of such an individual was considered impossible, and whichever judge had finally sentenced him had evidently believed that society had reached its tolerance for the man. Garvey knew that the only place he would ever go was another penitentiary. Now in his early fifties, a resident of Southern State for nearly two decades, he had established himself – by force, by blackmail, by sheer will – in his current assumed authority. To a man like Garvey, never to walk free again, never to perform the most ordinary functions of a human being, the position he held in prison was everything. For the vast majority of inmates, even those with twenty- and thirty-year sentences, there was hope, just as Sheehan had said. One day, if they survived Southern, they would sit at a table with family and friends, they would walk the street, buy things in a supermarket, hold someone's hand, feel the presence of another human being who was neither custodian nor threat. For Garvey, this would never happen. The reality he maintained was the only reality he would ever know.

Early on the Tuesday morning, breakfast done, Nelson was on a standard cell search. Searches were undertaken weekly – never the same times, never the same days, always with two officers to a cell. In truth, it was little more than a cursory check beneath mattresses, through the inmate's personal effects, the lining of clothes, the soles of shoes. The ways in which contraband and weapons could be hidden were both ingenious and numerous.

In Garvey's cell, Sheehan stood in the doorway as Nelson went through the routine.

Garvey, standing with his back against the wall beneath the narrow window, said nothing. He looked directly ahead, never once making eye contact with Nelson.

Checking the fixed tabletop at the end of Garvey's bunk, Nelson saw that something had been taped to the underside. As he reached for it, Garvey cleared his throat. It was subtle, but Nelson heard it.

'Next cell,' Sheehan said.

Nelson, still on his knees, looked up at him. He opened his mouth to speak, but Sheehan shook his head. He stepped over the threshold.

Nelson got up. He looked at Garvey, Garvey went on looking right ahead, neither at Nelson nor Sheehan. He didn't move a muscle, didn't utter a sound.

'We're all done, Mr Nelson,' Sheehan said. His tone was insistent.

Nelson hesitated. 'But—'

'We're behind schedule,' Sheehan said. He nodded towards the door. 'Let's go.'

Sheehan turned and left the cell. Nelson followed him. Out on the landing, Sheehan gripped Nelson's arm and walked him away down the gantry.

'What are you doing?' Nelson asked. 'There was something taped under his table.'

'You didn't see it,' Sheehan said.

'What d'you mean, I didn't see it? What if it was drugs, a razor blade...'

Sheehan held Nelson's gaze for seconds. His expression said all that needed to be said. Here was the agreement. Here was the give and take, the leeway that was granted to the Cains and Garveys of Southern.

Sheehan reached out and put his hand on Nelson's shoulder, a gesture that was more a warning than reassurance. 'You learn the difference between when you do something and when you don't and you'll get along just fine.'

By the time Christmas came, Nelson, had already started to feel the pressure of what he was doing. It was subtle, just as Hannah had said, but he knew that something was going on. Indefinable, perhaps exaggerated by his own imagination, but an insidious shift in perspective was taking place. He found himself watching people in the supermarket, at the gas station. He felt uncomfortable when someone was standing right behind him. There were awkward moments with Hannah too. Three or four times a week he would stay over at the Lakeport apartment. He wanted to be with her, but he also felt that the sense of individual identity he'd possessed before taking the job was slowly being absorbed by Southern State. Aspects of who he was were being replaced by aspects of who he was required to be. Perhaps it had been the same in the Sheriff's Department, and perhaps it was nothing more than the necessary change in attitude when doing a different job. That was how he explained it to himself, yet he was never fully satisfied with that explanation.

Nelson got to know Sheehan. He wasn't difficult to like. He had a sharp sense of humor, never took things too seriously, and – as was proven on several occasions in HS – he could be relied upon without question to give back up, to quell a conflict, to say the right thing to the right person and thus avoid escalating a small drama into a greater conflict. It was experience, of course, but there was something beyond that. Sheehan possessed the sixth sense that Ray Montgomery had spoken of – an innate ability to predict how someone was thinking, to see a different motive in an otherwise unremarkable action.

'Watch this,' Sheehan said one time as a man left his cell and started down the gantry. Another man approaching him appeared suddenly fearful and started to turn. The first man increased his pace.

Sheehan, slamming his baton hard on the railings, had stopped both men dead in their tracks.

'Back up, both of you,' he'd said. 'You don't want me to crack your skulls, right?'

The men had backed up, each returning to their respective cells.

Sheehan had come back later, found Nelson in the commissary. From his pocket he'd produced a toothbrush, one end of which had been sharpened to a point.

'That was heading for someone's kidneys,' he'd said.

'Those guys earlier?'

'We straightened it out.'

'What was it about?'

'A skin mag.'

'He was going to stab that guy because of a magazine?'

Sheehan had laughed. 'Oh, believe me, people have gotten themselves stabbed over a lot less.'

Following that incident, thinking back to the Garvey cell search, Nelson started to appreciate the invisible web of discipline that held Southern together. It was tenuous, fragile even, and it was maintained by nothing more than tacit consent between the captive and the captors.

Christmas Day was at the Montgomery place. The entire family showed up. It was the first time Nelson met not only Ray's wife, Charlene, but also got to share something more than a passing greeting with Hannah's other siblings.

Brian was Hannah's only older brother, the other three – Ray, Earl and Danny – were younger by just two or three years apart. Brian was an engineer by profession. He smiled infrequently, didn't drink, becoming animated only when Nelson asked him about his work. The consequence was a half-hour monologue about stress fractures in construction alloys, and how the standards of workmanship and material quality had sorely declined over the previous decade.

Earl was as unlike his father as it was possible to be. With shoulder-length hair, a faded jean jacket, a mustache that seemed set to catch everything headed for his mouth, Earl was a throwback to Haight Ashbury and the Summer of Love. His wife, Mary, a tall blonde woman with a seemingly uncontrollable habit of laughing raucously at the slightest provocation, spent most of her time in the kitchen with Hannah's mother, Miriam, appearing every once in a while to ask if anyone needed another beer.

Danny had been the one Nelson had met on his first visit to the house. He often disappeared into the extension on the side of the house. Nelson guessed he was smoking weed or something.

By the time dinner was served, the atmosphere in that house was everything that Nelson imagined a family celebration could be. Such things were unknown to him, an only child with estranged and aggressive parents, and, in its own way, the sense of togetherness and affection that these people had not only for one another but for Nelson himself was alien.

Frank stood up and raised his glass.

'A toast,' he said. 'To Miriam and Mary for putting on such a feast. To all of us for making it through another year with all our teeth and limbs.' He paused, looked at Nelson. 'And to Garrett here, the newest member of the clan, and hopefully the man who will help me with the insufferable burden that is my daughter.'

Hannah laughed. 'And let's not forget, Dad, who never wanted a girl in the first place and all the therapy I've needed to get over it.'

Mary laughed like a train full of hyenas. Brian wore the expression of a man who'd found himself at the wrong dinner table. Nelson looked at Hannah and wondered what the hell he'd done to deserve her.

Reaching for his hand after they'd all sat down, Hannah had asked him if he was okay. She seemed genuinely concerned that something was awry.

'I'm good, yes,' Nelson said. 'This is just a new thing for me.'

She frowned. 'What? Christmas?'

'No,' he replied. 'A family.'

15

It was less than a month before Nelson graduated his training and became a qualified correctional officer.

In the first week of February, he was assigned the position of Second-Tier Shift Supervisor in General Population. His duties were not a great deal more demanding than they'd previously been, and though he sensed a degree of unspoken resentment from some of the longer-serving officers, he soon demonstrated that he neither possessed a wish to establish any degree of superiority, nor did he treat anyone, either inmate or colleague, any differently.

Under his jurisdiction were twelve officers and a hundred and eighty-six prisoners. Reasons for incarceration ranged from assault and domestic abuse to burglary and grand theft auto. Some were there for as little as three months, others were looking at a decade.

The system was simple enough. The inmates ate, exercised, showered and shared community time by respective tier. First bell was six in the morning. Tier One took breakfast in the mess hall from 6.15 to 6.45. A fifteen-minute break allowed time for inmates to return to their cells, and for the catering crew to prepare for the Second Tier breakfast shift that started at seven. The Third Tier then arrived at 7.45. Thirty minutes for each meal sitting required a great deal of preparation. Assignment to the catering crew was a privilege afforded only those serving a sentence in excess of five years. Before acceptance, a man had to have served a minimum of two years without incident. Any infraction perpetrated by a catering applicant meant that his two years started over. Catering crew ate better. They were not assigned to external work programs. The position was fiercely sought after and guarded with equal ferocity once secured. Men had been goaded into fights and altercations, contraband had been planted before a cell search, all in an effort to take someone off the crew and thus create an opening for someone else on the roster.

Community time, known as 'social' amongst the inmates, was again scheduled by tier. Each tier had ninety minutes to engage with others outside their cells. Running from 7.00 to 8.30, 8.45 to 10.15, and then with the third beginning at 10.30, the evolution was completed by noon. Lunch, consisting of little more than a sandwich and a cup of weak, tepid coffee, was delivered to all tiers simultaneously at 12.15.

At 12.45, the work details began. At no time were more than eighty men – four groups of twenty that could each be supervised by two officers – permitted out of the block at the same time. Assignments included laundry, clothing repair, the wood shop, painting of the facility itself, cleaning and maintenance duties, external building and renovation, laying of pipe, and – during the harvest months – crews were sometimes shipped out to pick oranges, tomatoes, peppers and sugar cane.

The evening meal was again done in thirty-minute rotations, each tier taking yard time while another was eating. Once yard time was over, men went back to their cells and there they remained. Last bell and lights out was at 10.30.

It was a production line, established by Warden Young when he arrived and maintained without alteration ever since. If a man did not finish his breakfast in time, that was his loss. If a man upset the routine for any reason, he got a week in solitary. Known simply as 'the basement', solitary was below ground level under General Population. Twelve individual cells – dank, cold, measuring eight feet by six, nothing in them but a wooden palette and a thin horsehair mattress – welcomed anyone who disrupted the precise cycle of meals, social, work detail and yard.

Inmate hygiene was an issue. Cram six hundred men into a three-storey building with minimal ventilation, open toilets in each cell, a sewage system that had not been upgraded for more than five decades, and the air these men breathed, especially in the summer months, was close to unbearable. Showers were taken once every three days, fifty men at a time, but the combination of lukewarm water and cheap soap did little to temper the ever-present stench.

The incident that resulted in Nelson's reassignment to High Security in the latter part of March involved the prison chaplain.

General Population provided a small chapel, and here, once a month, a single Sunday was set aside for those who wished to attend. Due to space restrictions, the chapel could hold no more than twenty men at a time. Father Donald, a quiet, methodical man in his late sixties, had worked for more than four decades in a local community church. Though technically retired, he'd taken the position at Southern State because he genuinely believed he could be of service to the lost souls who inhabited the place.

'I am not under any assumption that I can make a huge difference here,' he explained to Nelson one afternoon in the commissary, 'but maybe there are a few who will benefit from a patient ear, perhaps a word of advice. I have known men punish themselves with guilt over something that really would be of no great significance to you or me. Having a chance, however slight, to unburden themselves of that guilt can sometimes have remarkable effects.'

Father Donald had paused then, looking at Nelson intently.

'Are you a man of faith, Mr Nelson?'

'Are you asking me if I believe in God?'

'I am asking if you believe in a creator, a divine power, perhaps just the possibility that there is something beyond the immediate mortal life that we live.'

'Big question,' Nelson said.

'For some, yes,' Father Donald replied.

'I didn't grow up with the church,' Nelson said. 'I guess that has some bearing.'

'What does your father do?'

'My father was a sheriff.'

'He passed?'

'He killed himself, Father. He was a bad man, corrupt, and his conscience finally got the better of him. For you, that's a mortal sin, right? Committing suicide.'

'It is, yes. We believe that life is granted only by God, and only God has the power to take it. Taking one's own life is viewed as an act of aggression against the Creator.'

'So he's in Hell.'

'That depends upon whether or not you believe in such things.'

'But if you believe in God, then you must also accept the concept of Heaven. And if there's a Heaven, there must be a Hell.'

'Do you know the work of Milton? A book called "Paradise Lost", perhaps?'

'I can't say I do, no,' Nelson replied.

'Milton said, "The mind is its own place and in itself, can make a Heaven of Hell or a Hell of Heaven."'

'We do it to ourselves. That's what he means, right?'

Father Donald leaned forward. He smiled with great sincerity.

'All men are basically good,' he said. 'I believe that. I don't have to believe it, but I choose to do so. In God's eyes, there really is nothing a man can do for which he cannot then be forgiven. I don't profess to understand the minds and motives of all men, but in the time that I've spent here I've come to understand a peculiar phenomenon. In almost every case, a man is caught because of something he himself did that led to his capture. The clue at the scene of the crime, the inexplicable need for a man to go back to the place something occurred, thereby alerting the authorities to his presence, the one small fact he shared with another that only he could have known. That, to me, proves that these men are fundamentally good. Perhaps they are incapable of withholding themselves from violence, from the diabolic urges they endure, and so, even subconsciously, they do something that will result in their confinement from society. Unable to stop themselves, they find a way for us to stop them.'

'It's an interesting theory,' Nelson said. 'But I'm no criminologist. I'm not really here to understand why they do what they do. I'm only here to make sure they don't do it again.'

'Most of those in General Population will leave,' Father Donald said. 'I feel it's my duty as a man of the church to try and give them something that will make their future more bearable than their past.'

Father Donald's once-a-month Sunday services began at eight in the morning. They ran for an hour or so – three, sometimes four throughout the day if there were enough who wished to attend – with a half-hour break in between each one. A single officer was assigned to supervise the gathering.

Whether the attack that took place in the chapel was planned or if it had merely been opportunistic, it later transpired that the men involved had maintained a long-standing feud.

Jerome Sallis was a small-time conman from West Palm

Beach. Serving a second term for theft, attempted bribery and the cashing of fraudulent checks, he was a bitter and twisted man. Now in his early thirties, he'd spent more than twenty years of his life peddling lies and deception. As young as twelve, he'd been sent to reform school for selling black market cigarettes to tourists in Lantana and Boynton Beach. Reform school seemed to have served only to cultivate a deep-seated mistrust of teachers, social workers, probation officers and police. He bore a grudge easily, harbored ill feeling toward pretty much everyone who crossed his path, irrespective of their intentions. Nelson knew him well enough, had put him in the basement on two separate occasions. Sallis had another two years before he could be considered for parole, but Nelson felt sure he'd not see beyond the walls of Southern until his full term was done.

Paul Bisson was a first-timer. A native of Lake Wales, he was a family man, seemingly law-abiding, a respectable and hard-working citizen. A car salesman by trade, the company he'd worked for had gone through hard times and he'd been let go. With a wife and two small children to support, he'd been at his wits' end. Feeling the ever-mounting pressure of his financial obligations, Bisson had started drinking. The bar he frequented was the haunt for a handful of grifters and thieves. One drink after another had led to a conversation about Bisson's prior place of employment, about the possibility of stealing a dozen or more cars in one go. Bisson knew the layout, knew that there was minimal security, especially over the Labor Day weekend, and thus a foolhardy and ill-advised plan was born.

Despite the fact that not a single car was taken from the lot, Bisson was charged with breaking and entering, damage to private property, attempted grand theft auto and conspiracy to rob. With no record behind him and a lenient judge, he got two years. That sentence had begun in January of the previous year. To date, he'd been a model prisoner. His wife visited frequently, often brought the children with her, and Bisson was all set to leave Southern in the early part of 1978. Bisson was also a churchgoing man, and had been part of Father Donald's congregation every chance he'd been given.

Only later, after Jerome Sallis had spent a month in solitary, did he give his reason for the attack on Paul Bisson. As Nelson had expected, it was of little substance. According to Sallis, Bisson had disrespected him, implying – at least to Sallis's understanding – that he was somehow different from everyone in Southern. In Sallis's twisted little universe, Bisson was taunting him, looking down on him, making a mockery of who he was. Bisson could never hope to understand the hard life that Sallis had endured. Sallis didn't have a wife and kids, he didn't have a home, and when he was finally released there was nothing for him to look forward to. Bisson had everything, and Sallis worked that envy up into a fury that he was no longer able to withhold.

Seated in front of Bisson, Sallis waited until prayers began. Men kneeled, their hands clasped together, their heads bowed as Father Donald first said the Lord's Prayer, and then began the recitation of a psalm.

'Blessed is the man who does not walk with the wicked, whose delight is in the law of the Lord. He is like a tree planted by water...'

It was in that moment that Sallis rose to his feet, turned suddenly, and, wrenching Bisson's head back by his hair, proceeded to stab him repeatedly in the face with a four-inch nail he'd taken from the woodshop.

Chaos, like a wave, broke out. The sound of hollering brought Nelson running from an upper gantry. The supervising officer seemed incapable not only of ascertaining what was happening, but responding appropriately. Bisson was already down on the ground, Sallis straddling him. Seemingly unsatisfied with merely brutalising the man with a nail, he was now determined to choke the life out of him.

Nelson came through the double doors as fast as his gait would permit. Immediately directing the primary officer with corralling Father Donald and the remaining congregation out of the chapel, Nelson vaulted the chairs and hit Sallis with his full body weight.

Sallis went down like a stone. Chairs clattered across the floor. A single baton blow knocked Sallis out cold. Nelson then proceeded to drag him bodily across the floor and handcuff him to a radiator pipe. Returning to the prostrate Bisson, he applied pressure to his facial wounds. By this time, two other officers had reached the chapel. Nelson sent one for a stretcher and bandages, the other for the prison doctor.

From the moment that Nelson had come through the chapel doors to the moment that Bisson was ferried out to the infirmary, it was less than six minutes.

Warden Young was contacted at his home. He arrived within a quarter of an hour. He found Garrett Nelson and another officer escorting the now-conscious Jerome Sallis out of the chapel and down to solitary. Nelson's face, his hands and his uniform were spattered with blood. Young didn't say a word. He merely stood back and watched as Nelson executed his duty.

Later that afternoon, Paul Bisson was taken to the hospital in Fort Myers. Bisson had lost his left eye, his face was badly lacerated, and the abrasions on his neck were so severe that another minute of such sustained pressure would have killed him. The attending doctor filed a report commending the immediate and effective action that had been taken by the first respondent. It was quite clear that Nelson had saved the man's life.

Nelson's command of the situation did not go unnoticed by Warden Young. A week after the incident – with Jerome Sallis awaiting arraignment and a trial date for the assault – Young called Nelson to his office.

'I had my reservations about you, Mr Nelson,' Young said, 'but let me be the first to say that those reservations have been proven completely unfounded. Your effective control of the situation last Sunday not only saved a man's life, but prevented this incident from becoming far graver.'

Young sat behind his desk. He did not ask Nelson to sit.

'This place can be likened to a powder keg. A spark is enough. We have had riots in the past, and the catalyst for such things is always unexpected, often insignificant. These men are under immense stress, as you well know, and it is only with discipline, complete authority and immediate and effective containment of such outbreaks of violence that we maintain order. What you did has unseen ramifications. It sends a message that we are in charge, that we know precisely what we are doing, and that we are always on our guard.'

Nelson was not invited to respond, and so he remained silent.

'I am provisionally transferring you to High Security,' Young said. 'I know you spent a short time there during your apprenticeship, but your presence of mind and lack of hesitation to act tells me that we are not utilising you as best we could.'

'Yes, sir.'

'Then it is settled. You will move next Monday. Second Landing. Prove yourself there, and we will have you Shift Supervisor within six months. Better pay, of course, but more importantly you will have opportunities to advance your career even further.'

'Thank you, sir.'

Young got up. 'Very good, Mr Nelson. That is all.'

Nelson turned and started towards the door. How he knew it, he could not tell, but he sensed that something had been left unsaid.

His hand on the doorhandle, Nelson paused for just a moment, and it was in that moment that Young spoke.

'Oh, one further thing.'

Nelson stopped, turned back towards Young.

'We are due to execute a man on April 6. I would like you to be one of the attending officers. I think it's time for your baptism of fire.'

16

It was an indication of the closeness of the Southern State family that both Frank and Ray Montgomery knew about the execution assignment within twenty-four hours.

On that Monday, Nelson had driven over to the house to have dinner with Hannah and her parents. Danny ate with them, but then went back to his own room. Ray showed up later with a six-pack, and while Hannah spent some time with her mother, the three men sat out on the porch.

'First time was pretty rough for me,' Ray told Nelson. 'That was back at the tail-end of '64. Twenty-three years old, green as grass. The thing that really got to me was that the kid we were executing was younger than me.'

'I remember that clear as day,' Frank said. 'I've seen a good number of them go to the chair over the years. Pretty damned sure he was the youngest.'

'Nathan Webster,' Ray said. 'That was his name. Skinny guy, hardly nothin' to him, but it took three of us to strap him down. Never would've believed a kid that size had so much strength.'

'It's instinctive,' Frank said. He leaned forward. 'Man is the only species that fears death. You hear about these Japs in the war, the kamikaze guys, you know? Honor and duty and dying for the empire and all that shit. They had those guys whacked out of their minds on amphetamines.'

'They drugged them?' Nelson asked.

'Sure as hell they did. I read about it. They called it Hiropin. They had some Japanese name for it. Senryoku something-or-other. A drug to inspire the fighting spirits. That's what they told them. Gave them shots of the stuff before they flew out. They gave them pills stamped with the crest of the emperor. Green tea powder mixed with more amphetamine. They were young as well, teenagers mostly. Off their fucking skulls they were. I mean, how the hell else you gonna get a kid to fly a plane into a battleship?'

'They gave that shit to the SS as well,' Ray said. 'And all them fellers that shot Jews at the side of trenches.'

Frank lit a cigarette. The flame of the lighter cast a glow around his face. It gave his features the cast of beaten copper.

'The other guys, they're gonna talk to you about it like it's some sort of initiation rite,' he said. 'That's just so much horse-shit. It ain't nothin' but a duty. Doesn't matter how old the guy is, he did what he did. He's been through the system. He got a fair trial, a competent defense, and a jury of his peers determined that whatever he did was bad enough to kill him. It's like an amputation. That's what it's like. Fingers got gangrene. They gotta go. Or taking a rotten tooth out of someone's mouth. You don't do that, then you'll let the infection spread and soon there's no way to stop it. Bad people are a virus. They are poisoned. Who the hell knows why? Sick in the mind, perhaps. That ain't our concern. You just man up, do what's needed, and you keep tellin' yourself that the world's a better place for it.'

'Warden Young called it a baptism of fire,' Nelson said.

Frank smiled. 'I'm sure he did.'

'I think he's got plans for you,' Ray said.

'Plans?'

'You done good here,' Frank said. 'You've got mettle. That situation in the chapel. You saved a bunch of lives, no doubt about it. Who the hell knows what would have happened if you hadn't done what you did.'

'I didn't think about it, to be honest,' Nelson said.

'And that's the difference between you and the other feller. He froze, you didn't. I'm guessin' that if you'd been on duty instead of that schmuck, then that guy wouldn't have lost his eye.'

'I heard that the other officer might lose his job.'

'He's gone, man,' Ray said. 'Warden deep-sixed him. Can't have shit like that goin' on and a guy standin' there with his pecker in his hand.'

'So what plans does the Warden have for me?' Nelson asked.

'Hell knows,' Ray replied. 'I just know that a good officer is hard to come by, and when you get a good one you do whatever's needed to keep 'em.'

Frank flicked the cigarette butt out over the porch railing into the yard. He stood up and arched his back.

Looking down at Nelson, he said, 'I liked you from the get-go, Garrett. You say what you think, and you think in straight lines. I also think you're good for Hannah. Some of the fellers she's been with, I wouldn't piss on them if they was burnin'. She's my only daughter, and she ain't fallin' over herself to get me no grandkids. I've come to terms with that. Not every woman is destined to be a mother. Only thing I want is for her to be happy, and she's happier now than I've seen her in a long time.'

'I care for her a great deal,' Nelson said.

'I know you do, son, and that means a lot to me. You keep on doin' whatever you're doin' because it's workin' just fine. An' if you decide that maybe you wanna get a place together so you ain't drivin' back an' forth between here and Fort Haines every damned day, then come talk to me. Me and Miriam got a bit set aside, and we'd be happy to help you out if you need it.'

Nelson stood up. 'That's really good of you, Frank. That really means a lot to me.'

Frank put his hand on Nelson's shoulder. He smiled warmly. 'You're a good man, Garrett, and I appreciate you bein' around.'

With that, Frank went back into the house. Nelson sat down again. He took a swig from his bottle.

'He's an old man,' Ray said. 'Mind's goin', I reckon. Me, I see you for exactly who you are, you gammy-legged fuckin' halfwit.'

Nelson near choked on his beer, the pair of them laughing like fools.

Nelson barely said a word on the drive back to Lakeport.

Not until they were in Hannah's kitchen did she ask what was up.

'Your father,' he said.

'What's he done now?'

'He surprised me is all.'

'Surprised you? How?'

'He told me that he thought I was good for you.'

'Well, he's right. You are.'

'And he said that if we ever thought of getting a place together then he and your mom would help us out if we asked.'

Hannah couldn't conceal her dismay. She sat down at the kitchen table.

'You serious? He actually said that?'

Nelson sat facing her. 'Does that surprise you?'

'Surprise is an understatement. Jesus, that is … hell, Garrett, I don't even know what to say.'

'Because?'

'Because my dad has his issues. Maybe *had* is more accurate.'

'With you?'

'With all of us,' Hannah said. 'But ours was never a regular family.'

'But you all seem so close.'

'Now, maybe. But not when we were kids. Mom and Dad got married young. Dad was seventeen, Mom a year younger. And they got married because she was pregnant.' Hannah gave a wry smile. 'And no, it wasn't planned.'

'That must've been rough.'

'Mom's family disowned her, basically. Didn't go to their wedding, not that it was much of a wedding anyway. Even when Brian was born, they didn't want to know. Not a word from any of them. My dad's mom took them in. Dad was working sales. Some godawful travelling job, back and forth across the state. But he kept it together, and by the time I was born in '39, they had their own place. He still had to work all hours God sent, but whatever else you might say about him, he ain't work-shy. Then she had Ray in '41, and got pregnant with Earl in July of '42. October of '42, Dad went to the war. Served in Belgium, France, even North Africa as far as I can figure. He wasn't here when Earl was born, and when he got back in the fall of '45 he was, understandably, a different man. Mom never really spoke of it. Even now, thirty years on, she changes the subject anytime any of us bring it up. I think he drank. I can't be sure of that, but that's the impression I get. Mom said he was moody, unpredictable, a real short fuse, you know?'

'And then they had Danny, right?'

'Yeah. He was born in March of '46. Five kids by the age of twenty-five. Can you imagine?'

'But they must've wanted you all, right? I mean, how the hell do you wind up with five kids if you don't want a big family?'

'I don't think they planned on having five,' Hannah said. 'Brian definitely wasn't planned, and I don't think Danny was either.'

'And how was he when you were a kid?'

'I don't really remember him being around. He started at Southern in about '48. He did long shifts, sometimes doubles, but I don't think he had any choice. Mom couldn't work, obviously, and the idea of not providing for his family would never have entered his mind.'

'So why are you so surprised that he'd want to help you now?'

'Because I know I'm a disappointment to him. He's old-school. A girl gets married, has babies, looks after the home, takes care of her husband. All that stuff. And, to be honest, I was a bit wild in my teens and early twenties. Smoking and drinking and going to the drive-in with boys wasn't his idea of what I should be doing with my life.'

'And what about your mom?'

Hannah smiled. 'My mom is the glue which holds the whole world together. That woman has layers, and then there's layers beneath the layers. She might seem like the dutiful wife, but she doesn't take any shit from my father. He doesn't get wound up so often these days, but if he starts, she only has to give him a look and he backpedals like a motherfucker. He'd never admit it, but she's the boss of the Montgomery clan.'

'So what's the deal with Danny?' Nelson asked.

'What about him?'

'He's, what, thirty? He lives in that room at the side of the house. He creeps away without a word. And then creeps on back, and if he ain't stoned then I'm a fucking houseplant.'

Hannah started laughing. 'Danny is the one that got away. He's always had it the easiest. Dad expects nothing from him, and nothing is what he's gonna get. Unless, of course, Danny decides to get his shit together and do something with his life. That boy hit seventeen and never changed, and Dad just lets it go as an apology.'

'An apology?'

'To my mom. To us. Letting Danny do whatever the hell he wants is my dad's way of making amends for being an asshole.'

'I gotta say, Frank has never been anything other than friendly to me.'

'You didn't see it,' Hannah said, 'but he was watching you like a hawk. A wrong move, and you would've been out of here on your ear. You know, for all the crap he gave me about the guys I went with, I have to say now that he was a pretty damned good judge of character. The ones he said were assholes really turned out to be full-time assholes. However, you were different. A cop for ten years, wounded in action. If that wasn't enough, you took the job at Southern, did your training with Ray, and then that thing happened in the chapel. Now you're Frank Montgomery's golden boy. If he'd have sat down and written a description of the kind of man he'd want for me, then you'd be it.'

'And what about you? You know, as far as kids are concerned?'

Hannah looked down, away, and then she sighed. 'I don't know, Garrett. Sure, there've been times I've wondered what it would've been like to have a family of my own, but it wasn't meant to be.'

'You think it's too late?'

Hannah turned to face him. It was the first time Nelson had ever seen her look at him that way. There were shadows, undeniably so, and he regretted asking the question.

'I do, yes,' she said. 'To be honest, the idea scares me. Not that I couldn't be a good mother. I think I could be, you know? I guess maybe it has something to do with Southern.'

'How so?'

'Living with people who work there reminds me how bad people can be. Bringing a child into a world that's this dark, this fucked up … I don't know. I think I'd be frightened to ever let a child of mine out of my sight.'

Nelson took her hand. 'I'm sorry I asked,' he said.

'It's okay,' she replied. 'Don't be sorry. If we're gonna make a real go of this, then these things need to be talked about.'

'I want to make a real go of it, Hannah. I also think that we should talk about moving in together.'

'Is that what you want?'

'Don't you?' Nelson asked.

'Sure, yes. Of course. But that kinda scares me too.'

'Because we haven't been together long enough for you to feel you know me?'

'No, it's not that,' she said. 'It's because you haven't been at Southern long enough for me to know how you're gonna change.'

17

In the days leading up to the execution, Nelson knew he wouldn't walk away from the experience unscathed. How it would affect him, he had no way of knowing. The weight of it burdened him with a sense of unease that grew heavier with each passing day.

In an effort to better understand what was going to happen, Nelson took the time to research the condemned man and the crime for which he'd been sentenced. Through newspaper articles at the Clewiston Library and the court records themselves, pretty much everything he wanted to know about the man was available.

Darryl Steven Jeffreys was a Florida native. Now forty-two years old, he'd been born in Fellsmere, Indian River County, in September of 1934. His parents, Harold and Catherine, were regular working people, and throughout his childhood there was no indication that their boy was anything other than a regular child. He neither failed nor excelled at school. He had friends, pursued interests in baseball, camping trips and fishing, and when he reached high school, it seemed clear that Darryl would wind up working outdoors. His father was in construction, and instead of going to college, Darryl took a job in the same firm. He was a hard worker. By the time he was twenty, he was running his own crew of six.

In the spring of 1965, Darryl left home. He moved into his own place out near the airport in Gifford. He saw his father routinely at work, he visited his family home frequently, and he started dating a local primary schoolteacher called Faye Bryant. They started living together in June of the same year.

In December of 1965, Darryl fell from the roof of a one-storey building. He suffered a broken shoulder, three cracked ribs and a dislocated pelvis. He was laid up for a month, and even when he was back on his feet, he continued to suffer incapacitating bouts of pain. Advil, Tylenol and Hydrocodone didn't make the grade. So began an ever-worsening dependency on stronger and stronger painkillers. Combined with the fact that Darryl started drinking more and more frequently, the deterioration in his physical well-being and emotional state was rapid.

Despite the fact that no callouts, cautions or charges were filed, friends and neighbors of the couple reported that Darryl and Faye argued often and loudly. Though explained away as accidents by Faye herself, there were clear indications that Darryl was physically abusive. On one occasion she was unable to work for more than a month. A note in her employment file at the school said that she was suffering from a protracted bout of pneumonia. The prosecution's cross-examination revealed that Faye had undergone surgery for a broken jaw.

In August of 1966, Faye, finally at her wits' end, left Darryl and returned to her parents' home in Palm Bay. Her father, Walter, giving testimony at the trial, said that it was as if a stranger had moved into their home. The vivacious, sociable young woman who had moved in with Daryl Jeffreys just over a year before was now withdrawn, introverted and argumentative.

The first police report filed against Darryl Jeffreys by Faye's father came just six weeks later. Due to the fact that Darryl did nothing more than sit in a car across the street from the Bryant house, no action could be taken against him. He was neither trespassing nor harassing them.

That Darryl took to standing in the Bryants' front yard at night, looking up at the house, chaining cigarettes, did warrant a caution. Darryl simply stood on the sidewalk instead.

The incidents grew in frequency and duration. On one occasion, Walter threatened Darryl with a golf club, finally venting his anger and frustration by striking Darryl's car numerous times. A half-dozen pronounced dents, a broken wing mirror and a cracked windshield resulted in Walter being charged with damaging private property. Walter Bryant had to pay for the repairs to Darryl's car, and was bound over to keep the peace for twelve months.

On Christmas Eve, 1966, having taken enough painkillers to floor the average man, Darryl Jeffreys kicked in the back door of the Bryant house. Charging up the stairs, Darryl was confronted by Walter. With a single blow, Walter was knocked sideways into the wall. He was out cold before he hit the landing. Walter survived. Faye and her mother, however, were not so fortunate.

Corralling the distraught mother and daughter in the parents' room, Darryl bound Faye's hands and feet together with the cord from a robe. Lying on her stomach, her arms pulled back behind her and tied to her ankles, she then had to endure the sound of her mother being fatally strangled by Darryl.

Darryl then proceeded to kick Faye Bryant to death.

According to the post-mortem, the young woman suffered more than forty broken bones. Giving an uncharacteristically emotive statement in court, the coroner said that the pain and suffering Faye Bryant must have experienced would have been far beyond the imagination of most people. Despite the defense attorney's rebuttal that such a claim was unsubstantiated, despite the judge's instruction that the jury should disregard the comment, the desired effect had been accomplished.

In a somewhat brief and perfunctory defense, Jeffreys' drug dependency and alcoholism were viewed not as mitigating circumstances as was hoped by his public defender, but as further evidence of his depraved and sordid character. Nothing that took place through the remainder of the trial served to change the opinion of the jury.

Darryl Jeffreys was found guilty of breaking and entering, assault, and two counts of first-degree murder on Wednesday, February 8, 1967. On Friday the 24th, he was sentenced to death and remanded to Southern State. When Furman v. Georgia ended the death penalty in June of 1972, Jeffreys believed that his sentence would be commuted to life without parole. With the reinstatement of the death penalty in July of 1976, it became clear that no such commutation had been proposed or implemented.

Darryl had been on Death Row at Southern for eleven years. Appeals had gone all the way to the Supreme Court. The Supreme Court had been unmoved. The murder of Faye Bryant and her mother had been considered not only heinous, atrocious and cruel, but also committed in a cold, calculated and premeditated manner without any pretence of moral or legal justification. Save last-minute intervention by the Governor of Florida – the likelihood of which was less than slim – Darryl was going to die, and Nelson knew he would be there to ensure it happened.

The morning of Wednesday, April 6, 1977 broke clear. The light was soft, like burnished metal. Moment by moment, the sky displayed all the colors of a gasoline spill.

Arriving at Southern just after six, he was met by Frank Montgomery.

'Today you make your bones,' Frank said.

Nelson didn't respond. He focused on the events that had brought Darryl Jeffreys to this point in time. Due process had been carried out. The man had received a competent defense, but the weight of his crimes had tipped the scales of justice too far against him ever to be balanced in his favor.

During his apprenticeship, Nelson had not been in the block itself. Once through the external doors, the palpable sense of shadowed claustrophobia was of greater intensity than anything he'd experienced in High Security or solitary.

Six cells ran face-to-face on each side of a wide corridor. There were no inner walls, merely floor-to-ceiling bars, a section of which was hinged to provide entry and exit. Every aspect of privacy was removed. A man slept, ate, washed, pissed and took a crap in full view of anyone in the hallway. Nine cells were occupied, and as Nelson followed Montgomery down to a doorway at the end, he felt every man present watching him. These people knew Darryl Jeffreys better than anyone else alive. They also knew that the fate that awaited him was also patiently waiting for them.

Unlocking the door at the end of the hall, Nelson and Montgomery stepped into a narrow secondary corridor. There were four further doors.

Indicating the two doors to the right, Montgomery said, 'Isolation cells. Man gets troublesome, in he goes.'

He then indicated the doors to his left. 'That one goes out through a covered walkway to the bell tower. And this one is where they spend their last night.'

Sliding open a hatch in the door, Montgomery looked through a circular aperture.

'Take a seat, Mr Jeffreys. We're comin' in.'

Montgomery waited a moment until Jeffreys complied, and then he unlocked the door.

Though spartan, the cell was twice the size of those in High Security. The floor was linoleum, the walls painted a pale yellow. To the right, close to the ceiling, was a narrow window through which came a good deal of light. The bed, the same iron design and construction as the bunks in the other blocks, was bolted to the floor. The sheets appeared to be cotton, the blanket of heavy wool, and beside the bed a single chair – also bolted to the floor – had a deep cushion. It was only when Nelson looked up that he realized that the cell had no ceiling. In its place were bars, an observation post, a guard on watch. A man spending his last night on Earth might very well be tempted to take his own life. He could strip the sheets and fashion a noose. A desperate man might choose to commit suicide in some final, futile demonstration of free will. Much like Nelson's own father.

Darryl Jeffreys, subdued and pale, sat on the edge of the bed.

Nelson remained standing by the door as Frank took a seat.

'You want to write a letter?' Frank asked.

Jeffreys, looking considerably older than a man in his early forties, shook his head.

'Nothin' to say,' he replied, 'and no one to say it to.'

'This here's Mr Nelson,' Frank said. 'He's gonna be with us when we take you over.'

Jeffreys looked up at Nelson. His gaze, implacable, unerring, pinned Nelson right where he stood.

When Jeffreys spoke, he barely moved his lips, as if every word he uttered was against his will.

'How ya doin' there, Mr Nelson?'

Nelson hesitated, and then he nodded. 'Okay, Mr Jeffreys.'

'You rode this wagon before, have you?'

Nelson gave an almost imperceptible shake of his head.

Jeffreys smiled knowingly. 'First time for me, too.'

'Is there anything we can get you now?' Frank asked.

'Still waitin' on my damned breakfast,' Jeffreys said.

'It'll be here soon,' Frank said. He glanced at his watch. 'Comes at seven. In fifteen minutes or thereabouts.'

'I asked for blueberry pancakes. Four o' them. Whipped cream.

Got me some bacon, too. Home fries. Pint of coffee. Told 'em I wanted it black and bitter.' He grinned. 'Like my fuckin' soul, I guess.'

Jeffreys lowered his head again. He laced his fingers together in his lap.

'Sweet girl,' he said, his voice little more than a whisper. 'Didn't deserve what I did to her. I know that. I got myself in a bad, bad place. Couldn't see nothin' but more darkness. The drugs I was takin', an' all that drinkin'. Drove me crazy it did. But hell, there's people in the same situation an' they don't go killin' innocent people, right?'

Jeffreys looked up at Nelson.

'Ain't a man here who doesn't wish he could go back and change one thing,' Jeffreys said. 'A minute, a second, that's all it took. One terrible fuckin' decision, and here we all are.'

Frank got up. 'We're gonna go check on that breakfast for you,' he said.

Nelson followed Frank out of the room. He waited until the door was locked. Frank indicated that they should leave the way they came in.

Frank led the way, Nelson right behind him, his hands varnished with sweat, a strange sense of disconnected weightlessness throughout his entire body.

18

At 7.45 on the morning of Wednesday, April 6, the prison doctor performed a final examination of Darryl Jeffreys. Though his pulse and blood pressure were understandably elevated, he was given a clean bill of health. It was, perhaps, the final irony. In the eyes of the state a man had to be well enough to die.

At 8.00, the prison barber, accompanied by another guard, attended Jeffreys' cell in order to shave his head and the calf of his right leg. It was during this procedure that Jeffreys pissed himself. It was another ten minutes before provision was made for him to shower and don a clean set of clothes.

At 8.35, Frank Montgomery and Garrett Nelson arrived at Jeffreys' cell. Here he was placed in handcuffs and legs irons. Jeffreys said nothing. He neither resisted nor aided them as he was shackled. It was as if he'd already quit his body.

Exiting the cell, Frank to Jeffreys' right, Nelson to his left, they walked him to the fourth door. A third guard unlocked the door and stepped through. Jeffreys went through first, the guard gripping him by the forearm and holding him until Frank and Nelson had come through. The guard then locked the door behind them.

The corridor that ran from the back of the block to the bell tower was no more than fifteen feet in length.

Walking ahead of them, the guard reached the door. He knocked once. The door was immediately unlocked and opened from within.

The guard went through first to receive Jeffreys, and then, once Frank and Nelson had entered the chamber itself, the door was locked behind them.

Jeffreys was instructed to sit on a bench against the wall. He did so without a word.

Standing beside the electric chair itself was a middle-aged man in a three-piece suit. Over this, he wore a leather apron. At his feet was a bucket. From his attire and demeanor, Nelson had no doubt this was the state executioner. Back against the wall the Warden and Father Donald stood motionless. To the right of the Warden was a wall-mounted telephone unit. Above it was a clock. The time was 8.46.

Glancing at his own watch, the Warden nodded to the executioner.

The executioner stepped forward. 'We begin,' he said quietly.

Frank got up. Unhooking his key chain, he knelt down and released the irons on Jeffreys' legs. He then removed the handcuffs. He nodded to Nelson, and between them they brought Jeffreys to his feet and walked him to the chair.

Once seated, Frank indicated that Nelson should strap down Jeffreys' right wrist. Frank strapped down the left. Looping the rear strap through from behind the chair, Jeffreys' chest was secured. From the underside of the chair, a fourth strap secured him at the waist.

It was only then that Jeffreys raised his head. He looked at Nelson, but Nelson had no sense that he was actually being seen. The man wore a strange, enigmatic half-smile, almost as if he was looking at some long-ago nostalgic memory that somehow served to separate him from the reality of what was now happening.

With the straps secured, Frank stepped back. Nelson followed his lead.

The executioner wheeled a small trolley forward. On it were the calf plate and the head cap. Taking a length of wet sponge from the bucket on the floor, the calf plate – semicircular, perhaps eight inches long and three and a half inches wide – was positioned over the sponge and then secured behind the leg by two leather straps. As the straps were tightened, small rivulets of water ran down Jeffreys' ankle and pooled on the floor. Before he stood up, the executioner took a clean towel from the trolley and mopped up the spillage.

Jeffreys closed his eyes. He took a deep breath and then released a long slow sigh. He then lowered his head and started to mumble something that Nelson could not understand.

The head cap was a circle of thick leather with two straps – one that secured the cap around the forehead, the other beneath the chin. Inside it was affixed an internal brass screen. The executioner took a small dry sponge from the pocket of his apron. He positioned it over the screen. He then took a second sponge from the bucket and placed it on top of Jeffreys' shaved head. Ensuring the cap was situated correctly, he then nodded towards Frank. Frank assisted in securing the straps. Once again, thin streams of water issued from the wet sponge and made their way down Jeffreys' face. It appeared that he was weeping, but not of his own volition.

The executioner glanced up at the clock: 8.54.

The guard who had assisted in Jeffreys' movement from the final holding cell then came forward. In his hand he held a cable. It was as thick as a finger. At its end there was a brass clamp that the executioner secured to the electrode at the edge of the head cap. Once complete, a second cable was produced. This was secured to the calf plate.

The executioner checked the straps, the cables, the electrode connections, and then, in a final moment that seemed almost tender, he wiped the last vestiges of water from Jeffreys' face.

Stepping back, he nodded at the Warden.

The Warden directed that the viewing curtain be drawn aside. The light from the room beyond illuminated the chamber, lifting all shadows and presenting the scene in the starkest clarity. Jeffreys involuntarily blinked, and when he saw the number of people – Walter Bryant amonst them – on the other side of the glass it was as if he only then fully comprehended where he was. He started to hyperventilate. He wrestled against the straps that held him, but they held him so securely that he barely moved.

The Warden cleared his throat.

'Darryl Steven Jeffreys. Having been tried and found guilty by a jury of your peers, it is the judgement of the court and the State of Florida that you be put to death. Before sentence is carried out, do you have any last words?'

Jeffreys stopped fighting. He closed his eyes and breathed deeply. When he again opened his eyes, there was that faint enigmatic smile. Jeffreys looked out towards the crowd of witnesses.

'You people ain't no better than me,' he said. 'Only one that deserves an apology is Faye, and she ain't here. The rest of you can go fuck yourselves. An' if I'm goin' to Hell, then I guess I'll be seein' you there.'

Jeffreys then turned to Warden Young. 'As for you . . . if there's a life beyond this one, I will come back and kill you. And it will be a pure kill, justified and clean.'

With a final sneer, Jeffreys lowered his head.

The Warden stepped back to the wall.

Father Donald opened the Bible in his hands, and, as he read a verse, the executioner proceeded to apply two-inch lengths of white tape over Jeffreys' eyes.

Father Donald finished his reading.

The Warden looked up at the clock. It was 8.59 and thirty seconds. He glanced at the telephone, then back to the clock. He looked straight ahead.

Nelson, unable to look at Jeffreys, focused on the clock as that final half-minute counted down. Passing the six at the bottom of the face, it was as if the second hand was fighting against gravity. Everything slowed down. A single second became five, then ten, and time stretched and played out like a distorted spool of film.

The nausea rose from the base of Nelson's gut to his chest, then to his throat. He closed his eyes, opened them again. He tried to breathe deeply, but without a sound. There was a rushing noise in his head and he couldn't make it stop. His scalp itched with sweat, his palms too, and it was a battle to stay upright.

Eleven seconds.

Nelson swallowed. His mouth was dry, his throat tight. Had he been required to speak, he didn't believe he would have been able.

Eight seconds.

Warden Young glanced at the telephone on the wall. He knew it would not ring, but he looked anyway.

Nelson looked at Frank. His expression was implacable.

Four seconds.

The executioner looked at the Warden. The Warden nodded in the affirmative.

The lever dropped.

A fraction of a second, and suddenly Jeffreys arched backwards. His mouth opened in a silent scream.

The sound of bone cracking was like a gunshot.

Jeffreys' body was rigid, held in suspension off the seat of the chair, his every muscle, nerve and sinew pulled taut, his entire frame as rigid as steel.

The smell of scorched sponge hit Nelson. At first he thought it was hair, but Jeffreys' head had been shaved clean. Nelson's mouth filled with vomit. He closed his eyes, gritted his teeth and swallowed.

The executioner raised the lever and the current stopped. Jeffreys' lifeless body slumped back into the chair.

Warden Young nodded at the doctor. The doctor stepped forward and placed a stethoscope against Jeffreys' chest. After a few moments, he stepped back.

'Again,' he said, his voice barely a whisper.

The second surge produced the same effect, lifting Jeffreys' body off the chair as if it was being dragged upwards towards the ceiling. His face stretched and contorted. A section of tape came loose and Jeffreys' right eye, blood-red and swollen, issued a thick viscous liquid.

The current halted, Jeffreys slumped into the chair once more. His head down, his chin against his chest, Nelson smelled the rich, acrid stench of burning skin.

The doctor once again checked for heartbeat and pulse. He looked at the clock on the wall. 'Official time of death, 9.04 a.m., Wednesday, April 6, 1977.'

Warden Young instructed that the viewing window curtain be drawn.

'Officer Nelson,' Frank said.

Nelson looked up. Only then did he understand that the Warden's instruction had been for him.

Stepping to the window, Nelson looked into the witness room. Bathed in a strange varicoloured light that came from the stained-glass window above, the faces that looked back at him were pale and drawn. No one moved. No one spoke.

Nelson drew the curtain, and then turned back to Jeffreys.

'Officer Montgomery,' Young said to Frank. 'You and Officer Nelson assist the doctor.'

'Sir,' Frank replied.

Young left, as did the executioner, Father Donald and the other chamber attendees.

Frank started to undo the straps securing Jeffreys' body to the chair.

'I'll call for the gurney,' the doctor said.

The straps freed, Frank handed Nelson a tool that resembled a small paint scraper.

'You'll need this,' he said. 'To get the plate off of his calf.'

Nelson took the implement. He looked at Jeffreys, then back at Frank.

'Best to just do it, Garrett. It don't get any easier the longer you wait.'

Nelson knelt at the foot of the chair. He looked at the metal plate, how it had burned into Jeffreys' leg, the radiation of scorch marks, the way the swelling had pulled the leather straps so very taut around the muscle.

He tried his very best, but he could not stop himself. It was then, as he leaned forward and retched violently into the bucket of saltwater beside the chair, that the bell in the steeple above him began to toll. The sound was brutal and relentless, and he felt it through every bone in his sickened body.

19

The smell of burning was in Nelson's clothes, in his hair, his nostrils and on his skin. It was the smell of dying and death, and he could not rid himself of it.

The weight of Jeffreys' body as they lifted it from the chair to the gurney was greater than anything he had ever carried. The bone in his own leg – long-since knitted and healed – ached with a dull pain. His mind was crowded with unwanted images, and the sound of the bell in the tower seemed to echo long after its tolling had ceased.

After the prison doctor completed his full examination and signed the death certificate, Father Donald came to oversee the placement of the body in the simple wooden coffin. He rested the flat of his right hand on Jeffreys' chest and he bowed his hand and he mumbled prayers. All the while, Nelson was unable to stop himself from looking at Jeffreys' face. The scalp had been badly burned. The blood in every vein had boiled furiously, if only for seconds, and this had brought them to the surface. The man's skin displayed a network of visible threads. Jeffreys' eyes had burst. The doctor, unable to close his eyelids, wound a bandage around the head to contain the fluid that still seeped from the ruptured sockets. Soon the bandages became sodden, and the resultant visage was disturbing and horrific. Jeffreys' face was an image of pain and torment that far exceeded anything that Nelson could have imagined. Darryl Jeffreys had died, but Nelson, experiencing emotions that were utterly unfamiliar to him, believed that a small aspect of his own humanity had also died in that chamber.

At last, the official procedures were complete. Four inmates from General Population were brought in, and, under the watchful eye of Father Donald, the doctor, Frank Montgomery and Nelson, the coffin was carried out of the bell tower to a flatbed truck behind the building. The inmates were dismissed. Frank and Father Donald climbed into the cab of the truck. Nelson sat beside Father Donald, wordless and without expression. He hoped no one would speak. He believed he would be unable to respond.

The drive from the bell tower to the main gate lasted a mere handful of minutes. Nelson saw no one as they went, but nevertheless had the impression that every eye in the compound was watching them. There was a sense of being judged, and though he knew it was nothing but imagination, he felt it so very strongly. He had aided in the killing of a man, a man he did not know, a man who had never done anything to him. Nelson had obeyed the law. He had fulfilled the obligation and requirement of the justice system. He had performed the duty and function of his post. But, all these things aside, he had nevertheless strapped a man down, watched him die in a truly brutal manner, and thus knew he would never be able to forget what he had seen.

God's Acre, the Southern State Penitentiary cemetery, was a tract of land no more than a quarter of a mile from the fence. Simple wooden crosses, many of them rotted into fragments, marked the burial of all those who had been executed throughout the prison's history. They were arranged in neat rows, and they led out to the edge of a wide expanse of trees. As the truck drew nearer, Nelson saw a guard and a group of four inmates awaiting their arrival.

Frank came to a halt along a rutted track that ran between the rows. He turned off the engine and he and Father Donald got out of the cab. The four inmates walked towards them slowly from the gravesite.

Nelson got out and went to the rear of the vehicle. He let down the gate. With simple nods of acknowledgement, two of the inmates climbed onto the bed and pushed the coffin towards the edge. Stepping down once more, the four men shouldered it between them and carried it from the edge of the road.

Ropes were slung beneath the coffin, and with a seeming ease that came from repetition, it was lowered into the ground. Frank stayed by the truck. He smoked a cigarette. He said nothing. Nelson watched as the hole was filled, as a wooden cross was hammered into the ground, as the guard and the four men – again without a single word – started back towards the compound. Within a few minutes they had passed out of sight. Father Donald then said a few final words. Nelson heard them but they did not register.

Frank got back into the truck. Nelson got into the passenger seat, Father Donald beside him.

'You okay?' Frank asked.

Nelson nodded in the affirmative. His throat was tight.

'You mustn't think about it,' Frank said. 'It is what it is. There's nothing you can do to change it. That man made his own fate. It was his decisions and his actions that brought him here. Not you, not me, not the Warden. He and he alone is responsible for the way he died.'

'I know,' Nelson replied.

'And if, like Father Donald here, you believe in God and redemption and forgiveness of sins, then wherever he is now has got to be a better place than Southern.'

Nelson looked at Father Donald. Father Donald just stared right ahead.

He looked back at Frank. 'Do you believe in that?' Nelson asked.

Frank didn't blink, didn't turn his head. 'Maybe. A long time ago. Now I don't know. Father Donald once told me that if you look hard enough, you'll find God's presence in everything. If that's true, then you'll find the Devil's too, right, Father?'

Father Donald didn't respond.

'I do know that there's nothing that people won't do to each other,' Frank went on. 'Men like Jeffreys have brought a world of hurt down on others. They lie with such conviction that they believe it's the truth. Some of them told so many lies they can't even remember the truth. They ain't the same as you an' me. I don't know why. Maybe they was born that way. Maybe God quit on them before they even got started.'

'The only thing I want to believe is that we're doin' the right thing,' Nelson said.

'Well, I guess we won't know that until our own time comes.'

Frank started the engine. He backed up the truck, turned it around, and headed towards the fence. Neither he, Father Donald nor Nelson spoke another word.

20

Nelson understood that the mind possessed shadowed corners, and within those corners resided the things he hoped he'd one day forget. Their presence was known to him, and the mere fact of ignoring them afforded them strength. His efforts to hide from these things not only confirmed their existence, but acknowledged their power to find him, to hurt him, to scar his soul. However he might try to run from what was inside of him, he knew he could never escape from who and what he believed he had become.

In the week following the execution, Nelson was subdued, so much so that Hannah began to question the nature of their relationship. He'd spent less time with her, had gone to the Montgomery house only once, had not stayed over at the Lakeport apartment as was his usual routine.

Finally, on the subsequent Thursday, she'd arrived unannounced and unexpected at his house in Fort Haines. Once in the kitchen, she had confronted him.

'You need to talk to me,' she said. 'I need to understand what's going on with you. With us. Something has happened, and if you won't share it with me then I... well, I don't know what we're going to do.'

'It's not you,' Nelson said.

'Well, from where I'm standing, I don't see who else it could be.'

'Really, it's not you,' Nelson repeated. 'And it's nothing to do with us.'

She frowned. 'Of course it's to do with us, Garrett. This is *us*. We're either together or we're not. You either trust me or you don't. If something happens and you can't talk to me about it, then I don't see how we can create a future together. If this isn't based on honesty and openness, then it ain't worth a damn.'

Nelson sat down at the kitchen table. Hannah sat facing him. He looked at her, all the while asking himself whether it was right and fair to draw her into the well of dark emotions that he was experiencing.

'I killed a man,' Nelson said.

'You what?'

'Last Wednesday. The man that was executed.'

Hannah's relief was instantaneous. 'Jesus Christ, Garrett, I thought you meant that you actually killed someone.'

'I've killed two,' he said. 'The one back in August, and now this one.'

'Is that what this is about? You think you are actually responsible for either of those?'

'I am,' he replied.

'Okay, you are, but it's not like you actually murdered anyone. That guy at the drug bust thing was all set to kill you and whoever else was in the way. That was self-defense. And the guy who was executed, that was your job. He was gonna be executed whether you were there or not.'

'I know that, Hannah. I understand that. But it doesn't change the fact that… that it tears me up inside to think about it.'

'So don't think about it.'

Nelson gave a wry smile. 'I'm not like your father, Hannah.'

'I know you're not. I love him dearly, but the last thing I want is someone like my father.'

'He's made of different stuff. He can handle it. He just sees it as part of his job, a necessary thing. Whichever way I look at it, I don't see how I can reconcile myself to being involved in this.'

'So don't be involved.'

Nelson frowned. 'How can I not be involved?'

'Don't volunteer again.'

'What? I didn't volunteer.'

Hannah hesitated. 'Execution duty is voluntary, Garrett. Sure, you get an extra fifty bucks for doing it, but it's not something you have to do.'

'So, you're saying that Frank volunteers for it?'

'Well, he ain't shoving people out of the way to get there, but there's very few people who are willing to do it, so he steps up.'

'I was told I had no choice. I was ordered to do it.'

'Maybe everyone has to one time, but it sure as hell ain't something you have to do again. At least that's my understanding of the situation.'

Nelson leaned his head back and breathed deeply. The feeling was one of being released from shackles.

'Okay,' he said. 'Okay, okay, okay. Jesus Christ, that is a weight off. This has been really tough, Hannah. This has been the toughest thing I've ever had to deal with. What happened back there was truly horrific. I haven't slept properly. I haven't been able to think about anything else. I've had nightmares, for Christ's sake. It's had me all twisted up inside.'

'And that's what's been going on with you this past week?'

'Yes.'

'Nothing to do with us, then?'

'God, no. Nothing to do with us at all.'

'You're sure?'

'Well, I guess there's been an element of doubt in my mind as to whether I can go on doing this job. That's made me wonder whether your father would have an issue with us going on seeing one another. But no, as far as you and I are concerned, nothing has changed about how much I love you.'

Hannah's eyes widened. 'How much you *love* me?'

Nelson realized what he'd said. It had just come out – unprepared, almost involuntary – but it was the truth.

'Yes,' he said. 'How much I love you.'

'You're telling me you love me?'

'I am,' Nelson replied. 'Why? Are you planning on dumping me?'

Hannah laughed. She got up from the table. She put her arms around his shoulders and kissed him.

'I was,' she said, 'but now you've changed my mind.'

'What?'

She was laughing then. Both of them were. She kissed him again.

'And I love you too, Garrett Nelson, even though you're all twisted up inside and a good deal crazier than most.'

21

At the end of May, Nelson and Hannah relinquished their respective properties and rented a house together in Port LaBelle. Close to Highway 80, they were thirty miles or so from the Montgomery place in Clewiston, and half that distance to Southern State. Hannah, still working varying shifts at numerous hospitals, was spending less and less time at her parents' place. The move made sense. It confirmed and solidified their commitment to one another. They fell into a routine that worked for both of them, and the ease with which it came defied the fact that they'd only been together for eight months or so.

Frank and Miriam Montgomery treated Nelson like another son. That, in itself, provoked an unexpected shift in Nelson's viewpoint about family. This sense of *belonging* was something with which he was unfamiliar. His father's violent unpredictability, his mother's depression, the fact that he'd been an only child, was all he knew of this fundamental human reality. Having never experienced it, he had never missed it. Now he saw how it could be, he began to recognize in himself the mental and emotional consequences of this omission. Having never felt truly loved, he was learning how to love. Whether he would ever finally come to terms with the disturbed loneliness of his own childhood, he did not know, but spending time with Hannah and the Montgomerys was perhaps the best therapy possible.

In the first week of June, Nelson was permanently assigned to High Security. Since April he had remained in General Population, had settled into the schedule relatively easily, and though there had been moments that tested his temper and his resolve, he had acquitted himself. Permanent transfer to High Security was considered a promotion. He was given a salary increase. Warden Young even iterated the fact that if he continued to work with the same degree of professionalism and diligence that had been previously demonstrated, there was a good chance he'd be considered for a Shift Supervisor position the following year.

In HS, the promise of conflict was ever-present. Nelson sensed it on the gantries and in the mess hall. It pervaded every cell, every walkway, every corridor. Those confined had perpetrated crimes sufficient to warrant their quarantine from society, and whatever had driven them to do what they'd done was still present. They brought the darkness with them, and it thickened the air with a sense of contagious malice. HS simmered quietly, and every once in a while, it boiled over.

During Nelson's training for the Sheriff's Department, elements of psychology had been covered, but only superficially. He remembered a seminar designed to give the attendees a glimpse into the mind and rationale of the career criminal. The lecturer, a respected criminologist with more letters after his name than in it, had focused on the fact that the moral code of a criminal was entirely different from that of a law-abiding individual.

'Here we're addressing the fundamental difference between ethics and morals,' he'd said. 'Morals are what the society and the law consider to be the correct code of conduct. You don't kill, you don't steal, you don't commit adultery. In effect, they are agreements we make with one another as to how we should behave for the good of all. Ethics is different. Ethics is your own decision, your own personal code. An honest individual reports instances of crime to the authorities. That is considered a good thing to do. In a criminal code, reporting criminal activities to the authorities is the worst violation of the agreements, albeit unspoken, within that group. You only have to look at *omerta*, the code of silence that has remained within the organized crime structure of the various mafias, as a clear example of the difference between morals and ethics. So, in effect, we are dealing with a different way of thinking, a different mindset altogether.'

The policing of De Soto County was not comparable to that of Miami, Tampa, even Port Charlotte. Crime was random and opportunistic. Breaking and entering, grand theft auto, even the rare instances of a gas station robbery were not perpetrated by established criminal gangs. There had been killings, perhaps two or three in the entire time Nelson had served, but in each case it had been unintentional. The closest he had ever come to a large-scale enterprise had been in Sebring – ironically the very thing that had ended his service.

The fundamental difference between his former and current careers was that he was now dealing with a wholly criminal environment. Whatever attitude he may have adopted previously – that the vast majority of people were law-abiding and decent, that people should be given the benefit of the doubt – was thoroughly challenged. In Southern State, a man was guilty until proven innocent, his intentions were assumed to be destructive, and every word, every action, every reaction, was viewed with suspicion. What an inmate said and what he meant were never the same thing.

The first indications of what would later be known as the Independence Day Riot started with rumors concerning David Garvey and William Cain. Nelson was familiar with Garvey from his previous stint in HS, but Cain was an unknown quantity. Having served eight years of a twenty-five to life, Cain was looking at another decade and a half before he could even apply for a parole hearing. Forty-eight years old, married with three children, he was a quiet, determined man. For the most part, he went unnoticed. He did not attract attention in the same manner as Garvey. Nevertheless, Cain was no less dangerous or influential. Cain also had a *consigliere* by the name of Jimmy Christiansen. Christiansen was point man, buffer, bodyguard and all else. If you wanted to speak to Cain, you went through Christiansen.

The enmity that existed between the landings rarely escalated beyond verbal challenges, scuffles and threats. Instances of actual physical violence were infrequent. A man would fall down a flight of stairs, another man would be found beaten unconscious in the shower room, but the code of silence remained intact. No one knew what had happened; no one had seen anything. The inmates were a tribe, and no matter the conflicts and rancor that might exist between different factions of that tribe, they nevertheless stood together as one in the face of the Warden and his officers. Men would rather go to solitary than break ranks, for they knew well enough that the penalty of speaking would be far worse than a week or two of solitude.

The true purpose behind what happened on July 4, 1977 would never be fully clarified. The reason that Cain and Garvey went to war was a strategized falsehood. Christiansen, acting under the direction of Cain, had sown the seeds of this apparent conflict weeks in advance. The official investigation that would later consume July and August would reveal mere fragments of the truth. The code of silence, which seemed to be as much a part of Southern as the walls and fences, would ultimately result in Warden Young's dismissal and departure.

The full truth would never come out, and that, for Garrett Nelson, was the beginning of the end.

July 4 would mark not only the turning point in his career, but the rest of his life.

22

Despite the inherent irony, American Independence Day was granted the appropriate degree of importance at Southern State.

Warden Young, a self-professed patriot, appreciated that to have ignored it would have been an invitation for resentment. Above all else, reputation was everything. Young was answerable to the Board of Prisons, themselves answerable to the Department of Justice, and his primary functions were twofold – the maintenance of order and the prevention of escape. The things that kept a man in line were few – visitation rights, adequate food, an hour of fresh air a day, access to mail, competent medical care, the certainty that, even in Southern, there was a sense of fairness and justice. If a man was wronged, he had a hope that his case might be heard, that the system might be on his side. If he wronged another, he could expect to be punished. The denial of privileges was a far greater penalty than solitary confinement. Threaten a man with the possibility that his wife and family might make a trip of several hours only to be told that they couldn't see him was more than sufficient to see him back down and concede defeat. Tell a man he would receive no mail for a month, and he soon shut his mouth.

Young's willingness to afford credence to Independence Day, Thanksgiving and Christmas was a method of control. Even in

HS, such days gave inmates an extra half-hour of outside time and a significantly better standard of food. It was also on those three occasions that the split meal shift was replaced with a single lunch sitting. More than a hundred and forty men would sit down to eat together. Eight provisional officers would be drafted in to supplement the existing twelve. It was observed that in the time leading up to these days, the atmosphere at Southern changed. There was a reduction in the number of incidents and a sense of calm pervaded the landings, for every man knew that with a single word, Warden Young could cancel the celebration and lock down the entire prison population.

Nelson had been working the second landing since his re-assignment to High Security from General Population. Though William Cain and Jimmy Christiansen were on the first landing, it was obvious that they cared less for maintaining order than Garvey on the second. Perhaps Cain wanted to run both landings, and Christiansen was the blunt hammer he used to make his presence and intentions known. Perhaps Christiansen was establishing as much authority as possible so that he could take over the first landing in the event of something happening to Cain.

Jimmy Christiansen would never set foot beyond the walls of a prison. Convicted of drug trafficking in late '65, it was rumored he'd been personally responsible for the deaths of a dozen or more men. Working out of Miami, the network of suppliers and dealers he'd established and maintained was greater than anything the state had seen before or since. Whatever level of protection Cain was afforded, Christiansen got the same. If something happened, Christiansen's direct involvement could never be proven. In all their years at Southern, neither Cain nor Christiansen had spent a single day in solitary.

*

The preparations for the Independence Day dinner were extensive. Aside from the additional officers that were drafted in, it was one of three occasions during the year when the inmate kitchen crews were supplemented by staff from an outside catering agency. The company employed, Florida Food and Drink, was always the same. Based in Fort Lauderdale, it maintained subsidiary offices in Coral Springs, West Palm Beach and Fort Pierce. With more than three hundred freelance caterers on their books, it had not been difficult for William Cain's people to identify, bribe, coerce and infiltrate the ranks with their own people. How Cain had engineered and organized this from a cell on the first landing of Southern State was the subject of subsequent extensive investigation. Cain knew people, and those people knew other people. It was as simple as that. The conclusion, though unproven, was that he'd sent word out via released inmates in the months leading up to July. The names of the catering staff sent in to Southern were on the books of the agency, and they possessed the right identification. That was sufficient for them to get through the outer gates and into the compound itself.

Work in the kitchens began early. By 6.30 a.m., as the first landing started filing along the gantry towards the mess hall for breakfast, the forty-man catering crew had unpacked three hundred pounds of shrimp, a comparable weight of ground beef, half as much in bacon and cheese, crates of lettuce, tomatoes, potatoes, beans and coleslaw. Instead of water, there was Dr Pepper and Coca-Cola. Two hundred apple pies and several gallons of cream went into the refrigerators.

Breakfast went ahead as usual. The second landing sat at 7.30. By 9.00, every man was back in his cell.

A little before half past nine, Nelson saw Frank Montgomery in the officers' commissary. Frank was the internal duty officer for the lunch sitting.

'You're on my crew,' he said. 'You weren't here at Christmas, so this is not something you've done before. You got a lot of bodies in the same place at the same time. You also got outsiders who aren't familiar with how things run. However much attention you usually pay, double it.'

'Is there word there'll be trouble?' Nelson asked.

'Hell, I don't know, Garrett. The only predictable thing about Southern is its unpredictability. Coupla weeks back there was word that Cain and Garvey had some beef about something or other. Whatever that was, it seems to have quietened down, if it was ever there in the first place. One thing I do know is that shit can stay buried for months, and then – all of a sudden – there's a catalyst and you have a real situation on your hands.'

'We have extra people, right?'

'Sure, but they ain't Southern.'

With that, Frank left the commissary and returned to the office to brief the draftees.

Nelson went back to the second landing. It was 9.42. At 10.00, the first yard shift would begin. Once complete at 11.30, the second would run from 11.45 until 1.15. Lunch was scheduled for 1.45.

The organization of seating and tableware, even the hanging of flags, had begun in the mess hall. Warden Young made an appearance around 10.20, made a cursory inspection, and then headed back to Central Admin.

The fact that Nelson had to directly engage with Jimmy Christiansen that morning was attributable to nothing more than the confusion generated by the introduction of additional personnel. It was Frank Montgomery who told Nelson to go down to the first landing and assist Max Sheehan. There were reports of a medical situation requiring attention from the prison doctor.

It was not until Nelson spoke with Sheehan that he became aware of the inmate in question. Sheehan was in Christiansen's cell. Christiansen, pale and sweating, lay on his bunk, his arms around his midriff, his breathing shallow and rapid.

'You stay here with him,' Sheehan said, and then left without another word.

In that moment, as Nelson stood in the doorway of the cell and watched Christiansen in seemingly considerable discomfort, he felt that something about the entire scenario wasn't right.

'What's going on with you?' Nelson asked.

Christiansen, grimacing with each word, said, 'All twisted up inside. Pain is somethin' fuckin' awful.'

'When did it start?'

Christiansen looked at Nelson. 'What the hell does it matter? He's gone for the doctor, ain't he?'

'Is it your chest or your guts?'

There was a flash of menace in Christiansen's eyes. Seemed that despite the pain, the man was still more than capable of being true to character.

'Just get the fuckin' doctor here, for Christ's sake.'

Nelson, goaded by the man's arrogance, felt his hackles rise.

'Talk to me like that and you ain't gonna see a doctor until tomorrow.'

Awkward silence for a moment, the tension between them palpable, and then Christiansen said, 'You bring him here. Bring him here now. You may be Frank Montgomery's little bitch, but that don't mean I can't get to you.'

Nelson took a step forward. Christiansen turned on his side, then pushed himself up and sat on the edge of the bunk. Still he managed to maintain the appearance of a man in pain. Nelson knew then that it was a performance. There was something else going on here, and whatever it was, it was trouble.

Just as he was about to speak, Sheehan entered the cell, the doctor in tow. Nelson glanced back, then turned again to see Christiansen down on his side once more, his arms around his body, his face twisted in pain.

The doctor attended to Christiansen. Nelson asked Sheehan to step outside.

'This is bullshit,' Nelson said. 'This is an act.'

'Doesn't look like that to me. Man seems pretty fucked up.'

'Trust me,' Nelson said. 'Something's going on here, and it sure as hell ain't a medical situation.'

'So what the fuck do you wanna do?' Sheehan asked.

'I don't know. Keep him here?'

'He's just as secure locked up in the infirmary,' Sheehan said. 'There'll be someone posted down there to keep an eye on him, for sure. Just let the doctor do his thing. We got enough to handle without—'

'He knew who I was,' Nelson said. 'I'm not even on this landing. He called me Frank Montgomery's little bitch.'

Sheehan frowned. 'You think these guys don't know everything they can about us? Jesus, Garrett, wise up. Someone like Christiansen? Hell, that man probably knows more about all of us than everyone in Central Admin combined.'

The doctor called Sheehan back into the cell. Sheehan went, returned a moment later.

'Stretcher,' Sheehan said. 'Go get one and we'll take him down together.'

Twenty minutes later, Christiansen was in an infirmary bed.

Nelson asked the doctor for his opinion.

'I don't know right now. Could be appendix, could be a minor cardiac event. Hell, it could be indigestion. I need to do a thorough examination. If it's his heart, then he'll need to go to the hospital in Port Charlotte.'

'I don't buy it,' Nelson said.

'You don't think he's sick?'

Nelson shook his head.

'Well, if he ain't, then he'll get an Oscar for the performance. Only way to find out is to let me do some tests.'

Nelson, still convinced that something was awry, left Christiansen in the care of the doctor and a temporary officer. Instinct told him he should speak to Frank, perhaps go right to Young, but he didn't. Why he didn't trust himself in that moment was a question he would never be able to answer. According to the doctor, interviewed at length after the event, Christiansen was subdued and cooperative. It seemed, despite the pain he was suffering, that his real concern was that he'd miss the Independence lunch. The medical tests were done as per protocol. Heart rate and pulse were steady with no anomalies in rhythm or regularity. The doctor was sufficiently confident that there had been no cardiac event, and thus concluded that a hospital transfer was not required. Christiansen was told to rest, that there would be periodic checks on his progress.

There were two other subsequent requests for medical attention – one at 11.40 a.m. by Lucas Fielding, a white-collar money launderer from St Petersburg, and the second at 12.06 p.m. by Richard Stein, an ex-Florida State Heavyweight boxing champion from Miami Beach serving ten-to-fifteen for aggravated assault, malicious wounding and unlawful possession of a firearm. Both men reported vomiting, dehydration, stomach cramps and diarrhea – textbook symptoms of food poisoning. As if to confirm this malady, they had shared an almond cake brought in by Fielding's wife the previous day. Both men were sent to the infirmary. Due to the limitations on officer numbers, no additional back-up was afforded the single man assigned to that watch. Under his inexperienced eye, he had the *consigliere* of the first landing, a known Miami enforcer and a man with access to a great deal of money in adjoining rooms. Add into that equation the fact that the infirmary was not only the closest building to the fence, but having only two interior doors and one secure door to the compound, and there was a potential situation that was not predicted. Once again, with hindsight, the coincidence of men and location would have raised alarm bells. Not so on Independence Day, when all eyes were focused on the mess hall.

At 1.20 p.m., Frank Montgomery, Garrett Nelson and four other officers began the supervised release of the second landing. Seventy-three men filed out of their cells and made their way along the gantry, down the stairs and along the corridor to the mess hall. Inside the mess hall itself, a further eight officers, one in each corner and one between them, stood sentinel. Once the second landing complement was seated, the duty officers on the first landing walked another seventy-one men into the mess hall.

At 1.40 p.m., Warden Young, flanked by Frank Montgomery and the senior duty officer from the first landing, stood on a small dais and addressed the men.

'Gentlemen, welcome. As is tradition, we are here to celebrate the independence of the United States of America. Two hundred and one years ago, we unburdened ourselves from the yoke of colonialism and began our progress towards our present position on the world stage. From this continent, we have not only witnessed some of the greatest technological and scientific advancements in the history of humanity, but we have been instrumental in bringing peace to Europe, to South-East Asia and to many other nations around the world. It goes without saying that I am proud to be an American, as I know you all are, and I trust that those of you who leave this place as free men will become hardworking, honest and contributing members of our great society. We will now stand for a rendition of our national anthem.'

Through the internal tannoy, the first strains of 'Star Spangled Banner' filtered into the mess hall.

Uncertain at first, though quickly gaining volume and enthusiasm, the inmates of Southern State High Security block broke into song.

> *O say can you see, by the dawn's early light, what so proudly we hailed as the twilight's first gleaming…*

The prison doctor, leaving a single officer to watch Christiansen, Fielding and Stein in the infirmary, then returned to the main block. On his way down he informed one of the drafted officers that he should go to the infirmary to assist in the watch. The drafted officer, unfamiliar with Southern's layout, got lost, turned back the way he'd come, and was then instructed by someone else to go to the mess hall. He did as he was instructed.

At 1.48 p.m., as the gathered inmates struggled through the last verse of the national anthem, Richard Stein called for assistance from the officer outside his door. Unlocking it, the officer stepped inside to find Stein doubled up on the floor in what appeared to be excruciating pain. Before he had a chance to unclip his radio and call for assistance, Stein kicked the man's legs out from under him and cold-cocked him with a right hook that broke his jaw in two places.

Stein, releasing both Christiansen and Fielding from their rooms, then bound and gagged the officer. He was secured to the frame of the infirmary bed with strips torn from a sheet. With the door locked behind them, the three men made their way out of the infirmary to the first internal door. There they crouched in silence and waited for 2.15 p.m.

23

Penitentiary protocol required that all weapons, ammunition, tear gas and riot shields were held in the armory behind the Central Administrative office. Only those officers on tower duty carried rifles, and standard procedure for the containment of an internal prisoner revolt required that those rifles did not enter the blocks. Irrespective of training and experience, sheer weight of numbers would always place the officers at a disadvantage. That day, even with the additional draftees, many of whom had little to no experience of a high security unit, twenty men would not win a war against more than a hundred and forty. Add firearms into the mix, and the potential for a bloodbath was increased a thousandfold. Containment was the key in all such scenarios. By any and all means possible, it was the duty of the officers to corral the prisoners in one location – in this instance the mess hall – and then to secure the doors with no penitentiary personnel inside. Once isolated, riot crews would employ tear gas to incapacitate the prisoners. Subsequently, strike teams of eight men wearing full riot gear and gas masks would make swift and decisive extraction forays into the crowd and bring out as many as they could. Beyond the doors, other teams would handcuff the evacuees and secure them in their cells. Such an operation had never before taken place in Warden Young's tenure at Southern.

The initial fight, orchestrated by Jimmy Christiansen, broke out between David Garvey and William Cain. It was Garvey who made the first move, returning from the buffet line with his tray of food. Passing Cain's table, he swung the tray sideways with all the force he could muster. The edge of the tray connected with the side of Cain's head. Cain, momentarily stunned, roared into action, hurling himself at Garvey and bringing him down to the ground. Garvey was a head taller than Cain, a good deal heavier, but Cain, propelled by sheer fury, was considerably more agile. Before Garvey had managed to gather his senses and work his way out from underneath the flailing fists, Cain had broken Garvey's nose and cut a wide gash above his left eye.

It was then that it became obvious that four members of the catering staff were there for a very different reason.

Frank Montgomery realized what was happening when he saw a white-aproned man vault across the serving counter with a foot-long length of heavy metal pipe. The first officer he reached went down with a single blow to the back of the head.

Screaming at a second officer to get out of the mess hall and raise the alarm, Montgomery pulled every man back to the double doors and formed a defensive line. Rapidly, the fight between Garvey and Cain spread throughout the hall in a wave. Tables were overturned, food was spilled every which way, and within minutes the sheer magnitude of the situation became evident.

The internal klaxon, close to deafening, screamed into life.

High Security went into immediate lockdown mode. It was then that Montgomery removed his men from the mess hall, taking with them the unconscious guard who had been first to fall.

Warden Young appeared within seconds. Despite Frank Montgomery's insistence that he leave men on the towers, Young directed that every able-bodied officer be deployed to the mess hall. Authorization to open the armory and issue riot gear and tear gas was given.

Through the heavy glass portholes of the mess hall doors, Warden Young, Frank Montgomery, Garrett Nelson and the remainder of the officer complement watched as the situation within escalated to a full-blown riot. It was 2.21 p.m.

In the infirmary, the sound of the klaxon could be clearly heard.

Christiansen, Fielding and Stein reached the external secure door that led into the Southern State compound. Later, upon examination, there were no signs of force. They had to have had a key. How they obtained the key was unknown, but it could only have come from an inside source.

At 2.32 p.m., the three escapees gained the compound, carrying with them mattresses and torn bedding. The towers were unmanned. The fence, now no more than thirty yards from the back of the infirmary, was the only thing that stood between them and freedom.

Tying the makeshift rope between two sections of the fence, a loop was created that was sufficient to hold Stein's weight. Once in position, he was able to pull the mattresses up and over the top of the barbed wire. Balanced on top, straddling the fence like a rodeo rider, Stein then tied a second length of knotted bedding to the other side of the fence. It was thus possible for Stein to pull Christiansen and Fielding up one by one. Lowering themselves down on the other side, the two men then waited for Stein. Before lowering himself to the ground, Stein managed to extricate the mattress from the barbs. Once he was on the ground, the men untied the bedding. They ran headlong towards the trees, carrying everything with them. By the time they reached cover, nothing remained inside or outside the compound to betray their point of escape.

Having gained the treeline and passed out of sight, the

mattresses and bedding were submerged into the first glade they reached.

Pausing for a moment, the three men looked at one another, then back at the outer fence of Southern State. Christiansen nodded to Stein. Stein nodded back. Fielding was taken completely by surprise. Before Fielding understood what was happening, Richard Stein came up behind him and closed his arm around his throat. With a single wrench, Fielding's neck was broken. The sound – the only sound beside the peal of the klaxon from the compound – was that of a branch snapping underfoot.

The shortest route – five, maybe six miles – to Highway 80 would have been directly north towards Goodno. Christiansen indicated northwest. It was double the distance and would bring them out on 22 near Alva.

They had twelve miles of inhospitable swampland, glade and forest ahead of them.

They started walking. Lucas Fielding's lifeless body was left right where he'd fallen. The alligators would take him before Christiansen and Stein had covered half a mile.

24

It was 4.16 p.m. before the last group of prisoners had been evacuated from the mess hall and returned to their cells.

A further twenty-two minutes elapsed before the escape was discovered. The three fugitives had been gone for two hours.

It was Garrett Nelson, haunted by the fact that he'd known something was wrong from the beginning, who reported the break to Warden Young. He said nothing to Young about his exchange with Christiansen in the cell that morning. He hadn't trusted himself sufficiently to insist on additional security in the infirmary. He felt a burden of responsibility that he knew could only be alleviated by the capture of the escapees.

Young, feeling that he'd already come out of a war zone by the skin of his teeth, assigned Nelson and Frank Montgomery as point-of-contact for the US Marshals Service and the FBI. Hendry County Sheriff's Department was alerted. At that stage of the game, they had no clear indication of the direction the escapees had taken. Beyond the Southern State fence lay six and a half thousand square miles of everglade and swampland. Despite the fact that the Marshals Service had access to planes and helicopters, the sheer density of forest and foliage cover beneath them made air-spotting impossible.

Federal units had arrived from Miami and Fort Lauderdale

by 6 p.m. Additional experienced prison officers, some of them now retired, were ferried in from Florida State Pen to replace the provisional officers assigned for Independence Day. The seriously wounded – two of whom were part of the agency catering crew – were transferred to a hospital in Sarasota under armed guard. Garvey was treated in the penitentiary infirmary and then returned to his cell. The walking wounded were treated by the prison doctor and a medical staff complement of EMTs, male nurses and doctors from hospitals in Clewiston, Lehigh Acres, Port Charlotte and Fort Myers. The Arcadia and Okeechobee Police Departments provided security within Southern State for the numerous personnel that were requisitioned from the various agencies around the state.

By 8 p.m., the US Marshals Service and the FBI had established roadblocks on Highways 80 and 78, Interstate 75 and many of the smaller roads that formed a perimeter around Hendry County. News bulletins began before 9 p.m., and the faces of the three escapees appeared on TV screens in every home and motel room, every diner and restaurant and bar.

And then there were the dead. Four inmates had been killed in the mess hall. Not only did Warden Young stand at the centre of the largest manhunt in Florida's history, he was going to be the focal point of an investigation that would encompass inmate homicides, more than a hundred injured men, the destruction of more than thirty thousand dollars' worth of government property, the staggering cost of the federal response and a barrage of press and public demands for his resignation.

By the time Frank Montgomery met with Nelson in the Central Administrative office it was past 10 p.m. Both men had been on their feet for more than fourteen hours.

'We're on search party tomorrow,' Frank said. 'Starting at first light. I suggest you get out of here, get your head down if you can. Tomorrow is gonna be even longer than today.'

'And you?'

'I'll stay. I gotta run interference for Young. He's falling to pieces right now.'

'But you need to get some sleep, Frank. You can't stay up all night and then go out there.'

'I'll snatch a couple of hours along the way,' Frank said. 'You go see Hannah. Tell her what's going on. Make sure she ain't worried, okay?'

'You want me to call Miriam?'

'Yeah, you do that.'

Frank turned to leave.

'Frank?'

'What?'

'I knew something was wrong.'

'What are you talkin' about?'

'This morning, in Christiansen's cell. I knew it was bullshit.'

'You knew, or you thought you knew?'

'Okay, I thought it. I sensed something was wrong.'

'And what good is that gonna do us now?'

Nelson shook his head. 'No good. I just wanted to say it.'

'So you said it. Put it out of your mind.'

Nelson hesitated.

'What?'

'You've been out there before... out beyond the wire?'

'Not like this I haven't, no,' Frank replied.

'How many of us?'

'As many as we can get. These are bad fucking people, Garrett, and they ain't gonna stop running 'til they're dead.'

It took Nelson close to an hour to get out of the Southern State compound itself. Beyond the wire, it took him another fifteen minutes to navigate the phalanx of news trucks, cameramen, reporters and onlookers. People were banging on the roof of his car, flashguns fired left, right and center, and he didn't make it onto the highway until 11.30 p.m.

It seemed to Nelson that every light in the house was burning. Even before he'd brought the car to a stop in the drive, Hannah was out of the front door and coming down the path to meet him.

She threw her arms around him and pulled him close.

'Oh my God, Garrett, it's all over the news. I didn't know what the hell was going on. Both you an' Dad were up there and—'

'It's okay,' Nelson said. 'Come on, let's get inside. We need to call your mom and tell her that your dad is fine.'

'You've seen him? He's okay?'

'He's good, Hannah. He's stayin' up there tonight. I gotta go back and meet him in the morning.'

Inside the front door, Hannah started in with the questions.

'How the hell did they get out, Garrett? I mean, that place is like a fortress.'

'I don't know all the details, Hannah, and I really shouldn't be talking about it.'

'And tomorrow?'

'Search parties. As many people as we can get together. I guess we'll have teams that take different routes away from the compound.'

'Into the glades? You can't go out there. What the hell, Garrett? Surely they can't expect you to go out there.'

'We gotta find 'em, Hannah. Dead or alive, we have to find them.'

Hannah sat down at the kitchen table. 'So, what you're telling me is that two of the most important people in my life are walking out into some of the worst country imaginable to look for people who would have no hesitation in killing you?'

'I guess that's as good a way of sayin' it as any.'

Nelson sat facing her. He reached out and took her hand. 'It's gonna be okay. Really. There's a lot of people. Dozens, maybe hundreds. I can take care of myself, and your dad can too. Before this I was in the Sheriff's Department—'

'Sure you were, Garrett, and we met because someone fuckin' shot you.'

Nelson tried to smile. 'Well, I guess the odds on me gettin' shot a second time are pretty slim then, eh?'

'Don't try an' make light of this,' Hannah said. 'This is a bad business, an' I don't want you involved in it.'

'I ain't got no choice. I can't let your dad down. An' I can't let these men hurt or kill anyone else. You think what would happen if they holed up somewhere and they get cornered. It'll make what happened at Southern look like a church picnic.'

'You know what? Selfish it might be, but I don't give a damn about anyone else right now. You and dad are the only ones I'm worryin' about.'

'Let me do the worryin', okay? I'm gonna do my job, an' then I'm gonna come back here, your dad too. It'll be all over before you know it.'

'But—'

'But nothin', Hannah. We're done with this. I need to take a shower an' get some rest.'

Hannah looked at Nelson for the longest time, and then she nodded in acknowledgement. What was going to happen was inevitable, and there wasn't a single thing she could do about it.

'You hungry?' she asked.

'Get me enough ketchup and I'll eat roadkill right off the tarmac.'

25

Nelson slept fitfully. He guessed he'd managed maybe three or four hours unbroken.

Down in the kitchen, Hannah was making coffee. Nelson switched on the TV and caught the end of the 5 a.m. weather report. Temperature was set to hit the mid-nineties. Humidity was aiming for seventy percent plus. People were being advised to stay hydrated and avoid any strenuous outside activity.

What lay ahead, he could not predict. He was uneasy, but it was a very different feeling from the one he'd experienced when he went out to Sebring to help with the drug bust. This time he had some idea of what he was getting into. Hannah had been right. The men they were after would not stop at killing anyone who was fool enough to get in their way. Though neither Christiansen nor Stein had ever been convicted of murder, Nelson had no doubt that they had been responsible, directly or indirectly, for the deaths of more than enough people. Beyond his own immediate survival, Nelson had a duty to ensure that they did not increase that number.

Hannah didn't want him to leave, but knew she could do nothing to stop him. She'd made sandwiches, a flask of coffee, and she fussed around him as if he was a child on his first day at school.

Nelson stood in the hallway ahead of the front door. Neither one spoke. He merely held his arms out and she came to him. He pulled her tight, absorbed the scent of her skin, her warmth, her closeness, and then he let her go.

Holding her face between his hands, he kissed her.

'I will see you later,' he said, his voice little more than a whisper, and then he left the house.

It tore at him as he drove away, watching her grow ever smaller in the rearview.

The sun was still beneath the horizon when Nelson arrived at Southern State.

The small army of reporters had decreased in number. There was a perimeter line of squad cars that ran as far as the eye could see along the fence in each direction. The watchtowers were double-manned. There was an uncountable number of unfamiliar faces inside the compound itself.

Nelson parked up and headed for Central Admin. Inside, the corridors were crowded with police, Feds, marshals and correctional officers. Assignments were being given, shotguns, rifles and sidearms were being issued, and the sound of so many voices in such a confined space was deafening.

'Garrett! Garrett!'

Nelson saw a hand above the throng, and caught a glimpse of Frank near the processing office. Elbowing his way through, he finally managed to reach him.

'Stay with me,' Frank said. 'Let's get you some gear, and then get out of here. We're being briefed out back by the Feds.'

That morning – Tuesday, July 5 – the sun rose at 5.48.

Behind Central Admin, more than a hundred men gathered in lines of ten as light broke over the horizon.

Warden Young stood up ahead. He looked as if he'd been

dragged to Hell and back by his heels. Beside him, Senior Special Agent Michael Gant introduced himself as the Section Chief from the Florida Bureau in Fort Lauderdale.

'As it stands, gentlemen,' Gant said, 'we have no report of our fugitives being sighted. South of here is more than thirty miles of glades until you reach Interstate 75. North, we have ten or twelve miles. We also have a far greater number of towns. We have ten teams, ten men to each team, and your team leader has been briefed on the directions you will take. We aim to reach Alva, LaBelle, Port LaBelle, Goodno, Lake Hicpochee, Benbow and Clewiston and pretty much everything in between before nightfall. This is gonna be a long, hard day. It's gonna be hot, humid and dangerous out there. You stay together. You do not get separated from your team. Your job is to do whatever you can to find these fugitives. However, it is not your job to get hurt or killed. We've had more than our fair share of trouble already, and we don't want any more.'

Gant paused to let his words sink in. He glanced at Warden Young to his left.

'Warden Young and I are running this operation. You will be in radio contact with us here at Southern. You will report in every thirty minutes. If a man is injured, your Team Leader will alert us as to your coordinates and release a flare. We will find you. The roadblocks on all highways are in place. If you reach a highway, report in to us. We will reassign you to a different section of the target territory. Sundown is at 8.16 today. No matter what, by the time darkness falls every single one of you needs to be out of there and in a safe position. Plan accordingly. Now, are there any questions?'

Not a single man in the ranks moved or spoke.

'As a final word, it goes without saying that these are escaped felons. We can only assume that they have already coordinated with outside help, and thus are armed and dangerous. They need to be considered as such. Do not underestimate the lengths that such people will go to in order to avoid arrest and detention. You are authorized to use lethal force. Do not engage, do not surrender your arms. Shoot to kill policy is in full force. Are we all clear?'

A resounding 'Yes sir!' was returned in unison.

'Dismissed!'

26

'I gotta tell you,' Frank said. 'Ray is seriously pissed that he's missing this shitshow.'

They stood in a single line, ten men, with Frank taking the lead. Wearing waist-high heavy-duty waders, combat boots and thick canvas shirts that were designed not only to resist insect bites but provide some degree of protection against snake bites, Nelson knew that within five hundred yards he would be running with sweat. Aside from a regulation pump action shotgun, a sidearm, a KA-BAR combat knife and a machete, they also carried flare guns, water canisters, heat tabs, handcuffs, thirty feet of rope, a first-aid kit, extra ammunition, a compass, a hand-held radio and marker flags to indicate tracks and potential evidence.

'He's got himself double shifts in Gen Pop,' Frank explained. 'Place is on high alert. A stunt like this gets everyone wound tighter than a two-dollar watch. You got the better part of six hundred men hoping to God that these fellers get away and they kill some of us in the process.'

Nelson looked out towards the dense acreage of vegetation and swampland ahead of them.

'You think they made it through that?' he asked.

'I think Jimmy Christiansen is pretty fucking smart. I also

think he knows a good deal of people. This wasn't opportunistic – this was planned for a long time. All it would take would be a couple of guys who knew the territory and a boat and they'd have been through this and out the other side before nightfall. They got seventeen hours' head start now. If they're still in there, then they're more 'an likely dead. If they're not, they could be out-of-state and into the wind. However, that does not change the fact that we got one bitch of a day ahead of us. An' it ain't gonna get no shorter if we stand here wonderin', right?'

Frank gave the order. The men filed out in a line, side by side, two arm's-length apart.

'Tread slow,' he said. 'Tread careful. If the water reaches your knees get the fuck out of there pronto. Do not lose sight of the man to your left or right. We're looking for clothing, broken branches, any sign of footfall, anything that seems out of place. Keep your fuckin' wits about you, okay? Ten of us are going out there and ten of us are coming back.'

With that, Frank Montgomery started out towards the glade breakline. Their plotting was due north to Highway 80 and the Hendry County line near Goodno. It was eight miles of mud, water, stifling heat and dense humidity. They would traverse the most inhospitable landmass in the state in the hope of finding three men who would do everything possible not to be found. Nelson believed Frank when he'd said that these people did not go into this ill-prepared. Ill-advised, perhaps, but something like this had been planned for a considerable time. Time and terrain were the greatest enemies. The fugitives had the advantage, no doubt about it, and as Nelson started hacking his breathless way through overhanging branches and dense shrouds of Spanish moss, he had a deep and abiding certainty that they were on a hide into nowhere.

*

Frank Montgomery had overestimated Jimmy Christiansen's influence beyond the walls of Southern. There was no one waiting for him and Richard Stein with dry clothes, a lightweight boat and a planned escape route. Additionally, no one understood that the escape had a purpose that was not merely self-serving.

After the killing of Lucas Fielding, Christiansen and Stein went into the glades blind and alone. They knew they had to keep moving, but moving through that territory in darkness was as treacherous an activity as could be found. They went slow, cautious, profoundly aware of the speed with which the ground beneath their feet could shift and change. A steady path could drop into a waist-high pool with no warning whatsoever. Anything greater than four or five feet was home for alligators, cottonmouths, diamondbacks and coral snakes. Christiansen was wise enough to appreciate that their odds of survival, let alone actual escape, were less than slim. Nevertheless, having spent the better part of twelve years inside, he considered that dying a free man was a better option than rotting away in an eight-by-ten for another three decades. As for Stein, there was a poison in his blood. Had he possessed the slightest degree of self-awareness, he would have understood that escaping was less a matter of getting away, and more a matter of defying anyone or anything that sought to inhibit his true nature. Even as a boxer, he had not been motivated by competition or challenge, but by the desire to crush and destroy. The letting of an opponent's blood did not temper his aggression, but rather fuelled it to ever-greater extremes. Even with a fighter cowed, defeated, backed against the ropes and ready to surrender, Stein would have to be wrestled away by the referee. To hammer a man into unconsciousness was not enough; he fought with the intention to kill.

In the first three or four hours, Christiansen and Stein defied even their own expectations. They made good progress, covering close to a mile an hour. The moon, though not full, was high and bright. By eight on the evening of the 4th, they were more than a quarter of the way towards Alva and Highway 22. Christiansen's intention was to then head west towards Buckingham. It would be another eight or nine miles on foot, but they would follow the road. Keeping back inside the treeline, they would make far faster progress than they had through the glades. If they kept going, if they did not veer or get lost, he hoped that they'd be in Buckingham before daybreak. He knew it was unrealistic, but better that than defeatism.

Once they arrived, it would simply be a matter of finding an isolated property, securing food, water, clothing and a vehicle. Despite the fact that a prison break was automatically a federal matter, he wanted to get out of Florida. The only direction was north into Georgia along Interstate 75 and up through Port Charlotte and Tampa. It was a six-hundred-mile journey. There would be news bulletins, roadblocks, helicopters, a US Marshals Task Force, and alerts to every Sheriff's Department from here to kingdom come. Christiansen had considered the possibility that he and Stein might split up and head in different directions, but decided against it. Boxed in, he wanted Stein at his side. Stein would kill without compunction, and that was a valuable asset. And once they were free and clear, Christiansen then had a secondary purpose known only to himself and William Cain. If anyone had taken the time to question why they had waged a war against one another, then that purpose might have been understood.

During the hours between eight and midnight, both Christiansen and Stein began to labor. Not only did the terrain become progressively more impassable – deep ruts filled with stinking water, the sucking mud, the never-ending maze of wrist-thick roots that made each step precarious and unsteady – but they were also suffering the significant effects of dehydration, hunger and exhaustion. Energy was not wasted on words. Their intent was clear. It required no discussion. They just had to keep going, come what may. Every bone, nerve, sinew and muscle ached and screamed for respite, but they did not stop. They were driven by determination, fear, and a firm belief that to make it to the highway was in some way a form of revenge against the system that had kept them caged like animals for so much of their respective adult lives. And if people came after them through this wilderness and escape was denied them, they would die here. Their last act would be to take as many of their hunters with them as possible.

Experiencing much the same sense of disorientation as Christiansen and Stein, Nelson stayed close to Frank Montgomery. Frank moved quickly, expecting every man in the line to keep up with him. Despite the fact that Frank was close to twenty years older than Nelson, his stamina was far greater. Nelson's leg ached mercilessly. He regretted not thinking ahead and bringing a substantial supply of painkillers with him.

The sun was strong, and though it did little to illuminate the depth of gloom that they soldiered through, it served to boil the air beneath the canopy above their heads. It was like marching through a pressure cooker. Sweat filled Nelson's boots. His socks, his underwear, the shirt he wore were sodden. Everything doubled in weight. The sting of salt in his eyes clouded his vision, each breath was a conscious effort, and he didn't know how much longer he could keep moving.

Three hours in, perhaps the same number of miles behind them, Frank stopped the line. They gathered together in a narrow clearing. No one had seen a thing. There was nothing to report. One man had twisted his ankle, and Frank instructed that he remove his boots and bind it tightly.

'You gotta keep going, son,' he said. 'It's as far back as it is ahead. Makes no difference now.'

They drank water, they ate, took heat tabs. Some of the men took off their shirts and made an effort to wring them out. Everything was soaked with filth and rot and the putrid stench of decayed vegetation.

Taking Nelson aside, Frank said, 'I seen you limping some. You sufferin' with your leg?'

'I'm okay,' Nelson replied. 'I've had it worse.'

Frank grasped his shoulder. 'Let's get through this. Hannah will fix you up when you're home.'

Frank radioed in again to the US Marshals Command Center. He gave a brief update. He also received word back that, as yet, no other team had located the fugitives or seen evidence of their passing.

With the order to once again spread out in a horizontal line, their trek towards Goodno resumed.

Against seemingly insurmountable odds, Jimmy Christiansen and Richard Stein reached flat land as the search teams were being organized at Southern before daybreak on the 5th.

It was still dark, and they lay on their backs behind the cover of trees and gathered their senses. Not knowing exactly where they were, they could still hear the distant passing of trucks on the highway. Christiansen guessed it was 22. In truth, it did not matter where they were. A road led somewhere, and somewhere along it there would be houses, towns or farms. Too exhausted to congratulate themselves, they were back on their feet by 6 a.m.

Before they started moving, Christiansen took a moment to look back at the black mass of landscape behind him. He experienced an epiphany. In the main, he could not believe that they had come this far, but he also interpreted their survival as an omen. They were meant to get out. He knew this with as much certainty as his own name. He also knew that search parties would not venture into that wilderness until daybreak. He and Stein had the upper hand. There was no question about it. Now all they had to do was evade the helicopters, spotter planes, roadblocks and, most of all, the simple fact that every man, woman and child in the state must have already been notified of their escape. Their priority was to avoid drawing attention to themselves, and that required a place to hole up, get clean, get changed, get some food and rest.

Christiansen indicated west and led the way. Stein moved with him, his face and hands black with mud, his eyes like that of a wolf scenting blood in the wind.

27

Three generations of the Richmond family had lived in the same house beyond the limits of Alva.

The current patriarch, Errol, a laconic, hardworking, uncomplicated man, was an engineer by trade. Now fifty-one, he spent much of his working week maintaining and servicing farming machinery across Hendry, Charlotte, Glades and Lee counties. Employed by the Agricultural Maintenance and Supply Company in St Petersburg, there wasn't a picking or sorting machine that he didn't know or couldn't fix. On the rare occasion that he was not carrying a needed replacement part, a long-established and efficient courier network would bring that part to a site within hours. AMSC prided themselves on their ability to keep the year-round harvest cycle running smoothly, and Errol Richmond was equally proud to be a working ambassador for them.

By eight on the morning of July 5, 1977, Errol and his wife, Grace, had finished breakfast and were sharing a pot of coffee before Errol's first calls came in. When the call would come and where it would take him, he didn't know. Once he'd departed for whatever farm or factory that required him, Grace would follow a routine that, to some, would have seemed banal and repetitive. For Grace, however, the simple chores of cleaning, making the bed, laundry, preparation of food, grocery shopping and family correspondence was a comfort. Grace Richmond was a creature of habit, possessed no lofty aspirations, pursued interests in needlework and gardening, and was more than content to live her life as a wife and a mother. Her own mother had been the same, her grandmother before that, and there was not a single thought in Grace Richmond's head that prompted her to buck tradition.

Errol and Grace had raised three children – a son and the eldest, Garth, and two daughters, Helen and Frances. Garth, now nineteen, was staying with friends in Cape Coral and would not be back until Wednesday evening. Helen and Frances were fifteen and sixteen respectively, and the pair of them, obsessed with some pop singer called Peter Frampton, had taken the early bus out to Lehigh Acres to buy a vinyl record at a store.

Just after 8.15 that morning, the phone rang in the front hallway. Knowing it was for him, Errol took it. He was needed in Bayshore, about twenty-five miles to the west. According to the on-site report, a farmhand had reversed a tractor into a grain cart and buckled the hook-up lines. If that was the case, then parts would be needed. Until he got there and made his own survey, the model numbers could not be ordered. Considering the distance, Errol guessed he might make it out there and back home for lunch before he was called out again.

Hanging up the phone, he called out to his wife.

'I'm out to Bayshore, sweetheart. I'll give you a call once I see what's happened, let you know if I can make it back here for lunch, okay?'

Grace did not respond.

Errol put on his hat. He took the keys for his truck from a wooden bowl on the telephone table, and went back to the kitchen.

'Grace? Where you at, honey?'

The scene that met Errol Richmond as he walked through the kitchen doorway defied all sense of reality and reason.

Grace was seated at the table, just as she had been when he'd left to take the phone call. The expression on her face was something Errol had never seen before. All color had drained from her features. Her eyes were wide with terror. Standing at the back door, almost in silhouette from the light through the window, was a man of enormous proportions. At the sink, a drinking glass in his hand, was a second man – shorter, and with a wiry physique. The pair of them were black with mud. Every inch of them was covered in filth. They were like visions from some horrific nightmare, and the menace they exuded was palpable.

'Take a seat, mister,' Christiansen said. His tone was cold and matter-of-fact.

'Wh-who a-are y-you? Wh-what do yo-you w-want?' Errol stammered.

'I want you to do as I said and take a fuckin' seat,' Christiansen replied.

Errol stepped forward, his guts like liquid, his knees already weak. He held onto the back of the chair and steadied himself before stepping around it and sitting down.

'What's your name?'

'Ri-Richmond,' Errol said. 'My name is Errol Richmond.'

'Good morning, Mr Richmond. An' I'm guessin' this is your good lady wife.'

'Y-yes.'

Christiansen paused. He raised his eyebrows. 'You're not gonna introduce us?'

'Gr-Grace,' Errol said. 'This is my wife, Grace.'

Christiansen turned on the faucet. He filled the glass and drank it in one go. He filled it again and passed it to Stein.

'My name is Jimmy Christiansen and this here's my buddy, Richard Stein. I'm pretty darn sure you know who we are, right?'

Errol looked at Christiansen, then at Stein. He shook his head.

'N-no,' he said. 'I have no i-idea who y-you are.'

'You are kiddin' me,' Christiansen said. 'Well, fuck me sideways, we ain't nowhere near as famous as I'd hoped. I don't know whether to feel relieved or disappointed.'

'Wha-what do you wa-want?' Errol asked. 'You want mo-money?'

'Sure, we want money, but we also want to get ourselves cleaned up. We want some clothes, a good meal, a vehicle. Hell, we want anythin' you got to give us.'

Christiansen nodded towards the front hallway. 'Go take care of the phone.'

Stein set down the empty glass and left the kitchen. A moment later, there was the sound of the telephone being torn wholesale off the wall. It landed with a crash on the floor.

Once in the kitchen again, Stein returned to the back door.

'So, Mr and Mrs Richmond, what's the deal with you today? I'm figurin' you're headed out to work or whatever.'

'I-I was, yes,' Errol said. 'I have to go to Bayshore.'

'An' what is it that you do in Bayshore?'

'I-I fix machinery,' Errol said. 'Farm machinery.'

'Well, that's as honest a day's work as you're likely to see,' Christiansen said. 'And what about you, Grace?'

'Grace is staying here,' Errol started.

Christiansen frowned. 'I am askin' your wife, Errol.'

'I-m s-sorry.'

Grace looked at her husband, and then turned and looked up at Christiansen. She opened her mouth to speak, but she didn't seem able to connect her thoughts with any audible response.

Christiansen smiled. 'Oh, she's a quiet one, eh? Best kind, if you ask me.'

Stein emitted a low guttural laugh.

'Right, well, I guess you should know that today's gonna go a little differently than planned. First thing I need to know is whether you're expectin' anyone.'

Errol shook his head.

'What?' Christiansen asked. 'You don't got no friends comin' over for coffee, no kids on their way back from someplace?'

'Our s-son's away until tomorrow,' Errol said, 'a-and our daughters aren't g-going to be home for s-several hours.'

'I gotta tell you that's just about as perfect an arrangement as we could've asked for,' Christiansen said. He gave a self-satisfied grin.

'Well, my first order of business is to take myself a long, hot bath. An' while I do that, Mr Stein here is gonna look after you folks, right, Mr Stein?'

Stein nodded in acknowledgement but didn't speak.

'It was mighty nice to meet you both,' Christiansen said as he started towards the door. 'An' I must say that you really are the most generous of hosts.'

By the time Christiansen reached the stairs, Richard Stein had cut Errol Richmond's throat from ear to ear with a bread knife. He then dragged Grace from her chair by her hair and threw her to the ground.

Over the sound of running water, her screams were still audible from the upstairs bathroom, but they didn't last long.

28

Frank Montgomery, Garrett Nelson and the other eight men of the Goodno team emerged from the everglades just before two that same afternoon.

By the time they reached Highway 22 outside of Alva, Jimmy Christiansen and Richard Stein had bathed, shaved, eaten and changed into clean clothes. They had taken Errol Richmond's truck and started west, joined the Interstate at Tice, and were halfway between Bayshore and Tropical Gulf Acres. Agricultural Maintenance and Supply's dispatch supervisor, hounded by an irate farm manager, receiving no response from the Richmond house despite numerous calls, had assumed that Errol Richmond had been sent elsewhere by a colleague. No alarm was raised, for such a mix-up was not altogether unusual. Someone else was dispatched and the phone calls stopped.

Radioing in to Command Center, Frank was told that a Charlotte County Sheriff's Department vehicle would be sent to pick them up and bring them back to Southern State. While they waited, they sat on the ground at the side of the road, took off their boots and waders, smoked cigarettes, all of them wondering if any of the other teams had achieved any greater success than themselves. Had Christiansen, Stein and Fielding been located, Frank felt sure he would have been informed. Though he wanted to believe they were dead, his gut told him something different. They had made it through, and thus proven that it was possible. Despite the advantages he and his crew had – better light, food, water, compasses and hand tools – there was a single, simple factor that would have driven the fugitives: they knew that if they did not make it through the glades, they would be dead or back in Southern. There would be additional charges, not only for the escape itself, but the preceding violence in the mess hall. More than likely, the State's Attorney General would want to slap them with a couple of manslaughter charges apiece. For men who'd spent years behind fences, that was perhaps the most powerful motivation possible to make it through to the other side.

Close to half-past three, the Goodno team boarded a vehicle that would take them back to the penitentiary. The driver took them east on 22, then headed south on 29. No more than fifteen minutes after their departure, they passed the bus coming in from Lehigh Acres. On board were Helen and Frances Richmond. The horror that awaited them at their family home was beyond all comprehension. The butchering of their father, the rape and strangulation of their mother, the clothes that Christiansen and Stein had left behind and the theft of the vehicle confirmed for the Feds, the US Marshals and all those at Southern that the worst-case scenario had actually transpired. Now it was not only a matter of three fugitives on the run, it was a state-wide manhunt for a trio of killers.

In the subsequent hour, once the Richmond girls had been taken to a safe place and their brother had been contacted, analysis of the house made it clear that only two sets of prison clothes were present. Stein's clothes were identifiable by their size, but Christiansen and Fielding were of similar build. Though the suspicion was that Fielding was the most likely not to have reached Alva, the authorities could assume nothing.

As far as the news bulletins and police alerts were concerned, nothing changed. The faces and physical descriptions of the three escapees along with the make and plate number of Errol Richmond's truck were on the wires. Additionally, though there was nothing to prove it, the consensus of opinion was that they were headed north and out of state. It would make no sense to head south. South would take them to the Keys and the Gulf of Mexico coastline.

Back at Southern, the news of the Richmond killings had arrived with the Marshals Command Center Unit. By 5 p.m., every additional resource that had been stationed at Southern had packed up and left. The men from High Security were still in their cells, a good few of them in solitary. General Population was quiet. Those killed in the riot had been certified by the coroner. An edict had already been issued by the Board of Prisons – they would not be buried at Southern as was ordinarily the case with an inmate death. The families of the dead would be afforded all accommodations. The cost of burials would be borne by the state, and each man would be interred according to the wishes of their kin. It was only one of numerous efforts to allay the possibility of further criticism and attack from the public sector. Whichever way it was viewed and whoever might be held ultimately responsible, it was a public relations disaster that reverberated to the highest rank of State officialdom. The Department of Justice had approved a 'fully transparent' inquiry into the situation. Rumors that Young would have to resign were numerous, and they did not dissipate.

A little after seven that evening, his every bone aching, Garrett Nelson got into his car and drove home to Port LaBelle. Frank headed back to Clewiston. They were due back at Southern at six on Wednesday morning, and they both intended to get as much sleep as they could.

It was in the car park beyond the fence that they shared their final words before leaving.

'There was never going to be a good ending to this story,' Frank said. 'But we did what was asked of us, and that's all that matters.'

Nelson was too tired to do anything but listen.

'Young will go,' Frank added. 'He's finished. Can't see any other possibility. Tough guy, sure, but not tough enough. Those animals in HS need a fuckin' lion tamer. People like that just don't have the same respect for human life as we do.'

Frank took a deep breath. 'Anyway, tomorrow is another day. Tell Hannah I send my love, an' I'll see you in the morning. An' come over for dinner on Sunday, why don't you? Miriam would really appreciate that.'

29

News of Christiansen and Stein finally came in the first week of August, serving once again to remind Nelson of the failure to trust his own instincts.

Despite the massing of forces and almost constant news coverage, they had made it as far as Gainesville. Changing cars, sleeping rough, staying off the Interstate once they'd crossed the Pasco County line, they had somehow managed to evade apprehension. Finally, in the small town of Arredondo, seventy or eighty miles from Georgia, they had robbed a gas station. The cashier was beaten to the ground in the process. Though rushed to hospital, the cashier suffered haemorrhaging that proved fatal. The proceeds from the gas station robbery amounted to seventy-eight dollars and four cents. It was a meagre amount for which to lose your life; comparable, perhaps, to the value Christiansen and Stein had afforded the lives of the Richmonds.

Unbeknownst to either man, an off-duty cop was filling his car at a pump and had recognized them. He knew who they were and he knew well enough what they'd done. Having called for assistance and then administered what little assistance he could to the cashier, he set out to follow Christiansen and Stein. Those few minutes gave them sufficient a head start to vanish once more.

That they were still on the run, that they were now responsible for a third killing, meant that the manhunt was ramped up once more. Even more men and resources were assigned to the task of finding the escaped convicts. The Florida Bureau put them at the top of the Most Wanted list.

The fact that only Christiansen and Stein had been seen at the gas station raised the question of what had happened to Lucas Fielding. It was assumed that he'd died or been murdered in the everglades beyond Southern. Whether it would be worse to die at the hands of Richard Stein or be dragged into the swamp by a twenty-foot 'gator was a matter of opinion. One thing was certain, however – for the 'gator it would have been a matter of instinct and survival; for Stein it would have been a matter of pleasure.

Though Nelson and all those at Southern sought some sense of closure, none was forthcoming. For Nelson, perhaps more than anyone, that shadow of guilt haunted him. He could have done something, but he did not. He had trusted someone else's analysis and judgement of the situation in preference to his own.

The Independence Day riot and the ongoing relentless campaign to find Christiansen, Stein and Fielding confirmed the fact that the perceived control of the men in their charge was just that – a perception. Men were not built to be caged. It flew in the teeth of instinct. Nelson asked himself whether being in the ranks of those who enforced this isolation was equally against human nature. Thinking beyond the job itself, beyond the necessity for salary, for the security and stability of employment itself, he could not help but question why he had so easily accepted the opportunity. At one time he had enforced the law. Unable to do that, he had chosen to detain those who had broken it. Once he began to question that, he began asking himself if he had joined the Sheriff's Department because that was what had been expected of him by his father. It was all within the same framework, and the framework appeared more and more as an artifice. Somewhere along the way, in the few short months since November of the previous year, a seed of doubt had rooted itself in the fertile substance of his mind. It unsettled him, gave him a sense of anxiety and introspection that – even to himself – seemed out of character.

Hannah noticed it on numerous occasions. Nelson circumvented and changed the subject time and again until they were driving back from the Montgomery house on the first Sunday in August.

'You need to talk to me, Garrett,' she said.

Glancing sideways as he drove, the expression on her face told him that she was not going to let it go.

'It's been a year,' Nelson said. 'Since Sebring.'

'Okay.'

'It feels like more has happened in the last year than in the rest of my life put together.'

'And that's a bad thing?' Hannah asked.

'Some of it, yes. A year ago I killed a man. Then I watched a man die in the electric chair. I hunted three other men through the fucking everglades, for Christ's sake. Seems more than likely one of them is dead, and then the other two killed a couple in Alva and then some guy in a gas station for the sake of a few dollars. All these people have died in the last twelve months, and every one of them had something to do with me.'

'What are you talking about, Garrett? We had this conversation before.'

'I don't know what I feel,' Nelson replied. 'Guilt? Responsibility? I know the first one was self-defense. The rest were... well, there were what they were. Like you said, that shit would've happened whether I'd been involved or not.'

'So what's happening?'

Nelson was quiet for a moment, and then he pulled over to

the side of the road and slowed to a halt. He switched off the engine and sat there, his hands on the wheel, and when he spoke, he did not look at Hannah.

'I guess I'm asking myself if this is what I want to do with my life,' he said. 'Not you, and not your family, but this ... this job. It isn't a job, you see? It's a way of life. It's a way of thinking. Like you said, it changes how you see people. You meet someone for the first time, and before you even know their name you're wondering if they're good or bad, if they have a record, if they've done things, bad things. I feel like I've lost my basic faith in humanity. It's like ... well, before this I would trust people until they gave me a reason not to trust them. It's now the opposite, like they have to earn the right to gain my trust.'

Nelson paused. He turned and looked at Hannah, held her gaze.

'There's a priest up at Southern. Father Donald. He believes that people are fundamentally good. I didn't really think about it, but I guess I've always believed that too, and I want to go on believing it. But ... but it's like there's a poison in your blood, you know? It's like some kind of slow-acting poison that gets into your mind and starts to color everything that you think, everything that you see. And I want to leave it back there, you know, at Southern. I want to walk out of those gates and leave all that shit behind me, but it sticks to you. It's like a scent. Like someone who works in a slaughterhouse can never wash the smell of blood from his clothes or his skin.'

'So leave,' Hannah said. 'You don't have to work there. You really don't. You don't need to impress my father. You don't even need his approval. I know him better than you, and all he really cares about when it comes to me is that I'm happy.'

Hannah reached out and closed her hand over Nelson's.

'And I am, Garrett. Happier than I ever remember being. And if this isn't right for you, then change it. Do something else.'

'I don't know what else to do,' Nelson said. 'I feel like my whole life has been indirectly dictated by the expectations of others, even when it was never spoken out loud. Hell, maybe they didn't even expect it of me. Maybe I just convinced myself that that's what they wanted. I guess I never gave myself a chance to find out what I wanted.'

'So, what *do* you want?'

Nelson gave a wry smile. 'That's the problem right there,' he said. 'I don't even know.'

'Okay, so what are you certain of?'

'Certain of? I'm certain of us. I'm also certain that we'll never be parents.'

'It's still possible, Garrett.'

'You're thirty-eight, Hannah—'

'I know how old I am,' Hannah replied. 'And I know that the risks increase as you get older, but all I'm saying is that it's possible.'

'Well, I guess that's another way in which this past year has changed me. I've thought about kids, you know? In the past. And if there was ever someone I'd want to have a family with, it would be you. But, like you, I'm seriously asking myself whether or not this is a world I'd want to bring a child into.'

'I know I said the same thing, Garrett, but it's not all darkness.'

'But it's a great deal darker than it used to be.'

Neither one spoke for a few moments. Hannah inched down the window to let some air into the car. She breathed deeply, almost as if she was trying to center herself.

'And what do you want?' Nelson asked.

'Me?' she asked. She did not look back at him. 'I guess I want us to be together, to create a future, to have a life that has value. When I get old, I want to be sat on a rocker on a veranda somewhere, and know that I did something meaningful with my time.'

Hannah smiled nostalgically.

'You never met my grandma. Mom's mom. She was most often batshit crazy. Other times she came out with things that really stuck with me. "What if?", she said, "is the question with which to begin your life, not end it." I remember her telling me that when I was about fifteen or sixteen. It took me a long time to really get what she meant. And in the hospitals I go to, every once in a while I get to treat someone who knows they're dying. And you know what they regret the most?'

Nelson shook his head.

'Not what they did, but what they didn't do.'

'Then I guess I'm asking myself if I want to be sat on that veranda with you remembering all the people I killed or locked up or sent to their deaths.'

'So dramatic,' Hannah said.

'I'm also asking myself if continuing to do this will turn me into a person you can't live with ... whether it would be better for you if—'

'No,' Hannah interjected. 'We're not going there, Garrett.'

'Maybe I already went. Maybe I already went so far that I can't get back.'

'Is this some, "It's not you, it's me ..." bullshit?'

Nelson turned and looked at her. There was hurt in her eyes.

'No,' he said. 'It's not that. It's just—'

'Stop talking. Enough already. Drive, Garrett. Take me home.'

'Hannah, look—'

'We talked about this when this started. Everyone needs someone to see the best in them, and then they need someone to take a gamble on it.'

'I know. I remember.'

'I took a gamble. Now you're tellin' me that I was wrong to do that?'

'That's not what I'm saying, sweetheart.'

'Sounds to me like you have no idea what the fuck you're saying.'

'Well, I guess—'

'You figure out whatever the hell you need to figure out, Garrett. Until then, keep your crazy thoughts to yourself.'

'I'm sorry, Hannah, but—'

'To yourself, Garrett. Now drive the fucking car.'

30

Perhaps Warden Young possessed some premonitory sense of what was to come. Towards the end of August, as word got out that the summary and findings of the Bureau of Prisons' independent inquiry were to be released, the mood at Southern changed.

Neither specific nor immediately identifiable, it was nevertheless reflected in an air of anticipation. Someone had to take the fall for the Independence Day riot and, by default, the killings of the Richmonds and the gas station attendant in Arredondo. It was never going to be a board member or a politician. It was always going to be the guy on the ground.

Emery Young served his last day as Warden of Southern State on Friday, September 2. His departure was intended to be quiet and unceremonious. He made no announcement to the prison population, and although he and the correctional staff hoped that he could slip away unnoticed, that was not how it turned out.

For over fifteen minutes, the combined populace of both High Security and General Population hammered relentlessly against their cell bars with anything that came to hand – cups, shoes, books – and the chant of 'Warden! Warden! Warden!' rose and swelled in unison as if from one mighty throat. Even from the gate, as Young drove out to an uncertain future, that swell of voices could be heard as it reverberated through every cell, along every gantry and corridor, and through the very foundations of the buildings themselves.

Young was neither loved nor admired, but he was a known quantity. There seemed to be a general consensus of opinion, both from the inmates and the officers, that 'Better the Devil you know' applied more than ever in such an instance.

For that weekend, Frank Montgomery was made Acting Warden. The new man, his identity as yet unknown, was due to arrive on Monday the 5th. Montgomery changed nothing. There was no point. His promotion was in name only, and even though he accepted it without question, it had no true significance.

On Sunday the 4th, Nelson and Hannah went for dinner at the Montgomery house. As was routine, Frank, Ray and Nelson went out onto the back veranda to have a beer and talk shop.

It had been a month since Nelson and Hannah had discussed their collective future, and it seemed that merely its exposure to daylight had desensitised the issue. Perhaps, for Nelson, it was also a matter of the known being preferable to the unknown. For fear of things deteriorating even further, people accepted the unacceptable, learned to live with them, reconciled themselves to what was, as opposed to what could be. Though it still took a conscious effort on Nelson's part, he had persuaded himself to acknowledge that it was just a job, a job he could do until something better came along. That the 'something' had to be looked for and found he knew well enough, but he traded his uncertainties for the apparent security of routine. He knew what he was doing. He also knew that such a compromise would serve to haunt him, even if he ignored it.

'So, not a clue who's coming?' Ray asked.

Frank shook his head. 'Nothing.'

'Fuck, I hope we don't wind up with some hard-headed ballbuster.'

'I'm guessin' whoever it is will be coming in looking to make an impression,' Nelson said. 'Southern's had a clean record for a long, long time. Whichever way you view it, this was a one-off. It'll be a knee-jerk reaction. Things are gonna get harsh.'

'I'm thinking the same,' Frank said, 'and that's what concerns me.'

'Whatever the fuck happens,' Ray said, 'I intend to stay in Gen Pop. I have no plans to wind up in HS with you pair. Fucking madhouse over there.'

'If that's what it is, then it seems it'd be the perfect place for you,' Frank said.

'What d'you think'll happen to Young?' Nelson asked.

Frank shook his head. 'He'll go run a Juvy or something. They'll stick him in some bumfuck, nowhere place and hope no one pays any attention. He knows and they know that he was just the head in the noose on this one. Hell, they probably paid him off to take the rap so they could cover their own asses.'

'DOJ?' Nelson asked.

'DOJ, prisons, Attorney General's Office, all of them. The whole bureaucratic pyramid that sits above us.'

'I've only been there a year,' Nelson said, 'but that shit is bound to happen eventually, right? I mean, there's always gonna be people who are gonna do whatever they can to get out.'

'Human nature,' Frank said. 'Accept it or do something to change it.'

The words reflected Nelson's own state of mind.

'And no matter who they bring in, that's not gonna change,' Ray said. 'There's always gonna be a handful who are trouble, another handful who are completely fucking nuts, and there's always gonna be people who can't think of anything else but running.'

'And we're supposed to be able to tell the difference and predict it,' Frank said. 'That's what they think, the desk jockeys. That's why they can point the finger and give their opinion about how things should be. Doesn't matter that they know fuck-all about it. They're just suits, and a suit is there to tell you how you should have done something different when things go to shit.'

'I keep thinking about that couple who got killed,' Ray said. 'They had kids, three of them. Makes you wonder what kind of people could do something like that.'

'Get a transfer to HS,' Nelson said. 'We've got no shortage of them over there.'

'Better still, Death Row,' Frank added. 'That's the cast of some truly horrific nightmares.'

Echoing Nelson's own sentiment, Ray said, 'One time was enough. Fucking thing gave me nightmares for weeks. I mean, sure, I get the "eye for an eye" philosophy, but that was... was just brutal.'

'You think too much,' Frank said. 'You always have.'

'So, how does anyone ever reconcile themselves to that?' Ray asked.

'Reconcile themselves?' Frank frowned, shook his head. 'You don't. It's the law, Ray. It's what we do. I've seen these people, talked to them, listened to all the bullshit stories about how they had difficult childhoods an' all that shit. Hell, half the population of the damned planet has had a difficult childhood, but half the planet ain't goin' around cuttin' people's fuckin' heads off and doing finger painting in blood on the walls, are they? The people on the row... Jesus, I have trouble even calling them "people". Those people are beasts. Okay, so killing them in an electric chair might be inhumane and a violation of their human rights, but where was humanity and rights when it came to the people they murdered? They did it for money or some twisted sense of power or whatever the hell, but they still did it. Every man sees the line, right? Every man sees the line, and it's the man himself who makes the decision to cross it. No one pushes him. I don't give a flying fuck how crazy you are or how traumatised you were when your daddy slapped your mommy around, that line is there and there's nothing anyone can say or do that's gonna convince me that they didn't see it.'

'And what about the ones that didn't do it?' Ray asked.

'What ones would that be, then?'

'It's happened, right? People have gotten executed for shit that they didn't do.'

'Collateral damage,' Frank said. 'Or maybe they did something else just as bad. Who the fuck knows, and to be honest who the fuck cares? Seems to me that if a guy winds up on the row then there's gonna be no shortage of reasons for him being there.'

'Is that what you really think, Dad?'

Frank sighed. 'What I really think is that I need another beer.'

With that, Frank got up and went back into the house.

Ray and Nelson were silent for a moment, and then Ray turned and looked at him.

'Welcome to the fuckin' family, Garrett,' he said, and raised his bottle.

31

Whatever preconceptions the staff and inmates of Southern might have had about the incoming Warden, no one could have predicted the man who arrived on the morning of Monday, September 5.

Harold Greaves was sixty-one years old. He had served in the Federal Bureau of Prisons for over forty years. Amongst the last complement of officers to leave Alcatraz when it closed in March of 1963, he'd then gone on to Deputy and Warden posts in Georgia, Alabama, New York State and Illinois. Greaves had never married, had no children, and had one brother with whom he'd severed all ties after his brother had been arrested for shoplifting in May of 1970. He did not smoke, nor did he drink, and such things as literature, music and academic studies were of no interest to him. Had he been asked what purpose his life served, he would have quoted the Bureau of Prisons motto: 'Courage. Respect. Integrity. Correctional Excellence.'

Every officer serving at Southern, irrespective of shift schedules, days off, medical appointments or family commitments, was summoned to the High Security mess hall at 5 a.m. that first morning. Greaves had brought with him the majority of the Sheriff's Departments of three surrounding counties to stand watch in the blocks for the duration of his introduction.

Close to a hundred men stood to attention as Warden Greaves entered the hall and stepped up onto a dais.

'My name is Harold Greaves,' he began, 'and for the foreseeable future I will be assuming the position of Warden of this facility.'

Greaves' physical appearance – slight and wiry in stature, iron-gray hair shorn close to the scalp, thin steel-rimmed spectacles – belied the impingement and reach of his voice.

'Just as you are not here to be friends and confidantes of the inmates in our care, so I am not here to be your friend and confidante. This is now my prison, and in my prison we do things my way. If, faced with any degree of uncertainty as to how you should act or respond to a given situation, you simply need to ask yourself one question. What would Warden Greaves do? The answer to that question will always be the right answer. I do not doubt that, and nor should you.'

Greaves paused. He gave a faint, emotionless smile.

'There will be changes, of course. I have no interest in what happened under your previous Warden, save to ensure that it never happens again. That is your job just as much as it is mine. If you fail, I am accountable, and thus you will not fail. Understand that, and understand it well. You are each reliant on one another to fulfil the remit of your duties in an exemplary manner, but that is where your team attitude comes to an end. Your loyalty is only to me and to the purpose of this facility. If you discover that another officer has been remiss, incompetent, insecure or has in some way been negligent, then it is to be reported and reported at once. Failure to report a known violation of penitentiary rules will carry the same penalty as that of the violation perpetrated.'

Again, Greaves paused as if to allow time for his edict to arrive.

'And no, I will not mellow with time. I have no interest in

reputation, save that of my position as Warden. I do not care if you like me or hate me. You need only respect me as your superior.'

Again that faint disconnected smile.

'And though it may be customary in such situations to ask if there are any questions, I am not going to make that enquiry. If you have heard what I have said, and I trust you have, then you will know that all the answers you need have already been given. We are here for one purpose and one purpose only. It is a common purpose, and together we will see it fulfilled to the letter.'

Having finished his presentation, Warden Greaves nodded towards Frank Montgomery and then marched out of the hall.

Frank walked to the head of the ranks and dismissed the men. They moved away in silence, perhaps too stunned to think, let alone speak.

One of the first changes that Warden Greaves implemented at Southern was the layout. To prevent the possibility that the inmates could engineer a means by which an escape could be made, Greaves brought in external crews under armed guard to carry out the construction work. Those on Death Row were moved to the solitary cells in the basement of High Security. The building that housed the Death Row inmates was converted to the infirmary, though a single cell closest to the bell tower was maintained. Known as 'final holding', this was for a condemned man on his last night. After substantially reinforcing the security of the infirmary, it became the new home for the prison armory. Once that was complete, the northernmost quadrant of High Security's lower floor was redesigned to allow for twelve individual cells. The cells would house those awaiting execution. The basement was once again available for any who warranted isolation.

Greaves' re-planning meant that an escape from the infirmary was as impossible as from the main block. His integration of Death Row into the HS block meant that the officer complement was no longer split between two buildings. Greaves also established a new shift rota. He divided the sixty officers at HS into three teams of twenty. He called them Alpha, Bravo and Charlie. He assigned a single officer not as a senior over each team, but as the relay point for all instructions and orders. Frank Montgomery was given Alpha, Nelson was given Bravo, and Charlie was assigned to a veteran officer called Don Trent. Warden briefings were short, to the point, with only those three men in attendance. In this way, the management and administration of HS was designed to be as uncomplicated as possible.

The final change related to the Death Row inmates. Though now contained within the same building, access was through two reinforced steel doors, akin to a submarine. The inner door could not be opened until the outer door was closed and locked. Once through the inner door, a corridor divided the unit with six cells on each side. Each cell had a solid outer door on horizontal rollers and a second internal series of bars that ran floor-to-ceiling. The gap between the two was sufficient for a man to stand in order to deliver food, mail, medication, books and magazines. As had been the protocol when Death Row was in a separate building, the inmates ate in isolation. The cells were also soundproofed so as to prevent the possibility of prisoners talking to one another. Even with an outer door open, an officer speaking with an inmate could not be overheard by another inmate.

'Alcatraz,' Frank explained to Nelson one evening in the commissary. 'They had isolation cells like that. Worse than what we've got now because there was no light. They used to throw fellers in there for days at a time. Went crazy, for the most part. They used to twist buttons off their tunic tops and flick them into the darkness, and then crawl around on their hands and knees until they found it. Then they'd do it again. Anything to keep the mind occupied. Capone was in there. If he wasn't already whacko with the syphilis, that would've done the trick, for sure.'

Death Row guard duty was known as Dead Watch. For a three-day duration, three men would work eight-hour shifts in rotation – 8 a.m. until 4 p.m., 4 p.m. until midnight, midnight until 8 a.m. Due to the impregnability of the cell layout and double doors, only one man was required to supervise the row. He sat or stood in the dividing corridor. He attended to the prisoner's needs. Everything went through him.

There were five teams of three, and thus each three-day cycle would repeat after twelve days. If a team member was sick or on leave, the next three-man team on the board would cover for them. Once the Dead Watch was completed, the men would return to regular HS schedules until their time came around again. Greaves required that only those who had demonstrated initiative in the face of adversity be assigned. Frank was chosen, as were Nelson and thirteen others, amongst them Max Sheehan who, along with Trent, would comprise Nelson's team.

Nelson's first Dead Watch was scheduled for the 4th, 5th and 6th of October. Nine of the twelve cells were occupied, and, directed by Warden Greaves, Nelson, along with the other fourteen assigned officers, was obligated to study the case files of those who were incarcerated there.

Since the execution of Darryl Jeffreys back in April, Nelson had done everything possible to exorcise the memory of that day from his mind. Perhaps in an effort not only to explain to himself why he was continuing to do the job, but also because he sought some sense of personal justification for the death penalty, Nelson took the time to understand the crimes the condemned had committed.

Sitting in a small office in Central Admin, he, Don Trent and Max Sheehan passed the files between them.

Trent was the first to speak. He simply said, 'I always wondered if some people were born evil. Reading some of this stuff, I think I have the answer.'

'Who's that?' Sheehan asked.

Trent leaned forward and spread the dossier on the table.

'This here is Thomas Mark Lancaster,' he said. 'Arson, armed robbery, attempted kidnapping and rape, and that was before he was old enough to vote. Twenty-two years old, he abducts Melanie Burnett, sixteen years old, from the grounds of Brevard County Fair near Lake Sawgrass. It's late, no one sees him snatch her. Her friends think she's gone off with some boy. It's her folks who call the cops when it gets to midnight and there's no word from her. They don't find her for a week and a half.' Trent shook his head. 'I say *find her*, but they didn't find all of her. They found her head and torso in a ditch about thirty miles away off of 192. Driver pulls over to take a piss at the side of the road and there she is. Our friend Lancaster has pretty much sawed her in half at the waist, pulled out her intestines and draped them around her neck like a fuckin' necklace.'

'And what happened to her legs?' Nelson asked.

Trent shrugged. 'Doesn't say. I'm guessin' they never showed up.'

'You got three-of-a-kind there,' Sheehan said. 'This is a full fuckin' house.' He took a page from the dossier. 'Anthony Ulysses Irving. Forty-six years old as of last Wednesday. Did a tour in Vietnam. Seems he got a taste for killing. Convicted of the murder of seven. Two families, both in the same town on the same day. No known connection to either. Broke in, tied them all up, raped the mother and then the thirteen-year-old daughter. Strangled them both. Then he beat the father and son to death. Second family was pretty much the same, but this time he did the rapes, then tied them up and set the place on fire. He left them to burn alive. He was seen leaving the house, and someone called the cops. They found him in a diner about four blocks away having himself a blue plate special. He asked them whether it would be okay if he finished eating before they took him away. Apparently he said, 'Believe me, this shit sure as hell gives you an appetite.'

So they continued reading the files for three or four hours – decapitations, fatal stabbings, convenience store shootings, poisonings and child murders. It made for sickening reading, and Nelson, repelled by the sheer depravity of some of the things that he read, began to feel that a swift execution was too good for some of these people. As Frank had said, *people* was too generous a term for them. It was irrational, obscene; these were acts of unforgiving brutality, seemingly devoid of any sense of humanity or mercy. These were not crimes of passion or fury, but premeditated cruelty. To rationalize the irrational was impossible, and yet these men – every one of them – had been declared of sound mind and thus able to stand trial for what they'd done. In most cases, appeals had been granted and processed, and in each case those appeals had been denied and the sentence had been upheld. These men were on Death Row at Southern because that's where they belonged. Had they been allowed into High Security or General Population, they more than likely would have killed again. Had they been released into society, there would have been yet another bloodbath, the devastation of yet another family, and all of it for what? For no clear or understandable reason. It was, in truth, beyond all reason.

That night, ending his shift a little before ten, Nelson drove back to Port LaBelle with images in his mind that he did not want. He arrived to find a note from Hannah. She'd taken a double shift and wouldn't be back until the morning.

Nelson was not a habitual drinker, but he knew he would not

sleep until the kaleidoscope of blood and mayhem that assaulted every sense had been quietened. The whiskey did little but slow it down, but slower was better than nothing. He felt sick to his stomach, appalled and disturbed, and he did not know how he would be able to cope when he saw these men in the flesh.

Nelson appreciated that his thoughts about Darryl Jeffreys had also changed. There was no denying it. He had not read Jeffreys' file, but if what he'd learned today was anything to go by, the man had deserved to die. Contradicting his prior viewpoint, Nelson even felt that the electric chair was too swift a killing. An eye for an eye. The punishment should fit the crime. A man's life should end in the same manner as those whose lives he'd ended.

Nelson fell asleep in the chair, an empty glass in his hand. Even as he felt his eyes begin to close, he prayed that he would not dream, and thankfully – mercifully – he did not.

32

Driving into work on the morning of Friday, September 23, Nelson switched on the radio and caught the tail end of a news report. The long-awaited verdict in the appeal of Clarence Jefferson 'CJ' Whitman had been reached. Back in May of 1971, Whitman had been found guilty of the first-degree murder of a travelling salesman by the name of Garth Kenyon in Wauchula. Whitman, a young black man of just nineteen at the time, had subsequently become the focal point of two groups of individuals – those who opposed the death penalty, and those who believed that Whitman was not only innocent, but had been railroaded for his color. Despite not having made a confession, the faceless machinery of justice appeared to have rolled right over him.

The final State Supreme Court appeal process had headlined briefly in December of the previous year. Nelson vaguely remembered the story, but had paid it no mind. Back then he'd been too preoccupied with his apprenticeship at Southern and his burgeoning relationship with Hannah.

Once at work, taking a cup of coffee at the commissary before his shift began, Nelson saw that the case was front page in the *St Petersburg Times*. He scanned the article, gleaning what little he could of the details. They were insubstantial, focusing primarily on the seeming controversy and division of opinion about the appeal itself. Nevertheless, what caught Nelson's attention was that Whitman was being transferred to Death Row at Southern on Monday, 26th.

Since his original conviction, Whitman had been incarcerated at Florida State in Raiford. An influx of condemned men – subsequent to the overturning of Furman v. Georgia – had stretched their resources to capacity. The Bureau of Prisons had elected that some be transferred to other facilities. The Attorney General also made no secret of an additional agenda. The furore generated by protesters and civil rights lawyers about capital cases was an inconvenience, not only to his department, but to Florida State Penitentiary itself. Though he didn't say it and would never admit it, Nelson guessed what was in the AG's mind: the vast majority of those protesting would be working-class blacks. They had jobs, families, local commitments and obligations, and adding a few hundred miles to the drive from FSP in Raiford to Southern State might serve to dampen their enthusiasm and quiet their collective voice. As was invariably the case with politicians, what they said and what they meant weren't even cousins of the truth.

Florida's AG, quoted after the appeal was overturned, made it clear that he had every intention of seeing that Whitman's sentence – as delivered by the court – was to be carried out as rapidly as possible. As far as he was concerned, the case had been solid, the original conviction entirely warranted, and now it was merely a matter of reducing the burden on the taxpayer by carrying out the execution. CJ Whitman had already been on Death Row for six years. Every possible line of appeal had been exhausted. The law was the law, and Florida's exemplary justice system was going to abide by it to the letter. Besides, as far as the issue of human rights was concerned, wasn't it more inhumane to prolong the suffering of a condemned man by keeping him locked up?

Why Nelson felt an impulse to learn more of the case, he did not know, save that here would be another inmate under his watch. Whatever case files or dossiers might relate to Whitman would not arrive at Southern for some time, so at 4.40 that afternoon, his shift complete, Nelson drove to the library in Clewiston to read the newspaper archives.

CJ Whitman, born November 10, 1951 in Wauchula, Hardee County, was the youngest of five. His father, Floyd, was an itinerant carpenter and handyman who'd seen his fair share of prison cells. Unusual for a man of Floyd's age, he had not served in the military. Somehow he'd avoided World War Two and Korea, and hadn't been drafted to Vietnam. Whitman's mother, Dorothy, was a good deal younger than her husband. Why the trial itself garnered so much press attention was due to the fact that so much of the State's case was based on circumstantial evidence. Garth Kenyon, seemingly an individual of no great consequence, had been the victim of what appeared to be a robbery gone wrong. Kenyon was shot at point-blank range in the head with his own .38. At the time of the robbery, he'd been alone in the house, his wife running errands in town. Canvassing of neighbors revealed that a young black man had been seen on the Kenyon property on numerous occasions. Like his father, Whitman earned a living by gardening and other odd jobs. He was paid cash, gave no receipts, did not maintain a bank account, nor any kind of record of those he counted amongst his clientele. Simply stated, Whitman could not prove that he worked for the Kenyons, nor could he provide an alibi for the time of the shooting. He was identified by three different people, all of them white middle-class law-abiding citizens. The truly damning evidence, and the thing that Whitman's defense attorney could not explain away, was the presence of a partial thumbprint on the handle of Garth Kenyon's revolver.

The case presented by the prosecution posited that Whitman

had entered the property with the intent to commit robbery. He had been discovered *in flagrante* and had been challenged by a gun-wielding Kenyon. Kenyon had a permit for the gun, and had every right to use it in defense of his life and property. A struggle had ensued, during which Whitman had wrestled the gun from Kenyon's grip. Whitman had then shot Kenyon and fled the scene, leaving the murder weapon behind. No one had seen Whitman enter or exit the property, but as far as the jury was concerned, that counted for nothing. The defense questioned the investigating officer's omission of a wax paraffin test for gun residue. The lead investigator, a Detective Kenneth Woodward of the Wauchula Police Department Homicide Division, gave a credible response that concurred with Nelson's own experience. The dermal nitrate test that had been in use since the 1930s was no longer considered conclusive. Not only was it possible for someone to fire a gun and leave no residue on the hand, but the presence of fertilizer, cosmetics, urine, even cigarettes, could give a positive reaction to such a test. Wauchula PD did not have access to a scanning electron microscope, and, besides, it was only necessary for a man to thoroughly scrub his hands in order to remove particles of gunpowder and its constituent elements.

The defense presented the possibility that Whitman could have touched the gun on one of his prior visits to the property. Perhaps, as one of the many and varied jobs that Kenyon had Whitman undertake, cleaning the gun could have been one of them. Could the defense provide evidence of Whitman having worked at the Kenyons'? No, he could not. Kenyon's wife, Sarah, did not take the stand, but an affidavit provided by the prosecution clearly stated that Mrs Kenyon did not know and had never met CJ Whitman.

Whitman's counsel, try as he might to introduce the slightest degree of reasonable doubt into the proceedings, did not change the minds of the jury. They came back with a unanimous verdict. CJ Whitman was guilty of first-degree murder. Though there was no indication of premeditation, and though it could not necessarily be considered heinous or cruel, it still qualified as a capital crime due to the fact that Whitman fatally shot Garth Kenyon while engaged in the commission of a specified felony. At this stage the jury could have decided not to impose the death penalty. Whitman had few character witnesses. His father was considered unreliable due to his own criminal history. There was nothing about Whitman's childhood or background that could have been considered a mitigating circumstance. He had not suffered any known domestic abuse, his parents were still married, his siblings, two sisters and two brothers, were all law-abiding individuals. There was no known classifiable mental disorder. He was not a drug addict. The mere fact that he was as ordinary as a man could be actually proved to be a disadvantage. The jury wanted him to go to the chair.

The six years Whitman had spent at Florida State in Raiford had seen his defense counsel pursue the standard appellate protocol. Once denied by the State Court of Appeal, he presented findings to Florida's Supreme Court. Possessing the prerogative to let the appellate court ruling stand, the Supreme Court opted to review the original trial and its subsequent appeal. The defense submission concentrated on the circumstantial nature of the evidence, the fact that Whitman had no history as a thief or housebreaker, that he was gainfully employed, that he had never before been convicted of a misdemeanor, let alone a felony.

In essence, the Supreme Court concluded that despite the lack of direct eyewitnesses and additional material evidence relating to the homicide itself, there was also nothing to prove that he did not do it. The fact that his thumbprint – partial or not – was on the gun could not be refuted. Whitman had also been picked out of a line-up by three independent and unrelated witnesses.

The AG wanted the matter closed, and closed it was.

Notwithstanding the possibility that a final plea for clemency was received and granted by the Governor of Florida, Whitman was going to die in the bell tower, and that's all there was to it.

Whitman was now a little over two weeks away from his twenty-sixth birthday, but the image of a wide-eyed, stunned nineteen-year-old staring back at Nelson from the archive screen had unsettled him and he didn't know why. Perhaps it had played out exactly as the prosecution had said. Perhaps it was nothing more than a single, dreadful mistake on the part of Clarence Whitman. Whatever the truth, it was not Nelson's job to dig any deeper. He was no longer a deputy sheriff. He was a Southern State Correctional Officer. His sole responsibility was to keep the man incarcerated until his date of execution arrived.

However, dismiss it though he tried, a single statement made by Whitman and reported in a short article just a week after his original conviction stuck in Nelson's mind.

'We're just the low-hanging fruit,' Whitman had said. 'Ripe for the picking. Hell, people like us are always guilty until someone more guilty comes along.'

33

On the evening before his first Dead Watch, Nelson and Hannah had dinner at a restaurant in Clewiston.

Over dessert – a shared key lime pie – Hannah told him that she wanted to start a family.

'Seriously?' Nelson had joked. 'Isn't the one you've got trouble enough for you?'

'You know what I'm saying, Garrett,' she said.

Nelson set down his fork and looked at her. 'But—'

'I know,' she interjected. 'I'm thirty-eight years old and the world is fucked up, and around every corner is a rapist or a kidnapper or a psychopath, but that doesn't change the fact that I want a baby.'

Before Nelson had a chance to change the expression on his face, she said, 'And you don't.'

'I didn't say that.'

'Your reaction says everything.'

'Well, then you're misreading my reaction. I'm surprised, that's all.'

'But you're not saying yes.'

'And I'm not saying no.'

Hannah leaned back in the chair.

'You really want to talk about this in a restaurant?' Nelson asked.

'Where we talk about it doesn't matter,' Hannah replied. 'I want to talk about it now and we just happen to be here.'

'And how long have you been thinking about this?'

'Since Independence Day.'

'That's very specific.'

'I knew where you were going, Garrett, and I knew why you were going there. The two most important men in my life disappeared into the fucking wilderness after some escaped sociopaths. I actually asked myself what I would do if you didn't come back. And don't say that I would've found someone else, okay? It's taken me this long to find you.'

'Okay, I won't say that, then.'

'So?'

'Jeez, Hannah, it's a big deal, don't you think? I mean, having a baby isn't like buying a new car.'

'I know what having a baby means, Garrett. Don't patronize me.'

'I'm sorry. I didn't mean it to sound like that.'

'Are you scared?' Hannah asked. 'Or do you just never want children? Or is it that you want children, but you don't want them with me?'

'Scared? Maybe a little. And no, it's not because I don't want children with you. I told you before, if I was going to have children, you would be the only person I'd want them with.'

'So what then? Give me one good, sound reason why we shouldn't do this.'

'I guess the only reasons would be the same reasons that everyone has for not starting a family. Time, money, the commitment, the fact that your life will never be the same again. And then there's the inevitable anxiety that comes with having children so late.'

'I get that. After thirty-five there's a greater risk of complications. I'm more likely to need a caesarean. There can be growth issues, hormone problems. I've read all of it, Garrett. And I'm in hospitals all the time. Half the physio I do is with pregnant and post-natal mothers. But here's the thing...'

Hannah leaned forward. She looked at him directly.

'After finding someone you want to be with, having a child is probably the most basic, natural thing you could imagine. We'd be good at it. I have no doubt about that. I think we'd make great parents. I mean, who the hell wouldn't want us to be their mom and dad, right?'

'You're really serious about this.'

'No, actually, quite the opposite. It shouldn't be a serious thing. It should be a life-affirming, joyful thing. I don't want to be serious about it. I want it to be exciting and fun, and I want us to do it because we *want* to do it.'

'Can we talk about it some more? Can we at least take some time to think about it?'

'What's to talk about? What's to think about? It either feels right or it doesn't. I don't even want it to be an analytical process. It's something that you feel instinctively. Go with your gut feeling, Garrett.'

Nelson didn't respond.

'Are you still twisted around in knots about whether I would be happier without you?'

'No,' Nelson replied, and it was the truth. Whatever reservations he'd had about continuing at Southern had been thoroughly dispelled by the events of Independence Day, the fatal consequences of the escape, and finally by appreciating the kind of people that wound up on Death Row.

'So, what does your gut tell you?' Hannah asked.

'I am asking myself what you'll do if I say no.'

'Are you saying no?'

'It's a hypothetical question.'

'I'll be disappointed,' Hannah said.

'And what would that do to us?'

'Nothing.'

'I don't see how it wouldn't change things.'

'We don't have kids now,' Hannah replied. 'It would just mean that we would go on not having kids. Everything would be as it is now.'

'Except that I would have denied you something that you really want. As far as I can tell, I haven't done that yet.'

'I would reconcile myself to it. I would tell myself that it probably wasn't such a good idea for a thirty-eight-year-old woman to consider having a baby. I would find a way to get closure on it.'

'And you think you could do that?'

'I guess I'll find out, won't I?'

'And I'm guessing that it's gonna involve quite a lot of that naked, sweaty stuff.'

Hannah smiled. 'Probably quite a lot of that, yes.'

'And when were you thinking of starting this?'

'No time like the present, right?'

'Okay.'

'Okay, what? Is that the end of the conversation?'

Nelson shook his head and smiled. 'Okay, Hannah Montgomery. Let's have a baby.'

Before they'd slept, Hannah had closed herself up against him. In that moment he'd been struck with how responsible he felt for her well-being and welfare. Before too long, if this really happened, then it would not only be Hannah for whom he was responsible. That notion stood tall on the horizon, and he knew there would be seismic shifts in his attitude and perspective toward everything.

'If I get pregnant, we tell no one,' Hannah had said as they lay in bed. 'Not Mom or Dad. No one. Not until I'm through the first trimester. I want to know that everything's all right before we say anything, okay?'

'Okay,' Nelson had replied. He'd thought to ask her more, but before he could formulate the questions in his mind, he'd sensed her breathing slowing down, and within minutes she was asleep. He'd fallen into the same rhythm, and then it seemed that there was just one of them beneath the covers, each breathing in unison, each comforted by the sense that they were not – and would never be – alone. Perhaps that was, after all, the true meaning of a good relationship. You stood back-to-back against the world, and no matter what happened out there, you always knew that there was someone who would face it with you. Too often, with the noise and clamor of everyday living, people turned and faced one another to level blame and criticism for what had happened. Their force divided, they then became all the more weak and vulnerable.

Perhaps nothing more than a sign of the shifting social consensus, but Hannah hadn't spoken about marriage. For Nelson, the bonding by blood that was inherent in the creation of a child was of far greater significance and meaning than a stamped piece of paper from City Hall. Possibly that would come, but, at least for now, they had agreed to do something that would tie them together for ever in the most inextricable way.

34

The irony of Nelson's situation – spending his first day on Dead Watch guarding ten men who were scheduled to die, all the while preoccupied with the conversation he'd had with Hannah the night before – did not pass him by. Driving in that morning, he was acutely aware of a sense of unease. Whether that was attributable to what would happen in the next eight hours, or if he was already questioning his own certainty about starting a family with Hannah, he did not know. He had slept, had not woken in the night, but as he drank his coffee and made small talk in the kitchen, each of them aware of the fact that they weren't talking about the previous evening, he felt as if his consciousness was struggling to identify the aftermath of a dream. He hadn't yet told Hannah about Dead Watch. He'd planned to, but had then put it off each time. Now, with the sense that life and hope for the future was their foremost priority, it seemed incongruous and morbid.

Nelson, Trent and Sheehan had agreed on their schedule for the first three days. Nelson would take 8 a.m. until 4 p.m., Trent would take the next eight hours, and then Sheehan would cover from midnight until 8 a.m. the following morning. Their subsequent three-day shift would begin on Wednesday the 19th, at which point Nelson would take 4 p.m. until midnight. The shift would rotate each time so no one covered the same hours on consecutive watches. Through the next eleven weeks, right until their last pre-Christmas shift on December 20, none of them had booked any leave.

In HS and Gen Pop, each officer carried handcuffs and a billy club. For Dead Watch, officers were also issued with a can of pepper spray.

Within each cell there was a button on the back wall just three feet from the floor, positioned this way in case the prisoner suffered collapse and could not stand. Pressing that button illuminated a red light above the door in the corridor. Installed for the sole purpose of alerting the duty guard that the prisoner was in distress, its unnecessary use was not only forbidden, but carried a penalty of reduced rations.

Each cell had its own latrine and a washbasin. Showers were twice-weekly, one man at a time. Exercise was also taken one man at a time during the first and second shifts, forty-five minutes per day in a narrow twelve-by-eight-foot caged section behind the block. The Dead Watch officer would release the inmate into the cage and lock the door behind him. The cage was overseen by an armed guard in a watchtower. The inmate did not wear handcuffs, but his legs were shackled at the ankles with a two-foot chain. Even for a man of average height, a full stride could not be taken. Books and magazines were permitted weekly from the penitentiary library. Again, they were delivered by an HS inmate on a trolley. A man could request a specific book in writing, but it had to be approved before being issued. Mail was collected and delivered monthly, save when incoming mail arrived from a legal authority and related directly to an inmate's ongoing appeal. Paper and pencils were distributed, a half-hour afforded for a letter to be written, and then collected once again. Inmates were not permitted to write the names of officers or other inmates in their letters. The content of letters could not include any references to schedules, quality of food, medical conditions or ongoing treatment, nor any explicit sexual matters. An inmate was permitted to receive photographs of immediate family members. Inmates were not permitted to receive pornographic literature or images. 'Fan mail' from individuals who professed admiration for whatever crimes the condemned had committed was destroyed at Central Admin. Visitation was permitted once every two months. Applications from individuals wishing to see a man on Death Row were personally approved or disapproved by Warden Greaves.

Each Death Row inmate was fed at the same time. Food was delivered by trolley from the HS kitchen. A member of the catering crew would bring it to the outer door. An external guard would let him through. The trolley would remain. The catering crew member would back out and the external door would be locked. The outer guard would notify the Dead Watch officer with a buzzer that food had arrived. The secondary door would be opened from within, the trolley would be wheeled through into the corridor between the cells, and then the inner door would be secured. The inner barred door of each cell possessed an aperture of sufficient width to receive a food tray. Men ate in their cells. They were permitted fifteen minutes. The duty officer's meal came in at the same time. Even for the officer, the trays on which the food was served were plastic, as was the cutlery.

In truth, a man on Death Row at Southern was utterly disconnected from the outside world. For over twenty-three hours a day he saw nothing but concrete. Though each cell possessed a twelve-by-eight-inch skylight in the ceiling, itself three layers of reinforced glass, it did little to alleviate the gloom and shadows within. A fluorescent tube, encased within a heavy-duty metal cage, switched on only after sunset, emitted a greasy yellow light and a relentless subliminal hum.

The corridor that divided the cells was brightly lit, thus affording the duty officer a clear view of every door. At the far end of the corridor was a single wooden chair. If a man was on suicide watch, the outer door would be opened to permit observation of the interior of the cell. The integrated roller doors were on Greaves' insistence. A door opening outward into the corridor could serve to obscure an officer's view.

The first thing to assault Nelson's senses when he stepped through the second doorway of Death Row was the smell. Sweat, shit, urine, and beneath that, the underlying odor of rotting food. Beyond the walls, the temperature was in the low eighties. Nelson had driven in with the windows wide. Even as he'd walked through HS, he'd begun to perspire beneath his uniform jacket. The internal corridor of Death Row had to exceed ninety. Above the chair at the far end of the walkway a single vent fought sluggishly to circulate the thickened air. Having instinctively recoiled and held his breath, Nelson exhaled suddenly. Inhaling once again, he almost retched. He tried to take short, shallow breaths, but it was impossible. He stood there in silence for three or four minutes, willing himself to resist the urge to get out of there. Slowly but surely the nausea subsided.

Nelson walked to the end of the corridor and took off his jacket. He draped it over the back of the chair.

He would be there for eight hours, the only interruptions being the delivery of lunch and the release of half the men into the external cage for exercise time. He had not thought to bring a book. His sole company would be his own thoughts. He too was a prisoner it seemed, but the decision to be there was his and his alone. The prospect of eight hours was daunting. For those incarcerated, the knowledge that this – for months, perhaps years – was the last place on earth they would see before a short walk to the bell tower was impossible to comprehend.

Nelson imagined that there were some amongst them who now longed for that day. Dying was their only means of escape, and it could not come soon enough.

35

Nelson was required to check on his charges on the hour, every hour. Each outer cell door possessed a thin aperture at eye level, no more than eight inches wide and three inches high. Over it was a plate that could be slid back to see within. Beside each door was a hook, upon which hung a clipboard. On the clipboard was a single sheet of paper marked out in grids. The date and time was printed in the left-hand column, and there was a small box in which the duty officer would write his initials to confirm that his hourly inspection had been carried out.

Above the clipboard were the cell number and the name of the prisoner.

Thomas Lancaster, the man who'd left the head and torso of a sixteen-year-old in a ditch off the highway, was in Cell 6. Anthony Irving, child rapist and killer of two families in the same town on the same day, was in 3. Clarence Whitman was in 8.

The names beside the doors were just names until Nelson looked through into the dim, claustrophobic confines. Lester Garry Burroughs, Henry Edmund Finch, Bernard Warren Fuller, Leonard William Gayle, Albert Emerson Reid, Clifford John Hewitt and Samuel Fitzgerald Curtis. Their expressions belied their nature. Those that looked back at him did so without surprise or resentment. Their faces were those of ordinary men, men who would not warrant a second glance if you passed them on the street. The banality of evil – that expression made so famous in reference to Adolf Eichmann – surfaced from Nelson's memory. The acts collectively perpetrated were beyond comprehension and conscience. The number of innocent lives lost to the hands of these people were numerous. The simple reality was that every single one of them had wound up on Death Row as a consequence of his own actions. Blame could not be apportioned elsewhere. Their seeming normality prompted a thought about Jimmy Christiansen. Christiansen had been the very opposite – both in the way he looked and the way he acted. The man had exuded an aura of menacing intimidation. His actions following escape had proven that he was more than capable of justifying Nelson's intuitive sense that he was a truly disturbed individual. Christiansen, if he was still alive, had been on the run for two months. It was merely assumption that he and Stein were still together, but, as was demonstrated within Southern, those of like mind tended to gravitate toward one another. Perhaps they sought company from the ranks of those who saw the world with their own malign perspective. Where they were now, how far they'd gotten, what other heinous crimes they had perpetrated since the killing in Arredondo, was unknown to Nelson. The manhunt, which he presumed was still ongoing, had ceased to be newsworthy.

Nelson went to Cell 9 last. Pausing before he slid open the viewing hatch, he was aware that his attitude towards Clarence Whitman was somehow different from the others. Whitman had not raped anyone; he had not kicked a man to death; he hadn't set fire to a house and burned a family alive; he had not abducted and butchered a teenage girl. If he was indeed guilty of the murder of Garth Kenyon – and Nelson could not allow himself to believe otherwise – it had been a single act of desperation by a man intent on fleeing the scene of a crime. Though it did not excuse Whitman's culpability, Nelson could only ask himself what he might have done had he been on the jury. Would he have elected for the death sentence? Or would he have been the solitary voice that questioned whether a young man such as this deserved to be in the company of sociopaths? Were the crimes of comparable magnitude and severity? He did not believe so.

CJ Whitman looked up at the sound of the metal plate sliding back. Though twenty-six, he still possessed that same youthful face that had looked back at Nelson from the newspaper. Not a single man in the other nine cells had spoken to Nelson. Whitman spoke, and his voice was quiet and calm and not far from a whisper.

'Is it lunchtime yet?' he asked.

'It's nine o'clock,' Nelson replied.

'Really?'

'Yes.'

'Man, it feels like breakfast was hours ago.'

Nelson didn't reply. He slid back the cover. He stepped away with the knowledge that for these men, time had no meaning. There was no clock, no definable rising and setting of the sun, no truly discernible division between night and day. It was a blur of seconds into minutes into hours into weeks and months. He remembered another story he'd heard an age ago about Alcatraz. Perhaps apocryphal, but it was said that New Year's Eve was the worst night of the year – a clear sky, a breeze coming in off the water, and if you held your breath and listened closely, you could hear the clink of glasses and the laughter of girls on the boats out in San Francisco Bay.

*

Nelson's shift concluded at 4 p.m. without any incident of note. Even with the delivery of food and then seeing five of the men into the yard for exercise, not one of them uttered a word to him. It was as if they were barely alive – hammered by darkness and solitude into submission.

Back in Central Admin, Frank caught sight of him and they shared a few words before Nelson left for the day.

'Grim, huh?' Frank said.

'Horrific.'

'Fitting end for most of them, though. Every one of them is going to Hell. That place is the dress rehearsal.'

'It's so much worse than where they were before,' Nelson said.

'I guess that's the point, isn't it? Seen a good few wardens in my time, and Greaves ain't fuckin' around. He wants this place tied up tight as it'll go. Independence Day got them some headlines they really could have done without.' Frank shook his head, and, as if to echo the thought that had earlier surfaced in Nelson's mind, he said, 'Ironic, huh? Those motherfuckers sure got their independence. Anyway, they sent him here to make sure nothin' like that ever happens again.'

'But that block… the smell of it, the darkness—'

Frank gave a wry smile. 'Oh, I wouldn't lose any sleep over it, Garrett. If Greaves has his way, none of them are gonna be with us for very long anyway.'

36

Wednesday, November 2 was much the same as every other day in Southern. Nelson was on extra cover for three days that week. Instead of 8 a.m., he was coming in at 6 a.m. and leaving at 4 p.m. There were no incidents, save the near-psychotic ranting of a first landing inmate when he was informed that a family member visit had been cancelled. He'd not seen his wife for more than two months. Apparently his seven-year-old daughter, also due to make the trip, had come down with mono. Fuelled by disappointment and frustration, the inmate had threatened his cellmate, tried to break the metal sink off the wall, and then jammed a magazine down the toilet. Flushing repeatedly, he'd caused an overflow that made its way out beneath the external door and onto the landing. Hauled screaming to solitary, he swore to kill not only both of the guards who took him to isolation, but also the Warden.

Lights out was at 10.30 p.m. Garvey had a one-man cell – again an engineered privilege that was accomplished by repeated reports of intimidation by those with whom he'd been previously berthed. No such intimidation ever took place, but it was prison policy that three reports, each resulting in a week in solitary for the supposed victim for his own protection, would then result in single cell confinement. It was a good trade-off: twenty days in the hole for the assurance that you no longer had to sleep with one eye open.

On each landing, a primary lever closed all cells simultaneously. There was an override control that enabled individual cells to be opened. Access to the override was achieved with two keys, each held by different duty guards. By radio, each officer could reach Central Admin. Central Admin housed the main switchboard, and from there also a single cell could be opened and closed irrespective of whatever was happening on the landing.

First bell was at 6 a.m. Cell doors opened at 6.10. In single file, second landing made their way along the gantry and down the stairs to the mess hall. Each man remained the same distance apart as they walked, and thus – at once – it was observed that there was an extended gap in the line between the men who occupied cells to the left and right of Garvey's.

It was Max Sheehan who went up there to find out what was going on. Garvey could be sick, of course, and there had been occasions when inmates had decided they were on hunger strike and wouldn't come out of their cells.

On this occasion, neither was the case.

Sheehan stepped over the threshold of Garvey's cell and skidded awkwardly in a wide pool of blood. Grabbing for the doorframe, he managed to regain his balance. Before he investigated further, he stepped out and shouted for Nelson to activate the alarm.

The alarm sounding, the second landing crocodile turned – almost as one – and ran back to their cells. They had thirty seconds before the doors closed. Any man outside of his cell would be hauled into solitary.

Nelson went back up to join Sheehan at the entrance to Garvey's cell. Sheehan radioed into Central Admin and told them to send the doctor.

'What's happened?' Nelson asked.

'Fuck only knows,' Sheehan said.

Once inside, both Nelson and Sheehan did their best to circumvent the blood. Garvey was on his back, his left arm outstretched, his right arm up against the corner behind the bed. It wasn't until they reached the foot of the frame that his head and face were visible. Even in the limited light, the black, gaping crescent across the middle of his throat was visible.

'Jesus Christ Almighty,' Nelson said.

Sheehan paled at the sight. He put his hand over his mouth and gagged.

'Step out,' Nelson said. 'Go take a breath.'

Sheehan did as Nelson suggested. As Nelson kneeled down to take a closer look, he could hear Sheehan retching on the landing.

From first impression, it seemed that David Garvey had cut his own throat. Scanning the floor, Nelson saw a six-inch strip of metal just inches from Garvey's left hand. Where it had come from, he had no idea, but somehow Garvey had gotten it into his cell.

Nelson heard footsteps approaching and got up. He backed out of the cell as the doctor arrived. Behind him was Frank Montgomery.

The doctor went in. Frank nodded towards Nelson and Nelson stepped around Sheehan and joined him.

'Dead,' Nelson said.

'What?'

'Looks like he cut his own throat.'

'This is Garvey we're talking about, right?' Frank asked.

Nelson nodded in the affirmative.

'What the fuck?'

Frank's expression clearly communicated his confusion and dismay. He looked up as the doctor came out of the cell.

'Get a couple of men and bring a stretcher from the infirmary,' he said.

'You're taking him out of there?' Nelson asked.

The doctor frowned. 'And what would you have me do, Mr Nelson? Leave him where he is?'

'What about an examination of the cell?'

'To determine what? That he killed himself? I think that's pretty conclusive already.'

Nelson turned as Frank put his hand on his shoulder. 'You're not in the Sheriff's Department, Garrett. It's not a homicide investigation.'

The hubbub of voices started up along the landing then. Word had got out.

Frank hammered his billy club repeatedly on the gantry railing.

'Quieten down!' he shouted. 'Quieten down, you men!'

The hubbub reduced, but soon crescendoed once more.

'Silence!' Frank hollered. 'Every single damn one of you shut the hell up or you're skipping breakfast!'

That did the trick.

Frank told Sheehan to get another officer and do as the doctor had instructed. They needed Garvey's body out of there and down to the infirmary for the coroner.

'What happens now?' Nelson asked Frank.

'Nothing. Coroner files a report. Garvey goes to God's Acre.'

'That's it?'

'That's it,' Frank replied. 'We clear out his cell, clean the place up, and we do whatever's necessary to stop the inevitable bullshit that goes along with two or three assholes trying to be the boss of this landing.'

Nelson opened his mouth to ask another question.

'Let it go, Garrett. Whatever's going on, let it go. This is Southern. People kill themselves, okay? This ain't the first time, and it sure as fuck won't be the last.'

*

Half an hour later, Garvey's blanketed body coming out of the cell on a stretcher, Nelson yet again couldn't shake off an instinctive sense of suspicion.

Garvey was right-handed. The strip of metal he'd used had been on the floor just inches from his left. Sure, he could have slumped into the corner of the room and dropped it, though Nelson didn't see how it could have then ended up on the opposite side of his body. And there was Garvey himself. Nelson knew the man. He was strong-willed and defiant. Not that Nelson was any kind of expert on the subject, but he certainly didn't seem like the kind of person who'd take his own life. In his time in the Sheriff's Department, he'd seen suicides – drugs, hangings, slit wrists, the barrel of a gun to the roof of the mouth. He'd never heard of someone cutting their own throat. There were interior and anterior jugular veins, but the sheer quantity of blood on the floor of the cell suggested that Garvey had reached the carotid. That, simply stated, was not an easy thing to do with a six-inch strip of metal.

Nelson thought to ask Hannah. She was medically trained and had extensive knowledge of the human body, but he didn't want to upset her with the gruesome news of an inmate suicide.

The doctor would detail his initial findings, the coroner would perform an autopsy, and the truth of what had happened in David Garvey's cell would be made known.

Frank was right. It was not Nelson's job to conduct an investigation, no matter what his instinct might dictate.

37

Lester Garry Burroughs was an overweight, balding, middle-aged man from Bonita Springs. Seemingly innocuous and mild-mannered, he'd spent his time attending local churches, gradually working his way into the good graces of elderly women, all of them widowed or unmarried, all of them taken in by his gentle, polite persona. In the main, they were lonely, and that sense of loneliness was their undoing. Burroughs was a conversational companion, a man who offered to assist them with grocery shopping, odd jobs around the house, never once asking anything in return. He was considered a 'kind soul', a 'true gentleman', even 'an angel'. In reality, he was a devious sociopath, utterly without moral compass or compunction, deriving immense pleasure from the knowledge that he was slowly poisoning one victim after another.

Burroughs had once worked as an exterminator. Having accumulated numerous pesticides, his preferred poison of choice was thallium salts. Following his eventual arrest, boxes of it were found in a crawl space beneath his house. Highly toxic, near-undetectable, the effects of microscopic doses of thallium were not unlike the symptoms of gastroenteritis – stomach pain, nausea, vomiting and diarrhea. Additionally, growing ever more frequent and pronounced, there was numbness and tingling in the extremities. Burroughs' victims were old, and thus often plagued with poor circulation, low blood pressure and other physiological complaints. Burroughs would drive them to the doctor, sometimes the hospital, sitting with them, comforting and reassuring them, all-too-eager to ask the consulting physician what he could do to make the patient more comfortable. His quiet, caring manner, his seeming attentiveness, endeared him to everyone. Asked by one nurse why he was so tireless in his devotion, Burroughs stuttered and stammered, his eyes brimming with tears.

'My mother,' he explained. 'She had the cancer. It was a terrible death. I felt so powerless, so useless. I felt there was nothing I could do to ease her pain. After she died, I don't know... I just felt I had to do something, anything, to help people. And these are my dear friends from church, you know? Most of them have no one else. It breaks my heart to think how things would be if I wasn't there for them.'

The nurse, close to tears herself, had hugged him and told him he was 'Heaven-sent'.

It was later discovered that Burroughs' mother had deserted the family when he was just three years old. He and his sister had been raised by an aunt. The mother, though a drunk, was alive and living in California with a vacuum cleaner salesman.

All the while, carefully and conscientiously administering thallium, Burroughs continued to look after his church companions as the toxin worked its way into every organ, vein, artery and nerve channel. Detectable in the system for such a very short period of time, the resultant deaths were ascribed to a wide variety of conditions. In no instance was a post-mortem ordered or carried out. Had it not been for an astute trainee mortuary assistant in North Naples, Burroughs would have perhaps worked his diligent, methodical way through the entire congregation of half a dozen local churches.

Burroughs undoing was due to hair loss. Attending to a recently deceased woman by the name of Myrtle Wilson, the mortuary assistant – Robert Cutler – noted that she was one of the three women within a four-month period who'd evidenced advanced alopecia with no outward indications of anaemia, thyroid disorders or psoriasis. The fact that he understood the primary causes of alopecia was attributable to his having completed a year of pre-Med alongside his Mortuary Science studies. Cutler discussed his observations with the Collier County Coroner. The coroner was sufficiently conscientious to speak with the pathologist. Neighbors and fellow congregants were asked about Myrtle's deteriorating physical condition in the weeks prior to her death. They reported that she'd complained of headaches, dizziness, muscle spasms, intense fatigue. They'd also said that had it not been for the care of Lewis Burroughs then her final days might very well have been a great deal worse.

The coroner ordered an autopsy. Myrtle's body was transferred to St Savior's Hospital in Fort Myers where a full toxicological analysis and mass spectrometry could be performed.

The presence of heightened levels of thallium was detected and confirmed. Myrtle Wilson's house was searched. No presence of any substance containing such a toxin was found. Ruling the cause of death as suspicious initiated a police investigation. It was not long before the Bonita Springs Police Department investigator assigned to the case came across the name of Lewis Burroughs.

On the morning of Wednesday, March 6, 1968, Detective Greg Brandt made a visit to Burroughs' home. Burroughs was calm and polite. He appeared to have no issue with talking to the police and he welcomed Brandt into his home. Brandt was shown into the living room. When asked about Myrtle Wilson, Burroughs referred to her as 'one of my ladies'. Though she'd been dead for less than two weeks, Burroughs' seeming lack of emotion seemed incongruous considering the degree of affection he professed to have held for Myrtle.

Brandt was bold. He asked Burroughs outright why he'd poisoned her.

Burroughs looked away towards the window. There was silence for a long time.

Brandt later said that he was aware of nothing but his own elevated heartbeat.

Finally, after what seemed to be a small eternity, Burroughs smiled faintly and said, 'Because it seemed like the kindest thing to do under the circumstances.'

By Burroughs' own admission, Myrtle Wilson was the last of fourteen victims. His slow-motion killing spree had spanned four years, nine separate church congregations and three different towns. Exhumations of six other named victims were requested and approved. In each case, thallium poisoning was cited as cause of death. The other families of the deceased declined to authorize the exhumation orders.

On Thursday, June 6, 1968, as America reeled from the assassination of Robert Kennedy, Lewis Garry Burroughs was found guilty of seven first-degree homicides. He was sentenced to death at a hearing just three weeks later. Even with the death penalty moratorium between 1972 and '76, he had remained on Death Row at Southern.

While HS at Southern was on lockdown after the death of David Garvey, notification had arrived that Burroughs' execution had been signed off by the judge that tried him. Burroughs had – to date – refused any course of appeal. Up until the moment he knew exactly when he would sit in the chair, he'd been nothing less than a model prisoner. As had been observed by all those who knew him before his conviction, he was quiet and well-mannered, sometimes disconcertingly so considering his situation.

That façade fell apart dramatically when the prison chaplain arrived in the late afternoon of November 4 to tell Burroughs that at 9.00 a.m. precisely on the morning of the 11th, he would go to meet his Maker. He would stay on Death Row until the day before execution. Only then would he be transferred to final holding at the rear of the infirmary.

The first time that Burroughs' light went on, it was close to 2 a.m.

Nelson opened up the outer door to find Burroughs on his knees sobbing. He was ordered off the floor and back to his bunk.

Burroughs didn't comply.

'What's wrong with you?' Nelson asked. 'Are you sick?'

Burroughs, halting and gasping, mucus spooling from his nose and down his chin, looked up at Nelson through swollen, bloodshot eyes.

'Tell them I am s-sorry,' he gasped. 'Tell them I di-didn't m-mean it. I take it b-back. I-I t-take it all b-back.'

Nelson stood there and watched the man as he crawled forward on his knees towards the inner barred door. Burroughs gripped the bars and pulled himself up. He extended his right hand out through the aperture as if to grasp Nelson. Nelson stepped away.

'Back up,' Nelson said. 'Back the fuck up right now or you're getting sprayed.'

Oblivious to Nelson's words, Burroughs reached even further towards him.

Nelson was appalled – the man's tear-streaked face, the mucus, the pathetic desperation in every hitch and sob, as if he could somehow gain sufficient pity to extricate himself from the situation.

'Back up, Burroughs!' Nelson said. 'Last fucking warning!'

Burroughs, once again, failed to comply with the order.

Anger rose in Nelson's chest. He took the can of pepper spray from his belt and aimed it towards the bars.

'You want this? Is that what you want, you fat fuck?'

Burroughs, seemingly offended by the remark, sobbed louder. He fell back onto his haunches and then sat on the ground, his head in his hands.

Nelson realized then that he'd been holding his breath. He exhaled suddenly. For just a moment he felt lightheaded, a little disorientated.

Looking back at Burroughs, he said, 'Keep it down. I don't want to hear another fucking word out of you.'

Nelson closed and locked the outer door.

He stayed where he was for a few moments, and then returned to the end of the corridor. Once seated, he tried to take stock of what was happening, not with Burroughs but with himself.

He'd felt rage, disgust and revulsion. He'd felt the urge to get into that cell and club the man senseless. Burroughs' hopeless pleadings had provoked anything but pity. What he'd felt was a real sense of fury, as if he had the right to exact retribution for what the man had done.

To experience such an emotion was not only out of character, it was anathema to everything Nelson believed himself to be. It was primal, almost instinctive, and he could not deny the fact that the urge had been close to unstoppable.

That Burroughs' light went on time and again through the next four or five hours only served to exacerbate Nelson's rage. He ignored the man in the cell, but he could not ignore the very real perception that Southern had slipped insidiously under his skin and was beginning to change him.

38

Back in Port LaBelle, Hannah was home. Nelson hadn't expected her to be there.

'I got my shifts mixed up,' she said. 'Doing a late tomorrow, not today.' She smiled enthusiastically. 'So you get the pleasure of my undivided company all the way to breakfast tomorrow.'

Nelson, though pleased, seemed unable to disguise the unease he was experiencing.

'Did something happen at work?' Hannah asked.

Nelson sat down at the kitchen table.

'Dead Watch,' he said matter-of-factly. 'You know what that is, right?'

'Sure I do.'

'I'm on it. New system, new rota. Three days every couple of weeks.'

'How bad is it?'

'It's just fucking awful, Hannah. Never seen anything like it. I mean, I know some of the things that these people have done.' Nelson paused. He shook his head resignedly. 'On one hand you're appalled and you can't help but think that they deserve everything that's happening to them, but on the other hand—'

'On the other hand, you're a human being,' Hannah said. 'You're trying to reconcile the irreconcilable. You won't ever make sense of it. I know about some of the people who've wound up at Southern. Ray used to tell me stories until I told him to stop. Some people have a darkness inside of them, Garrett. That's just the nature of things. Trying to make sense of things that just make no sense is ... well, it just doesn't happen. You won't figure it out because you can't ever comprehend the mind of someone who's driven to hurt and kill other people.'

'I know,' Nelson replied. 'I've thought about it a good deal.'

Hannah smiled understandingly. 'And you're not really any the wiser, right?'

'No. If anything, the more I think about it, the more complicated it becomes.'

'So don't think about it. I know it's easy for me to say that, but even in my job there are things that I struggle with. Why does a sweet little kid get cancer? Why does someone who's never harmed a hair on anyone's head get hit by a car and paralysed for the rest of their life? You can look all you want, but I don't think there's an answer. It seems random because it is.'

'You're right,' Nelson said. 'I need to stop thinking about it. It serves no purpose.'

'You do the best you can. You make a difference where you can. You try and keep your own sanity and humanity intact while you deal with the insanity and inhumanity of others. These people make up the tiniest minority. Most everyone else is good and kind and decent. Those are the people you spend the rest of your time with, and you do your best not to bring Southern home with you. My dad and Ray went through the same thing. My mom saw it and she said pretty much the same things I'm saying to you now. You're not doing a bad thing, Garrett. You're doing a necessary thing, and you have to try not to forget that.'

Nelson had tried, but it was too hard to forget. A darkness

had invaded his thoughts and emotions. The depth of that shadow was such that he believed he might never walk out from beneath it.

The news of Hannah's pregnancy at the beginning of the following week pulled Nelson out of whatever funk he'd slipped into.

'It's early,' she said. 'And, you know, we have to be aware of the possibility that—'

'That we're going to have a baby,' Nelson interjected.

He got up from the kitchen table and threw his arms around her. She started laughing, and then he was kissing her, squeezing her tight, as if to let go of her might mean letting go of everything that this moment represented.

'How long?' he asked. 'You did a test, right?'

'No, Garrett, I cut open a bird and looked at its entrails. Of course I did a test.'

'So how long?'

'I don't know. Not exactly. I mean, my period was due about two weeks ago, so it could have happened anytime in the month before that.'

'So it could already be six weeks or so?'

'It could be.'

'Oh my God, Hannah. This is just incredible!'

'You're happy, right? I mean genuinely, positively, definitely happy about this?'

'What are you talking about? Of course I'm happy. It's what we wanted, what we agreed. I don't think I've ever been happier in my life.'

Nelson hugged her again, feeling a sense of love and hope that went beyond any words he could express.

'And you're not to tell anyone,' she said. 'Not yet. I want to get a proper check-up and find out how many weeks. We wait three months, okay? Like we agreed.'

'Yes, yes of course. I won't say a word.'

'However, I have to say that if you go to work looking like you do right now then the whole damned world's gonna know that something's going on.'

Nelson assumed a serious, downcast expression. 'I'll play it straight,' he said. 'I'll keep my Southern face on everywhere but home.'

Hannah sat down. 'If this happens... I mean if it really does happen, then everything will change. You do get that, don't you?'

'Change for the better,' Nelson said. 'That's how it'll change. How could this be anything but good?'

'To be honest, I don't know what I'm feeling right now. I mean, this is... well, it's not something I ever believed would happen.'

Nelson said nothing in response.

'What?' Hannah asked.

'Thinking about how we met.'

'That you had to get shot.'

'Yes,' Nelson replied, but that hadn't been what he was thinking. What he'd been thinking was that he'd had to kill someone.

'So, we wait and see,' Hannah said. 'I'll schedule an appointment for when you're not on shift so we can go together.'

'Yes, absolutely. Every part of this we're doing together.'

'Morning sickness, swollen feet, endless back rubs, weird cravings for pickles and Tootsie Rolls at three in the morning?'

'Everything,' Nelson said. 'Hell, I've got time to go get some stuff now.'

Hannah reached out her hand. Nelson took it, and for a few seconds they just held one another's gaze across the table.

'We're doing this,' she said. 'And there isn't anyone else in the world I'd want to do it with.'

39

Arriving at Southern before six on the morning of Monday 11th, Nelson was not surprised that the protesters – however small in number – who routinely accompanied every execution had not turned out for Lester Burroughs.

Though he wasn't assigned to the bell tower, Nelson was on watch in final holding between 6.00 and 8.45. He would be there to serve Burroughs' last meal, to supervise the final visit from Father Donald and the doctor, and to transfer Burroughs back to Death Row in the event that a reprieve came through from the Governor. There wasn't a man in Southern or the State of Florida who expected such an outcome. Burroughs was going to die, and no one – least of all the Governor – was going to do a thing to stop it.

Burroughs did not sob or plead. He sat quietly on the edge of the bed, and barely uttered a word. When his last meal arrived – chicken noodle soup and saltines, two pork chops with creamed potato, beans and gravy, and a dessert of buttermilk pie and whipped cream – he tucked a napkin into his shirt collar, closed his eyes and mouthed a few words, and then methodically cleared every plate on the tray before him.

When he was done eating, the doctor came down. The entire examination began and ended with barely a sound from

Burroughs. Responding to the doctor's questions about his physical conditions, Burroughs gave a monosyllabic series of affirmatives and negatives, and when the doctor reached the door to leave, Burroughs said, 'Thank you, sir,' and smiled with such apparent sincerity that Nelson appreciated how an elderly, lonely woman might consider him both gentle and charming. To Nelson, it seemed that Burroughs was two people, each of them trapped within the same body, each of them driven by entirely conflicting impulses – to help and to harm, to love and to hate, to care and to kill.

Father Donald arrived at 8.15. He asked Burroughs if there was anything he wished to say, if there was anything else he wanted to confess while he still had time.

'Everything I did, I did with no understanding of why I did it,' he said. 'I didn't want to kill anyone, but I couldn't stop myself. And if I hadn't been found out, I think I would have gone on doing it for ever.'

'Even in our own souls,' Father Donald said, 'there are things we will never understand.'

Burroughs looked at Father Donald. His expression was artless and transparent.

'I am going to Hell, aren't I?' Burroughs asked.

Nelson wondered how many times Father Donald had been asked that question.

Holding Burroughs' hand, Father Donald smiled compassionately. 'We are blessed with a merciful God,' he said. 'Of that I have no doubt. I can't tell you what will happen to you, Lester, but I know that if you have contrition in your heart, then God will look upon you with favor and forgiveness.'

Burroughs nodded slowly, and then he half smiled. 'No,' he whispered. 'I know I'm going to Hell.'

*

As Nelson made his way back across the Southern compound to the commissary, the bell in the tower rang clear and strident.

It was 9.16 a.m., and Lester Garry Burroughs was dead.

Turning slowly, Nelson stood and stared at the old mission steeple. With the stone cross at its apex, it had once been a beacon of refuge and sanctuary in this unforgiving landscape. Now it signified nothing but fear and death.

Nelson wondered what kind of merciful God could permit his house to become such a place.

40

Hannah booked a doctor's appointment for the afternoon of Tuesday, 15th. Nelson had arranged a half-day at Southern so he could go with her.

Leaving the commissary, Nelson saw Father Donald walking towards him along the corridor.

Acknowledging him as he passed, Nelson sensed that there was something Father Donald wanted to say. Evidently Nelson's expression conveyed some degree of anticipation.

'You wanted to ask me something, Mr Nelson?' Father Donald said.

'Actually, no. I thought you were going to say something.'

'Do you want me to say something?'

Nelson frowned.

'At some point everyone comes to me,' Father Donald said. 'For answers.'

Nelson felt awkward.

'I know you're not a man of faith, Mr Nelson.'

'No, Father, I'm not.'

'And you think I might have some issue with that?'

'I guess most everyone who doesn't have a religious belief might feel… I don't know, they might feel…'

'Uncomfortable?'

'A little, perhaps.'

Father Donald nodded understandingly. 'What are you doing now?'

Nelson glanced at his watch. 'I have to leave in about half an hour. I'm taking my girlfriend to the doctor.'

'Is she sick?'

'No, she's just getting a check-up.'

'So come spend half an hour with me.'

Before Nelson could respond, Father Donald turned and started walking. Nelson could do nothing but follow him.

Aside from a simple wooden cross on the wall behind his desk and a small shelf stacked with books and pamphlets, there was nothing about Father Donald's office that evidenced his position at Southern.

Indicating that Nelson should sit, Father Donald remained standing for a moment. It appeared that he was collecting his thoughts, perhaps preparing himself for a sermon he'd given many times before.

Once seated, Father Donald took out a pack of cigarettes. He offered one to Nelson. He declined.

'So,' Father Donald said. 'The first question, usually, is how a man of God can be in a place like this. After all, isn't God all about mercy, forgiveness, salvation, redemption? The parable of the lost sheep. A shepherd leaves his flock to find the one who's strayed.'

'I think the vast majority of men who find themselves here have strayed too far to be found, Father.'

'You don't think people can be rehabilitated?'

'I think that depends on your definition of "people".'

'I understand that you were in the Sheriff's Department.'

'I was, yes.'

'For how long?'

'Eleven years or so.'

'And I understand that you were invalided out due to an injury.'

'I was shot in the leg. If you haven't noticed, I have a relatively pronounced limp.'

'So did you choose to come here, or was this the best option that was available to you?'

'At the time, it was the simplest option.'

'So, it would be fair to say that this is not your vocation.'

'It would, yes,' Nelson replied.

'And you've been here for how long?'

'Coming up to a year now.'

Father Donald leaned forward and tapped the ash from his cigarette into the ashtray.

'What are your views on the death penalty?'

'My view is that it's the law,' Nelson said.

'That's not what I'm asking.'

'I know what you're asking, Father.'

Father Donald, awaiting an answer, raised his eyebrows.

'Well, let me ask you the same question,' Nelson said. 'What is your view about it?'

'Leviticus 24, verse 17. "Anyone who takes the life of a human being is to be put to death." Exodus 21, Verses 22 to 25, "The punishment that must be paid is life for life, eye for eye, tooth for tooth, hand for hand, foot for foot, burn for burn, wound for wound, and bruise for bruise."'

'That's pretty clear, then.'

'That's Old Testament, Mr Nelson,' Father Donald said. 'Matthew 5, Verses 38 to 48, it says, "Turn the other cheek", "Love your enemies, and pray for those who persecute you." In Romans, you'll find, "Repay no one evil for evil", that vengeance is the Lord's. It also says that you should obey the government because there is no government anywhere that God has not placed in power.'

Nelson laughed reflexively. 'You're not telling me that Jimmy Carter is in the White House because God wants him there.'

'I'm not trying to tell you anything, Mr Nelson,' Father Donald replied.

'Okay, so what are we actually talking about here?'

'Reconciliation.'

'With what?'

'Your own conscience, first and foremost. For the vast majority of men who work here, it has nothing to do with God or faith or Heaven and Hell. It has to do with whether or not they feel that their adherence to the law, and that includes capital punishment, is right or wrong. The law is the law. For a few years there were no executions here because the law deemed it unconstitutional or inhumane. Then it was reinstated. The death penalty was, for a time, illegal. Now it is legal once more.'

'And what about God's vengeance?'

'What about it?'

'Well, take Lester Burroughs, for example. He seemed certain that he was going to Hell.'

Father Donald put his cigarette out. He was quiet for a moment, and then he said, 'Before I came here, I worked in numerous churches around the state. I met Lester Burroughs on several occasions. I knew four of the women he murdered.'

'So is your attitude towards someone like that Old or New Testament?'

'My attitude is that the decision to kill a man like Burroughs comes from the courts, the state, the President himself. My mission is to counsel the condemned man, to be an empathetic ear, to take his confession. My mission is not to question a legal edict.'

'So what you're saying is that men will go to the electric chair no matter what we do? If we don't do the job, someone else will.'

'Exactly so.'

'And we have to reconcile our own moral and ethical issues with our civic duty.'

Father Donald gave a wry smile. 'Morals are social regulations. Ethics is a purely personal matter, Mr Nelson. Morally, it's right for Burroughs to be put to death. Ethically, you can disagree with capital punishment, but still accept that it's morally right.'

'Because it's the law.'

'Because having a man like Burroughs continue to do what he did is a greater evil than killing him.'

Nelson was pensive. There was an internal struggle, and yet he did not know where it was coming from. He glanced at his watch.

'I need to go, Father,' he said.

'Yes, of course.'

'Thank you for your time.'

Father Donald got up from his chair. 'I'm here if you want to talk further,' he said. 'Understand that there are very few men at Southern who haven't wrestled with this subject at one time or another. Those who stay have come to an agreement with themselves. Those who haven't... well, they move on.'

Nelson extended his hand and the two men shook.

Father Donald opened the door.

Once in the corridor Nelson looked back at him.

'Why did you become a priest, Father Donald?'

'In the hope that I would come to understand the true nature of life.'

'And do you?'

Father Donald paused for just a moment, and then said, 'Let's just say that I believe that hope is the very thing that gives us a reason to live.'

41

It was too early to determine precisely how long Hannah had been pregnant, but the estimate was something in the region of six weeks. If her pregnancy ran the full term, she and Nelson would be parents in July of the following year.

They sat together in the doctor's office as he edged cautiously around the issue that was foremost in both their minds.

Finally Hannah voiced what he couldn't.

'I know it's late,' she said. 'I'm thirty-eight. I appreciate that there are risks.'

'Well, you're in excellent physical health, Miss Montgomery,' the doctor said. 'Blood pressure and heart rate are both of a woman ten years your junior. No indication of any thyroid or glandular issues. No apparent hormone imbalance. We'll keep you under close observation, of course, and if you feel any contra-indicatory phenomena like dizziness, fainting spells, lack of appetite or inordinate levels of fatigue, then you must contact us immediately and we'll see what's going on. Aside from that, I can only congratulate you and wish you all the very best for an uneventful pregnancy and a successful birth.'

'Is there anything we should be doing?' Nelson asked. 'Recommended diet, exercises, things like that.'

'With the results I have here, I'd recommend that you keep on doing what you're doing. We only need to look at doing something different if something changes.'

Seated in the car, Nelson held Hannah's hand. They sat without speaking, each coming to terms with the fact that there had been no mistake, that the pregnancy had been confirmed, that whatever lay ahead of them, unknown though it was, it would be something that they had embarked upon together.

'I think it's going to be okay,' Hannah finally said. 'I *feel* it, Garrett. That we made the right decision.'

Nelson remembered Father Donald's words – that hope gave us a reason to live.

Perhaps hope was also the reason to create life. And perhaps this was a way to find the reconciliation he needed. He hadn't thought about leaving Southern for a long time. He'd accepted that this was now his job, that he was inextricably tied to the place and the people. His life was now connected to the Montgomerys, and to turn in his badge and billy club and head in some other direction would have been to upset the *status quo*.

Now, more than ever, he believed he should accept where he was and what he was doing. If he stopped fighting it, then it might very well stop fighting back. The internal conflict was just that – internal – and he was the one who was feeding it. If he gave it no further nourishment, then it would die.

Nelson started the car. Pulling out onto the highway, it felt like he was driving away from the past and into the future.

42

Just as was the case with news about Christiansen and Stein, so there seemed to be radio silence regarding the suicide of David Garvey. The last report of the escaped convicts had been in the first week of August, more than three months earlier. The assumption was that they'd continued north into Georgia. Where they were now, whether they were even alive, was unknown. The riot itself, the departure of Warden Young and all else that pertained to the events that transpired in July, was not discussed – neither at Southern itself nor in the Montgomery household.

Garvey had been dead for two weeks. The coroner's report stated suicide. If there had been any kind of comprehensive inquiry into the circumstances of Garvey's death, it was unknown to Nelson. The alternative explanation – that Garvey had been murdered – presented a possibility that was profoundly troubling. Access to Garvey's cell by an assailant would've been impossible without assistance from someone on the landing itself or from Central Admin. A serving officer or administrative official would have to have been complicit in the killing. Perhaps that was understood by Greaves, by the Board of Prisons, and they had not hesitated to shut down any further investigation. The last thing anyone needed was for Southern once again to be dominating the headlines in Florida.

*

Back on Dead Watch in the third week of November, Nelson was running the 8 a.m. to 4 p.m. shift.

Notification of execution dates had come down for Leonard Gayle and Albert Reid. Without reprieve, they would both be executed in the first two weeks of December.

Gayle was younger than Nelson. Just thirty-six years old, he'd shot and killed his wife and her lover in a motel on 41 near Del Tura. After the killings, he'd called the police himself, confessed over the telephone, and then waited for them to arrive. Waiving his right to legal counsel, Gayle had confessed once again. He then proceeded to retract his confession on the grounds that he'd been intimidated and violently threatened by the arresting officers and the interviewing detectives. Undertaking a competency evaluation to determine whether Gayle could stand trial, the court-appointed psychologist rapidly came to the conclusion that Gayle not only knew precisely what he'd done, but also what he was now doing. His intent seemed to be to cause as much trouble for the legal system and the state as he could.

With the original confession now in question, a trial was scheduled. Gayle refused a public defender and acted for himself. Knowing nothing of court protocol, he repeatedly stood up to shout 'Objection! Irrelevant!' until the judge ordered he be removed by the bailiff. Having accumulated more than a dozen contempt charges, Gayle finally agreed to behave himself. The trial resumed. On the first day he was quiet. On the second day, there beneath the table, Gayle urinated in a plastic water beaker. Once full, he waited until the State Prosecutor was within range, and threw the contents of the beaker over him.

The trial continued with Gayle in a harness, his hands cuffed, his legs shackled. In his closing statement, Gayle proceeded to describe the imagined sexual proclivities of each juror in turn. He stated that he had evidence that the State Prosecutor had been arrested for fucking a dog, and that the judge was a known pedophile.

The jury was out for twenty-seven minutes. It was the shortest deliberation in circuit history.

Gayle had never spoken to Nelson aside from the odd grunt of acknowledgement when his food was delivered. Today, however, Nelson was in the firing line.

Opening the outer door, Gayle was cross-legged on the floor.

Looking up at Nelson he said, 'Hey, man, what's wrong with your fucking leg?'

'Lunch, Gayle,' Nelson replied. 'Thirty seconds or I'm taking it away.'

Gayle slowly rose to his feet. He inched his way towards the bars, dragging one leg behind him in mockery of Nelson's limp.

'What the fuck, man? Are you a fucking retard, or what?'

'Take the tray,' Nelson said, 'and then back up.'

Gayle stopped moving. 'Seriously. What's the deal? Were you born like that or what?'

Nelson looked at Gayle. He felt nothing but contempt for the man.

'As it happens, I injured it kicking a man to death,' Nelson said. 'You want me to come in there and show you how?'

'Oh, oh, oh, we have ourselves a wiseass, ladies and gentlemen!' Gayle sneered. 'Yeah well, why don't you come on in here and we'll have ourselves a little tango, Mr Nelson?'

Nelson withdrew the tray. 'Thirty seconds is up,' he said.

Gayle, immediately contrite in appearance, held up his hands in a conciliatory fashion. 'Okay, okay,' he said. 'I'm sorry. I was just kiddin' with you. I'll take it.'

'Not another fucking word out of you,' Nelson said.

'I promise. Cross my heart.' Gayle lowered his hands, and then proceeded to mime an X on his chest and a zipper across his mouth.

Nelson put the tray back through the door.

Gayle took the food and walked back to his bed. He sat down slowly, all the while staring at Nelson with a dismissive, condescending expression.

'Now, go hobble the fuck away, you murderous fuck.'

Nelson had to consciously withhold the urge to go on in there and pepper spray Gayle. Knowing that there were no witnesses or record of the exchange, Nelson was impotent. Anything he did would be considered an unprovoked act. The only winner would be Gayle.

Nelson closed and locked the door to the sound of Gayle's laughter.

Opening up Cell 8, Clarence Whitman was standing with his back against the furthest wall with his eyes closed.

'Whitman. Lunch.'

Whitman remained silent and motionless for a second, and then opened his eyes.

'Mr Nelson,' he said. 'Thank you.'

Whitman walked forward and took the tray. Looking down at the meagre ration, he smiled and shook his head.

'Not so good, is it?'

'It is what it is,' Nelson replied.

Whitman looked up. 'Like life.'

Later, thinking back, Nelson could only describe the feeling that he'd then experienced as a profound sense of grief. It was neither sympathy nor pity, but an almost preternatural impression of hopelessness.

'You okay, Whitman?' he asked.

'Okay? Sure, I'm okay. You know, considering the circumstances.'

Whitman backed up and sat down on the bed. He set the tray on the mattress beside him.

'You sick or something?' Nelson asked.

'No, I'm not sick, Mr Nelson.'

'So eat your lunch, then.'

'Why?'

It was a simple question, but for which there was no real answer.

'Because it's lunchtime,' Nelson said, and even as the words came out of his mouth, he knew how inane and ridiculous they sounded.

'Spent my whole damned life doing what I was told,' Whitman said. 'Doing the things I was supposed to, you know? Followed the rules, colored inside the lines, kept my mouth shut, and for what? Here I am.'

'I have to deliver lunch,' Nelson said.

Whitman looked up and smiled. 'You go on and do your job, Mr Nelson. I'm sorry for troubling you. You ain't the reason I'm here now, are you?'

Nelson stepped back and closed the door. The sound of the lock snapping back into the striker plate was like a pistol shot in the narrow confines of the corridor.

43

Nelson's usual meal routine was to zigzag down the corridor. Starting at the inner door of the block, he would work his way to the far end. He would then wait until lunchtime was over and return to the inner door, collecting the trays from each cell as he went. Whether he began on the left or the right, his final collection would always be the ninth. On Sunday, he picked up at Cell 9 and came back to Cell 8 last.

Whitman was cross-legged on the floor, his back against the wall, a book in his hands. Closing the book, he set it down and got to his feet.

Passing the tray to Nelson through the aperture, he then returned to the bed.

Nelson did not step back and close the door. He stood there looking at the man, and once again felt this strange sense of sadness.

Whitman looked up at him. He smiled in a way that made Nelson feel as though he was being pitied.

'You shouldn't feel sorry for me,' Whitman said.

'Sorry for you?'

'It's not your job to sympathize with us, Mr Nelson. It's only your job to make sure that we're still here when the time comes.'

Nelson knew he should close the door, but he couldn't. The

man possessed a strange sense of calm, as if he had somehow achieved the reconciliation of which Father Donald had spoken.

'After all, perhaps I'm paying for sins from some former life.'

'Do you believe in that?'

'I'm trying,' Whitman said. 'Because if there's a past, then that means there must be a future.'

Nelson stepped back. He had the key in his hand.

'You don't have to,' Whitman said. 'I mean, what harm is there? It's not like I can get out through those bars, right?'

'No, you can't.'

'Do you ever feel like an inmate, Mr Nelson?'

'Me? An inmate? No, of course not. Why would you ask that?'

'I don't know. I just get the idea that you ain't so happy to be here. I mean, the other officers, some of them at least, give me the impression that they enjoy some sense of power over us. But you're not like that, are you?'

'Power over you?' Nelson asked. 'I don't have any power. I'm just doing my job.'

'But it's not really a job, is it? Not like being a mechanic or a landscaper or a plumber or whatever, is it? Don't you think that a man who does this has to be a particular kind of man?'

'I think he has to have faith in the law,' Nelson said.

Whitman smiled. 'The law. Right.'

'You don't believe in the law?'

'Sure I do. That's why I've never broken it.'

'But—'

'Think what you want. Believe what you want. It don't make any difference. I know what I know, even if everyone else tells me I don't. And when you're dealin' with folk who've made up their minds, you ain't never gonna change them. Sometimes people like a story so much they don't wanna hear that there might be a different ending.'

The buzzer sounded at the inner door. Lunchtime was over. He was behind schedule.

Nelson went back down the corridor to return the trolley and empty trays. Back at Cell 8, Whitman was still standing there at the bars.

'I ain't upset with you, Mr Nelson,' Whitman said. 'You didn't put me here. An' when the time comes, I'm hopin' you'll be the one to take me over to the bell tower.'

Nelson didn't respond. He closed and locked the door.

Nelson carried out only one cursory cell check in the remaining three hours of his shift. He indicated on the paperwork that he'd completed three. The remainder of the time he sat on the chair at the end of the corridor. Try as he might, he couldn't stop the questions in his mind. Whitman was neither aggressive nor angry. He didn't direct insults or defamatory comments. Never once had he raised his voice, at least not to Nelson. It really was as if he'd accepted what was happening to him. Other men like Darryl Jeffreys behaved as though their penalty was not only unjust, but some sort of unwarranted personal vendetta in which every single police officer, prison guard and state employee was complicit. Whitman knew he was going to die. He understood that there wasn't a single thing he could do about it. And despite the fact that Nelson had been on Dead Watch for just six weeks, at no time during that period had Whitman ever received a visitor or a single item of mail. It appeared that not only had the courts and the prison system given up on him, but his legal counsel and family too.

Twenty-six years old, the last six years of his life in darkness and solitude, and CJ Whitman was asking himself whether his present circumstances were somehow a penalty for something he'd done in a former life.

Something was different about the young man in Cell 8.

Nelson knew he shouldn't question it, shouldn't think about it. He knew that what had happened, and, more importantly, what was going to happen to him, was none of his business. If he had faith in the justice system, then he also had to have faith in the criminal investigation that had brought Whitman to this place. He'd spent more than ten years in the Sheriff's Department. There had been mistakes, of course, but none of them intentional. Men had been wrongfully arrested. Evidence had been misplaced. These things inevitably happened. But, in his own experience, the truth had always come to light in the end. Having said that, he'd never managed a homicide case directly. Such things were directed, more often than not, by the police, not the Sheriff's Department. The relationship between the two law enforcement bodies was long-established. There were protocols and procedures. Assistance from detectives had been requested and had always been forthcoming. The integrity of those investigations was something Nelson had never questioned – not because he hadn't wanted to question it, but because he'd never been given cause to do so.

Nelson knew nothing beyond what he'd read in the newspapers. Why he felt the urge to learn more, he didn't know. But the urge was there, and the more he considered it, the more it seemed to consume his attention. He also wanted to know why Whitman had received no communication from the outside world. Perhaps it was nothing more complicated than the delays inherent in a prisoner transfer. Mail received at Florida State would have to make its way through the system. As for Whitman's family in Wauchula, they were now half the distance from Southern compared to State in Raiford. That they were unaware of his transfer seemed beyond the bounds of possibility.

Back in training for the Sheriff's Department, the instructors and visiting detectives hammered the same point home time and time again: If something does not make sense, you are being misled. Beneath every contradiction of facts, there was a lie. It was repeated so many times and in so many different ways that it became a mantra, almost second nature. In the same way that Garvey's apparent suicide made no sense, so Whitman's situation and his attitude towards it was similarly disconcerting.

Nelson also knew that a question could be answered in such a way as to give the appearance of an answer without ever being such. Those who fabricated stories as to the whereabouts and the sequence of events never changed those stories. Those who told the truth routinely remembered additional facts as their memory became clearer.

There was something about the killing of Garth Kenyon – the fingerprint notwithstanding – that troubled Nelson. He knew enough of his own nature to appreciate that it would continue to occupy his thoughts until he found a satisfactory resolution. If Whitman went to the bell tower an innocent man, it would be a travesty of all that the law and the judicial system represented.

Nelson also knew that if Whitman had his wish and he was on duty to see him executed, then it would haunt him without respite for the remainder of his life.

44

Hannah's sickness was tough on her.

If Nelson needed any further confirmation that he was now responsible not only for her but for a child, it was the number of mornings he sat on the bathroom floor and held Hannah's hair back as she retched into the toilet. He helped her as best he could, but there was nothing he could do to minimize the discomfort she was experiencing. He wished that he could share it, but he also knew that everything that now happened for the next eight months was about Hannah and Hannah alone.

If their estimate had been correct, she would be through the first trimester at the beginning of January. Her body was changing, and with it came the swings in mood, the sense of frustration, all of it interspersed with moments of uplifting elation about the future. It was an emotional and psychological rollercoaster. They both had tickets, and once it had started, they couldn't get off.

Hannah took time off work to rest. Considering the fact that she was freelance, there was no issue with the hospitals which she worked. Her friends and colleagues expressed concern for her welfare, and Hannah, resolute in her decision to say nothing of the pregnancy until the new year, continued to tell them that she merely needed some time to herself, that she'd worked without a break for most of the year. Nelson added a couple of shifts to his schedule to compensate for the lost income, but that meant that Hannah was spending more and more time alone. Suggesting that she go to Clewiston and spend a few days with her folks, Hannah said, 'And what do I tell them when I'm puking in the toilet every morning?'

'Tell them the truth, Hannah.'

'We agreed what we agreed.'

'What are you afraid of?'

'You know exactly what I'm afraid of, Garrett.'

'And if something like that happens, you think that your family wouldn't be there to support you?'

'The only person I want supporting me right now is you,' she said.

Nelson recognized that tone of voice. It was the end of the conversation.

Despite Hannah's best efforts, her plan for secrecy came undone in the first week of December.

Once again on Dead Watch from the 3rd to the 5th, Nelson was called out on the Monday with a message from Central Admin. Don Trent was subbed in to cover for him.

Over at Admin, the message was simply that Nelson was needed at the hospital in Fort Myers.

His heart racing, Nelson tore out of the car park at Southern. He took 29 up to 82, headed west, flooring the car all the way. It was something in the region of thirty miles, but the half hour it took to get there seemed like an eternity.

Pulling to a stop outside the building, he ran inside without locking the car.

At reception he gave his name, asked for Hannah Montgomery. He was told to wait and someone would see him.

'I need to see someone now,' he insisted.

'Mr Nelson, I have paged the—'

'Now, goddamnit!'

A middle-aged woman appeared.

'Mr Nelson?'

Nelson turned.

'I'm Doctor Clarke. I'm one of the resident Ob Gyns here.'

'Where is she?' Nelson asked. 'What happened?'

Doctor Clarke smiled reassuringly. 'Hannah is absolutely fine, Mr Nelson. She had a fainting spell. Her blood pressure is a little low, but nothing to worry about. You can come and see her now.'

'I passed out,' Hannah said. 'I'm okay. I just thought it was best if I get checked over.'

Nelson sat at the side of the bed in the examination room.

'How did you get here?' he asked.

Hannah looked at him sheepishly.

'Hannah . . .'

'I called a cab.'

'What?'

'Do you have any idea how hard it is to get through to anyone at Southern?'

'You got me a message—'

'Garrett, I've been here for over two hours.'

Nelson took her hand. 'That's it,' he said. 'I need to be around for you—'

'No,' Hannah interjected. 'We're not doing that.'

'But—'

'But what? You're gonna quit your job? Come on, be serious now. We need the money. I'm already off work as it is. And nothing bad has happened, okay? This is normal. Women have been doing this ever since there were women.'

'Yeah, but none of them have been carrying my child, have they?'

'I'm not going to be fussed over, Garrett. I'm more than capable of taking care of myself. The doctor says everything is fine. We're a month away from being able to tell people. I'm not as sick as I was. Things are just happening inside me, and… and you just need to accept that this is the way it's going to be.'

'And if it's serious? If you fall or something?'

Hannah inched up the bed into a sitting position. 'Nature is nature. You can't change it. This is going to work or it's not, okay? Worrying about all the things that might or might not happen is utterly pointless. I see it all the time, you know? The ones who worry most about whether they're going to get better are usually the ones who take the longest time to recuperate. You just need to calm down, okay? You need to go to work, pay the bills, cook all the meals, clean the house, do the laundry, go to the supermarket, and cater to my every whim and everything will be just fine.'

Nelson laughed. 'And if I don't?'

'Then I'll send Brian, Ray, Earl and Danny over and they will thump you senseless.'

'You're really okay?'

'Yes, Garrett. I'm okay. Clean bill of health. Everything is good.'

'So can we go home?'

'Sure we can, but we need to stop on the way.'

'Where?'

'A supermarket. I have a craving for blue cheese and pineapple jelly sandwiches.'

45

Of the two men scheduled for execution in the first half of December, Albert Reid was first.

When Nelson arrived at Southern on the 6th, he was told that he and Frank Montgomery would be supervising Reid's transfer from Death Row to final holding after dinner. Reid's execution was not due to take place until 9 a.m. on the 8th. Though a condemned man was only supposed to be in final holding for twenty-four hours, Warden Greaves had ordered the move regardless. When asked why, he said, 'Because that's what I want.'

'He has a mind to empty the place as fast as he can,' Frank said to Nelson outside Central Admin. 'He's the kind of man who thinks that executions should be carried out the day after sentence. He sees Death Row as an unnecessary financial burden. Why keep them alive any longer than is absolutely necessary?'

'Appeals,' Nelson said. 'Wrongful conviction, clemency, reprieves, and there's always the possibility that capital punishment gets outlawed again. It's happened before.'

'Yeah, sure, I know all of that, but this is Greaves we're talking about.'

Frank saw a question in Nelson's eyes.

'What?'

'I keep thinking about Garvey,' he said.

Frank nodded. 'You're not alone.'

'Meaning?'

'Exactly how it sounds, Garrett.'

'You think that Garvey—'

'I think that cutting your own throat with a six-inch strip of tin would be like skinning a deer with a butter knife.'

'So—'

'Let it go, Garrett. Really. That, my friend, is a hide into nowhere.'

Nelson understood what Frank was telling him. Don't rock the boat. Up against Warden Greaves, Nelson would be the only one who'd drown.

'Anyway, we haven't seen you at the house for a good while. You really are makin' it your business to be strangers. Miriam says that Hannah doesn't call.'

'She's been sick,' Nelson said. 'Flu. Nothing serious.'

'She better?'

'Getting there.'

'Well, soon as she is, you come over and visit, okay?'

'Sure thing. I miss Miriam's cooking.'

Albert Reid was as crazy as a shithouse rat. If he wasn't before he arrived at Southern, then Southern had done an excellent job.

Reid had killed every member of his own family in a spree of butchery and horror over the Thanksgiving weekend of 1972. Having suffocated both his brother and sister in their beds during the night, Reid got up early and waited for his parents in the kitchen. He killed the pair of them with a single shotgun blast to their respective heads, and then took a shower and washed his hair. He drove his father's pickup from Cornwell to Buckhead Ridge, entered his paternal uncle's property at the rear, and then proceeded to club his uncle into unconsciousness with a length of timber. When his aunt appeared, Reid fatally stabbed her with a bread knife from the kitchen counter. He then used the same knife to near-decapitate his uncle. Reid's final gesture was to strangle the family dog. He left the lifeless corpse of the animal in the sink.

With every living relative murdered, Reid drove to Okeechobee and had lunch in a Mexican restaurant. He then returned home and awaited the inevitable arrival of the police. Unaware that Reid was the perpetrator, a single officer attended Reid's home to convey the news of the killings.

Reid invited him into the property, and when he was informed that his mother and father and both of his younger siblings were dead, Reid said, 'So you didn't get to Uncle Walt and Aunt Clara yet? They're over in Buckhead Ridge. I can give you the address if you like.'

In truth, had Clarence Darrow acted in defense of Albert Reid, it was never going to be anything other than a slam-dunk for the State. Reid even quoted verbatim the legal definition of sanity. He took the stand on his own volition, despite all advice to the contrary. He testified under oath that he knew exactly what he was doing. He had thought about it for a good while. He also said that he was just waiting for a weekend when he knew everyone would be home.

During the short walk from Death Row to final holding, Frank on one side of Reid, Nelson on the other, Reid repeated the same phrase over and over. His voice was barely a whisper, but after three or four repetitions, Nelson could make out what he was saying.

'A soul as black as dead of night, a heart as cold as ice. If given the chance to do it again, I'd kill the fuckers twice.'

Once secured, Frank walked back towards Central Admin with Nelson.

'I'm on that one,' Frank said. 'Thursday morning, bright and early. Crazy motherfucker.'

'What the hell is going on with someone like that?' Nelson asked. 'I mean, he killed six members of his own family, for Christ's sake.'

'Well, if they were all as crazy as him, then maybe it was for the best, eh?'

Nelson was sent down to Death Row to clear out Reid's cell. As he was doing so, the duty officer took one of the other prisoners out to the yard.

Nelson's mind was preoccupied with Hannah. He had the urge to call her to make sure everything was okay. He knew she'd tell him not to worry. She also knew that he more than likely wouldn't. He had to trust her to get a message relayed if she needed him. He longed for January, not only because she'd be through the first trimester, but because everyone else would know. Her parents and four brothers would be available for anything she might need.

When the light came on over Cell 8, Nelson's first thought was to bring the duty officer in to deal with it. He decided against it; it would be quicker to attend to it himself, and he also wanted to know what was going on with Whitman.

Whitman was seated on the bed. When Nelson opened the outer door, he didn't look at Nelson.

'What's up, Whitman?' Nelson asked.

'Reid has gone, right?'

Nelson didn't respond. Inmates on Death Row were not meant to know who was scheduled for execution, nor when.

'Reid. Albert Reid. He's gone to final holding already, hasn't he?'

'How do you know that?' Nelson asked.

'I was told.'

'Who told you?'

Whitman looked at Nelson. 'Now that would be telling, wouldn't it?'

'You're not supposed to know what's happening with other inmates.'

'We're not supposed to know, but we do. Some of the officers like to remind us.'

Nelson frowned. 'What's been said?'

'That we're next. That we're on the roster. That they can't wait to see us kick and scream and piss ourselves as we're dragged into the bell tower.'

'You need to tell me who's said these things to you, Whitman.'

'I ain't gonna tell you anything of the sort, Mr Nelson.'

'Whitman—'

'And say I did? What would you do then?'

'I would file a report to the Warden.'

'And what the hell do you think the Warden's gonna do, eh? Maybe he has a word with some of your colleagues, tells them to back off, gives them a slap on the wrist. And then you can't even begin to imagine what would happen to us? Our food gets spat in. They forget about exercise time, shower time, and all of sudden there's no books to read and no mail is gettin' through.'

Nelson knew Whitman was right. It would be futile and counter-productive.

'Talking about mail, why don't you get any, Whitman? And why no visits from your family?'

''Cause I told 'em not to write and not to visit.'

'Why?'

Whitman leaned forward and put his elbows on his knees. He lowered his head and sighed. When he looked up towards Nelson, there was that same half-smile on his face.

'Say you was here, Mr Nelson, would you wanna be constantly

reminded of everyone and everything you'd left behind? Would you want stories about Christmas and birthday parties and how your brother and his girl done had another kid? Would you want that? Or would you want them to move on with their lives, to forget about everything that happened?'

'I don't know... I mean, I don't think I'd ever be able to answer that question because—'

'Because you ain't sat where I'm sat, Mr Nelson. That's why. An' until you're sat here, and I hope with every prayer I could make that such a thing never happens, then you'll never know what it's like to be waitin' on your own death. My folks, they hurt enough already. They damned near killed themselves writin' letters and makin' them bus trips an' whatever. After a coupla years I said no, don't come no more. The more you see me, the worse it gets, an' there ain't a darn thing you can do to change what's gonna happen. My ma, she near killed herself with cryin', but she knew I was right. She knew she had to let go, and I knew that the only way she'd do that is if I refused all mail and visitations. That, to me, seemed the kindest thing to do.'

'I can't even begin to imagine what that must have been like,' Nelson said.

'Well, don't try. That ain't gonna do neither one of us any good now, is it?'

'No, I guess not.'

There was silence for a few moments. The air between them was replete with unspoken thoughts and emotions.

'Hey, Mr Nelson?'

'Yes, Whitman.'

'You been there, ain'tcha? In the bell tower. You know, when someone gets executed.'

Nelson nodded. 'Yes, I have.'

'Is it bad?'

'Why are you asking me this, Whitman? What do you want me to say?'

'I know it's bad. It's gotta be, right? I'm just wonderin' how bad is bad.'

'I can't tell you that,' Nelson said. 'I think it's fast. Real fast. I think your lights go out and that's that.'

'Then why do they hit you with it twice?'

'Whitman, come on. Enough already.'

'I'm sorry, Mr Nelson. You's the last person in the world I'd wanna upset.'

'Why do you say that?'

'Hell, because you're pretty much the only one who treats me like a fellow human being. Seems it don't matter what I might or might not have done, you still talk to me like maybe I ain't already dead.'

'And are you?' Nelson asked, knowing at once that the question should never have left his lips. 'Are you guilty of what they're killing you for?'

'We're all guilty in our own way, Mr Nelson.'

'What's that supposed to mean?'

'I guess it means that everyone gets what's comin' to them, even if it ain't for the right reasons.'

Nelson wanted to say more, but he knew he'd already said too much. He was violating one of the cardinal rules of the job: Don't get close.

He stepped back, closing the door as he did so.

'I got work to do,' Nelson said. 'And don't push that button again.'

Leonard Gayle went to the bell tower less than a week after Albert Reid.

It was the final execution at Southern before Christmas and the last of the year. Nelson was assigned to chamber duty. He made tentative inquiries amongst his fellow officers to see if there was some way to be relieved, but there was not. Once the Warden had assigned a team, it could not be changed save for a valid incapacitating medical condition or the death of a family member. It seemed so very ironic to Nelson. The only means of escaping the business of putting someone to death was if he was on death's door himself or someone close to him had died.

Nelson couldn't clearly recall the crimes for which Gayle had been condemned, and he didn't make the effort to remind himself. Every man on Death Row had killed one or more people. How and why seemed not to matter anymore. All except Whitman. Whitman was an enigma. Some nights, lying there in the dark, he had replayed the conversations they'd shared. Those conversations were strictly against penitentiary policy. They were offences for which Nelson could be fired. Nevertheless, there was something that kept pulling him back. He told himself it was sympathy, even basic human instinct, but it was neither. There was something about Whitman that made Nelson want to understand exactly what had happened that fateful day in January of 1971. Had he been asked, all he would've been able to say was that something about it felt wrong. Perhaps the most significant thing was that Whitman did not cry injustice. He never asked about appeals or the possibility of reprieve. He sat quietly in his cell. He reads books. He told Nelson that he played games of chess in his mind. He never complained or criticized, even in light of the things that had been said to him by other officers. Even the worst of those on Death Row expressed emotions – albeit impotently – about the prospect of dying. But not CJ Whitman.

The execution of Gayle sickened Nelson to his stomach.

The sheer force of that electric charge dislocated Gayle's pelvis as his body lurched away from the chair. Nelson heard it as clear as the bell that sounded just fifteen minutes later.

He was in the truck when Gayle's body was taken out to God's Acre. He stood there watching as he was interred. The air was thick, the atmosphere oppressive, and he wanted nothing more than to escape. He thought back to Whitman's question: *Do you ever feel like an inmate, Mr Nelson?*

46

It was on the following Friday that Hannah acceded. Now three weeks away from the end of the first trimester, she agreed that they would tell her family at Christmas.

With both a sense of joy that they could share the news of her pregnancy and the reassurance that there would be more than enough help readily available if Hannah needed it, Nelson felt that a burden had been lifted from his shoulders.

It was in the same conversation that Hannah asked about Nelson's mother.

They were in the living room. The TV was on, but neither of them was really watching it.

'You never speak of her,' she said. 'The only time you ever mentioned her was when I first started treating you in hospital.'

'She's not part of my life, Hannah. Hasn't been a for a long time.'

'You don't think she'd want to know that she's going to be a grandmother?'

'I think she's already forgotten she has a son.'

'What did you mean when you said she was crazy?'

'That she's crazy. She eats wasps and barks at the moon.'

'No, be serious.'

'Correct me if I'm wrong, but I seem to remember you saying something about not being serious.'

'About having a baby, not about your mother.'

Nelson turned to her. 'You don't want my mother in our lives, Hannah. Trust me on this.'

'So trust me to try and understand. I mean, I come along with half of Clewiston in tow, but you have no one. The only person in your family that I've even spoken to is you.'

'So what do you want to know?'

'Whatever you want to tell me.'

Nelson breathed deeply. 'Where to start.'

'At the beginning?'

'My father was rotten to the core. There's no other way to put it. He didn't beat me. Well, sometimes he did but there was good enough reason to do so, at least in his mind. He didn't hurt my mother physically, but he tortured her emotionally, mentally. It was psychological warfare. That's the only way to describe it. I knew she wanted nothing more than to get away, but she would never have left me behind. And there's no way my father would have let her take me. If she'd done so … well, I wouldn't have put it past him to track us down and kill us both.'

Nelson got up. He walked to the TV set and switched it off.

'She drank,' he went on. 'Secretly at first, and then it didn't matter. Then she went to see a doctor and he gave her pills, one kind after another, but pills weren't going to do anything but make her think that what was happening wasn't really happening. My father played that game. He took advantage of it. He questioned her memory. He told her things had happened that hadn't. He told her that things she was sure of were just her imagination. And he dragged me into it, made me feel like I was somehow complicit. We'd be having dinner, and he'd go on and on about some fishing trip that he and I had taken. There were no fishing trips. My mother would get confused and ask questions. He'd tell her some other bullshit and then wink at me and smile like he was really getting a kick out of it.'

'Why?' Hannah asked.

'Because he was just a bad fucking person. And he was corrupt. He took bribes, he got involved in drug deals, probably killed some people. I don't know everything, and I really don't want to know. And then finally, when it looked like he wasn't going to be able to cover his tracks and lie his way out of whatever the hell he'd gotten himself into, he stuck his service revolver in his mouth and blew the back of his own head off.'

'Were you the one that found him?'

'No,' Nelson replied. 'He made sure it would be my mother. One last kick in the teeth, you know?'

'And then what happened?'

'She went into a state psychiatric facility. However bad she was, she was worse when she got out. I don't even know what they did to her, but she was unrecognizable. When I said that she's forgotten she has a son, I wasn't kidding. I saw her a couple of times, and she looked back at me like she'd never seen me before. And I guess the fact that I look a lot like my father really didn't help matters.'

'You don't feel anything for her?' Hannah asked.

'She's my mother. How can I not? I just know that visiting her would serve no purpose, and that looking after her is more than a full-time job. I genuinely believe that she doesn't know who I am. I would just be some other stranger feeding her and cleaning up after her. And besides, even now she spends more time in hospital than out of it. What could I do that isn't already being done? Whoever my mother was, she's long-since gone.'

'So, all this time – what, twenty years? – you've been on your own.'

'I guess I got used to my own company.'

'But you've had girlfriends, right?'

'I thought so, yes.'

'Thought so?'

'No one important. No one to make a life with.'

'All things considered, you turned out pretty good,' Hannah said.

'But you've only known me a little over a year.'

'Meaning what?'

'That crazy shit is hereditary. In fact, all of a sudden I've got a compelling urge to go bark at the moon.'

'Hey, knock yourself out. Don't let me get in the way.'

Nelson put his arm around Hannah's shoulders and pulled her close.

'I guess you don't know what you've missed until it shows up,' he said. 'And then you couldn't imagine your life without it.'

47

News of Jimmy Christiansen and Richard Stein reached the Southern grapevine in early December.

They had indeed continued north into Georgia as was originally suspected. They both made it beyond Macon, perhaps aiming to reach Atlanta and disappear into the crowded city, but Stein made it no further.

Why the events of Wednesday, December 7, 1977 did not reach the airwaves more broadly was perhaps attributable to federal authorities wishing to save themselves from any further criticism or censure. With the combined resources of both the Florida and Georgia Bureaus, activation of broad media publicity, the police and Sheriff's Departments of innumerable counties on high alert, and a bi-state manhunt with a 'shoot to kill' policy in force, Christiansen and Stein had nevertheless evaded capture for five months. The fact that the search for Stein ended on US 41 between Forsyth and Barnesville was not due to the diligence of the local police, but Stein's seeming lack of foresight and preparedness.

Taylor Chapman – one-time US Army major – was a laconic, easy-going man. Despite his three-decade military background, had you not known he was a soldier you would never have guessed it. Retiring on a full pension, he'd gone back to Barnesville – the town of his birth and where he'd spent the majority of his childhood – and settled. He had no aspirations to travel, for he'd seen far more of the world than most people. The fact that he'd seen only places of conflict did not seem to matter. He'd spent thirty years following orders, going where he was told, doing what was required of him, questioning nothing. He'd earned the right to do as he pleased for the rest of his life, and what pleased him was running a general store that stocked everything from flour to floor polish, hardware to holdalls, stepladders to shoelaces. Outside of the store, a number of local farmers hawked their produce – everything from fresh meat and fruit to preserves and pickles. Chapman's Place, as it was known, had become a community hub, and the proprietor was both liked and respected.

In hindsight, the way events unfolded that morning would appear incongruous and out of keeping with all that had earlier transpired. Stein, despite his immediately identifiable physical appearance, had been nigh on invisible ever since he'd reached the treeline beyond Southern back in July. He and Jimmy Christiansen had engineered an escape from a federal penitentiary, traversed miles of swampland, and aside from the Richmond killings and the murder in Arredondo, they had both remained off the radar for the best part of half a year. To then derail whatever plan they might have had for the sake of a cup of coffee made no sense whatsoever. Perhaps the exchange that took place between Stein and Taylor Chapman was ultimately inevitable. If it hadn't happened there, it would have happened someplace else. An escaped felon, no matter how bright, no matter how conscientious, will always be nothing more or less than a wanted man. He would be ever-conscious of this fact, even if others weren't, and his behavior would be influenced accordingly.

As was his routine each morning, Chapman was alone when

Richard Stein appeared as nothing more than a silhouette outside the doors of the general store. It was early, just a little after daybreak, and Chapman hadn't yet opened up.

At first, Chapman thought it was a delivery – perhaps bread and pastries from the bakery in Forsyth – but deliveries were routinely made to the rear of the building. Taking into consideration the size of the man and the insistence with which he was knocking on the door, Chapman sensed something wasn't right. Perhaps a traveller in difficulty, someone with a busted car. Maybe there'd been an accident up on the highway and a telephone was needed. Whatever was going on, Chapman, a veteran of most everything a man could endure, was not concerned for his own welfare. That was a thought that never entered his mind. His impulse was to find out what was going on and do what he could to assist.

Opening the front door, Chapman stepped back and let the man inside.

Stein paused before speaking. He seemed to be surveying the interior of the store.

'This your place?' Stein asked.

'It is, yes. You after something in particular?'

'You alone here?'

Immediately, Chapman's intuitive sense of self-preservation kicked in.

'What's up, fella?' Chapman asked.

Stein, a good head taller and twice as wide, looked down at Chapman.

'You got some coffee on, mister?'

'Ain't right now, but wouldn't take long to brew some up.'

'And there ain't no one else here?'

'Just you and me,' Chapman said. 'And you wanna wait while I make that coffee, you're more than welcome.'

'You expectin' people?'

'Soon enough, sure. Place gets pretty darn busy first thing. Truckers, local folks on the way to work and what have you. Got deliveries comin' in too.'

Stein nodded slowly, all the while looking this way and that.

'Go ahead and make that coffee.'

'Sure thing,' Chapman said, smiling in as relaxed a manner as he could. 'Take a look around,' he added. 'See if there's anythin' else you need while you're here.'

Out back, Chapman called the Sheriff's Office in Barnesville. No, there was no robbery in progress, and no, the man had not made any indication of threatening behavior. Was he armed? He didn't appear to be, but Chapman couldn't confirm that one way or the other. The sole reason that the dispatcher agreed to send out a car was because there was already a car less than a mile away and Chapman's place happened to be en route to where it was headed. The dispatcher also knew Taylor Chapman well enough to appreciate that here was a man who wasn't easily spooked.

Chapman appeared from the back with a jug of fresh coffee just moments before the police car pulled up out front.

Stein, cup in hand, watched as the car drew to a halt. He looked back at Chapman, then out to the car again. He said nothing at all as Barnesville Deputy Sheriff, Dale Radick, made his way up the steps and came through the door.

'Mornin' there, Taylor,' Radick said.

Chapman raised his hand in greeting. 'Hey, Deputy. You're an early bird.'

'Headin' on up to Griffin. Figured I'd get me a cup of coffee for the drive.'

'Just made some fresh for this fella here,' Chapman said.

Radick looked at Stein. 'Hey, mister.'

Stein didn't reply. He stood motionless, cup in hand.

'You passin' through?' Radick asked.

Stein nodded.

'You sightseein', or you got business here?'

'Business,' Stein said.

Radick nodded, smiled. 'What business you in then? If you don't mind me askin', of course.'

'Nothin' special.'

'Don't see no vehicle out front,' Radick said. 'Where you parked up?'

Stein, his body language edgy, indicated out and to the left. 'Back there a way,' he said.

'That so? And where'd you come from this mornin'?'

Stein frowned, shook his head. 'I do somethin' wrong here?' he asked. 'I'm just gettin' some coffee here, mindin' my own business.'

Radick smiled, laughed. 'Hell, you're right, mister,' he said. 'I'm sorry. Force o' habit. Too damned eager to get up in everyone's business.'

Chapman came through from the back with a cup of coffee for Radick.

'You should hang on a handful of minutes,' Chapman said. 'Pastries and whatnot are comin' in.'

'That sounds like a fine idea,' Radick said.

'I need to get going,' Stein said.

'Wait up for the pastries,' Radick said. He looked at Chapman. 'They comin' in from that place in Forsyth?'

'Sure are,' Chapman said.

'Best bear claw you ever ate, I guarantee you,' Radick said to Stein.

Stein hesitated. Radick set down his cup. Chapman took a couple of steps backward and put the jug of coffee on the counter.

'We have a problem here, fella?' Radick asked.

Stein said nothing.

'You got yourself a gun there? You come in here with a mind to rob this place, or what?'

Again, Stein did not respond.

Radick's hand was on the handle of his revolver. Chapman, moving slowly, made it around the edge of the counter and was now standing behind it.

'I ain't done nothin',' Stein said. 'And now I'm gonna leave.'

'I wanna see some ID,' Radick said.

Stein closed his eyes. He breathed deeply. Later, Radick would say that there was just the slightest hint of relief in the man's expression, as if some burden had been lifted from his shoulders.

Looking back at the deputy, Stein said, 'I ain't got no ID. It's back there in my car.'

'Well, I got a few minutes to take a walk with you, mister,' he said.

Stein did not hesitate. He hurled the contents of his coffee cup at Radick, and before Radick had a moment to appreciate what was happening, Stein was running. Bringing the full weight of his body against the door, the frame just split like kindling. Stein lost his footing and went down the steps and landed on his hands and knees. He was up and heading for the police car as Radick came out behind him, gun raised, hollering for Stein to stop.

Stein had no intention of stopping. Radick fired a warning shot high over the man's head, but Stein was already in the driver's seat. Only then did he appreciate that there was no way out of this. The pump action on the passenger side was locked in its rack. The keys were not in the ignition.

Pulling the door closed, Stein just sat there, his hands on the wheel.

Radick advanced slowly, gun levelled directly at Stein's head.

'You need to come on out of there,' Radick said. 'I got a whole party headin' on over here. You ain't goin' no place in that vehicle.

An' if you come out of there with your hands anywhere but over your head, I'm gonna take your knees out. We understandin' one another?'

Stein lowered his head, and then he gave an affirmative nod.

Radick glanced toward the store. 'Taylor!'

Chapman appeared in the busted doorway.

'Fetch that old .45 you got stashed behind the counter.'

Chapman returned after a moment, the .45 in his hand.

'Come on down here and keep a bead on this fella while he gets himself out of there.'

In the sights of both weapons, Stein complied with every instruction Radick gave. He exited the car slowly, hands raised, and knelt on the ground. He didn't say a word as he was cuffed, nor when a second car arrived at the scene and two more officers from the Barnesville Sheriff's Department joined the party.

It was only when Stein was secured in a cell back in town that anyone realized who he was.

The Barnesville Sheriff, Tom Proctor, put a call in to the Florida Bureau in Fort Lauderdale, and Senior Special Agent Michael Gant, the same agent who had overseen the search for Christiansen and Stein, chartered a flight to Atlanta. With two other agents, his instruction was to return Stein to Southern State Penitentiary, and there Stein would be questioned regarding Christiansen's whereabouts. Despite having escaped Southern, it was still the most secure facility to hold Stein until a new arraignment could be instructed for the additional charges of escape and murder. It was Gant's superior officer who ordered the press remain uninformed. Until Christiansen himself was either apprehended or dead, there would be radio silence.

The direct involvement of both Nelson and Frank Montgomery began when Stein was delivered to Southern the following day. There was no question in Greaves' mind where Stein should be held. Once convicted of the Richmond murders and that of the gas station attendant, Stein would be on Death Row anyway, so that was where he would remain while the Bureau's interrogation proceeded. Greaves had Nelson and Montgomery complete Stein's processing back into custody, and they were the ones – under the watchful eye of Michael Gant – who delivered him to Lester Burroughs' old cell.

True to form, and as most everyone anticipated, Stein was initially as uncommunicative as it was possible to be. It was only when Gant assured him that cooperation would encourage the Attorney General not to insist on the death penalty that he conceded. The impulse for self-preservation, perhaps the greatest human motivation, could be found even in someone so inhumane as Richard Stein.

The escape had been orchestrated by Cain and Garvey. Fielding was dead. He was dead within minutes of the escape. The intent, albeit poorly planned and hugely optimistic, had been for Christiansen and Stein to get free and clear of Southern, to lie low for a while, and then to engineer a second escape for Cain and Garvey.

When Stein was informed by Gant of Garvey's suicide, he said, 'You make a list of the people who would never kill themselves, Garvey would be the first.'

'You have any notion of who would want him dead?' Gant asked.

'No better notion than you,' Stein replied. 'Though it seems to me that getting one person out of here would be a great deal easier than two.'

'You think Cain might've had Garvey killed?'

'What I think ain't important. You wanna know details about any of this, then you'd best ask Jimmy.'

'I would like to ask him,' Gant said, 'but I need to find him. And that's what you can help me with.'

Stein shook his head. 'He's gone. Into the fuckin' wind. I don't think you'll ever find him.'

'Was he with you out near Barnesville?'

'Sure. We been joined at the hip since we got outta here.'

'And you planned on robbin' that store?'

'I didn't plan on robbin' nothin'. I just wanted a cup of coffee.'

'So where do you think he would've headed? Gone on further north?'

Stein shrugged. 'Hell knows. That's what I woulda done, but I ain't him and he ain't me.'

'After Barnesville, where did you plan to go?'

'Atlanta.'

'Did Christiansen have contacts there?'

'If he did, he didn't say nothin' to me. We were just wingin' it. We took each day as it came. He talked about how he had to get Cain and Garvey out, but he didn't never seem to do nothin' about it. I ain't got no idea of what was goin' on in his mind.'

Gant was then quiet for a time. Stein seemed content just to sit there until the next question was forthcoming. As it stood, and with the information that Stein had given him, he was none the wiser as to Christiansen's whereabouts.

'I want to talk about something else,' Gant finally said.

'You go ahead and talk.'

'If William Cain had David Garvey murdered, then he must have had some inside assistance. Someone got into that cell to cut that man's throat. The only way it could've happened was if someone had opened Garvey's cell from the landing itself or from Central Admin.'

'Sure.'

'And you had a key for the escape. I am assuming that the key came from the same person who opened Garvey's cell.'

'Could be, sure.'

Gant didn't speak. He knew that silence was the best invitation for a subject to go on talking.

Stein looked up at him. He frowned, and then he smiled. 'You think I know who that is?'

Again, Gant stayed silent.

'How the hell would I know? Whatever happened back then, and whatever happened with Garvey… seems to me the only person who might have an answer for you is Cain.'

'Or Jimmy Christiansen.'

'Sure, maybe Jimmy knows who's on Cain's payroll, but like I said, I have no fuckin' idea where he's at.'

Stein was right and Gant knew it. Stein had never been anything more than a hired hand, a pair of fists, an enforcer. Cain and Christiansen had worked on this together. If Gant's suspicions were correct, then Cain had never intended to help Garvey escape. However, cooperation between the landings had been required to stage the July 4 riots.

Cain was already a lifer. He had not been implicated in the escape or any of its consequences. There was no further pressure to be brought on him; there was no reduction in sentence that could be offered for his cooperation.

Gant needed Jimmy Christiansen in custody, not only so his own office and the Bureau as a whole could save face, but because he believed it was the only way to discover the identity of Southern's inside man.

48

Soon after the return of Richard Stein to Southern, Nelson was caught up in the Montgomerys' preparations for Christmas.

A year before, the first time he'd met the entire family, he'd merely arrived on the day as a guest. Twelve months on and they considered him part of the tribe.

For them, it was a big deal. For Nelson, it was yet another reminder that his own childhood was nothing remotely like the childhood that Hannah and her brothers had enjoyed.

Nelson still felt a degree of disconnection. It was as if they spoke a different language – not only their words, but their emotions and attitudes – and here he was, a stranger from some foreign country struggling to comprehend the nuances of dialect and humor. His understanding was often literal and basic. He couldn't express himself in the way that he intended. He would learn in time, perhaps, but for ever there would be that sense that this was not his mother tongue.

Nelson's last Dead Watch shift of the year was on Tuesday, 20th. Having Richard Stein on the row was disconcerting. As far as Nelson was concerned, he shouldn't have been there. With his presence, both intimidating and aggressive, the atmosphere changed. Nelson didn't believe the atmosphere could be any bleaker, but somehow Stein accomplished that effect.

Only once, as Nelson was delivering meals, did Stein speak to him.

'I know who you are,' he said. 'What did Jimmy used to call you? Montgomery's little bitch, right?'

Nelson ignored him. That was the only way with which to deal with such an individual.

On the evening of the 22nd, Nelson and Hannah went out to the mall in Clewiston to get gifts for her parents and siblings.

Nelson needed new shirts, and while he was paying for them, Hannah left him at the cashier and headed to the lower floor of the department store. He found her fifteen minutes later in the babywear section. She was just standing there looking at tiny shoes.

'Hey you.'

She turned and smiled. 'Look,' she said.

'I see them,' Nelson replied.

'Why do I want to cry?'

Nelson set down his bag and put his arms around her. 'It's okay,' he said. 'You go on and cry if you want to.'

Hannah laughed at herself. 'Look at me,' she said. 'I'm behaving like an emotional wreck.'

'I think you're behaving like an expectant mother.'

'It still feels so unreal, Garrett.'

'Let's buy some,' Nelson said.

'Really?'

'Why not?'

Hannah looked up at Nelson. 'You don't think it's tempting fate?'

'The opposite. It's agreeing with fate.'

Hannah nodded, but there was uncertainty in her eyes.

'Those ones,' Nelson said, pointing to a pair of pale blue woollen bootees.

'Those ones,' Hannah echoed.

Nelson picked them up and handed them to her. They were so small that they barely covered the palm of her hand.

'Okay,' she said.

'Maybe it's time we stopped thinking that things might go wrong,' Nelson said. 'And started believing that it's all gonna be all right.'

Hannah didn't reply, but she pulled Nelson closer.

The cashier smiled so sincerely. 'For you?' she asked. 'Or are they a gift for someone?'

Hannah's eye brimmed with tears. 'For us,' she replied.

'Oh my, how wonderful. My congratulations to you both. Are you having a boy or a girl?'

'We don't know yet.'

Holding up the bootees, the cashier smiled knowingly and said, 'If these were the ones you chose, then maybe the little one is telling you already.'

'What's your name?' Hannah asked.

'Jennifer,' the cashier said. 'Jenny.'

'Do you have children, Jenny?'

'I do, yes. Two. Lucas is five and Nancy is three.'

'This is going to be our first.'

'Well, you have the greatest adventure of your lives ahead of you. All that stuff that people say about children and how much it costs and how much trouble they are, it's all nonsense. A house is not a home until there's children. It's like getting to see the world for the first time all over again. Children are a gift from God. That's what I say, and I mean every word of it. They're there to remind you that the magic you've stopped believing in is still around every corner.'

Jenny laughed. 'Now listen to me rattlin' on...'

'No, not at all,' Hannah said. 'That's a beautiful thing to say.'

Jenny reached out and took Hannah's hand. She squeezed it reassuringly.

'Bless all three of you,' she said. 'And a Happy Christmas.'

Christmas dinner went by in a blur.

Nelson drank beers, then wine, and when Ray broke out a bottle of ten-year-old Sazerac Rye, a roar went up from the gathering.

Perhaps no one had noticed, but when Frank started filling shot glasses and Hannah refused, it was Earl's wife, Mary, who said, 'You ain't had a drop all day, sweetheart. You're not in the festive spirit?'

Hannah looked at Nelson. Nelson held her gaze for a moment, and then the pair of them looked at the people around the table.

Miriam put her hand to her mouth. 'Oh my,' she said.

Nelson reached into his jacket pocket and took out the tiny blue bootees. Placing them on the dinner table without a word, the collective gasp seemed to suck every breath of air out of the room.

Everyone descended on them – Frank, Miriam, Ray, Charlene, Earl, Mary, Brian and Danny – hugging them, shaking hands, laughing, crying. Nelson was dragged to his feet and Frank embraced him, held his face in his hands, saying, 'My God man, this is such great news. I am so proud. I am so happy. I couldn't be happier.' And then Frank was pulling Hannah to him, and he wrapped his arms around her like a bear. Hannah was crying, Miriam too, and Danny was holding a glass aloft and urging everyone to drink a toast to the first Montgomery grandchild.

'We never thought... you know, we never believed...' Miriam started, and then she had to sit down so she didn't lose her balance.

The life and love amongst them was contagious. Nelson's heart swelled. He looked at Hannah. She mouthed *I love you*, and he leaned down and kissed her.

Someone started singing, and the sound was a blur of words that Nelson didn't hear. Everything beyond the walls of that room disappeared. Nothing else mattered. He felt a rush of unfamiliar emotion that was yet so undeniably powerful. Had he tried to describe it, he would have been unable.

What it would mean to be a father, he didn't know. But that didn't matter. Nothing mattered. Nothing else in his life compared to what he felt in that moment. It was a tidal wave, and he relinquished everything that held him back. It was set to carry him into the future, and he let it take him without a second thought.

49

Ray was drunk. He sat out on the back porch with Frank and Brian.

Nelson had offered to help Miriam, Hannah, Charlene and Mary as they cleared the table and finalised a host of desserts, but he was shooed out of the kitchen.

Danny and Earl had gone off to Danny's annexe. Nelson guessed they were smoking weed and listening to music.

Nelson went out the back door.

'Hey, pops,' Ray said. He held up his glass. 'Come share a drink and smoke with us.'

Nelson hadn't smoked for years, but he felt he could not decline.

Frank handed him a cigar and a box of matches. Nelson took a glass of rye from Brian, and the four of them sat in a semi-circle looking out over the back yard of the Montgomery house.

'I have to say that I kind of gave up on Hannah,' Frank said. 'Just as far as being a mom was concerned. An' then I got four sons and not one of them seems to have fulfilled their duty. Useless crowd of losers, if you ask me.'

'We'll get there,' Ray said. 'An' it sure ain't like we haven't tried.' He looked at Nelson. 'You have no idea the earful of noise I'm gonna get on the subject now. Just wanna say thanks for that, buddy.'

Nelson laughed.

'Well, at least I got a girl, eh, Brian?' Ray said. 'Me an' dad here are startin' to wonder if maybe you're . . . you know—'

'Fuck off, Ray.'

'Brian is gonna get himself a girl,' Frank said. 'Brian is gonna handle this the way he handles everything. Sure, steady, methodical, precise. It's gonna be a one-time deal, right, Brian? Once you get her, that's it for life.'

'That's the plan,' Brian said.

'See what I mean?' Frank replied. 'The man's an engineer.'

Nelson's cigar had gone out. He reached for the matches.

'Don't bother,' Frank said. 'You don't wanna smoke it, don't smoke it.'

Nelson rested the cigar in the ashtray.

'So we have some changes comin',' Frank said. 'Can't tell you how thrilled Miriam is. She thinks you're the Angel fucking Gabriel. Garrett this and Garrett that. You're the golden boy now, believe me.'

'Well, I don't know what to say, aside from how welcome you all have made me, and how happy me and Hannah are. The last year has been the best of my life, no doubt about it.'

'You don't have your own family to see at Christmas?' Brian asked. 'There isn't anyone you—'

'Brian,' Frank said, cutting him off.

'It's okay,' Nelson said. 'No, I don't have family. My father's dead, has been for twenty years, and my mother and I don't see one another.'

'I'm sorry,' Brian said. 'It's none of my business.'

'Well, it kind of is,' Nelson said. 'Seein' as how you're going to be an uncle soon enough.'

'I hated my father,' Frank said. 'He was a mean son of a bitch.

They're all gone now, Miriam's folks too. My father should have gone first, but he outlived all of them.'

'Your dad was a cop, right?' Ray asked Nelson.

'Sheriff over in Charlotte County – '48 to '56. They kicked him out. Took them eight years to realize that he wasn't in the job to serve anyone but himself.'

'What happened to him?' Brian asked.

'He killed himself.'

'Oh fuck. Really?'

'It happens, Brian,' Frank said.

'Yeah,' Ray added. 'Like David Garvey, right?'

There was silence for a moment.

'Who's David Garvey?' Brian asked.

'Ray, that's enough,' Frank said.

'Up at Southern,' Ray said, ignoring Frank. 'A guy who killed himself in a way that was impossible to kill yourself.'

'And now you've gone and killed the festive fucking spirit,' Frank said.

Ray shrugged. 'Just makin' conversation.'

'That's as may be, but it's not the kind of conversation we're gonna be havin' this evening,' Frank said.

'And there lies the problem, doesn't it? This shit happens an' everyone just keeps their mouth shut and carries on like nothin' happened.'

'Ray, you're drunk.'

'Well, he ain't the first and I have no doubt he won't be the last.' Ray raised his glass. 'To David Garvey, may he rest in pieces.'

Nelson wanted to say something. Ray had just expressed an opinion in agreement with his own. Ray was in Gen Pop, and yet he knew about Garvey's apparent suicide. What did he know? What was being said over there?

'Well, if your little penitentiary club doesn't want to share whatever gory details you've got, I'm gonna go get me some cake,' Brian said. He got to his feet awkwardly, almost lost his balance as he made his way to the back door, and went into the house.

'You don't talk about that shit to anyone, you hear me?' Frank said.

'The guy didn't kill himself, Dad. You know that better than anyone. Jesus, it's all but common knowledge. An' if he didn't kill himself then someone got into that cell. And that, whichever fuckin' way you look at it, means we got someone on the landing or someone in Central Admin who opened that fucking door.'

Frank turned to Nelson. 'You don't have to listen to this, Garrett. Ray is drunk and talkin' out of turn.'

'I never believed he killed himself,' Nelson said. 'I was in there. I saw him. Aside from the fact that doing something like that is pretty near impossible, the whole scene was wrong.'

'That's exactly what I'm sayin',' Ray said. 'And all this noise about Cain and Garvey. This escape that Christiansen was supposed to organize once he got out. Everything that went down, that pair must've had some smarts to stay on the run for five months, right? Got me wonderin' whether getting Stein back in Southern was intentional.'

'Stein's on the row,' Frank said. 'He ain't organizin' shit from down there.'

'I'm just sayin',' Ray said.

'Well, you've said more than enough,' Frank said, his tone direct and unflinching. 'We're not discussing this. You think something is awry, you report it. But you better be sure you know whose weeds you're pissin' on before you do that.'

Frank leaned forward and picked up his shot glass. He downed the whiskey in one go and stood up.

Without another word, he stepped past Nelson and went into the house.

Ray grinned. 'Looks like we just gone an' pissed on his weeds, eh?'

Hannah drove them home. Nelson had drunk more that day than he had in the previous six months. She talked incessantly. Nelson listened, smiled, laughed, but at the back of his mind were the questions Ray had asked and how quickly Frank had shut him down.

Hannah slept soundlessly. Nelson did not, at least not for a good while. He lay awake, his mind a mess of conflicting emotions. He felt that his loyalties were split. Devoted to Hannah, dedicated unconditionally to the future they were planning together, he was nevertheless troubled by Southern and all it represented. To oppose Southern would be to oppose Frank. That had the potential of causing a rift between Hannah and her family, and that was the very last thing he wanted to do. But, at the same time, he knew Ray was right. He'd gone into that cell with Max Sheehan. He'd seen Garvey's body. The man had not committed suicide. And if that was the case, it was also the case that someone had opened Garvey's cell. Nelson didn't doubt that Cain was the most likely instigator of Garvey's murder, if not because of their rivalry, then because he believed that he had a greater chance of escaping alone. But more importantly, who was on the inside, and why were they aiding and abetting escapes and murders?

It was a question Nelson did not want to ask for fear of the answer. However, he also recognized it was his duty, both as a prison guard and a one-time law enforcement officer, to expose the truth.

Between them, Frank and Ray had over forty years of history at Southern. Nelson had been there a year. Frank was close to retirement. He would have a vested interest in maintaining the status quo. Like those who'd known what Nelson's father was doing and yet feared for their own livelihoods, maybe Frank had let things slide, turned a blind eye, convinced himself that as long as he wasn't complicit then he was innocent.

Nelson's last thought as he finally drifted off to sleep was for CJ Whitman. He had allowed himself to get too close. He had become the man's confidante. Whitman acknowledged neither guilt nor innocence in the matter of Garth Kenyon's murder. He'd merely said that everyone was guilty in their own way. Would Nelson now be guilty too? Would his sense of self-preservation override his integrity? Would he too just let everything slide for the sake of keeping the peace? Or was he going to do something – about Garvey, about Whitman, about discovering the real truth of Southern and the ghosts within its walls?

50

As Nelson had predicted, the Montgomery family and its various resources rallied around Hannah. In a sense, Nelson experienced a sense of resentment, as if her reduced dependency upon him somehow made less of his worth. He wanted to feel needed, and now the value of his contribution was relegated. He knew it was irrational, a knee-jerk reaction, and he also knew that her parents and brothers had nothing but both their best interests at heart. Nevertheless, it provoked a quiet sense of vulnerability. Without him by her side, there would be no shortage of help. On the flip side of that, he couldn't imagine how he might feel if she was no longer there for him. It was ludicrous to think such things, but in the dim silence of the Dead Watch corridor, the Devil found comfort in an idle mind.

During the first three-day shift in January, Nelson made a conscious effort to engage with neither CJ Whitman nor Richard Stein. Whitman, in turn, did not make an effort to engage with him. He seemed uncharacteristically subdued and withdrawn, and seemed to spend much of his time sleeping. On the other occasions that Nelson opened the viewing hatch to check on him, he found Whitman standing and looking towards the narrow window high in the cell wall.

Stein, however, grew ever more vocal as his residence continued. The number of interrogations had decreased. Nelson knew, from the rumor mill that was Southern, that Gant and the Bureau were after Christiansen's whereabouts. Even if Stein had known this at the time of his arrest, Christiansen would have long-since vanished. Perhaps they hoped that Stein could name Christiansen's external contacts, and thus they could initiate surveillance. Whether or not Ray's suspicion that Stein's capture had been intentional had any basis in fact was unknown. As Frank had said, even if Stein was back at Southern to help facilitate the escape of William Cain, he was in no position to do anything from his cell on the row.

Finally, an hour or so before his shift ended on the Wednesday, Nelson opened up the door and asked Whitman what was going on.

'Nothing, Mr Nelson,' Whitman replied.

'You're quiet. You haven't said a thing to me in three days.'

'My understanding is that we're not meant to speak.'

'Even so, we have, and a good number of times.'

'We have, yes, and it's been appreciated, but the last thing I'd want to do is get you in trouble.'

'No one knows,' Nelson said, 'and no one will find out unless you tell them.'

'We can talk, but I don't really have anything to tell you,' Whitman said. 'I mean, every day is the same as every other day, right?'

'Are you afraid?'

'Of dying?'

'Yes, of dying.'

Whitman sat down on the bed. 'The worst way to die is for nothing, Mr Nelson.'

'What do you mean?'

'People who spend their whole lives waiting for it to start. People who live their lives according to someone else's expectations. People forever trying to be something they aren't. They're the ones who get to the end and ask themselves if anything they did was important.'

'Is that the way you feel? That you've done nothing important with your life?'

Whitman shook his head. 'When I die, Mr Nelson, it will be the most important thing I've ever done.'

'I don't understand—'

'And you don't need to,' Whitman interjected. 'There's nothing that you or anyone else needs to understand.'

'So you're telling me that you're dying for a reason?'

Whitman walked to the end of the cell and looked up at the window.

'Maybe the best reason, Mr Nelson. In the end, maybe the only reason that really matters.'

Whitman turned and smiled then, and it was that same expression – reconciliation, acceptance, even self-assurance – and Nelson didn't know what to say.

'I think we'll hear soon enough,' Whitman said. 'A date, you know? And yes, I'm afraid. I don't see how anyone couldn't be. But it will also be a relief, I guess. The waiting is worse than the penalty. Maybe that's the real punishment here.'

Nelson stood for a moment longer, and then he nodded in acknowledgement. He closed and locked the door. He went back to his chair at the end of the corridor. Closing his eyes, he tried to imagine what it would be like to have the ever-present specter of your own death haunting every waking and sleeping moment. He imagined the nightmares these men must have, only to wake and realize that it was not a nightmare at all.

The hairs rose on Nelson's scalp. He felt suddenly cold and

desperately alone. It was a truly awful thing to consider, and he forced himself to think of something else. He was wrestling with everything he was feeling, and he was scared that he was going to lose.

51

'Something's troubling you, isn't it?' Hannah asked at breakfast the following morning.

'Just a work thing,' Nelson replied.

'And you're not going to tell me.'

'That's the issue right there.'

'That you can't talk about it?'

'That I have been talking to someone that I shouldn't have.'

'On Death Row?'

Nelson nodded.

'And?' Hannah prompted.

Nelson didn't respond.

'You don't have to tell me details, Garrett. However, if you're upset then it's only right that you discuss it with me. After all, I have to live with you, even when you're being morose.'

'I'm not being morose.'

'I beg to differ.'

Hannah picked up her coffee cup and held it between her hands. She looked at him over the rim.

'I don't know why, I can't even explain it, but there's someone I think shouldn't be there.'

'You think he's innocent?'

'Well, that's just it,' Nelson said. 'I don't know. I can't put my finger on anything. His attitude, his manner, the way he talks, the fact that he's never said he's innocent.'

'I thought that pretty much everyone in prison was innocent. At least, that's what they'd have you believe.'

'He's different. It's like he got arrested, charged, convicted, tried and sentenced, and he just seems to have accepted all of it without a single word of protest. He talks like ... like he knows he's going to die and he wants it to happen. That's the only way I can describe it.'

'He wants it to happen? Like he's committing suicide, but he wants the state to do it?'

'Maybe. Christ only knows, Hannah. There's something about the whole thing that I don't understand and it's really getting to me.'

'So what are you going to do about it?'

'I don't know.'

'You have to decide then. Do something or don't do something. It's one way or the other. You can't just sit on the fence feeling like crap.'

'I know.'

'You were a cop. Figure it out. Go ask some questions. If you don't want anyone to know about it, don't tell anyone. I won't say anything.'

'And if I'm wrong?'

'Then you're wrong. He did whatever they said he did and he'll be executed. How can finding out more about it make it worse?'

'Because I might be opening up a can of worms that affects my job, my career, you know? And I have to think about us, about the baby.'

'You're worried you might lose your job?'

'I'm not a cop anymore, Hannah. I go digging around in some

case that's already been tried, I can imagine that there's gonna be some people that get pissed about it.'

'You can get another job, Garrett. This guy, whoever he is, isn't going to get another life.'

After work, Nelson came home to find a note from Hannah. She was over in Clewiston with her folks and wouldn't be back until late. There were pork chops for his dinner in the refrigerator.

Nelson called information and got the Port Charlotte telephone number of George Levitt, the public defender who'd represented Clarence Whitman back in 1971. Levitt was out, but his secretary took Nelson's number and a message.

Nelson was eating when Levitt called back.

'Garrett Nelson?'

'Speaking.'

'This is George Levitt. You left a message for me to call you.'

'I did, yes. Thanks for getting back to me. I wanted to know if it was possible to come and see you at your office.'

'What's this about, Mr Nelson?'

'You probably won't remember, but you defended someone back in the early part of 1971. Clarence Whitman?'

There was a long silence at the other end of the line, so much so that Nelson wondered if the call had been disconnected.

'Mr Levitt?'

'Yes, yes, I'm here.'

'I was just saying—'

'I heard what you said.'

'So you remember him?'

'Very well, Mr Nelson. I remember him very well indeed.'

'I wanted to ask you about the case.'

'In what capacity are you making these inquiries?'

Nelson hesitated, and then said, 'I'm actually a retired deputy sheriff.'

'And you were involved in the original investigation?'

'Not directly, Mr Levitt, but I'm aware of its history and that Whitman is on Death Row at Southern State.'

'And there is new evidence that brings the conviction into question?'

'That's what I wanted to discuss with you.'

'You say you've retired from the Sheriff's Department. So, are you now acting in a private investigatory capacity?'

'I would just like to meet, sir. That's all. If you'd just be willing to give me a little of your time, it would be really appreciated.'

Levitt was quiet again. Nelson waited.

'Tomorrow,' Levitt said. 'Say around six o'clock at my office here in Port Charlotte.'

'Thank you, Mr Levitt,' Nelson said, and then he hung up before Levitt had a chance to withdraw the invitation.

52

Nelson drove to Tice and then headed north on 41 to Port Charlotte. The route took him through Charlotte County, the place he'd been born and raised. He'd once known it like the back of his hand, but now it was unfamiliar country. This was the landscape of his past, a past he'd all but erased from his memory. Things unspoken, things never shared, the lies and deceptions, the ways in which the truth had been twisted and manipulated to make fact into fiction – this was how he remembered everything that had happened in the years leading up to his father's death.

At the junction of 164, he was less than ten miles from Murdock and the family home. Whether his mother was still there, if the house had been sold, the proceeds vanishing into the vast maw of medical costs that she more than likely required, he didn't know. In truth, there was always the possibility that she was dead. This he doubted, however. He was easy enough for the authorities to find, and Nelson was her only kin.

Nelson hit traffic on the outskirts of the city, and then had some difficulty finding Levitt's office.

By the time he arrived, it was quarter past six. He hoped that Levitt hadn't changed his mind and used Nelson's lateness as an excuse to bail out.

Nelson needn't have worried. Levitt – a diminutive man in his fifties with heavy horn-rimmed spectacles – was waiting for him in the hallway as he came up the stairs.

'Mr Nelson?'

'Yes,' Nelson replied. 'I'm sorry I'm late.'

'Come on through.'

Levitt went into the reception area. Nelson followed him.

'I'd offer you coffee or something, but no one else is here and—'

'I'm good thank you, Mr Levitt.'

Levitt sat at his desk.

'Take a seat, Mr Nelson, and tell me what this is all about.'

'I didn't really want to share any details over the phone,' Nelson started. 'This is... well, to be completely honest, I don't quite know what this is.'

'From what you said, there appears to be some new evidence regarding the murder of Garth Kenyon. Is that not the case?'

'No, sir, that's not the case.'

Levitt frowned.

'I work at Southern State,' Nelson said.

'Southern State Penitentiary?'

'Yes.'

'You're a correctional officer, then.'

'I am.'

'I'm sorry, I'm not sure what—'

'I have Clarence Whitman on Death Row, Mr Levitt.'

'At Southern? I thought he was at Florida State.'

'He was, but he was transferred back at the end of September. I'm actually surprised you didn't know.'

'Why would I?' Levitt asked. 'It's a closed case.'

'But you're his defense attorney.'

'I was. And I might very well have continued to be so had my client pursued the appeal process. I went through the motions, of course, but it's mighty hard trying to help someone who doesn't want to be helped.'

'I remember hearing about the verdict being upheld,' Nelson said. 'Didn't it go to the Supreme Court?'

Levitt leaned back in his chair. 'Why are you here, Mr Nelson?'

Nelson knew there was no point playing games. If he wanted to find out the truth, then he himself needed to be truthful.

'Something's not right, Mr Levitt. I'm sure of it. Ask me what, I wouldn't be able to tell you, but I've spoken with Clarence Whitman on a number of occasions and he's a good deal different from any other prisoner who's waiting to die.'

'Do you know the significance of today, Mr Nelson?'

'Significance?'

'Today is the sixth of January. It's exactly seven years since Garth Kenyon was murdered.'

'I didn't realize.'

'You were a deputy sheriff, you say?'

'I was, yes. Over in De Soto County.'

'And can I ask why you are no longer in De Soto County?'

'I was shot, Mr Levitt. I was invalided out on medical grounds.'

'I'm sorry to hear that, Mr Nelson. And then you took a job at Southern.'

'Yes.'

'And how long have you been there?'

'A little over a year.'

'I work for the state, Mr Nelson, just as you do. Over the past thirty years I've come to know a good many police officers. Some of them are now retired. Some of them I still see every once in a while on a social basis. And you know what every one of them has in common?'

Nelson shook his head.

'The one that got away. The one case they didn't solve. The one victim that haunts the back of their mind.'

Levitt opened a drawer and took out a packet of cigarettes.

'They call it a ghost. Well, Clarence Whitman is my ghost, Mr Nelson.'

'Because you think he didn't kill Kenyon?'

'I don't know. I really don't know if he did or he didn't. It's my duty to provide as good a defense as I can, no matter what the accused has done. I've defended people I knew were innocent, a great many more that were undeniably guilty. I've represented people from every walk of life, every sector of the community, and almost without exception they've wanted the best defense possible. In my opinion, Clarence Whitman didn't want any defense at all. And we had very little to go on. Circumstantial evidence, the fact that a handful of people saw him at different times around the property, the thumbprint on a gun. And he had no alibi for the time in question. More accurately, he didn't make any effort to provide an alibi. There should have been reasonable doubt, and it should've been sufficient to throw the entire matter into question, but we had a black man accused of murdering an upstanding white man with a young wife, a man who had a good job, no criminal record, and nothing to suggest that the motive was anything other than an attempted escape after a botched robbery. We also had an all-white jury.'

'And they wanted him to be guilty.'

'They wanted justice for someone with whom they identified.'

'And you think Whitman wanted to be found guilty?'

'I have no idea what he wanted. All I can tell you is that it's damn near impossible to build a defense for someone who isn't working with you. And after his conviction, I did what I always do. I followed the protocol for appeal. I crossed the t's and dotted the i's, and yes, it went all the way to the Supreme Court. Anything less would've been negligent. But I had nothing of substance to work with, Mr Nelson. No new evidence, no other potential suspects, no doubt about the chain of evidence or the way the interrogation was carried out. Most of all, I had a defendant who wasn't playing the game. It was an administrative exercise, nothing more than that, and we got the outcome that I expected.'

'And his family?'

'Parents are alive, as far as I know. Two sisters, two brothers, all older than Clarence. He was just nineteen, Mr Nelson. Barely said a word in court, just sat there as the state prosecutor painted him in the worst possible light. He had no criminal history, no prior arrests, and yet to hear Ronald Jacobs, Clarence was a cruel teenage delinquent who took delight in shooting Garth Kenyon in the head with Kenyon's own revolver. By the time Jacobs was done, Clarence was the personification of everything that was wrong with the younger generation and a primary contributor to the inevitable collapse of modern society.'

'And what do you think, Mr Levitt? What do you think really happened?'

'I can't help you with that, Mr Nelson, and that's why Clarence Whitman is my ghost.'

53

Nelson left Levitt's office with the names of Clarence Whitman's parents and siblings. He had no current address or phone numbers on record. Levitt also knew nothing of the whereabouts of Garth Kenyon's widow, Sarah. All he could tell Nelson was that her maiden name was O'Brien. Levitt seemed to remember that she'd moved out of state, but he wasn't sure.

The conversation with Levitt had done nothing but affirm and strengthen Nelson's resolve. The need to find the truth was more addictive than any drug.

Nelson had another ten days ahead of him before he was back on Dead Watch. He would maintain his 8 a.m. until 4 p.m. shift in HS, and that would give him the latter part of the afternoon and evening to make his inquiries. Notwithstanding the possibility that Hannah needed him to run errands or take her out to Clewiston, that would be ample time to make some headway.

Nelson felt some sense of connection to Whitman, albeit misguided and far beyond the remit of his job, but he couldn't deny that it was there. What happened to Whitman was important, not only for Whitman himself but for Nelson's conscience.

*

Hannah was home.

'Where'd you go?' she asked.

'Port Charlotte. I went to see the guy that defended the person I was talking about.'

'Can you tell me when you're not going to be here?'

'Sure. I'm sorry. I just had to rush out of work to get there in time.'

'So what did he say?'

'He said it was the toughest case he's ever had to defend.'

'Because the evidence was so overwhelming?'

'Because he was representing someone who didn't appear to want a defense.'

Hannah frowned. 'Because he did it.'

'That's what I'm trying to find out.'

'So what about the original investigation? There must have been something on him or he wouldn't have been tried for it.'

'A thumbprint on the murder weapon.'

'Which was?'

'A gun.'

'And this was this person's gun?' Hannah asked.

'No, it belonged to the guy that got killed.'

'So this person stole someone's gun and then used it to kill them.'

Nelson hesitated before speaking. 'Why do you want to know all this, Hannah?'

'Because I'm interested in what you're interested in.'

'I still feel like I shouldn't be discussing it.'

'Where did you find out what you already know?' Hannah asked.

'I went to the library and looked it up in the newspaper archives.'

'So everything you're telling me is already public knowledge.'

Nelson nodded in the affirmative.

'So what harm is there in telling me what you read in the papers?'

'None, I guess.'

'So take your jacket off, sit down and tell me what you think is going on.'

Nelson told her what he knew and gave her a brief rundown on his conversation with Levitt.

'You're gonna go find his family, right?' Hannah asked.

'That's what I was thinking, yes.'

'And is there any way you can get hold of the original interrogation notes?'

'Not without breaking the law, no.'

'You couldn't maybe get one of your old Sheriff's Department buddies to do you a favor?'

'Police and sheriff are two different things entirely. Officially someone could request files, but if they did it unofficially it'd be no different than me breaking in and stealing them.'

'Which is something you're not going to do. I'm not having a baby while you're locked up in Southern.'

'I need to know you're okay with this,' Nelson said.

'I'm okay with you doing something that you feel you need to do. I'm not okay with you getting into trouble.'

'I have no intention of getting into trouble, but it does mean that I want to keep it between us.'

'You don't want me to mention it to Dad.'

'Or Ray.'

'You need to know that I'm pretty much the world's worst liar, Garrett. I won't volunteer anything, but if I'm put on the spot you can guarantee I'll crumble in the first ten seconds.'

'So this idea I have about you and I robbing a bank to pay for all the baby stuff is off the cards?'

'I'd go with that being a non-starter, yeah.'

'Good to know,' Nelson said.

'You want me to help track down some of these brothers and sisters?'

'I don't really want you to get involved, Hannah.'

'I think it's a bit late for that, sweetheart. I'm here during the day. You're at work. I can get on the phone and find some numbers and addresses and whatever.'

'But don't speak to them, okay?'

Hannah looked at him like he'd lost his mind. 'Oh, so you don't want me calling up his mom and saying, "Hey, lady. My boyfriend thinks your son might be innocent. What've you got to say about that, then?"'

'You know what I meant.'

'I may be a hyper-hormonal, mood-swinging, candy bar-craving lunatic, but I'm not altogether stupid.'

'Then yes, that would be really helpful.'

'Good. I'm glad we got that settled.'

Nelson sat back in the chair and sighed deeply.

'Do you want him to be innocent?' Hannah asked.

'I just want to know the truth. If he didn't do this, then I want to know why he's letting the world believe he did.'

54

Nelson's plan to spend the time following up on CJ Whitman's family before his next Dead Watch went to hell.

For a week following his conversation with Hannah, she was sick. At first lightheaded and dizzy, she then complained of stomach pain and immense fatigue. Nelson ferried her back and forth to the hospital in Fort Myers for tests, even took two days off work to look after her at home. Though Dr Clarke's conclusion was that Hannah was suffering from nothing more serious than anemia and a urinary tract infection, she did advise plenty of rest. They were finally sent home with iron tablets and antibiotics.

It was the 15th of January before Hannah was back-to-battery, and Nelson told her to wait until after his Dead Watch shifts before they did anything further.

From the 17th, he was on the 4 p.m. until midnight schedule on the row. Ray was on 8 a.m. until 4 p.m. in General Population. He said he'd keep an eye on Hannah and take her anywhere she needed.

Mid-morning of Wednesday, January 18, Richard Stein was finally transferred from Death Row to a secure federal facility in Fort Lauderdale. The arraignment process was scheduled for the following Monday. Whether he would be transferred back to Southern to await trial was unknown. From all accounts – none of them official – Stein hadn't given the Bureau anything of worth regarding the possible whereabouts of Jimmy Christiansen.

On Wednesday afternoon, Thomas Lancaster's execution date came down. He was scheduled for the bell tower on Friday the 27th.

Lancaster was the one who'd abducted the teenager from Brevard County Fair and then left her head and torso in a ditch off of Highway 192. He had nine days to tell someone where he'd dumped her legs. Nelson was certain he'd go to his death with no one the wiser.

Nelson also felt sure there was no possibility of a stay or reprieve for Lancaster. Lancaster knew it too, and late that same evening, around nine, the light went on over the man's door.

Opening up, Nelson was assaulted with the stench of human excrement. Lancaster had daubed the walls and sink with shit. He stood in the middle of the cell naked, and when Nelson recoiled, he just started laughing.

'This is what I think of all you motherfuckers!' Lancaster shouted. 'Fuck you, fuck your families, fuck everyone you know! I hope you all fucking die!'

The process of getting him out of there securely, transporting him to the showers, and then cleaning the cell took over two hours. Nelson had to call in other officers to assist.

Even though he was handcuffed and shackled in the washroom, Lancaster continued to shout and threaten and curse as he was hosed down. He was back in his cell just half an hour before Nelson's shift ended.

The noise and clamor that Lancaster created prompted some comments from some of the other inmates. A couple of them – seemingly aware of the murder for which Lancaster had been condemned – remarked that things would be a great deal better for everyone after the 27th.

Throughout those three days of duty, Nelson did not see CJ Whitman, aside from the evening meal deliveries. CJ did not speak to him, and Nelson didn't initiate a conversation.

Nelson arrived home close to one on the morning of the 20th. Hannah was sound asleep. Nelson merely took off his uniform and crawled into bed beside her. He was out for seven hours straight and woke to find Hannah still sleeping.

He left her a note before he departed for work.

At Southern that morning, Nelson was met with the news that there had been another suicide.

Though there was no indication that it was anything other than suicide, it would generate bad press for Greaves and Southern itself. It had only been ten weeks since the death of David Garvey.

Jackson Forsyth was twenty-eight years old. He was three weeks away from his first parole hearing, and there was every indication that the application would be successful. According to Forsyth, a young man with no prior criminal record, he had been strong-armed into driving the getaway car in a bank robbery back in late '68. The three men who perpetrated the robbery itself were all in their forties, each of them possessed of a long track record of violence, burglaries, assault and theft. Whether Forsyth's account was true or not didn't seem to matter. A bank teller was killed, a second left with life-changing injuries, and their attempted escape culminated with a high-speed police chase through downtown Miami that left a wake of destruction behind it. Finally boxed in by the police, the robbers came out guns blazing. Forsyth crawled into the passenger seat footwell as bullets tore through the body of the car. His three associates were decimated in a hail of gunfire. Somehow Forsyth survived unscathed. Forsyth was charged with the robbery, but escaped the charge of accomplice to murder. Perhaps to make a point, perhaps to satisfy the public demand that justice had to be seen to be done, he was given an eight to twelve. With a decade of model behavior behind him, the father of a nine-year-old daughter he'd not seen save through reinforced glass and steel bars, Jackson Forsyth was all set to head off into a crime-free future.

It was Southern protocol that a potential parolee was transferred to a single-berth cell for a month before his hearing. Lifers could be bitter, deeply resentful of anyone who was due for release, and incidents of intimidation and violence, spurred by nothing but jealousy, had been known.

Forsyth was found hanged after first bell on Friday morning. He'd fashioned a rope from the fabric that covered his mattress. Forsyth did not appear to have any known enemies within the walls of Southern itself, nor had he secured a shorter sentence by striking a plea deal and giving up his accomplices. There was no one to give up; all three of them had been killed as they fled the bank.

Once again, just as had been the case with Garvey, an initial examination of the cell was carried out. Due to the fact that the cell could not be opened by anyone but those on landing watch and those in Central Admin, the possibility that someone got into the cell was ruled out. The doctor signed the death certificate with suicide by hanging as the cause of death, and the coroner confirmed it. Forsyth was still a serving prisoner. He would be buried in God's Acre and the matter would be closed.

During social, it was impossible not to overhear snatches of conversation amongst the inmates in HS. The talk was that Forsyth had been murdered, and that it had to have been with the knowledge of the correctional officers or those in Central Admin.

Warden Greaves got wind of the scuttlebutt. He ordered a lockdown. He cancelled social. He gave a briefing to the complement of officers in HS that their duty was to ensure that rumors that denigrated the integrity of the prison and its internal security were to be stamped out, and stamped out hard. He did not give any indication as to how such a thing should be accomplished.

Inmates with nothing to do latched onto anything that would occupy their otherwise empty minds. Over the coming days, the air of tension did nothing but escalate. Scuffles broke out at mealtimes. A man was beaten unconscious in the shower room. Word also arrived regarding Stein. His arraignment had gone ahead as scheduled on the 23rd. The decision had been made not to return him to Southern, but instead to transfer him to Florida State until his trial.

On the night of the 25th, Nelson was over at the Montgomery place in Clewiston for dinner.

After they'd eaten, Frank took Nelson aside and said, 'This thing isn't going to calm down, you know? Soon as Greaves lifts the lockdown, the place is going to boil over.'

'Meaning?'

'A riot. Bad fucking news. My advice, take some time off. Stay away from there for as long as you can.'

'But—'

'I've seen it before, Garrett. Seen it too many times to know that it ain't something to be involved in. You're with Hannah now. That changes things. You've got a kid on the way. I feel it's my responsibility to keep you out of harm's way.'

'You really think this is going to happen?' Nelson asked.

'I can't be sure, but it wouldn't surprise me. Say what you like about Garvey, but he was respected. Feared sure, but also respected. And he sure as hell wasn't a guy I'd take for a suicide. And now this thing with Forsyth. Good kid, made a fuckin' bad mistake. A few weeks from parole and he hangs himself.' Frank shook his head. 'All I know is that when things don't make sense, there's something about the story you ain't being told.'

'If they weren't suicides, then someone had to have been—'

'Let's not get ahead of ourselves, eh? That's not the kind of thing you want people to hear you saying.'

Nelson looked at Frank. Frank held his gaze for a moment, and then looked away.

It was fleeting, nothing more than a perception, but Nelson had the definite feeling that Frank knew the missing part of the story. He also couldn't escape the notion that the deaths of both Garvey and Forsyth were somehow connected to the Independence Day riot and the escape of Christiansen and Stein. And that, in turn, made the reality of an insider – someone they knew, someone they worked with and trusted – all the more certain.

Frank put his hand on Nelson's shoulder. 'You're not my son-in-law,' he said, 'but you're as good as. I'm not having my daughter raise a child on her own. No matter what goes down, that is never gonna happen.'

55

Thomas Lancaster went to the chair like a terrified child.

This time, Nelson was not on chamber duty. He was, once again, assigned to final holding during the night of the 26th. Had Nelson not known the details of Lancaster's case, he might have been able to muster a degree of sympathy for the man. However, he did, and thus could not. Nelson didn't doubt that Lancaster had brutally raped Melanie Burnett, but taking into account the fact that he'd cut her in half, there was no way to prove it.

Lancaster did not sleep. He paced, he cried, he prayed. He asked for water and cigarettes. He talked to Nelson and to himself, repeatedly asked to see Father Donald – a request that was denied time and again – and cycled through phases of despair, rage, grief and apathy.

At one point, somewhere around two in the morning, he went into a rambling monologue about how there had to be demons inside of him. The demons had driven him to do what he did. The demons had always been there. They compelled him to take her. They wanted him to sacrifice the girl. There was nothing he could do to stop it.

Nelson tried not to listen, but Lancaster kept on going.

As dawn broke and the time of his death grew ever closer, he became more and more agitated and disturbed. Finally, exhausted with trying to contain the tornado of emotion and hysteria, Nelson called for the doctor. A mild sedative was administered. Afterwards, Lancaster didn't sleep, but lay on the bed mumbling to himself.

Nelson, frayed around the edges, longed for the end of the shift. The last couple of hours dragged interminably.

At last, with the chamber crew arriving at 7.45, Nelson was able to leave.

Once out of the building, he handed in his keys at Central Admin and walked to the car. He did not immediately drive away, but sat there in silence and allowed his mind to settle.

To Nelson, it seemed that the opportunities to focus on himself were becoming ever-more infrequent. Perhaps self-created in an effort to avoid any direct confrontation with his own conscience, his days had been filled with all the things he was duty-bound to do, rather than those things he wanted to do. He couldn't remember the last time he and Hannah had really had a day to themselves. He couldn't remember the last time they'd gone out to a restaurant or the movies. Between work, visits to Clewiston, hospital trips and errands for Hannah, his own life had been absorbed. He pursued no personal interests, he maintained no hobbies. Perhaps more telling than anything, he had no family or friends outside of those who were directly connected to Southern. Southern was his life, and even though he had taken the job voluntarily, he felt as if the consequences of that decision had not been of his own choosing.

And then there was CJ Whitman. Nelson's next Dead Watch started on February 1. There would be hours of silence and thought. Whitman would sleep, and Nelson would be out in the corridor with all his unanswered questions. It had been three weeks since he and Hannah had talked about reaching out to Whitman's family. Neither one of them had done anything to progress that initiative. He was now in two minds, though the part of him that compelled action seemed greater – even if only slightly – than the part that urged acceptance. Whitman was where he was because of Whitman, not because of anyone else. If Nelson believed that, then any effort to change that reality was neither obligated nor required. This wasn't something he wanted to do, but still the need remained. Why he felt such an impulse could be explained no more easily than Lancaster's impulse to abduct and kill a girl. Nelson had always believed himself to be a good person. He had no wish to harm or hurt; he had no wish to be anything like his own father. A man like Lancaster was the other side of the coin. He was driven by something else entirely, and the shadows that resided inside of him had eventually escaped and painted the world with darkness.

Nelson must have dozed. He was woken right there in his car by the sound of the steeple bell.

Thomas Lancaster was dead, and in truth he couldn't help but feel the world was a better place for it.

Nelson started the engine, put the car in gear, and headed out of the compound to home.

56

Warden Harold Greaves would not be a scapegoat like his predecessor, Emery Young.

The riot that broke out moments after the death knell for Thomas Lancaster was met with a level of response that was both immediate and brutal.

Nelson was already asleep when the call came in. Every serving Southern officer, irrespective of their shift, was summoned for duty.

Arriving at the compound just two hours after he'd left, Nelson was issued with riot gear and a mask. HS was already filled with tear gas and smoke. Mattresses had been set alight and thrown from the gantries. The infirmary already at capacity, wounded inmates were being brought out and transferred to General Population for treatment. Greaves had given the order that no outside agencies were to be contacted or brought in. This was a Southern situation, and Southern was going to contain it.

Entering HS in teams of three, officers had been instructed to corral inmates and get them confined. It didn't matter how they were corralled, and it didn't matter how many were crammed into cells. Via radio, Central Admin was instructed to open and lock cell doors individually as required, and people were being herded in en masse. The landings and corridors were at first impassable due to the number of people and the lack of visibility. Men already floored by the gas were nevertheless being clubbed and dragged bodily down stairways and into cells. Nelson felt that he'd stepped into Hell.

The roar of voices was deafening, beyond that the screams of men as they were wrestled to the ground, cuffed and subdued. The floors were awash with water, making steady footing an impossibility. Vision was restricted due to the gas masks, and people seemed to come from all sides. It took time to determine who they were – inmate or guard – and more than once Nelson saw a colleague go down under the club of a fellow officer.

For an hour it was relentless. Nelson, already exhausted from his shift, was driven by nothing but adrenalin and survival instinct. Twisting his ankle as he came down a stairwell, he dropped to the ground. Had he not, he would have been blindsided by an inmate wielding a chair leg. Nelson kicked out reflexively and the assailant lost his balance. Thundering down the remaining risers, the inmate lay spread-eagled on the ground, only to then be trampled by half a dozen men trying to flee a phalanx of baton-wielding officers.

By noon, the Southern High security block was back under control. Still the task of separating the men and returning them to their respective cells remained. It was done one by one, a lengthy and demanding procedure, and it went on for hours. To Southern's advantage, the fight had been beaten out of the inmates. Many were still reeling from the effects of tear gas, others were injured, some were found unconscious. There were four inmate deaths, three of them falls from overhead landings into the main area below, the last one having been trampled to death in a stampede. Only one officer – Max Sheehan – had been seriously injured. Word came back that evening from the hospital in Fort Myers. His right arm and leg had been broken, he had three fractured ribs, but the primary concern was the seven-inch length of metal with which he'd been stabbed. The entry wound was in his lower back, perilously close to the base of his spine. As of that moment, there was no indication that he would suffer any paralysis, but he was being monitored closely.

As far as Warden Greaves was concerned, he had succeeded in his primary objective. The riot had been contained, no outside agency had been employed, and the unit was under lockdown. Now he would not only instruct the massive repair and clean-up operation, but also enforce the most stringent regime of restrictions and penalties that Southern had ever seen. Social was cancelled, as were visitations, incoming and outgoing mail, exercise time, books, magazines and chaplain services. Last bell and lights out was brought forward by an hour to 9.30 p.m. All personal privileges – cigarettes, gum, drawing materials, photographs, pictures, playing cards and any personal effects – were confiscated. Men were to remain in their cells for twenty-four hours a day. Anyone giving up information that resulted in the identification of those who orchestrated the riot would be moved to isolation and their privileges would be restored. If no one came forward, then Greaves' own internal investigation would soon root out the ringleaders. The regime would continue until further notice.

As could have been predicted, no one spoke out. The code of silence was maintained. Nelson was on double shifts, as were most of the men in Alpha, Bravo and Charlie units. Dead Watch was covered by additional officers brought over from General Population. That the riot had not spread to Gen Pop was a miracle, perhaps attributable more to the fact that the vast majority of inmates had short sentences. In Gen Pop there was the promise of release, and thus a far greater unwillingness to do anything that might jeopardize it.

By the end of February, more than four weeks after the riot, Warden Greaves was still frustrated by the lack of information forthcoming about those responsible for what had happened. The consensus of opinion seemed to be that those in High Security had learned a hard but necessary lesson. Greaves was not Young. If he was crossed, he would retaliate with unprecedented force and penalties. There were those amongst the officer complement who appealed to Greaves to lift the lockdown. Greaves was at first single-minded and unmoving, but finally conceded on the basis that control could better be maintained now that the inmates knew what was at stake if they attempted anything similar.

On Wednesday, March 1, Greaves lifted the restrictions. Those men brought in from General Population went back to their former posts. The shift system and schedule that had previously existed was re-established. Starting at eight on the morning of the 3rd, Nelson was back on Dead Watch. He arrived to find that not only had Anthony Irving, a pedophile child killer from Vero Beach, gone to the bell tower on February 22, but that Clarence Whitman's execution date had already come down. Notwithstanding intervention, he was scheduled to die on Friday, May 19.

CJ Whitman had four months to live, and Nelson, caught between duty and conscience, had to decide whether he was going to do anything about it.

57

Nelson was aware that he'd neglected Hannah.

The rigors of double shifts and the demands of the Southern lockdown had not only greatly reduced his time at home, but had also meant that even when he was there his mind was preoccupied with things other than the baby. Hannah was now five months along and it showed. She no longer suffered morning sickness, and there had been no further instances of fainting or dizziness. Her latest test results had shown her blood pressure to be stably in range, no indication of iron deficiency, and that whatever infection she'd suffered had long since cleared up.

Hannah didn't want to know if they were having a boy or a girl. Nelson wanted to know, but acceded to her wishes.

'The only thing that matters is that we have a healthy child,' she said. 'There are too few surprises in life. Let this be one of them.'

On Thursday evening they were eating at the kitchen table.

'What's happening with the guy on Death Row?' she asked.

'He got his date,' Nelson said.

'When?'

Nelson looked at Hannah but said nothing.

'You can't tell me, can you?'

'No, I can't.'

'Is it soon?'

'Soon enough.'

It was Hannah's turn to be silent. Nelson looked up from his meatloaf.

'I don't know,' he said. 'Honestly, I really don't know.'

'What's changed? You seemed intent enough when we spoke about it.'

'I know. I was. Now...' Nelson shook his head. 'Now it seems like it could only make trouble.'

'For us?'

'For us. For Southern. That would then make trouble for Frank, for Ray.'

'He's got no one else, Garrett. His lawyer can't do anything unless he's instructed, and if he's a public defender then I'm sure he's buried under a thousand other cases that take priority. Just imagine if the roles were reversed.'

'That's not fair, Hannah. I didn't kill anyone.'

'And maybe he didn't kill anyone either. That's what you told me, right?'

'Right.'

'So if you were in there for something you didn't do, wouldn't you want someone to at least try. I mean, that's all we're doing, right?'

'We?'

'We've had this conversation, Garrett.'

'Why is it important to you?'

'Because he's a person,' Hannah said. 'And no, it's not hormones or motherhood filling me with some notion about the sanctity of human life. It's no different from what any decent person would feel. If something's not right, then it needs to be fixed.'

'Eleven weeks.'

'That's what he's got?'

'Yeah. Eleven weeks.'

'What's his name?'

'Hannah...'

'Say his name, Garrett.'

'His name is Whitman, okay? Clarence Whitman. CJ.'

'CJ.'

'That's how he's known. CJ Whitman.'

'And how old is CJ Whitman?' Hannah asked.

'He's twenty-six.'

'And does he have a wife and kids?'

'No.'

'And he won't take visits or letters from his family.'

'No.'

'So you really are the only one he has, aren't you?'

'Yes,' Nelson said resignedly. 'It would seem that way.'

Hannah put down her fork and sat back in the chair.

Nelson had lost his appetite.

'When will you see him next?' Hannah asked.

'Tomorrow morning.'

'Talk to him, then.'

'We're not supposed to talk to them, Hannah.'

'We're not supposed to do a lot of things, but that doesn't mean we shouldn't do them.'

'And what is it that you would like to know, sweetheart?'

'Don't be facetious, Garrett.'

'Okay, I'll talk to him. Happy now?'

'Yes, I am. Now stop sulking and eat your meatloaf before it gets cold.'

58

'We missed you,' CJ said.

Nelson stood at the open door of the cell and looked at Whitman through the bars. It was Saturday night. It had taken Nelson a day to summon the will to speak to him.

'I was busy,' Nelson replied.

'So I heard.'

'From the replacement guards.'

CJ smiled. 'No, man, it was all over the news. We all sat around and had a beer and chilli dogs and watched it on TV.'

'What did you hear?'

'That shit went crazy. That you've had everyone on lockdown for a month. I'm guessin' the folks in HS didn't win the war, right?'

'No, they didn't.'

'I'm guessin' you also heard that I got my date.'

Nelson nodded in the affirmative.

'Goin' to church for the very last time, eh?'

Whitman's expression didn't change – that same calm acceptance in his eyes, an expression that George Levitt must have seen so many times during the trial.

'Do you want to die, CJ?' Nelson asked.

'That's the first time you've called me that.'

'That's how you're known, right?'

'It was, yeah. Before here. Now I'm just a number like everyone else. And no, Mr Nelson, I don't want to die.'

'Then why are you accepting it? Why no appeal?'

'What good would it serve? They got me painted wrong before I even opened my mouth.'

'And you've just accepted that there's nothing you can do about it.'

'I ain't accepted nothin' but the inevitability of the thing. That's a monster out there. A big fucking monster an' it's got teeth and claws, and once they feed you into it there ain't no way you're wrestlin' free.'

'But you're not even struggling,' Nelson said. 'The other men here—'

'The other men here might be in the same place, but they ain't here for the same reasons. We're all different. We all got different histories and different circumstances, an' just because we're all gonna die doesn't mean we're anything alike.'

'I didn't mean that.'

'I know what you meant.'

'I can't understand how—'

'You don't need to understand anything, Mr Nelson. It ain't your job to understand an' if I were you, I wouldn't go makin' it your job.'

'But if you didn't kill that man, then what? You're going to die and the person who did it is just gonna get away with it?'

'Now why would you think I didn't kill him? What the hell's put that notion in your head?'

'Because—'

'Because what? Because I ain't fightin' it? Because I didn't want no appeal? Because I don't want my family around here worryin' themselves crazy about the injustice of it all?'

'Because you don't seem like the kind of person who could kill a man.'

Whitman smiled. 'You ever kill anyone, Mr Nelson?'

Nelson didn't reply. The answer was in his expression.

'Well, you don't seem like the kind of person who could kill a man neither.'

'I killed someone in self-defense,' Nelson said.

'You don't have to tell me nothin' about it. What happened is between you and God.'

'Do you believe in God, CJ?'

'Whether or not I believe in God don't matter much. Anyways, I'm gonna find out soon enough, ain't I?'

'Last time in church.'

'Yes, siree.'

'What will you do if there's a stay?' Nelson asked.

'There ain't gonna be no stay.'

'If there was. Say something happened and there was.'

'And why would you ask that, Mr Nelson? You got a mind to make something happen?'

'It's a hypothetical question, CJ. Nothing more.'

'Well then, I guess we'd have a little more time to continue our conversations before I got a new date, wouldn't we?'

'And what if I wanted to do something to help?'

Whitman looked at Nelson. A light of defiance flared in his eyes. For the first time, Whitman showed some emotion that was neither reconciliation nor acceptance.

'Only thing you can do to help me is nothing,' Whitman said. 'I ain't askin' for your help or anyone else's. I know you got a good heart, Mr Nelson, but there's only one thing I've ever asked of you and that ain't gonna change.'

'You want me to be there when you die.'

'That's right.'

'And if I'm not willing?'

'That's your decision, Mr Nelson. And maybe you have no say in the matter. Maybe even if you ask, you ain't gonna be on duty that day or whatever. But, aside from that, I don't want anything from you.'

'Okay.'

'I guess you better shut the door now. Before anyone finds out you've been fraternizing with the condemned again.'

Nelson stepped back and closed the door.

Later, driving back to Port LaBelle, Nelson knew he'd made his decision.

Despite all that Whitman had said, he was now resolved to find out what happened in January of 1971 and why a man he believed to be innocent was going to the bell tower.

59

Before Nelson left on Monday 6th, Don Trent told him that Max Sheehan was being moved from the hospital in Fort Lauderdale to Fort Myers, the same hospital where Hannah had been treated, and where in all likelihood she would give birth. Nelson figured he would make the time to go see Sheehan. They had worked together for more than a year, and it was the very least he could do. Had Hannah still been working, she more than likely would have been one of his physiotherapists.

Arriving home a little after five, Hannah told him that she'd been to the library.

'I read all about it,' she said, and handed Nelson a slip of paper. 'And that's where his parents live.'

'How did you find this?' Nelson asked.

'I called Information.'

'Hannah, I really don't want you to—'

She smiled artlessly. 'Too late.'

'Okay, but—'

'I made you some sandwiches and a flask of coffee. If you get changed quickly and start out now you could be there by seven.'

Nelson smiled. 'Am I being sent on a mission?'

'I guess you are.'

'You know, I have no idea what we're getting into,' Nelson said. 'It might be a whole world of trouble.'

'I know you've already decided, Garrett. You're gonna go ask them some questions. That's all you're gonna do right now. Depending on what they say, you can make another decision, and then another.'

'What kind of sandwiches are they?'

Hannah smiled. 'Considering I made them, they're probably gonna be the best you ever had.'

Nelson headed north to Palmdale and joined 27. He would go as far as Lake Josephine and then head west into Wauchula on 66. The junction of the two highways was a handful of miles from Sebring, the place where all of this had started. He thought back to that morning, how he'd left home like any other day, how he'd stopped en route to pick up coffee and share a few words with April in the diner on Lakes Avenue. Had he not been in work that day, had Eugene Bigsby not sent him out to Highlands County, had he been posted in some other location, then he wouldn't be where he was right now. Against that was the fact that he would never have met Hannah, and he wouldn't be four months away from fatherhood. Life turned on a dime.

Just as Hannah had predicted, Nelson reached the outskirts of Wauchula at 7 p.m. He pulled into a gas station and asked for directions. The Whitman place was just three or four blocks away.

He found the house without difficulty. It was a single-storey shotgun house, but wider than most. The yard was well maintained and the paintwork fresh. CJ's parents evidently prided themselves on the appearance of their home.

The woman who opened the door was clearly Dorothy Whitman. The resemblance between her and CJ was striking. She looked at Nelson through the screen door. Her expression was one of caution.

'Yes?' she asked. 'Can I help you?'

'Mrs Whitman?'

'Yes. What do you want?'

'I wondered if it would be possible to speak with you about your son.'

'Which one?'

'Clarence, ma'am. I wanted to ask you some questions about Clarence.'

Dorothy looked at him askance, immediately suspicious. 'Who are you? Police? I've had more than enough of the police, young man.'

'I'm not police,' Nelson said. 'I know your son from Southern.'

Dorothy's surprise was visible.

'Wait there,' she said, and closed the door firmly.

Moments later the door opened once again. Floyd Whitman looked Nelson up and down and said, 'What are you doing here? Why you askin' questions about Clarence?'

'Because I want to help, Mr Whitman.'

Floyd sneered dismissively. 'That boy, he's beyond all help.'

'Why do you say that, Mr Whitman?'

Floyd paused for a moment and then shook his head resignedly. 'You ain't police.'

'No, sir, I'm not police.'

Floyd hesitated once more as if considering whether this was something he really wanted to deal with.

'I guess you better come on in,' he said, and opened the screen door.

When Nelson told Floyd and Dorothy Whitman how he knew their son, the tone of the conversation changed dramatically.

The air of suspicion was gone, and in its place was nothing but interest and a heartfelt concern for CJ's welfare.

'He thinks he's saving us by not letting us visit,' Floyd said, 'but that's about as far from the truth as you could get. He won't see any of the family, and he and his brothers and sisters were as close as could be. He won't accept mail and he hasn't written a word to us in all the time he's been in prison.'

'It's like he's pretendin' to himself that we don't exist,' Dorothy said.

'And we've got some kind of idea why he might want to do that, Mr Nelson, but I gotta tell you that it sure as hell ain't doin' us no good.'

'Does he ever speak of us?' Dorothy asked.

Nelson couldn't lie to them. 'No, Mrs Whitman. Like you say, he acts like he doesn't have a family.'

'We tried to visit him in Raiford,' Floyd said, 'but he wouldn't see us there neither. We left letters for him and they got sent back. Maurice, my eldest, even went to see the Warden there but the Warden told him that folks in prison don't have to see visitors if they don't want to.'

'How did you find out that he'd been transferred to Southern?' Nelson asked.

'We just got a letter from the Bureau of Prisons,' Dorothy said. 'I mean, we're his next of kin so I guess there's some sort of requirement that they let us know when he gets moved.'

'Yes,' Nelson said. 'He came to us at the end of September.' He wondered if the Whitmans knew that CJ had received an execution date. He should have asked, but he couldn't bring himself to do it.

'How is he?' Dorothy asked. 'Is he all right?'

'He's okay, Mrs Whitman,' Nelson said. There was nothing else he could say.

'You see him every day?'

'No, ma'am. I am in that section of the prison every couple of weeks.'

'On Death Row,' Floyd said.

'Yes, sir. On Death Row.'

Floyd sat back in the chair and lowered his head. He put his hands together as if in prayer, and then he looked up at Nelson.

'I still don't know what happened. None of us do,' he said. 'He was a good boy. Hard worker. People liked him. I mean, he wasn't never gonna go to college or whatever, but he had a mind to make something of himself. Had his heart set on moving to Miami and starting some business or other. All that yard work and fixin' things was just a means to make some money. He saved a good deal, as well.'

'And he worked for the Kenyons, right?'

'He did, sure. Worked for them for a good while.'

'And do you know anything about them?'

'Nothin',' Floyd said. 'He said they was nice folks, but then Clarence was the kind of person who said that everyone was nice folks.'

'And he never said anything about any difficulties with them? You never heard him angry about something that might have happened?'

Dorothy leaned forward. 'He was here when they came to get him, Mr Nelson. He was right here when the police came through the door and put him on the ground. They dragged him out of here like he was some kind of wild animal. He didn't fight them. He didn't say a damned thing. He just let them take him away and that was that. Next thing we heard he'd been charged with that man's murder and he was going to trial.'

'Did you go to the trial, Mrs Whitman?'

'We all went. The whole family. We was there every single day watching that thing and he never looked at us more than once or twice. It was like we wasn't even in the room.'

Nelson took a breath. There was a question he had to ask, and there was no good way to ask it.

'Do you think your son could have killed Garth Kenyon?'

'Any man can kill another man,' Floyd said. 'Just because he can doesn't mean he would.'

'I'm talking about this situation, this murder. Do you believe that CJ went to rob that house and wound up killing that man?'

'I'll tell you something, Mr Nelson. This was a good few years back. We was goin' through a tough time. I'd lost my job and we was strugglin' to put food on the table. Clarence and his brothers were cleanin' cars and deliverin' papers and whatever else they could do to help out. One time I sent Clarence down to the supermarket to get some groceries. I give him a ten-dollar bill. He comes back and he gives me the change and there's too much. Whoever was there gave him a couple dollars more than they should have. What did Clarence do? He took them dollars and gave them back. The man down there gave him a quart of milk for being honest. On the lives of all my children, that's a true story. Clarence would no more rob a man's house than he would fly to the moon and then come on back for supper.'

Nelson left the Whitmans with the names and addresses of CJ's four siblings.

The brothers – Maurice and Errol – shared a house and ran an auto shop together in Punta Gorda. Alma was married. She lived in North Port with her husband and a four-year-old daughter. The youngest sister, Jennifer, had apparently never settled. Last they'd heard she was singing in nightclubs in Port Charlotte. She called and visited often enough, but she never seemed to put down any roots.

The last words from Floyd Whitman as Nelson went out the door and down to his car were, 'Next time you see my boy, tell him his family loves him. And whatever he might or might not have done, he's still as much a part of this family as he ever was.'

60

Arriving at Southern the following morning, Nelson immediately sensed that something was awry.

It wasn't long before he tracked down Frank and asked him what was going on.

'Word got out about the riot,' he said. 'That got someone interested enough to start asking questions. They found out about Garvey and Forsyth. Two suicides in two months. That's a personal best for Southern. Add into the mix the ones that got killed in the riot, and Greaves has one fuck of a headache. Bureau of Prisons is sending some pencil pusher to check things out.'

'Is there gonna be trouble for us?' Nelson asked, aware of how naïve he sounded even as the words left his lips.

'Depends on whether they find anything. Seems plain as fucking daylight to me that the pair who offed themselves don't make a great deal of sense.'

'Garvey was on my landing,' Nelson said. 'They're gonna want to talk to me, for sure.'

'You weren't on that night, were you?'

'No, but I was here when they found him. I was doing a couple of hours extra some of the mornings that week.'

'Then it ain't your shit to shovel, is it?'

'Unless someone makes it so.'

Frank leaned forward and lowered his voice. 'Look, it's simple. You saw nothing, you heard nothing. You weren't on duty when Garvey killed himself, and Forsyth was not on your landing. As for the riot, Greaves ran the whole operation. We just followed orders. When he got here, he took away supervising officers, unit leaders, everything. He wanted to be the big boss of the hot sauce, so now he gets to deal with this shit on his own. To Greaves, every single one of us is the same, and we're all subordinate to him. Well, that might be fine while everything's running smoothly, but it didn't, did it? Now he gets to clean it up.'

'Understood,' Nelson said. 'Keep me up to speed, okay?'

'Will do,' Frank said. He put his hand on Nelson's shoulder. 'We look after our own, Garrett. We close ranks. All of us. Never forget that.'

Nelson watched Frank walk away with the definite impression that what Frank had said and what he'd meant was not the same thing at all.

A while later, Nelson was in the commissary with Don Trent. Conversation turned to the Bureau inspection, and it was Trent who raised the subject of Jackson Forsyth.

'Everyone keeps asking themselves why he would hang himself when he was so damned close to release,' Trent said. 'That's the point though, isn't it? He was getting released. I mean, you can't do anything but make a guess, but there's been noises.'

'Noises?'

'Idle minds, maybe, but until the truth comes along then people're gonna fill the vacuum with whatever they can.'

'So what have you heard?'

'Nothin' that I haven't heard before. Man gets released, sometimes he's gotta take care of things on the outside for someone.

People get protection in here, you know, and then there's a debt to be paid.'

'You think that's what was goin' on?'

'Wouldn't be the first time. Maybe he was supposed to be doing something when he got out. Maybe he changed his mind. Maybe he got scared and told someone. The guy had a wife and a kid out there. Someone on the outside gets to them. Word comes back to Forsyth that if he doesn't send in drugs or help set up an escape or whatever, then they're gonna make things bad for him and his family. He goes along with it, then all of a sudden he decides he can't do it or maybe he goes to the Warden. That's the fuckin' end of Jackson Forsyth.'

'And Garvey?'

'I don't know, Garrett. It's a stretch to think they're connected, but who the hell knows, eh?'

'But for someone to get into either cell, there had to be someone on the landing or in Central Admin who opened the doors.'

Trent looked at Nelson. He didn't speak, but the look in his eyes said everything.

'Do you really believe that someone would—'

'Like I said,' Trent interjected. 'I been here long enough to know what people are capable of, an' I ain't just talking about the ones who are locked up.'

Nelson had spent the majority of his life in the shadow of corruption. Ever since his father's suicide, it had been like a memory he couldn't forget. No matter which way he turned, no matter how hard he tried to believe that it was all behind him, it was not.

Perhaps his reluctance to have anything to do with his own mother wasn't only because he didn't want to be reminded of their history, but also because he couldn't convince himself that she'd been unaware of what her own husband was doing. The money he spent, the things he bought – this could not have come solely from a sheriff's salary. They were married for more than twenty years. Could someone remain ignorant for that long? Or was it a case of selective blindness? People see what they want to see, and so very often convince themselves that what's right in front of them is something else entirely. It was human nature to give people the benefit of the doubt, but all human beings were not the same. There were those who trusted others until given a reason not to, and there were those who trusted no one until they had proof that they weren't going to be betrayed.

An hour before he left that day, Nelson received word that a Bureau of Prisons inspector would be coming to Southern on Thursday. His focus would be High Security and the events since Greaves' arrival. Word went through the ranks rapidly. Just as Frank had said, the message was clear. Garvey and Forsyth committed suicide. The riot was successfully contained in a matter of hours. The fatalities were as a result of other inmates, not the correctional officers.

Just as there was a code of silence between those incarcerated at Southern, so there was a code amongst those who worked there.

Nelson had nothing but unfounded rumors. Don Trent had done nothing but substantiate them with further suspicions. It was instinct that told Nelson that something was wrong, just as was the case with Clarence Whitman. Now he felt surrounded by shadows, and the feeling of being closed in by them was suffocating and claustrophobic.

Yet again, CJ's words came home with greater significance than ever. Maybe he was just as much a prisoner as the men behind bars.

61

On Wednesday evening, Nelson drove out to Punta Gorda to see Maurice and Errol Whitman.

He didn't call beforehand, knowing full well he might not find them at home or in their auto shop. He felt it was better to take that risk that rather than forewarning them and being told not to come.

Reaching the outskirts, he knew that if he kept on driving for another ten minutes, he would have been in Murdock. Seemed that whichever direction he took and no matter which way he turned, the ghosts of his past were waiting for him.

The Whitman auto shop was a modest little business on the Charlotte Harbor side of town. The roller doors were up, and there were men in overalls working under the glare of portable lights. Somewhere in the back was the flash and spark of an oxyacetylene burner.

Nelson got out of his car and crossed the street. A young man saw him coming and smiled.

'I'm sorry, mister,' he said. 'We're actually closed.'

'I was hopin' on seein' Errol or Maurice,' Nelson said.

'Maurice ain't here right now. Should be back soon. Errol is in the office.'

'Through there?' Nelson said, pointing to a doorway on the left-hand side of the garage's interior.

'Hang fire, let me go check.'

Moments later, Errol Whitman came out of the doorway and onto the forecourt.

Had Nelson seen him in the street, he would have looked twice. Errol, though a little taller, was the image of CJ, so much so that they could have been twins.

'Mr Whitman,' Nelson said. 'My name's Garrett Nelson. I was hoping you might have time to speak with me.'

'My pa called me,' Errol said. 'I know who you are.'

Nelson didn't respond. He stood waiting for an invitation into the office. He felt awkward and out of place.

'Let's go inside,' Errol finally said. He turned, a sense of resigned inevitability in his body language, and Nelson followed him through the doorway.

Seated in the cramped office amidst mountains of paperwork, boxes of auto parts, a small refrigerator and a copy machine, Errol seemed ill at ease.

'I have no idea what you're tryin' to do,' he said, 'but if you're tryin' to help him, then good luck with that.'

'That's pretty much what your parents said.'

Errol shook his head. 'Didn't make sense then, and it sure as hell don't make any more sense now. I mean, we're not much more than a year apart. Grew up livin' out of each other's pockets. Hell, all of us did. Maurice ain't here right now, but he'll tell you the same. Whitman kids were their own little tribe. Then this happens, and hell if he don't make us all feel like we ain't blood no more.'

'No mail, no visits—'

'Nothin'. Zero. Like hollerin' into a hole and waitin' for an echo that don't come.'

'Do you have any idea why he's doing this?'

'We didn't talk about much else for the first year or so. He was up at Raiford. We figured he was trying to distance himself, you know? Like he thought that cutting all ties would somehow make it easier when it... well, you know, when he...'

Errol stopped talking. He breathed deeply. There were tears in his eyes. When he again spoke, his voice cracked with emotion.

'No one 'cept someone who's been in the same situation could ever understand what it feels like to know your own brother, your own flesh and blood, is gonna be executed. I mean, I gotta be honest, I had no issue with the death penalty. We're church people, always have been, and it's all eye-for-an-eye an' all that. He who lives by the sword should die by the sword. And then it happens to someone that's kin and there ain't no way to feel about it 'cept it's wrong. To make matters worse, if they could be worse, he seems to have just folded up and accepted it like... well, like he wants it to happen.'

'That's how it seems to me, Mr Whitman.'

'You talk to him, right? You see him down there at Southern?'

'I do, yes.'

'He talk about us?'

'No, Mr Whitman, he doesn't. To be honest, he doesn't talk about much at all.'

'He gone crazy or what? I mean, them people are in their cells most every hour of every day. That's gotta do somethin' to a man's mind, right? That ain't gonna do anything but mess him up bad.'

'He's not crazy,' Nelson said. 'I don't know what to tell you. He's quiet, polite, even calm. Like you said, it just seems that he's accepted his fate and there's nothing anyone can do to help him.'

Nelson glanced to the right as the door opened.

The man in the doorway was altogether different from Errol

– shorter and heavier-set – but the similarity in features was undeniable.

'You the feller from Southern?' Maurice asked.

'I am, yes,' Nelson said.

Maurice came in and closed the door.

'I came here to talk about Clarence,' Nelson said.

'Why?' Maurice asked.

'Because there ain't a great deal about this whole situation that makes sense.'

Maurice closed the door and leaned back against it.

'I spoke to your parents a couple of nights ago,' Nelson said. 'I was just talking to your brother here about why Clarence won't see you and why he won't take any mail.'

'If you think we got better answers than you, then you're wastin' your time,' Maurice said. 'We been askin' ourselves the same thing for seven years now. Why won't he appeal? Why won't he talk to anyone? What really happened back then?'

'What do you think happened?' Nelson asked.

Maurice looked at Errol, and then back at Nelson.

'Somethin' happened, that's for sure,' Maurice said. 'Seems to me only three people really know, and one of them is dead.'

'Garth Kenyon.'

Right. 'And then there's Clarence and the widow. And Clarence ain't sayin' shit.'

'And she's gone, man,' Errol said. 'Over the horizon. We tried findin' her a while back, but she's like a fucking ghost. I mean, I can understand why someone might wanna move away after something like that happened. We did our best, but we had no luck trackin' her down.'

'I can try,' Nelson said.

'You don't think he killed that man, do you?' Errol asked.

'I don't know,' Nelson replied. 'Your father said that any man is capable of killing another man. I see people every day who've killed plenty. All I can say is that Clarence—'

'Clarence just don't fit,' Maurice interjected.

'That's as good a way of saying it as any,' Nelson replied. 'Something about it is wrong, and I have no idea what it is.'

'So what are you plannin' on doin'?' Errol asked.

'Keep looking,' Nelson said. 'See if I can find Kenyon's widow.'

'Only thing I was able to find out was that she had folks in Bartow,' Maurice said. 'Never got to see 'em, and I have no idea if they're still there. That lawyer, Levitt, was the one who tracked them down but they wouldn't talk to him. Seems everyone who might know something is keepin' their mouths shut tight.'

'I'll see what I can find out,' Nelson said.

'How long you been out there at Southern?' Errol asked.

'A year,' Nelson said.

'And before that?'

'I was in the Sheriff's Department over in De Soto County.'

'Why you no longer there?'

'I got shot in the leg. Can't run worth shit anymore.'

'So you know people,' Maurice said. 'People who might be able to find this woman.'

'Officially, no.'

'But then you ain't here on official business are you, Mr Nelson? And that makes me wonder why you're doin' this. What's in this for you?'

'For me?' Nelson asked. 'There's nothing in it for me.'

'One thing I learned in this life, no one ever does nothin' 'cept when there's somethin' in it for them. Usually that'd be money, but there's a whole world of reasons out there.'

Nelson looked at each man in turn. He felt the blood rising in his face.

'To make amends,' Nelson said. 'Maybe that.'

'Amends for what?' Errol asked. 'What did you do? Kill a man?'

'No,' Nelson replied, 'but I guess you could say that I let a man kill himself. Maybe I could've stopped it happening. I don't know. Maybe nothing would have been different. I didn't try, that was all. I could've tried and I didn't.'

'That'll do it,' Maurice said. 'Burden of guilt.'

'Is that the same for Clarence?' Nelson asked. 'Is that why he's willing to die?'

Maurice shook his head resignedly. 'I have no idea. But you find out, you be sure and let us know.'

62

Under the spotlight of the Bureau investigation, Nelson erred on the side of caution and held off pursuing any further leads relating to CJ Whitman.

Beginning on the Thursday morning, the interviews, second interviews, requests for inmate reports, briefings, and all else that the internal inquiry required, went on for the better part of a month.

The duty roster in High Security went to Hell. Once again, staff from General Population were drafted in to cover for those who were being questioned. On two occasions, Nelson had Ray Montgomery on shift with him.

Southern was subdued. There was no other way to describe it. Though it was quieter than Nelson had ever known it, the tension was palpable. Patience was frayed at the edges, tempers were short, but no one raised a voice or clenched a fist.

Nelson's own interview was relatively perfunctory, all things considered. He was asked questions about other officers, about Wardens Young and Greaves, about the days leading up to both the July and January riots, the escape of Jimmy Christiansen and the others, the deaths of David Garvey and Jackson Forsyth. Sitting in front of three Bureau of Prisons officials, he felt neither paranoid nor anxious. The tone of the inquiry was businesslike and methodical. That he'd only been at Southern a year meant that the answers he could provide were minimal.

At one point, giving substance to Don Trent's hypothesis about Forsyth, Nelson was asked whether he was aware of any relationship that might have existed between Forsyth and other inmates.

'Relationship?' Nelson had asked. 'In what way?'

Raymond Gould, the Bureau inspector who seemed to be leading the proceedings, responded with, 'What we're looking at, Mr Nelson, is that there may have been some pressure brought to bear upon Jackson Forsyth, something that prompted his suicide.'

'Pressure to do what?'

'That is what we're trying to ascertain.'

'Forsyth was not on my landing,' Nelson said. 'I knew of him, of course, but the landings are kept pretty much separate as far as their management is concerned.'

And so it went on. Though there was no direct reference to officer corruption or collusion in the riots, the deaths, the escape itself, Nelson came away with the definite impression that the inspectors believed there was an insider, and they were intent on identifying him.

On Wednesday, April 5, the inspectors packed up and left. How long it would take for them to summarise and publish their findings wasn't known, but Southern seemed to breathe a sigh of relief.

Greaves made it clear that officers should not engage in discussions about the inquiry, but that was altogether unrealistic. Southern and all that happened within its walls was their business, their collective livelihood, and Greaves, Warden or not, had no authority concerning what they could or couldn't say.

Nelson hadn't been on Dead Watch throughout the entire period. His next scheduled shift would begin on April 17. He knew that when he next saw CJ Whitman, they would be a month from his date in the bell tower.

Foremost in his mind was finding Garth Kenyon's widow. Having spoken to Whitman's parents and both his brothers, he didn't believe that they could provide anything beyond what he already knew. That, in essence, was nothing save confirmation that CJ had seemingly put up no resistance, no rebuttal, no defense.

The day after the inspectors left, Nelson completed his shift and went home. He told Hannah that he planned to go to Bartow to see Sarah Kenyon's parents. He'd gotten their address from Information and he didn't want to delay.

'I think we need to spend some time together,' she said. 'You've been really stressed recently and I feel like I hardly see you.'

'I know,' Nelson said. 'This whole inquiry thing has been playing on my mind. But it's over now. Maybe things will get back to normal.'

'What's happening with that?'

'The inquiry? What do you mean?'

'Dad's been kinda weird. Maybe it's just me, but . . .' Hannah shook her head. 'I don't know. He's not himself. And he asked me about you.'

'What about me?'

'If you talked about work at home. If you'd spoken about this inquiry that's going on. He also asked me if you'd ever mentioned someone called Max.'

'Max Sheehan?'

'He just said Max.'

'The only Max I know is Max Sheehan.'

'And who's he?' Hannah asked.

'He is – was – one of the guys on my crew. He was injured in the riot. They had him in Fort Lauderdale, but now he's been moved to Fort Myers. I was plannin' to go see him.'

'He's okay?'

'He's alive, sure, but I'm pretty sure he won't be coming back to Southern.'

Hannah didn't say anything. For a moment, it seemed she was altogether elsewhere.

'What is it?' Nelson asked.

'I've seen Dad and Ray out in the yard a couple of times. They're obviously talking about something pretty important. Ray's not the kind of guy to get wound up, but he seems really stressed too.'

Nelson thought back to Garvey's suicide. Sheehan had been the first up there. Sheehan had also been on duty that night. However, his reaction to the discovery of Garvey's body was of a man appalled and upset.

Had something happened that Frank knew about, and did it somehow involve Max Sheehan? Why else would Frank be asking his daughter if Nelson had mentioned Sheehan's name?

Nelson pushed the questions out of his mind. His priority right now was CJ Whitman. He had a month, and he needed to find Garth Kenyon's widow.

'I'm running out of time,' Nelson said. 'If I'm going to stay on this thing with Whitman, then I need to stay on it. When it's over, whatever the outcome, we'll take some time out, okay? We'll go somewhere, even if it's just down to the Keys for a few days.'

Hannah put her arms around him, turning her body slightly so as not to put pressure on the baby.

'I don't want to make a choice, Garrett,' she said.

'A choice about what?'

'Between us and my family.'

Nelson looked down at her. 'Why would you say that?'

'I feel like something bad is going to happen,' she said. 'Or maybe something bad has already happened and my dad was involved or he knows about it. Don't ask me why, and maybe it's just me being crazy, but sometimes you get a sense of something and you can't get it out of your mind.'

'I don't think anything bad is gonna happen,' Nelson said, 'and if it already has, then I don't think your dad was involved.'

'I'm not saying that he's done something. I'm just saying that knowing about something and not making it right can be just as bad.'

'Do you want me to stay tonight?' Nelson asked.

'No,' Hannah replied. 'Go to Bartow. This needs to end.'

63

Nelson headed north, on up through Sebring and Avon Park, until he hit the intersection of 60 outside of Lake Wales. He was in Bartow by 8.30 p.m.

Throughout the journey he'd tried his best not to ponder questions that couldn't be answered. There were pieces of a puzzle, and yet none of them seemed to fit. Perhaps they were all unrelated. Perhaps there was no bigger picture to see. Maybe what he was feeling – a profound sense of disquiet – was attributable to the Whitman case, impending fatherhood, the pressure of a month spent under investigation by the Federal Bureau of Prisons. Prior to Southern his life had been his own. He'd built walls around himself, refrained from socializing, making friends, getting married, raising a family. He didn't believe that madness was hereditary, but he did appreciate that living your life around crazy people could only have a detrimental effect. That effect was not only intimate and personal, it also served to color one's perception of all people. There was an innate distrust, and only since he'd met Hannah had it started to ease and surrender. Now it seemed to be back in full force. He was questioning not only himself and his perspective on recent events, but now a seed of doubt – about Southern, about Max Sheehan, even Frank Montgomery – was haunting the edges of his mind. He was indeed surrounded by ghosts, and he had to ask himself whether these ghosts were entirely of his own creation and without substance. Time would tell, but time – for Whitman, for Hannah's pregnancy and the attendant concern that everything would be okay, even for the findings of the Southern inquiry – seemed to have become his enemy. He felt crowded and claustrophobic, yet by nothing he could see or touch.

Hannah was right – it had to end.

The reception from Sarah Kenyon's parents was, at best, unsympathetic.

Howard O'Brien opened the door and said, 'Whatever you're sellin', we're not interested.'

Nelson mustered as warm a smile as he could manage.

'Mr O'Brien?'

'That's me. And who are you?'

'My name's Garrett Nelson. I wondered whether it would be possible to ask you a few questions?'

'You from the police?'

'No, sir, I'm not.'

'What are you, then? A reporter?'

'No, sir, I've come up from Southern. I wanted to ask you if you knew the whereabouts of your daughter.'

O'Brien didn't speak for a few seconds. His expression darkened, and then he shook his head disapprovingly.

'You're one of them so-called human rights people who keep hammerin' on about the death penalty, aren't you? What about the human rights of the victims, eh? You seem all too eager to forget about the terrible things some of these people have done—'

'No, sir. I work at Southern. On Death Row.'

'Is that so?'

'Yes, sir.'

'That's where he is now, isn't it? The one who killed Garth.'

'Yes, he is.'

'I heard they moved him from Raiford. He not dead yet?'

'No, he's not, but he will be in about a month.'

'Hell of a waste, eh? All that money bein' spent keepin' them people alive. Take them out the back of the courtroom and shoot them in the damned head, that's what I say.'

'You're probably right there, Mr O'Brien,' Nelson said, at this point willing to say pretty much anything if it got him in the door.

'So what do you want with my daughter... what d'you say your name was?'

'Nelson. Garrett Nelson. I just wanted to find her, that's all. I had a couple of questions that I thought she might be able to answer.'

'Well, I guess you best get yourself inside,' O'Brien said.

Rosalyn O'Brien, a nervous, rail-thin woman, hovered around the kitchen as if she didn't know whether to stand or hide or run away.

O'Brien asked Nelson to sit.

'I'd offer you a drink, but you ain't gonna be here long enough to finish it,' O'Brien said. He then turned to his wife. 'Rosalyn, let me and this feller here have a few words. You go on upstairs and do some laundry or something.'

Rosalyn, without a word, left the room.

'She's an anxious woman,' O'Brien said. 'Always has been. I love her dearly, but she don't ever settle. Drives me crazy sometimes, but what can't be cured must be endured, right?'

'I apologize for not calling you,' Nelson said, 'but I didn't want you to tell me not to come.'

'Well, you're here now, son, so why don't you say what's on your mind.'

'I know this man, the one that killed Sarah's husband,' Nelson explained. 'He's going to the electric chair in the middle of May. That's the law, an' I have no issue with it. If I did, I sure as hell wouldn't be working at Southern. But there's things that trouble me about it, Mr O'Brien, and most of that has to do with the fact that he's never made any effort to defend himself or pursue the lines of appeal that are available.'

'I guess some folks know what they've done and just accept the penalty.'

'Not the ones I've met, Mr O'Brien.'

'So what are you saying, Mr Nelson? You think this boy didn't do it? Seems to me they had him bang-to-rights. That was Garth's gun. Had Whitman's prints on it. And he knew Garth and Sarah. From what I understand, he was there plenty of times doin' yard work an' whatever else.'

'But he wasn't a thief, Mr O'Brien.'

'No one's a thief until they want somethin' they can't get any other way.'

'Do you think that Clarence Whitman killed your son-in-law, Mr O'Brien?'

'Not my question to answer,' O'Brien said. 'That's for the police and the courts to decide. They had their evidence, they did the trial, jury found him guilty. As far as I'm concerned, that's the end of it.'

'And what did Sarah think?'

'Sarah never spoke about it. Didn't then and doesn't now. A month after Garth's death she was gone. I guess I could understand that. I mean, it was a hell of a thing. You wouldn't want to stay in the house where your husband was killed, would you?'

'Where did she go?'

'Last I heard she was in Georgia.'

'Last you heard? She doesn't keep in touch with you?'

O'Brien sat back in the chair. He shook his head and sighed audibly.

'I guess, in a way, Sarah takes after her mother. Fragile. That's the word I'd use. She's our only child, Mr Nelson.' He paused, looked at Nelson. 'You have children?'

'Not yet,' Nelson replied. 'I have one on the way.'

'Well, when they get here you'll understand what I mean. There's a bond there. Doesn't matter who they are or what they do, that bond can never be broken. There's something of yourself in them, and you can't erase it. You want them to be happy. You want them to live a good life. Sometimes that don't happen, and it's a raw deal.'

'You think she wasn't happy in her marriage?'

O'Brien shrugged. 'You sense things, I guess. What someone says and what's really going on ain't always the same thing. Garth was … well, he was older than her, sure. She was just eighteen when they got married. He was twenty-six or thereabouts. He had a good job, he had some money, drove a fancy car, an' I guess as far as Sarah was concerned, he was the best she was ever gonna get. I didn't have to like him. That's not to say that I didn't, but he was the kind of person who wanted things to be a certain way, you know? He wasn't much for conversation, neither. All the years they were together we never really got beyond pleasantries. I know Sarah wanted children. I figure he didn't because they never had any. They lived their own lives, we lived ours, and the more time that passed, the less we saw of either of them. Hell, they only lived down there in Wauchula, but it might well have been the other side of the moon.'

'Do you think Garth didn't want her to see you?'

O'Brien frowned. 'Why would you ask that?'

'Maybe there was something going on between them that he didn't want you to know.'

'What, like he was violent towards her or something?'

'I don't know, Mr O'Brien, but it seems strange that your daughter would get married and then just vanish out of your lives.'

'I think maybe you're trying to write a story that ain't there, Mr Nelson. I think if he'd been violent towards Sarah, we'd have known about it. And she didn't vanish. We knew where she was, and my wife spoke to her on the telephone every Sunday afternoon like clockwork.'

Nelson didn't say what was on his mind. Abuse and mistreatment was not always violent. He only had to think of his own parents' relationship.

'Okay,' Nelson said. 'So, last you heard she was in Georgia. And you've not seen her since the trial?'

'She came here once. Two years ago. Showed up out of the blue. Said she was passin' through. She was here a day, and then she was gone.'

'And how did she seem?'

'Herself. On edge, a little nervous. Aside from that, she seemed okay. Sarah is a sweet, kind girl, but she ain't never gonna set the world alight.'

'Did she give you an address?'

'I have a phone number, that's all,' O'Brien said. 'I've called it a few times, but no one has answered.'

'If you'd be willing to give me that, it would be really appreciated.'

'Sure, I can give it you, but I don't hold out much hope you're gonna get anywhere, Mr Nelson. Seems to me that she don't wanna be found.'

O'Brien got up, and, just like Floyd Whitman, he said, 'But if you do find her, you tell her we love her. We're her family, and no matter what's happened she'll always be welcome here.'

Nelson had a theory – unfounded, unsubstantiated, based on nothing more than a collection of suspicions and possibilities – but if he was right, then it would explain why CJ was so unwilling to talk about what had happened on January 6, 1971.

Nelson also knew that he'd go all the way to Georgia to track down Sarah O'Brien, but he wasn't going out there until he had something more than a two-year-old phone number.

Irrespective of what he believed, he had to be cautious not to make everything fit some pre-determined conclusion. He had to maintain an open mind. So often in police work, an assumption was made and then later facts were manipulated to fit that initial hypothesis.

Arriving home after the return journey from Bartow, Hannah was still up.

'You found them?' she asked.

'I did, yes.'

'And they know where the daughter is?'

'No. Last they heard she was in Georgia. They've seen her once since the trial. Her father gave me a phone number. He's called it a few times but never reached anyone.'

'So she's just vanished off the face off the earth?'

'Seems that way.'

'Well, she's gotta be somewhere, hasn't she? We just have to find out where that is.'

'I want you to call the number in the morning,' Nelson said.

'Why me?'

'So if someone answers the phone, you can pretend that you're an old friend of Sarah's. See if you can find out where she's gone, if there's a forwarding address.'

'Am I being deputised to the deputy?'

'You are.'

'Do I get a badge or something?'

Nelson smiled. 'I'll ask.'

'So, are you coming to bed, or are you gonna sit up and do some more sheriffin'?'

'Bed,' Nelson said. 'I'm beat.'

64

'I spoke to someone,' Hannah said when Nelson got home on Friday. 'Called again and again, and finally someone picked up.'

'You found her?'

'No, not Sarah,' Hannah said. 'And the person I spoke to didn't give me anything helpful.'

'What happened?'

'It was a woman. I told her I was an old friend of Sarah's and we'd lost touch. I just said that this was the last number her folks had and I wondered if she was still there or if there was a forwarding address.'

'And what did they say?'

'She said that there was no one there of that name, that I should stop calling, and that the person I was looking for didn't want any contact with anyone from her past.'

'So this person knows her?'

'It would seem so, yes.'

'So we need the address for that phone number. Maybe I'll get some more information if I turn up in person.'

'Or if *I* turn up in person.'

'What?'

'I want to come. Like you said, a woman is better. It's less intimidating, especially being pregnant an' all.'

Nelson opened his mouth to say something.

'Let's not have whatever conversation you're intent on starting right now, Garrett. If you're going all the way to Georgia, then I'm coming with you.'

'We're talking four hundred miles here, Hannah. That's six hours or more just to get to the state line.'

'Well, you're not working this weekend, are you? Did you have something special planned?'

In a last-ditch effort to dissuade her, he said, 'But what if something happens on the way?'

'With the baby? I'm pregnant, Garrett, not an invalid. Okay, so we need to stop for the restroom a few more times than usual, but I want to come. I want to get out of this place, even if it's only for a day or so.'

Nelson knew he couldn't win, and so he gave up trying.

Nelson called Information. He told them he was the Deputy Sheriff of De Soto County. Once he gave his badge number, they were more than happy to oblige. The phone was registered to an address in Thomasville. Hannah wrote it down as Nelson repeated it.

Planning a route together, Nelson figured it would be a good eight hours on the road.

'Let's go now,' Hannah said.

'What are you talking about?'

'It's still early. We can do three or four hours, find a motel, stay overnight, do the rest in the morning. If we start out again after breakfast, we could be there by lunchtime. It's either that, or a straight eight hours tomorrow.'

It made sense, and – once again – Nelson couldn't argue with the logic. The prospect of a single run all the way to Thomasville was daunting.

'It'll be our first vacation,' Hannah said.

'More like a long road trip with a guarantee of nothing at the end.'

'Yeah, but think how lucky you are. Once again, you get my undivided attention for a whole day.'

'I didn't consider that.'

'We can decide on some names. We choose three each, both boys and girls. If we do that in the first hundred miles, we can spend the rest of the time arguing until you give up.'

'Well, that's really something to look forward to.'

'I'll get us a change of clothes,' Hannah said.

'And dinner?'

'We'll get something on the way,' she said. 'That way it's a dinner date as well.'

They left before seven. Nelson figured they could make it as far as Ocala and then find somewhere to stay.

For those hours as they drove north, they spoke about the baby, about the future, about the possibility of buying a home together. They did not speak of CJ Whitman, of the bell tower, nor of an execution date that was rapidly approaching. Thoughts of Frank Montgomery and Max Sheehan, the blood-spattered cell of David Garvey, the lifeless body of Jackson Forsyth hanging from the window bars with a makeshift rope around his neck, the endless hours in the everglades as they looked for any sign of Jimmy Christiansen and his fellow escapees, seemed to slip from his mind.

Nelson lived in two worlds. That's how he felt. To be away from that – even for a short while – was a welcome reprieve.

65

Nelson sat in the car at the side of the road in a town he did not know.

Across the street, the mother of his child was talking to a stranger about a woman who'd apparently disappeared.

Perhaps in her early thirties, dark-haired and taller than Hannah, she was listening but seemed to be saying nothing in response. Looking down, her arms folded, everything about her body language implied defensiveness and anxiety.

Hannah glanced back at the car a couple of times, and even though Nelson couldn't hear what she was saying, he knew she was doing everything she could to convince the woman that they weren't here to cause trouble. Or perhaps they were. He did not know.

The conversation continued for just a few minutes, but time seemed to stretch and bend in such a way as to make it seem like forever.

Finally, and much to Nelson's surprise, Hannah looked right at him and waved him over.

Nelson hesitated, and then he got out of the car and crossed the street.

Hannah, smiling, said, 'Garrett, this is Caroline Southwell.'

'Miss Southwell,' Nelson said. He did his best to appear as relaxed as possible, but it was a challenge. Inside, he was a fury of unanswered questions, and he wanted to ask them all at the same time.

Caroline smiled, but it was forced and uncertain.

'I don't know about this,' she said. 'I really don't think this is a good idea.'

'We're not here to make things difficult, Miss Southwell,' Nelson said. 'You have my word on that.'

'I appreciate that, but I still don't understand why you're here.'

'Because we're trying to help someone,' Nelson said.

'And what if the person you're trying to help doesn't want to be helped?'

Hannah reached out and put her hand on Caroline's arm.

'Do you think it might be better if we went inside?' she asked.

Again, Caroline hesitated. She looked at Hannah, at Nelson, and then she nodded her head once.

'Okay,' she said. 'But if I ask you to leave then you have to leave.'

'Of course,' Nelson replied.

Caroline Southwell sat in a chair by the window.

Against the light she was little more than a silhouette. Regardless, she seemed to exude an aura of paranoia.

'I won't tell you where Sarah is,' Caroline said. 'That would be... well, it would be a betrayal. I made a promise, and I always keep my promises.'

'I can understand why she would want to move as far away as possible,' Nelson said. 'Why she would want to disconnect from everything that happened.'

'Yes,' Caroline replied.

'I can't even begin to imagine what she must have gone through,' Hannah said.

'I wouldn't wish it on my worst enemy,' Caroline replied. 'It very nearly destroyed her. I mean, there were times when she thought of taking her own life.'

'And we have no wish to cause her any more distress,' Nelson said. 'We just want to know what happened.'

'But why? After all this time? It's over now. That's the main thing. She survived it, and though what happened is heartbreaking, there's nothing anyone can do to change it.'

'You're right,' Nelson said, 'but there's things that don't make sense and I would really like to understand them.'

'What doesn't make sense? He did what he did. That was who he was. Sarah could have been killed, you know? I really believe he was that crazy. A truly dangerous man. He was the worst kind of human being, and as far as I'm concerned, he got what he deserved.'

'To be honest, I really don't know anything about him,' Nelson said.

'Well, people wear a face for the world, don't they, Mr Nelson? There's who they want everyone to believe they are, and then there's the truth. That man could lie so easily. No conscience, no consideration for anyone's feelings, nothing. He smiles and he says nice things, he does his job, he goes to church, and all the while he's manipulating and twisting everything to suit his own interests. I don't understand it myself. Maybe it's not possible to understand. I mean, why would someone want to control people like that?'

Nelson was struggling. What he was being told and his own experience, though limited, didn't seem to connect with the picture Caroline Southwell was painting of CJ Whitman.

'The description you're giving me and what I understand are two different things,' Nelson said.

Caroline laughed, but it was not out of humor.

'And there's the trick. That's what he did. And he had this… this ability. I don't know what else you'd call it. If there was a disagreement or an argument or something, even if he was in the wrong, somehow he'd manage to twist it all around so you'd end up apologizing to him. It would leave you confused, you know? You'd begin to doubt your own recollection of events. Sometimes you wondered if you were going crazy.'

Caroline took a deep breath.

'But, there it is. It's done and over with. She got away with her life and most of her sanity. Now she just wants to be left alone. It's taken a long, long time for her to come to terms with it all, but she's a survivor. And I have to be honest, Mr Nelson. No matter what it is that you're trying to do, I won't do or say anything that brings that trouble back into her life.'

'No one's trying to cause any trouble for her,' Hannah said. 'We just wanted to understand what happened so that there isn't any more injustice.'

'Injustice?' Caroline asked. 'Is that what this is about? The world is filled with injustice. If that's your reason for being here, then I think you've made a wasted journey.'

'Is it possible that you'd give her a message from us?' Nelson asked.

'I don't know,' Caroline replied. 'I guess it would depend on what it was. You have to understand that with everything that she's going through right now, she doesn't want to be reminded of it at all. To be honest, I don't even talk to her about it. She cries a lot. She's heartbroken, as you can probably appreciate.'

Nelson frowned. 'I'm sorry, I don't understand. Heartbroken about what?'

'About the fact that he's going to die.' Caroline looked at Hannah. 'She told me you work at Southern. You do know that they're going to execute him, don't you?'

'But you have just told us how evil he is, how he manipulated and controlled her.'

'You thought I was talking about Clarence?' Caroline asked, her tone incredulous. 'Clarence rescued her, Mr Nelson. Clarence was her savior. I wasn't talking about Clarence. Lord forbid! I was talking about Garth.'

66

For almost an hour, Nelson didn't speak.

Trying to recall every word he'd shared with CJ, he was grappling not only with an understanding of what had happened, but also the sense of defeat that came with the knowledge that he could do nothing to avert the inevitable.

Clarence Whitman had killed Garth Kenyon. Clarence was going to die. Driven by whatever sense of duty or love he felt for Sarah O'Brien, Clarence had killed the man that was tormenting her. It was not self-defense, nor even a crime of passion. It was murder, plain and simple. Considering the nature of Garth Kenyon's apparent intimidation and emotional persecution of his wife, nothing could be proven. He had not beaten her, had not locked her in the house, but the echoes of his own father's attitude and conduct towards his mother made Nelson very aware that mental and emotional abuse could be just as devastating as anything physical. The scars were hidden and unknown. If you spoke of it, you could be refuted. In a way, it was the very worst kind of punishment.

After detailing the unrelenting psychological abuse that Garth Kenyon had inflicted on Sarah, Caroline Southwell had said little else. Despite further questions from both Nelson and Hannah, she remained constant in her resolve to exclude Sarah from what was now happening. She did not divulge details regarding whatever relationship might have existed between Clarence and Sarah, though it was clear from the way she spoke of him that it was something of substance. She referred to Clarence's death as a sacrifice, for that's what it was. Clarence was giving up his own life having already saved the life of another. If ever there was an injustice, this was it, but Nelson knew he was impotent.

Caroline did allow that she and Sarah had been friends for a long time. They were close before Garth Kenyon made his appearance. Garth had then driven a wedge between them, as he'd done with Sarah's family and other friends, and it was only after Garth's death that she and Sarah were once again able to reunite. When Sarah moved away from Wauchula, Caroline went with her. Then and now, she felt it was her responsibility to do everything she could to protect her friend from further distress and pain. The fact that CJ was now going to be executed for killing a man who had set out to destroy any hope Sarah might have had of happiness was the last, crushing blow. In a way, Caroline said, one nightmare had ended only for another to begin. Sarah knew she couldn't change the course of events, but that didn't make it any easier.

Hannah had asked if Caroline would tell Sarah that they'd visited. It might be that Sarah wished to relay a message to Clarence through Nelson, if only to say goodbye. Hannah gave her their phone number.

Caroline said she would think about it. She promised nothing.

Hannah let Nelson drive. She could see his mind was elsewhere, and she didn't interrupt his thoughts.

It was only as they crossed the Florida state line that she broke the silence.

'He's going to die, isn't he?' she said. 'And there's nothing we can do about it.'

'He killed Garth Kenyon. No matter the reason, that's what he did. And no, there's nothing we can do about it.'

'And his silence?'

'I don't know,' Nelson said. 'I can only guess that he wanted to protect Sarah. If Garth Kenyon was really as bad as he sounds, then I imagine CJ felt she'd been through enough. She was a victim, too, after all. Maybe the prospect of dragging her back into all of this with endless appeals and Lord knows what else was the last thing he wanted.'

'He loved her,' Hannah said. 'He must have done.'

'Enough to die for her,' Nelson replied.

'It's heartbreaking.'

'It's a travesty. It isn't justice. I don't know what it is.'

'When will you see him again?'

'Nine days,' Nelson said. 'I'm on Dead Watch on the 17th.'

'I can't bear to hear you call it that. It's just too morbid.'

'I'm sorry. That's just what it's called.'

'Are you going to tell him that we spoke to Caroline?'

'I don't know.'

Nelson didn't say anything for a while.

'What is it?' Hannah asked.

'Thinking about Southern,' Nelson said. 'How much longer I can do this.'

It was Hannah's turn to be quiet. The road stretched out ahead of them like a ribbon and the atmosphere in the car was tense.

'If you want to quit...'

'I can't, Hannah. We have a baby on the way.'

'You can,' she replied. 'There are other jobs. I have a little money saved. We would manage.'

'I need to think about it,' Nelson said. 'I need to think about a lot of things.'

'Whatever you decide, we're in this together. You do know that, right?'

'I do, yes. And the only way I'm coping with this is because I've got you.'

'And you can't think about what Dad or Ray or anyone else might say. You have to make your own decision.'

'I know.'

Nelson felt Hannah looking at him. He kept his eyes on the road.

'There's something else, isn't there?'

'He wants me to be there.'

'Who?' Hannah asked.

'CJ.'

'When he's executed?'

'Yes.'

'Oh my God, Garrett. He actually asked you to be there?'

'He did.'

'Why?'

'He said I was the only person that really treated him like a human being.'

'And what did you say?'

'I didn't say anything, Hannah. I didn't know what to say. I was speechless.'

'So, what are you going to do?'

'Hope that it's not my choice, I guess.' Nelson sighed and shook his head. 'All this time I've thought he was innocent. I had no explanation for his silence, his unwillingness to defend himself, the fact that he didn't even try to give an alibi, but that didn't change the fact that I genuinely believed he wasn't the one who shot Garth Kenyon. Now I know he did, and now I have an idea why he's willing to die for it, it changes things. It can't help but change things. And I think he'll refuse to have his family there. Sarah won't be there, that's for sure. If it were me, would I want someone there who understood what really happened? I think I would.'

'But we don't have to be the only ones who know what happened, Garrett. Talk to that lawyer – what was his name?'

'Levitt.'

'So talk to him, tell him what we've found out about Garth Kenyon.'

'He'd need proof. As it stands, it's hearsay. It's one person's testimony against another's, and one of them is dead. Garth Kenyon can't deny anything. Not even Caroline can help in that regard because all she knows of Kenyon is from Sarah. By the time they got back together, Kenyon was already dead.'

'So talk to CJ. Tell him we came out here. Tell him that he needs to explain what happened. It might be enough to get a stay, and then maybe we'd have time to find people who could corroborate what Caroline told us about Kenyon.'

'You're forgetting one thing.'

'What?'

'CJ already knows what happened. He already knows about Kenyon. Seven years, and he hasn't said a word in his own defense. This is a man who wants to die, and I don't think anything's going to change that.'

Hannah didn't reply. She looked out of the window to her right. Nelson understood her frustration and despair. He felt exactly the same way.

67

Called into a briefing on the morning of the 19th, Nelson found Don Trent, Frank Montgomery and a half dozen other officers waiting in silence.

'What the hell's going on?' Nelson asked Frank.

Frank shook his head, indicated that he should just take a seat and wait with the rest of them.

Nelson caught a worried glance from Don Trent as he did so.

Minutes passed. People Nelson had never seen before walked back and forth past the office. Every once in a while, someone would pause and glance in through the narrow window in the door. They appeared to be counting the men inside, perhaps taking a mental note of who they were, and then moving off.

A good twenty minutes elapsed. No one spoke. The room was filled with cigarette smoke.

Finally the door opened. One after the other, a line of five men came into the room without a word. Four of them stood with their backs to the wall, one of them stood front and center. Everything about him said Florida Bureau of Investigation, and when he spoke, Nelson's assumption was confirmed.

'I am Senior Special Agent Richard Carlson. The men behind me are also Florida Bureau agents. We are here to conduct a formal investigation prompted by the most recent Bureau of

Prisons internal inquiry. The findings of that inquiry are yet to be published. They will not be made public, however, and you are all under the strictest orders as federal employees not to discuss any matters pertaining to our presence here.'

Carlson paused for a moment to let his final words sink in.

'Evidence has come to light that an officer within this correctional facility was compromised as a result of personal situations. Instead of reporting this matter, the officer in question chose to engage in a conspiracy with individuals both inside and outside this prison. His actions, ill-advised and illegal, both directly and indirectly resulted in the escape of three men, one of whom appears to have been murdered by his accomplices, the others going on to commit three further homicides. One of those men is now in custody at Florida State and will be tried in due course. The second of those men continues to evade capture. Beyond that, we are investigating the circumstances of two reported suicides. The officer in question was injured in the most recent riot here at Southern—'

'You're talking about Max Sheehan, aren't you?' Frank asked.

Carlson ignored the question. 'Rumors will no doubt be widespread, but I must caution you that if information pertaining to this investigation is relayed to the press or to any other individuals outside the employ of Southern State, then not only will the person responsible lose their job, but prosecution to the full extent of the law will be pursued and will be successful.'

'Is this all you're going to tell us?' Don Trent asked.

'In the course of individual interviews, we may divulge specifics about the events I have outlined,' Carlson said, 'but that will merely serve to give context to the questions we are asking. And, once again, this is a federal matter, and as employees of the federal government, you are required to maintain absolute confidentiality, even between yourselves. Is that clear?'

There was a murmur of acknowledgement from the gathering.

'Very good. As far as your own duties are concerned, it will be business as usual until you hear otherwise.'

'Is Warden Greaves staying?' Frank asked.

'I am not able to answer that question, Officer—?'

'Montgomery,' Frank replied. 'Not able or not willing to answer it?'

Carlson didn't respond.

'Seems to me that if Young got the chop for what happened back in July, Greaves is gonna go the same way.'

Carlson visibly tensed, and then he seemed to change his mind about what he'd planned to say. For a second, the brusque and businesslike persona yielded.

'Let me be straight with you,' Carlson said. 'I appreciate that you want to know all the details. I also understand that you're a team, that you work side by side, that you perhaps socialize outside the prison. If I were in your place, I'd be asking the same questions. However, we don't have all of the answers. Until we do, we have to make sure that innuendo and rumor don't influence your recollection of events. Not only that, but your professional reputations and the reputation of Southern State as a whole is in the spotlight. If we don't deal with this as discreetly and conscientiously as possible, then we're going to have a media feeding frenzy on our hands. I don't know about you, Officer Montgomery, but the idea of journalists camping in my front yard and hounding my family for statements is the last thing I'd want.'

'Okay,' Frank said. 'What you're saying makes sense. I'm not disagreeing with you. But, as a courtesy and as one federal employee to another, I think we deserve to know a little more about what's happened here. You don't have to work here. You don't have to wonder whether someone you know and trust has been involved in this. Are we talking about Max Sheehan?'

'Yes, Officer Montgomery. Mr Sheehan is currently under investigation for his involvement.'

'And is that why he was injured in the riot? Did someone try and kill him to keep him quiet?'

'That would appear to be the case, yes.'

'Okay, so the thing we need to know, and this is just for personal security and assurance, is whether the person who tried to kill him was one of us or one of them.'

'I assume when you say "them", you mean one of the inmates.'

'Yes.'

'Everything we have, though not a hundred percent conclusive, tells us that Sheehan was attacked by an inmate.'

It was Don Trent's turn to ask questions, and he seemed as determined as Frank to get some answers.

'So, Max got into some trouble. I'm guessing it was financial. He gets compromised, and he was the one who helped engineer the escape of Christiansen and the others.'

Trent looked to Carlson for an acknowledgement. Though he said nothing, the fact that he gave no denial was answer enough.

'And you're also telling us that he was implicated in the deaths of Garvey and Forsyth, right?'

Again, there was neither confirmation nor denial from Carlson.

'He must have opened the cell doors,' Frank said. 'Either from the landing or from Central.'

'And the person who killed Garvey and Forsyth is still here?'

Carlson looked down at his shoes. He seemed to be gathering himself, trying to give the group of men a response that would end the questions without giving up any further details.

'It's Cain, isn't it?' Frank asked. 'It has to be Cain. Christiansen and Stein were s'posed to get him out. Forsyth was involved somehow. I'm guessin' he was meant to be the man on the outside after his release. They all fucked up, and Cain—'

'The investigation is ongoing,' Carlson interjected. 'We are confident that the identities of all those involved will be revealed in time.'

'That's what we're getting?' Trent asked.

'I'm sorry, gentlemen, but at this stage that's the most I can give you. All I can ask for is your cooperation, your patience and your agreement to maintain confidentiality. This is a matter for the Florida Bureau, the Bureau of Prisons and for Southern itself. Until we have pursued all lines of investigation and are ready to make any kind of public statement, what has happened within these walls needs to stay within these walls.'

With that, Carlson and his men left the room.

'This is bullshit,' Frank said. 'This is gonna be another fuckin' whitewash. They aren't interested in the truth. They just want to make sure that their own asses are covered. If Sheehan helped Christiansen and the others escape, and if he really did open up cells so someone could get in there and kill Garvey and Forsyth, then I guess he gets whatever's comin' to him. But that doesn't do us any good right now, does it? If Cain can get Garvey, Forsyth and Sheehan, then who the fuck knows what else he's capable of.'

'Frank, we've got two landings crammed with fucking psychopaths,' Trent said. 'We don't know who killed them.'

Frank shook his head resignedly.

Echoing Nelson's own thoughts, he said, 'For fuck's sake, I think I've had just about as much of this shit as I can handle.'

'I agree,' Trent said, 'but what you gonna do? Quit? Like the man said, it's business as usual. There's gonna be Feds all over this place. They're gonna do whatever they have to do. Maybe we'll get all the answers, maybe we won't. Seems to me that Cain or whoever killed those guys isn't gonna be killin' anyone else for a while, right? Just get your heads down, do your jobs, and we'll see what the deal is when the dust has settled.'

Frank sighed heavily. 'Yes,' he said. 'But I sure as shit ain't gonna get fucked over on this. I'm not so far from retirement. I wanna make sure I get there.'

'Why the hell would you get fucked over?' Trent asked.

'Because this is our prison, Don. These people are our fuckin' responsibility. Good or bad, whatever happens here falls on us. You don't think they're gonna be lookin' for scapegoats. We already lost Young. They brought Greaves in an' there's been more shit in six months than there was in the previous fuckin' decade. You think they're gonna wanna admit that they made a mistake?'

'I think you're taking this too personally,' Trent said. 'I don't think anyone's gonna be gunning for us. They got Sheehan. Garvey and Forsyth are dead. Stein is in Florida State, and it's only a matter of time before Christiansen shows up and they either arrest him or kill him. They're gonna do everything they possibly can to contain this. If they throw a bunch of us under the bus, then they're running the risk of us talking to the press, filing for unfair dismissal, God only knows what. I agree with you. This is bullshit. But it will end. It always fucking ends. We know we weren't involved. Let them do their jobs. Hell, let them do their worst. We stick together. We back each other up. That's all we need to do.'

Frank nodded. 'Yes,' he said. 'It just makes me so fuckin' mad.'

'You've done thirty years,' Trent said. 'A few more and you're out of here. Hang in there. We've seen storms before, and we've survived. This might be the worst yet, but we'll come through it, just like we always do.'

Frank got to his feet.

'Right,' he said. 'Back to work. Stay on it, watch each other's backs, eyes everywhere. I sure as hell do not want to hear that someone else got killed on my watch.'

68

Frank Montgomery's admission that he'd had enough of Southern – even if it was nothing more than a knee-jerk response to the stress of the situation – gave Nelson hope that he himself might be able to walk away from the job.

In the subsequent days, all the way through the weekend, it seemed that every aspect of the prison's routines and security protocols were under the microscope.

Whatever Carlson may have hoped, the fact that he'd relayed only a handful of details regarding Sheehan served to fuel the fire of rumor and speculation. The Southern grapevine bore fruit, and it was bitter and unpalatable.

Some said Sheehan was a gambler, others said he was doing drugs; yet more said he had a mistress, or that he was seeing hookers. In the absence of fact, there was a vacuum, and that vacuum was rapidly filled with all manner of hearsay.

On Sunday evening, Nelson and Hannah went for dinner at her parents' place in Clewiston. Afterwards, as had become their routine, Nelson, Frank and Ray went out on the back porch to have a drink.

Ray, never having been posted anywhere but General Population, had heard fragments.

Frank, one of the longest-serving officers at Southern, had

worked every line and called on every resource possible to ascertain what he could.

'I don't know what he was into,' he said, 'but he was compromised. That we know for certain. Whoever got to him was connected to Christiansen. We can assume that it was Sheehan who got Christiansen the key to the infirmary.'

'And what about Garvey and Forsyth?' Nelson asked.

'We're tyin' stuff together here,' Frank said. 'Maybe we're all wrong, but as far as I can tell, Christiansen was supposed to get Cain and Garvey out. Maybe Sheehan knows who killed Garvey, and the Feds'll get it out of him. Forsyth was involved somehow, maybe to be another external contact for Cain's escape. Whoever was working for Cain outside got to Forsyth's wife. They made it clear that Forsyth had no choice but to help them. Of course, Forsyth had all the up-to-date info they needed. Layout, shifts, officers' names, everything. Difference here was that it looks like Forsyth reported it. I'm guessing he spoke to Max Sheehan. He wouldn't have known that Sheehan was in Cain's pocket. Anyway, my guess, for what it's worth, is that both Cain and Christiansen can implicate Sheehan in everything and vice versa.'

'And you think Sheehan knows where Christiansen is?' Ray asked.

'I very much doubt it,' Frank said. 'Christiansen will be moving. He won't be hangin' around any place for long, that's for sure.'

'Jesus Christ,' Ray said. 'Remind me never to accept a transfer to HS.'

'It's a rat's nest,' Frank said. 'I've spent more than thirty years of my life dealing with these assholes. They're a different breed.'

'Have you had enough?' Nelson said.

Frank looked at him, and there was a profound tiredness in his eyes. 'I think I have. I didn't think I'd ever say that, but this last year has been a fucking burden on me. I mean, hell, it ain't a job you look forward to, that's for sure. You do it out of duty, a sense of… what? Responsibility? Because you believe in the law? Because you have faith in the justice system and you think you can make a difference? That's all well and good if you're dealing with people who know the difference between right and wrong, but we ain't, are we?'

Frank lit a cigarette and reached for his beer.

'I am fifty-nine years old,' he said, 'and I am fucking worn out.'

'Take your retirement, Dad,' Ray said. 'Fuck it. What are you gonna lose if you go now? A few thousand dollars a year from your pension. You ain't ever gonna sit around watching daytime TV and tellin' war stories. You'll do something else. I know Mom would love to have you out of there. She talks about it all the time.'

Frank smiled. 'Your mother has been talking about it since Kennedy was elected.'

'So, why don't you?' Ray asked.

'Because now is not the right time. I think I know enough of what happened to leave it behind, but walking out now is gonna leave a question in peoples' minds.'

'About what?' Nelson asked.

'About whether I've gone into hiding.'

'Who gives a fuck what people think, Dad?'

'I do, Ray. I do. I give a fuck. You don't give three decades of your life to something and not feel a sense of obligation to it. Southern is all I've known since you were babies. I've done a good job. I've done it to the best of my ability. If I walk away, I want to go with my head held high and the knowledge that I didn't bail out when it got tough. You may not understand that, but that's who I am.'

'I understand it,' Nelson said. 'It was the same in the Sheriff's Department. If I'd have had a choice, I'd have stayed.'

'That's right,' Frank said. 'That's what I'm talkin' about.'

'But I don't know that I can stay much longer,' Nelson said. 'I'm gonna be a father. That's something that I never expected. I have a duty to Hannah and a duty to our child to be out of the line of fire, if you know what I mean.'

'You're a good man, Garrett,' Frank said. 'I know you've only been at Southern a little while, but you proved yourself as well as anyone could. You have to make your own decisions, and you can't let anyone else dictate or influence what those decisions might be.'

Frank reached out and closed his hand over Nelson's.

'I'm biased, sure, but Hannah's my only daughter. I know how much she loves you. I know that you and her are gonna have a great future together. If you stay at Southern because you're concerned about what I might think, what anyone might think, then set that aside. What I think doesn't amount to a hill o' beans in the face of what's right for my daughter.'

It was as if every nerve in Nelson's body had been wound to breaking point, and then with those few words had been suddenly released. The relief he felt was immediate and profound.

'So I'm gonna be left high an' fuckin' dry?' Ray said. 'Last man standing.'

'You're in General Population, Ray,' Frank said. 'You don't know shit.'

Ray pretended offense, and then started laughing.

'Hang in there for a little longer, Garrett,' Frank said. 'Let's get through the other side of this, at least.'

'Sure,' Nelson said, knowing full well that the real reason he would stay was CJ Whitman.

Nelson had made a decision. Tomorrow morning he would tell Whitman about the trip to Thomasville, about Caroline Southwell, but most of all he wanted to hear from CJ's own lips that he'd killed Garth Kenyon for love.

69

'You ain't never gonna stop bein' a cop, are you?' CJ said. 'I mean, to even do that in the first place, I guess it's gotta be in your nature.'

Nelson had taken the chair along the corridor and set it outside CJ's cell. They were looking at one another face-to-face through the bars.

At first, there had been anger, and then CJ had fallen quiet as Nelson told him what he thought had happened. CJ neither refuted nor denied anything. He did what he'd always done and stayed quiet.

'It's my nature to find the truth,' Nelson said. 'How I do that doesn't matter.'

'And say all of this is true, what difference does it make?' CJ asked. 'Don't change the fact that the man is dead, and it sure as hell don't change the fact that I'm gonna die too.'

'But there's mitigating circumstances,' Nelson said. 'If we can get a stay of execution, that will give us time. Maybe Sarah would be willing to come forward—'

CJ leaned forward. He gripped the bar with his hands. He looked at Nelson with such defiance that Nelson felt himself withdraw.

'You leave her be, you hear me? She's gone. She's away from all of this, has been all these years, and that's how it's gonna be.'

'But—'

'But nothin', Mr Nelson. That's the end of it. And even if she was willin', which she wouldn't be, then they'd have to hear me out too, wouldn't they? I'd have to give my version, and that's the version they'd wanna hear. They already got me for this. I already been tried, convicted and sentenced. They gonna execute me, Mr Nelson, and that ain't never gonna change, no matter what you try and do.'

'You killed Garth Kenyon to protect her,' Nelson said. 'If what her friend said is true, then he was a cruel and dangerous man.'

'Prove it.'

'I can't.'

CJ let go of the bars and sat back in the chair.

'Then you're chasin' shadows, Mr Nelson. You know it, I know it, and you're just too damned stubborn to accept it.'

'I don't want to see a man die for doin' the right thing,' Nelson said.

'Who says it's right? You? What you think is right and what the law says is right ain't the same, then. She could've gone to the police. She could've left him. She could've done a whole lot of things, but she didn't.'

'She couldn't,' Nelson said. 'My mother was in the same situation...'

CJ smiled knowingly. 'Oh, so now we're gettin' to the heart of it. This isn't about me or Sarah or any of this. This is about you.'

'No, it's not, CJ. It's not about me at all. I just meant to say that I know how someone can get trapped in a situation like this, how they can become so frightened and intimidated that they're incapable of doing anything to change it.'

'You're makin' amends for your own failure.'

'I don't see it that way.'

'Because you don't want to see it that way, Mr Nelson. People say evil is the hardest thing we ever have to face. I don't agree. I think it's the truth.'

Nelson was frustrated. He felt it welling up inside him. He was trying to remain calm, to be reasonable, but he was up against a man who'd made a decision that would never change.

'This is not your life, Mr Nelson,' CJ said. 'It's mine. More importantly, it's Sarah's. You want to know if I loved her? Yes, I loved her. She's the only person in my life that I ever truly loved. I was angry and hurt and confused and desperate. I knew what she was going through, and I knew she couldn't do anything about it. No, he didn't hurt her, not physically, but the hurt he caused was deeper, even more cruel, and it was killing her. It was like watching someone being tortured to death. There weren't any bars or locks, but she was in prison, and it was a far worse prison than this. And so when he came home that day, she wasn't there. I was working, fixin' somethin' in the house. He wanted to know where she was. I had no idea. He said he'd told her he was comin' home, that she should be there, that she didn't have permission to leave. He got a gun, Mr Nelson. He got a fuckin' gun and he said he was gonna find her and kill her. I believed him. I actually thought he was that crazy. What was I gonna do? Let him murder her?'

CJ closed his eyes and lowered his head.

'No, Mr Nelson. That wasn't never gonna happen.'

'So you took the gun from him and shot him?'

CJ didn't respond. He didn't need to.

'Do you want me to get a message to her?'

CJ looked up. 'No, Mr Nelson. I want you to leave her alone.'

Nelson had to admit defeat. He had to accept what was going to happen with the same reconciliation as the man in front of him. How he would do that, he didn't know, but – as CJ had said – he was chasing shadows and they would never be caught.

'There's only one thing I have ever asked of you,' CJ said, 'an' I already told you what it is. Even more so now, Mr Nelson. Because, aside from Sarah, you an' me are the only people who know the truth of what really happened.'

70

Throughout the subsequent two days of Nelson's shift, he and CJ didn't speak. Even when Nelson delivered his food, CJ took it in silence.

Perhaps Nelson had known all along that this would be the outcome, but still he resisted it. The senselessness of what was happening was irreconcilable. It was justice, at least by the standards of law, but it was neither equitable nor fair. The judicial machine was without conscience or mercy. To Nelson, it seemed driven by nothing more than a hunger for misplaced vengeance.

Nelson couldn't bring himself to discuss it with Hannah. She asked, of course, but Nelson was vague in his responses. He believed that she was wrestling with the same emotions. She too had listened to everything Caroline Southwell had said. She knew that nothing could be proven. She also knew that CJ Whitman had killed Garth Kenyon in cold blood. There was no denying that fact, and they had nothing to prove it had been otherwise.

Nelson couldn't bring himself to cover Dead Watch again before the 19th. Whitman would not change his mind. Of this, Nelson was certain. If there was one last thing Nelson could do before CJ went to his death, it would be to respect his decision.

Nelson arranged to take vacation days during the first week of May, and then again at the start of the third week. His shifts were covered by Don Trent.

Asking after CJ, Trent was puzzled by Nelson's interest.

'Nothing you need to concern yourself with,' Nelson said.

Trent, perhaps conscious not to get involved in anything questionable while the Feds were still in the building, did not inquire further.

'He's the same as always,' Trent said. 'Maybe he's in shock. Never known anyone so quiet.'

A week before CJ's sentence was due to be carried out, Nelson went to see Father Donald. He told him that he wanted to be on chamber duty.

'You're volunteering?' Father Donald asked.

'I am, yes.'

'But why?'

'Because that's what he wants, Father.'

'You've spoken to him?'

'I have, yes.'

'You appreciate that you're not permitted to.'

'I'm speaking to you as a man of God,' Nelson said. 'You have faith. I wish I did, but I don't. I have tried, believe me, but I guess some of us just don't find it. You can report me for breaking the rules, or you can help me come to terms with something that I feel I have to do.'

'And why do you feel you have to do this, Mr Nelson?'

'Because I care, Father. Because I want it to be as quick and painless as possible. Because I want him to be judged for what he's done by the only thing in this universe that I feel has a right to judge him.'

'So you do believe in God?'

'I don't know what I believe,' Nelson said, 'except that what is happening here, the lives we live, the few years we have on this earth, can't be all there is to it. I want to believe that there's something more, something beyond, and if that is God, and God is as merciful and forgiving as we're told, then CJ Whitman might just find the peace he's looking for. The peace he deserves.'

'Deserves?' Father Donald asked. 'You think he didn't kill that man?'

'He killed him, Father, but he killed him for the right reasons.'

'Then doesn't this open up a possibility for an appeal?'

'The reasons he did it might be right, Father, but they're not reasons that can be proven.'

'And you think I can influence who is assigned to chamber duty?'

'I don't know,' Nelson said. 'Maybe I just wanted to tell someone, to hear myself say it out loud.'

'In all the years I've been here, I've never known anyone ask to carry out an execution.'

'If you can't help me, that's fine. I'll go to the Warden.'

'No, no. Wait a minute,' Father Donald said. 'I can look and see who's assigned. If you're not assigned, I can imagine it'd be easy enough to ask one of them to step aside. I can do that. I have to be present, of course, so if we're a man short I can recommend that you replace them. I can't make any promises, but I'll see what I can do.'

'Thank you, Father.'

'And what about you?'

'Me?'

'Yes, Mr Nelson. If you've been speaking to this prisoner and he has become sufficiently attached to you to ask this of you, then you must be feeling a great deal of personal conflict.'

'I can't think about that, Father,' Nelson said. 'I can't afford myself the luxury of emotions. Afterwards, who knows? Maybe we'll end up spending a great deal more time together, eh?'

'I'm here if you need me,' Father Donald said. 'If for no other reason than to talk.'

'Thank you, Father.'

Nelson got up and extended his hand.

Father Donald took it, and said, 'I'm going to pray for you,' he said.

'Pray for Whitman, Father,' Nelson replied. 'Right now he needs God a great deal more than I do.'

Two days later, Father Donald came up to the second landing.

'I didn't need to do anything,' he said. 'You're already on chamber duty for the 19th.'

Nelson didn't reply.

'Maybe a prayer was enough, Mr Nelson.'

'Do you know who's on final holding the night before?'

'Mr Trent. And he'll be with you on chamber, too.'

'Okay,' Nelson said.

'The assignment hasn't been released yet, so—'

'Thank you, Father,' Nelson said, and walked away.

On the morning of the 17th, the execution roster assignments made known, Nelson again went to see Don Trent.

'The night before,' he said, 'when you're on final holding, I want you to look after Whitman.'

'Look after him?'

'I just want you to see that he's okay, Don. If he wants to talk, let him talk. If he needs something to eat, make sure he gets it.'

Trent frowned. 'What is with you and this guy?' he asked.

'He shouldn't be there,' Nelson said. 'He really shouldn't be there, but there's nothing me or him or anyone else can do about it.'

'Hey, if you know something—'

'I don't,' Nelson said, cutting the question short.

'If you're so interested in what's going on with him, why did you have me cover your last two shifts?'

'Can you do this for me, Don? Can you just make sure he gets what he needs.'

'Sure thing, Garrett, but one day you're gonna have to explain this to me.'

'One day,' Nelson said. 'And thanks. I owe you.'

71

Perhaps the future would always be eclipsed by the past.

Perhaps Nelson's life from that day forward would be forever overcast by regret. Regret for his mother, for the end of his career, for the decisions both he and others had made that had brought him to where he was in that moment.

There was Hannah, of course, and there was the child – now three months away – but these things all paled into insignificance in the face of what was about to happen.

Nelson did not sleep. He had known he wouldn't, and so he didn't fight it.

The sense of impotence crushed every other thought into docile submission. No matter which way he tried to navigate a means to rescue CJ Whitman from his fate, he was faced time and again with the most fundamental obstacle: CJ Whitman did not want to be rescued.

The vividness and clarity of that awful day when Darryl Jeffreys went to the chair haunted Nelson. It sickened him to his stomach. Twice he rose from the bed, the half-light of nascent dawn shadowing everything in blue and grey, and he leaned down into the bathroom sink. He felt sick, but he couldn't make himself be sick. His head hurt, every muscle ached, every nerve was on fire with fear, anticipation and disgust.

For the third time in his life, he was going to kill a man.

Light broke across the horizon. Colors returned in slow motion.

Hannah slept soundly, and he hoped with everything he possessed that he could rise and dress and leave the house without waking her.

For a while he stood by the window watching her. She lay on her side, her hair spooled out across the pillow. She seemed at peace with all things. He thought of the child growing inside of her – his child – and he prayed that whatever universal sentience might exist in the universe would not punish him for what he was about to do.

A life for a life.

Carrying his clothes downstairs, Nelson dressed in the living room. He did not draw the curtains. He wished everything to remain as dark as possible. He wanted somehow to erase the separation between night and day. He knew that his mind would absorb and retain every second, every fragment of this. If he did not think, did not speak, if he could recall everything in monochrome, then perhaps the experience would remain in the shadows, buried somewhere in the darkest recesses of his mind.

Minutes from leaving, he heard footfalls on the stairs.

He didn't move. Perhaps she wouldn't see him. It was a foolish, impossible thought, but he thought it all the same.

'You didn't wake me,' Hannah said.

'No.'

'You're leaving now?'

'Yes.'

'Have you eaten anything?'

'No.'

'Coffee?'

'No.'

'Do you want some?'

Nelson looked at her, the artless simplicity of her expression, and he knew he'd never before been cared for as much as Hannah cared in that moment.

'I want to go,' Nelson said. 'I want it to be over.'

'I know,' Hannah replied. 'I want it to be over, too. But not this way.'

Nelson remained still as she came towards him. He held out his arms and pulled her close, so aware that he was holding not only Hannah but also their child. He wanted nothing more than for them to be safe.

'Perhaps there will be a stay,' she said.

'There won't.'

'You don't know, Garrett. Maybe Caroline spoke to Sarah. Maybe—'

Nelson pulled her tighter. She fell silent.

He knew. They both knew. It was all so much wishful thinking.

Nelson asked her not to come outside, but she did.

Standing inside the open front door in her robe, she watched him as he walked down the path to the car.

Everything slowed down.

The sound of the door opening, closing, the key in the ignition, the guttural rush as the engine fired into life.

Nelson looked out through the windshield at Hannah.

She raised her hand, and then she held it against her heart.

A snapshot to keep for ever.

Nelson closed his eyes. He breathed deeply. He put the car into gear, and reversed. Turning at the end of the drive, he paused before moving off. He looked back at Hannah. She gave a single wave, and then she stepped back into the house and closed the door behind her.

There was a small death in every goodbye.

There were people at the gates. They held placards and they shouted slogans. Nelson did not look at their faces. He put the radio on, turned it up loud.

Guards outside the fence held people back so Nelson could enter the compound.

Glancing in the rearview he saw them – the Whitmans: Floyd, Dorothy, Maurice, Errol, and then the two sisters. He could not remember their names. He did not want to remember their names.

The gates drew shut behind him.

Having signed in at Central Admin, Nelson walked back across to HS.

The commissary was empty but for two or three people. He took a cup of coffee. He sat by the window and looked out at the endless fence that surrounded them. The sun was up, the sky was cloudless. The stark silhouettes of the watchtowers loomed over Southern.

Nelson managed half a cup. He left it there and started the walk to final holding.

With each step closer to the bell tower, his heart grew heavier.

The day was already warm, but the warmth didn't find him. Everything was cold, inside and out.

Entering the chapel, Father Donald walked towards Nelson. His expression was anxious.

'He had a bad night,' he said. 'He's asked for you. We don't have long.'

Nelson followed Father Donald without response.

*

Clarence was a child.

Perhaps he'd never been anything other than a child. The bitterness and cynicism that so insidiously steals innocence and honesty as each year passes had never taken from him the simple nature of youth.

He sat on the edge of the bed in final holding. His feet were bare. His head down, he looked up as Father Donald and Nelson entered the cell.

'Garrett,' Don Trent said, and nodded an acknowledgement. He seemed then to slip from the room without a sound. He was there, and then he was gone.

Nelson drew up a chair. He sat down ahead of CJ.

CJ did not look up at him, even when Nelson reached out and took CJ's hand.

'How long now?' CJ asked.

Nelson looked at Father Donald. Father Donald closed his eyes.

'A little while more,' Nelson said.

'Did my family come?'

'Yes, they did,' Nelson said. 'I saw them outside.'

'They mustn't come in here,' CJ said. 'You can't let them see this.'

'I won't, Clarence.'

CJ looked up then. Everything about his features seemed so much younger than Nelson recalled. Everything except his eyes. His eyes were those of the old man he would never become.

'I missed you,' CJ said. 'I haven't seen you for a month.'

'I know,' Nelson said, 'and I'm sorry.'

'I understand why you couldn't come.'

CJ smiled. In that moment, Nelson knew he was being forgiven.

'There are things I want to say, Clarence.'

'No, Mr Nelson. It's all been said.'

'But—'

CJ closed his hand over Nelson's.

Nelson fell silent.

'I have prayed,' CJ said. 'Prayed alone, and with Father Donald here. It's okay, Mr Nelson. It's okay. And prayers get answered. I believe that. Not always in the way we expect, but somehow they get answered.'

CJ looked up towards the ceiling.

'I don't know what's going to happen. Father Donald tells me there's a better place. I guess I'll find out real soon. But if that place is anything even close to how I felt when me and Sarah was together …'

CJ's voice trailed off into silence.

'Do you want me to find her, Clarence?' Nelson asked. 'Do you want me to tell her anything?'

'There's nothing you could tell her that she don't already know, Mr Nelson.'

Nelson looked at CJ. He held his gaze and he smiled. He leaned forward then, and he put his arms around CJ's shoulders.

Moments later, as if from another room, Nelson heard Don Trent's voice.

'It's time,' he said.

72

After the doctor's final examination, the barber shaved Clarence Whitman's head and the calf of his right leg.

Nelson stood against the wall and watched the routine progress as he had done before.

This time it was different. This time he knew exactly what was going to happen.

Father Donald asked CJ if there were any last words he wished to share, if he wanted to pray again. CJ thanked the Father for his counsel and his friendship, but said he'd done all the praying he needed.

CJ then got to his feet without being asked. He knew the way and he started walking.

Nelson was on CJ's left, Trent on his right, and when they entered the corridor that divided final holding from the bell tower, Trent led the way, Nelson behind CJ, Father Donald at the rear.

Trent knocked on the door at the end of the walkway.

There was but a moment's hesitation, and then it opened.

Trent went on through, turned to meet CJ, and put his hand on CJ's shoulder as if to ensure that he did not slip or fall.

Warden Greaves stood with his back to the wall, the telephone beside him.

The prison doctor stood near the viewing window.

The state executioner, there beside the trolley, was motionless, his face devoid of any expression.

The execution ritual began. The leather restraints, the sponges, the calf plate, the head cap, the sound of CJ's labored breathing the only thing that punctuated the silence in that room.

As each new step was completed, Nelson touched some part of CJ's body – his hand, his shoulder, the side of his face. He wanted CJ to know that he was there, that someone who understood what he was doing and why he was doing it was present in that moment.

As if securing a child in a harness, Nelson checked the straps were tight enough to hold him, yet not so tight as to cause discomfort.

The electrodes secured, the instruction was given to open the viewing curtain.

Light filled the room.

Nelson looked out into the chapel. Two men sat waiting. They still wore their hats.

Warden Greaves stepped forward.

'Clarence Jefferson Whitman. Having been tried and found guilty by a jury of your peers, it is the judgement of the court and the State of Florida that you be put to death. Before sentence is carried out, do you have any last words?'

CJ – eyes wide, tears coursing down his face, his hands gripping the arms of the chair as if he could somehow hold onto life for ever – looked at Nelson.

'I-I j-just want t-to thank you for being here, Mr Nelson.'

CJ closed his eyes again.

Trent moved.

Nelson raised his hand. 'I'll do it,' he said.

Nelson took a towel. He wiped the tears from CJ's face. He

gently placed the tape over his eyes, ensuring it was secure on his forehead and cheeks.

In a last gesture, Nelson leaned close, his hand on CJ's forearm, and he whispered, 'Goodbye, my friend.'

The clock labored. It gave up each second as if fighting the passage of time itself.

The phone hung silent on the wall.

The executioner's hand hovered over the lever.

CJ's breathing slowed. His chest rose and fell. His hands relaxed. A single tear broke out from beneath the tape.

Father Donald started reading.

'Yea, though I walk through the valley of the shadow of death, I will fear no evil; for thou art with me; thy rod and thy staff, they comfort me. Thou preparest a table before me in the presence of mine enemies; thou anointest my head with oil; my cup runneth over…'

Warden Greaves gave the word.

The lever dropped.

73

Nelson drove the flatbed truck to God's Acre.

He could still hear the echo from the bell tower. He believed he'd perhaps hear it for the rest of his life.

Standing beside Father Donald, he watched as Clarence Whitman's coffin was lowered into the ground.

His mind and his heart were hollow. He felt nothing.

It would come, of course – the tidal wave of grief, of despair, of horror – but perhaps by some divine good grace, he had been given leave of such things for now.

Nelson wanted nothing more than to go home, to close the doors, to shut out the light of day, to hide from the cruelty and injustice of the world.

And he wanted to see Hannah, for she, more than anyone in the world, would understand what he had endured.

Clarence Whitman was dead. If not for Nelson, the truth would have gone with him.

The world wanted to believe that Garth Kenyon had died a sudden and unnecessary death, that he'd been murdered without conscience or mercy. That he'd not deserved to die. Perhaps that would always be the belief, and there would be nothing that Nelson could do to change it.

But these were thoughts for a different day, and, for now, he had to let them go.

Nelson chose to walk back to the compound.

Father Donald walked with him.

For a long time, they did not speak.

Nearing the gates, Father Donald stopped. Nelson went a few steps ahead, and then turned back.

'You have to believe that there is something greater, Garrett,' he said. It was the first time Father Donald had used his name. 'Otherwise it all becomes meaningless.'

Nelson looked down. 'I want to,' he said, 'but it's hard.'

'And perhaps the hardest thing that is ever asked of us,' Father Donald said. 'To trust in the intangible, to have faith in something we cannot see or hear or touch. To believe that there's some sense and reason amidst the madness we call life.'

Nelson looked up.

'I'll try, Father,' he said. 'That's all I can do.'

74

On Friday, May 26, 1978, having served just eighteen months, Nelson walked out of Southern for the last time.

Handing in his uniform and keys at Central Admin, he felt as if he was not only being released from the prison itself, but the emotional and psychological confines of some self-imposed sentence. He'd done his time. He was a free man. What the future held, he did not know, and, in truth, he did not care. He would find work. He did not doubt that. All he knew was that it would be as far from the law and the judicial system as he could find.

That sense of release was just as quickly snatched away less than a month later. The events that unfolded on Tuesday, June 20, brought home to Nelson the fear that he'd harbored ever since leaving Southern – that his connection to the place, the way it had insidiously invaded every aspect of his life, was powerful enough to drag him right back into it without forewarning.

Having dropped Hannah out to the hospital for a routine check-up, he drove into town. It was a little after noon. Hannah was the one who told him to leave her there, that he should head into Fort Myers and find a delicatessen. She wanted pastrami and coleslaw, root beer, and – if he could find them

– chocolate-covered almonds. He made some crack about her being high maintenance. She told him to brace himself, that her demands were only going to become more impossible.

Nelson got everything but the almonds. He stopped for coffee at a diner, took a walk for a few blocks, and then headed back to the car. In hindsight, as was always the case, he would ask himself why he hadn't stayed at the hospital.

Before the main building came into view, Nelson knew that something was amiss. Cars were backed up for a good five hundred yards ahead of the turn-off. At first he figured it had been some kind of accident, but then the sound of sirens peeled through the air. Heading towards the hospital from the other side of the highway, a convoy of vehicles, cherry bars flashing, was visible. Nelson knew there was no way to reach the hospital in his car, so he got out and started walking.

A window came down as he passed the third or fourth car in the queue.

'What's going on?' the driver asked.

'No idea,' Nelson said. 'Looks like something at the hospital.'

The driver asked another question, but Nelson was already past him and running.

By the time he reached the exit, the approaching police cars were already establishing a cordon to block the highway itself. Officers were running every which way as tape was strung between the vehicles and across the entranceway to the hospital compound.

Nelson tried to get closer, but was stopped in his tracks by a Lee County Sheriff's Department officer.

'You can't come up here, sir.'

'What's happening?'

'Reports of a shooting. That's all we know. Now, if you can make your way back down there to your car, we're gonna do everything we can to get everyone moving and out of here as quickly as possible.'

'I have someone in the hospital,' Nelson said.

'As do a lot of people, sir. You need to let us do our job, okay? Go back to your vehicle and wait for further instructions.'

Nelson's heart was racing.

'But—'

'Sir,' the officer said, his tone adamant. 'Go back to your vehicle. You cannot be here.'

The officer turned and walked away. Nelson watched him go, the sense of dismay and disbelief matched only by the feeling of complete impotence. Hannah was in there. Who had been shot? Why was there even someone in there with a gun?

Nelson, panic rising in his chest, ran back to his car.

Reversing off the highway and turning back the way he came, he stopped at the first telephone he saw. He called the Montgomery place. He had no idea if Frank would be home. The phone rang and kept on ringing. No one answered.

Nelson rang Southern, got through to Central Admin, insisted that someone find Frank Montgomery and get him to the phone. It took a small forever, Nelson looking back towards the hospital, trying to comprehend what was happening, trying to make any sense at all of what was going on, experienced emotions that he'd never felt. He'd been afraid before – out in Sebring, during the attack on Paul Bisson in the chapel, during the riots in July and January – but none of them had provoked the emotional impact of what was taking place. This was personal, this was directly connected to him, and, as it stood, there seemed to be nothing he could do to take control of the situation.

'Garrett?'

Frank's voice at the other end of the line.

'Frank, I'm out in Fort Myers. I brought Hannah to the hospital. Someone's in there. There's been a shooting—'

'What the hell are you talking about, Garrett? A shooting at the hospital?'

'That's what I've been told. I can't get in there. Hannah's inside, Frank. Hannah's in the fucking hospital...'

'Jesus fucking Christ. I'm on my way, Garrett. I'm leaving now.'

The line went dead.

Nelson stood there with the receiver in his hand. He looked down at it, and just for a moment, it was as if he was standing a distance away looking at his own body. He went through the motions of hanging up, stepping away from the phone, gathering up the handful of coins he'd dropped on the sidewalk, heading back to his car, and yet it seemed that he was watching someone else entirely.

Only when he was once again in the driver's seat, the sound of the engine turning over as he started the car, did he snap back into reality. But it wasn't a reality; it was a surreal nightmare that had somehow exploded into his life with no warning.

Hannah, the woman with whom he intended to spend the rest of his life, the mother of his child, was trapped in a building with a gunman.

Nelson drove back towards the hospital. The queue of cars was now three or four times the length. People were out on the grass verge, huddled together in groups, each of them asking another what was happening.

Nelson pulled over and got out. He started walking towards the hospital. More police cars had arrived, and now there were black SUVs, an ambulance, a number of suited men gathered at the rear of one of them.

Nelson approached a uniformed officer.

'My girlfriend is in there,' Nelson said.

'I understand, sir, but I need you to go back to the highway and—'

'I'm De Soto County,' Nelson said. 'Deputy Sheriff. I'm off duty. Can you tell me what's going on?'

The officer shrugged and said, 'I don't know details, but it looks like there's some kind of hostage situation.'

'And someone was shot?'

'That's what we're being told, but this is federal jurisdiction now.' He nodded towards the group of suits.

'Federal?' Nelson asked. 'Why federal?'

'Your guess is as good as mine. I'd imagine that because whoever is in there is already on their radar, or he was chased across state lines.'

Nelson knew then. He felt sure of it. 'You get a name?'

'Of the guy in there? Can't help you with that.'

'I have a name,' Nelson said.

'You know who it is?'

'I have a damned good idea.'

The officer hesitated for a moment, and then he said, 'Wait here.'

Nelson did as he was asked. The officer ran down towards the SUV and spoke with the Feds. They looked back at Nelson. One of them said a few words to the others, and then started walking out to the cordon.

Reaching Nelson, he showed his ID. 'Special Agent Harman,' he said. 'You're a Deputy Sheriff from De Soto County?'

'I was,' Nelson said. 'I've been out at Southern State for the last year. I think I know who's in there, and I think I know why.'

75

By the time Frank Montgomery arrived at the hospital, it was close to two.

When he gave his name to one of the uniforms, he was told to come through the cordon and speak to the Feds.

Nelson was there with Harman and two others. They were looking over a floor plan of the hospital.

'It's Christiansen,' Nelson said. 'Jimmy Christiansen is in there. He came for Max Sheehan.'

'Sheehan is still here?' Frank asked.

'He was moved some weeks ago,' Harman said.

'And Hannah? Do we know anything about the people in there? Did someone get hit?'

'There was a gunshot,' Harman said. 'Maybe two. We're not sure. It happened as someone was leaving the building. That's all we've got. No one else has come out, so we don't have any more up-to-date information.'

'But you know it's Christiansen, right?' Frank asked.

'We do, yes. We had a negotiator call in to reception. He picked up.'

'And he made demands?'

'He wants Stein out of Florida State,' Nelson said. 'He wants William Cain out of Southern. He wants Max Sheehan brought here. Once that's done, he wants half a million dollars and unrestricted passage to Mexico.'

'The guy's completely insane,' Frank said. 'None of that is gonna happen.'

'He says he'll kill everyone in the building, himself included.'

Back towards the highway, there was the sound of cars starting. The Lee County Sheriff's Department had facilitated a route that would allow the queue of traffic to disperse and leave.

Harman watched them go. Frank just looked at Nelson. Nelson could see that he was experiencing the same blunt force trauma of an incomprehensible situation.

Frank snapped to. 'So, what's the strategy?' he asked Harman.

'Right now, the both of you go debrief the negotiator. You tell him everything you can about Christiansen. Anything you know, anything you can remember, no matter how unimportant it might seem. The more information he has, the better job he can do.'

'You have sight of him yet?' Frank asked.

'Not yet. But we want to draw him out, get him into a dialogue. We have snipers out here. If we can get him to a window, anywhere with a clear line of sight that doesn't jeopardize a hostage, we can take him out.'

'Or one of us goes in,' Frank said. 'He knows me. I've had the man on my watch ever since he arrived at Southern.'

'I appreciate the—'

'My daughter's in there, Agent Harman. You appreciate that?'

'I do, sir, but that doesn't follow any standard hostage scenario protocol.'

'Fuck your protocols. I know Jimmy Christiansen. You want a dialogue, I can get you a dialogue. Otherwise we're just out here pissin' in the wind and praying that he'll give himself up. That man's been on the run for the best part of a year. He and his buddy killed two people in Alva, another one in Arredondo.

He's not fucking about. You don't seem to understand the kind of person you're dealing with. He says he's gonna shoot up some people in there and then kill himself, I don't doubt that for a second. We get him, he's going to the chair. That's his other option right now, and if you believe that he thinks how we do, then you're very much mistaken.'

'You need to speak to the senior officer,' Harman said.

'And who is that?'

'Senior Special Agent Michael Gant. He's en route from Fort Lauderdale. He should be here anytime now.'

It was a further twenty minutes before Gant arrived. With him came a further fleet of SUVs, a tactical squad, a second negotiator and a medical unit. Before he spoke with anyone else, Gant was briefed on the current status of the situation by Harman. Harman came back to see Nelson and Frank Montgomery. He told them that Gant would speak to them in one of the vehicles.

Gant sat in the passenger seat. Nelson and Frank were in the back. He spoke to them without turning his head.

'Harman tells me you want to go into the building?'

'You have someone better?' Frank asked.

'And if your daughter wasn't in there?'

'Then I wouldn't even be here,' Frank replied. 'I'd still be at Southern.'

'Which tells me that you are about the least objective person—'

'Objective? Who the hell needs objective right now? You tell me there's someone here who has more to lose by this thing going to Hell than me, and we'll send them instead. How about that?'

Gant didn't speak for some time. Nelson could see his reflection in the rearview. He didn't believe he'd seen anyone so conflicted and intense.

'And what are you hoping to achieve, Officer Montgomery?'

'Dialogue. That's what you want, right?'

'What I want is to kill that motherfucker.'

'Harman said you got shooters. I get him near a window, any place with a clear sightline, and you can take him out.'

'In theory, yes.'

'In theory?'

'One of my people hits a hostage, perhaps even you, and they don't kill this guy, then we both know what will happen. There'll be a bloodbath in there.'

'And how long do you think we've got before that happens anyway? He's made these demands, demands that will never be met, not under any circumstances. You think he's gonna sit in there for a week while we keep tellin' him that we're workin' on it? Is that what you think's gonna happen? The guy is a fucking animal. He's a psychopath. Believe me, patience sure ain't in his repertoire. Two hours, three, and he's gonna get wound so tight he'll shoot someone in the head and throw them out of the window just so we know he's not fucking around.'

Gant turned then. He looked back over the seat at Frank.

'You think I'm not prepared to do whatever it takes to get my daughter out of there, Agent Gant? Well, I am, and I will. Comes to it, you get a shot at him and I go down, then that'd be fine by me.'

'That's not something I can even consider.'

'Well, start considerin' it. I've put my life on the line for decades. And for what? A paycheck. You think I'm not prepared to do that for my only daughter, then you're readin' me all wrong.'

Gant looked at Nelson.

'And you? Are you willing to go in there too?'

'He ain't goin' nowhere,' Frank said. 'He's weeks away from being a father. My girl's coming out of there, and she's coming out to him and her future.'

Gant turned away. He looked straight ahead – at the vehicles, the agents, the Sheriff's Department officers, the flashing lights, the barriers and the hospital beyond.

'If Christiansen agrees to speak to you, then you go in together, or not at all,' Gant said, his tone that of a man reconciled to a course of action because there appeared to be no alternative.

'I don't want—'

'It's not a case of what you want, Officer Montgomery,' Gant said. 'Nelson here is a trained legal enforcement officer. He has firearms experience. No longer in active service, maybe, but that doesn't change the fact that he has experience that you don't.'

Gant looked at Nelson.

'Are you willing to go in there, Mr Nelson?'

It was a question that didn't need to be asked.

The Florida Bureau negotiator sat with Nelson and Frank Montgomery for close to an hour. He talked about personal connection, use of first names, de-escalation of tension, distraction, the separation of Christiansen from the hostages, the continuous affirmation that whatever Christiansen wanted he could have, but it would take time. Time was everything. Time was the key.

'And if there's some reason to bring him to a window, even a doorway, perhaps to see that we're out here and we're working on meeting his demands, that will give the tactical agents every opportunity to neutralize the threat.'

'But first he's got to agree to see us,' Nelson said.

'Yes, of course, but we're dealing with that right now.'

Within minutes Gant appeared. 'He's willing to talk,' he said, 'and he's willing to release a hostage.'

'Who?' Frank asked.

'One of the nurses was hit. A flesh wound, apparently. She was treated by one of the doctors inside. I asked him to let her go as a sign of his willingness to negotiate, and he conceded. He also said that only one of you goes inside.'

'Well, that's as it should be,' Frank said. He made a move to leave the vehicle.

'He wants Nelson.'

'What?'

Nelson looked at Frank, then at Gant.

'He said that the only person he'd let inside was Nelson.'

'Did he say why?' Nelson asked.

'He said it was because he'd known you for less time and so had less of an impulse to kill you. He also said that we were dumb if we thought he was going to let himself be outnumbered.'

'You can't do this, Garrett,' Frank said.

'And you can? It's all right for you to put your life on the line for Hannah, but not me? Who do you think I am, Frank? She's in there and so is my child.'

Nelson looked at Gant. 'Are we done here? Is there anything else I need to know?'

'We're done,' the negotiator said.

'Then let's get the fuck on with this.'

76

The wounded nurse appeared in the foyer of the hospital. Nelson could see her through the glass. Looking pale and disorientated, her left arm in a sling, she made her way slowly toward the exit.

Nelson went up the steps and opened the door. Back down near the road, the medical unit were waiting for her.

'How many are in there?' Nelson asked.

'I'm guessing maybe sixty or seventy staff, and I don't know how many patients. He's got most everyone in the staff canteen. The ones who can't be moved have been locked in their rooms. They need help. Some of them require constant monitoring.'

'Nelson!'

It was Christiansen, out of sight, calling for him from somewhere inside the building.

Nelson looked down towards the road. 'Go see the medics. There's an agent called Gant who'll come to talk to you. Tell him everything that's happened, everything you've seen.'

The nurse closed her eyes for a moment and took a deep breath. 'I don't understand how someone—'

'You better get yourself on in here, Nelson,' Christiansen shouted, 'or I'm gonna shoot one of these sons of bitches in the head!'

'Go,' Nelson told the nurse.

*

Once inside the foyer, there was still no sign of Christiansen.

The door closed behind him.

'Take your jacket off,' Christiansen said.

Nelson did as he was told.

'Pull up your shirt. Turn around slowly. Then roll up each pant leg slowly. Let me see you got nothing hidden there.'

Again, Nelson did as instructed.

'Okay. You walk towards the door ahead and to the right. Walk slow. No sudden moves.'

Nelson reached the door, and it was only then that he sensed Christiansen beside him. Next to the doorway was a narrow alcove, and it was from here that Christiansen appeared and pressed the muzzle of a gun against the side of Nelson's head.

'Open the door.'

Nelson turned the handle, stepped back to pull it wide.

'You go on through ahead of me, down that corridor, second door on the left.'

Nelson moved slowly. Christiansen was a good six feet behind him. Had he kept the gun close to Nelson, he could've dropped and turned, kicking Christiansen's legs out from under him. His senses attuned to every movement, every sound behind him, he reached the door and opened it.

On the other side was a small office. To the right a window looked out into the staff canteen.

As the nurse had said, there must have been close to a hundred people in there. Most of them were seated at tables, some sat on the floor, even more stood against the wall. There was silence. Scanning the faces, Nelson searched for Hannah.

'Sit on the floor in the corner,' Christiansen said. 'Cross your legs, hands on your head.'

Christiansen dragged a chair to the other corner of the room.

From there he could see both Nelson and those through the window.

Nelson didn't comply immediately. He kept looking, searching for Hannah, scanning every aspect of the room to see if she was present. Concluding that she must be elsewhere in the hospital, he took a step backwards toward the chair, and it was then, even as he started to sit, that he caught sight of her. She was seated against the wall on the far left-hand side, her head back, her eyes closed. The rush of emotion he felt in his chest left him almost breathless.

Doing his utmost to give nothing away, he did as Christiansen had instructed and sat down.

'You here to tell me I ain't gonna get what I asked for?' Christiansen asked. 'If so, don't waste your breath. I know they ain't gonna do a damned thing.'

'So what are you going to do?' Nelson asked.

'You're gonna get me outta here.'

'You seen what's out there, Jimmy?'

Christiansen smiled. 'You call me Mr Christiansen, and yes, I know exactly what's out there.'

'So, why me? How am I any more use to you than any one of those people in there?'

'Because you're smart. Because you know who you're dealing with.'

'I know you didn't kill those folks in Alva,' Nelson said. 'An' I'm guessin' that Stein did that guy in the gas station too, right?'

'You want me to give myself up?' Christiansen sneered. 'Fuck you. Fuck all of you. I go back to Southern, I'm dead in an hour.'

'Because of Cain?'

'What the fuck do you know about Cain?'

'I know you were supposed to get him out. You know they got Stein, right? He's up at Florida State. And Garvey is dead.

Jackson Forsyth too. And you came here to get Max Sheehan, but they moved him a while back.'

Christiansen leaned back in the chair. He looked at the ceiling, and – just for a moment – he closed his eyes. Everything in his body language spelled exhaustion, but not for a second did he relax his grip on the gun. It was still pointed unerringly at Nelson's chest.

'So you know what you know,' Christiansen said.

'I also know the law.'

'Is that so?'

'You turn yourself in, they'll give you another handful of years for the escape. If Stein killed those people, then he'll go to the chair. That doesn't have to happen to you.'

'The law don't mean shit. You think they're gonna worry themselves over which one of us is tellin' the truth? Hell, you are naïve as fuck. They want both of us dead, no two ways about it.'

Christiansen was right, and Nelson knew it.

'So, how do you see this happening?' Nelson asked.

'You make a call to your buddies down there. They bring a car up here. Take it to the back of the building. You and I walk out. We drive away. They follow us, you're dead. It ain't complicated.'

'And where are you gonna go?'

'That ain't none of your damned business.'

'You alone in this, or you got people out there to help you?'

Christiansen frowned. 'If I did, why the fuck would I tell you? Are you really as dumb as you sound right now?'

Nelson knew he was just playing for time. Why, he didn't know. Perhaps for no other reason than to engage with Christiansen in any way possible; perhaps, as a consequence, to diminish any impulse Christiansen might have to kill him once they were out on the highway.

'You need to make the call,' Christiansen said.

*

Nelson spoke with Gant from the phone in reception.

Christiansen had Nelson hold the phone in such a way that Christiansen could hear everything that was being discussed.

When Gant told Christiansen that he would get a car out back of the building, that he wouldn't be followed, and that he and Nelson could drive away, he requested – as a condition – that all the hostages be freed.

Christiansen took the phone. He told Nelson to step away.

'You'll get what you're asking for,' Gant said. 'And you'll have Nelson. So let us get those people out of there.'

'And as soon as I'm gone, you can come in and get them,' Christiansen said. 'What the fuck difference does it make to you?'

'How do I know you don't have explosives? How do I know that you haven't rigged the doors?'

Christiansen laughed. 'Who do you think I am?'

'I think you're a man in a desperate situation. You let this go and we can talk—'

'Your buddy Nelson's already given me the sales pitch. I ain't buyin'. Get me a car. Handcuffs too. You got fifteen minutes. Once I'm out on the highway, you can come in here. I see anyone following, I see a chopper in the fuckin' air, I'm pullin' over an' shootin' this motherfucker in the head. Then I'm gonna get back in that car and drive on like nothin' happened. You get me?'

'I get you,' Gant replied.

Christiansen hung up.

'Out the back we go,' he said, and shoved the muzzle of the gun into Nelson's ribs.

77

Standing near the service door that opened into the rear car park behind the building, Nelson tried to evaluate every possible scenario.

If he rushed Christiansen, he would more than likely be killed. The man was desperate, just as Gant had said, and it wouldn't take a great deal to push him over the edge. With Nelson dead, Christiansen would take another hostage. A pregnant woman was as good a hostage as Christiansen could get. The odds were a hundred to one, but even that was too great a risk to consider.

If Nelson was wounded, Christiansen would still take him along. At the earliest available opportunity, he would get Nelson out of the car. Where that would be, and how long it would take for someone to find him, was unknown. He could be left there on the highway to bleed out.

Getting Christiansen out of the hospital and away from the other hostages was Nelson's priority. He asked himself whether he would've had the same viewpoint if Hannah had not been there. He believed he would. There was a fundamental impulse to do the right thing, to do whatever it took for the greater good. In the minutes that elapsed between the end of the phone call and the sound of a car pulling up outside the door, Nelson asked himself if that was the real motivation for joining the Sheriff's Department. To make amends. To do right after all the wrongs that had been perpetrated by his father.

Nelson's mind was a confusion of thoughts and emotions – fear, anger, hopelessness, the threat of losing not only his life, but the life he had created. Before Hannah, there was nothing. His life had been hollow, a predictable routine, a matter of one day after the next. Now there was meaning and purpose, a future ahead of him, and he was willing to do whatever it took to keep it.

A single knock on the door.

'Rock an' fuckin' roll,' Christiansen said.

Nelson went out first. One of the black SUVs, engine running, doors open, was no more than ten feet from the exit.

A pair of handcuffs was on the ground a few feet away.

'Cuff your wrist,' Christiansen said.

Nelson did as instructed. He cuffed his left hand.

'Get in back and put the other cuff through the door handle.'

Christiansen checked that both cuffs were secure.

'You sit upright,' Christiansen said. 'Your head the same height as mine. You stay that way until we're free and clear.'

Christiansen knew what he was doing. There were sharpshooters out there. He wanted Nelson as close to him as possible.

Christiansen got into the driver's seat and closed the door. He tilted the rearview so he could see both Nelson and the road behind him. No more than five miles an hour, creeping backwards down towards the main exit of the hospital, Christiansen reached the first cordon and stopped.

With the engine idling, he waited for the Feds and the Sheriff's Department vehicles to move slowly away.

Once the path to the highway had been cleared of obstructions, Christiansen backed out and turned. He moved slowly, again no more than five or ten miles an hour, ranks of law enforcement watching him.

Nelson caught sight of Gant, Frank Montgomery beside him, and the expression on their faces was one of grim resignation.

Reaching the last of the cars, Christiansen hit the accelerator and the SUV roared into life. Nelson looked back. He could see people running towards the hospital. Frank would go with them, and he would find Hannah. She would want to know what was happening, and Frank would have to tell her.

Gant was good to his word. For the first five miles or so there was nothing overhead, nothing behind them. They were heading north on 41, out towards Punta Gorda. The road was clear, remarkably so, and it was only as they crossed the town limits of Del Tura that Nelson understood what Gant must have done. Restricting traffic into Fort Myers, he would also have established a roadblock up ahead. Whether Christiansen was struck by the lack of vehicles on the highway, Nelson didn't know. He didn't say anything at all. His hands on the wheel, the gun in his lap, Nelson could see the unerring focus and determination in the man's eyes. This was his chance, the very last one he might have, to evade custody. He would not be going back to Southern. He would not see Death Row or the bell tower. He was intent on escaping or dying in the process.

Nelson inched sideways. Moving in incremental degrees, he worked to establish as great a distance between himself and Christiansen. He shifted forwards, bending his knees and lowering himself inch by inch. He felt sure Christiansen would notice, but so focused was he on the road ahead that he was oblivious to what was happening in the back seat.

A handful of miles out of Del Tura, Christiansen followed the road as it turned, and came over the crest of a rise. It was then that he saw the flashing lights, the barricade of cars, the way they fanned out and away from the highway so as to create as wide a barrier as possible.

'Motherfuckers!' he screamed, and hit the brakes. The car slewed awkwardly to the right. Christiansen wrestled with the wheel and regained control. The SUV went another twenty or thirty yards before juddering to a halt. It sat sideways to the roadblock, now no more than fifty yards ahead.

Christiansen ducked down. Nelson dropped low too. Christiansen looked at him through the gap between the front seats.

'Sons of fuckin' bitches,' he said.

Christiansen opened the driver's side door. He came out low to the ground. He edged towards the rear, the full length of the SUV obscuring his movements. Once the back door was open, he reached in and unlocked Nelson's handcuff.

'Out,' he said.

Nelson, keeping his head down, slid along the seat and got out of the car.

Christiansen, on his knees, moved away just a couple of feet.

'On the ground,' he said.

Nelson complied.

'Hands out,' Christiansen said, and handcuffed Nelson once more. Hauling him up onto his knees, Christiansen pressed the muzzle of the gun into Nelson's neck.

'If I'm going, you're fucking going with me,' he said.

Nelson felt the hatred and anger in the man's voice. He felt the cold metal of the gun. He could smell Christiansen's sweat. Everything was defined in the sharpest detail.

For what seemed like an age, nothing moved. Aside from the sound of the SUV's engine, there was silence.

'Guess this is the end of the fucking road, eh?' Christiansen said. 'Guess some of us are born never to get old.'

In the distance, Nelson heard the approaching sound of a helicopter.

'Never trust a fuckin' Fed, eh, Mr Nelson?'

'If you're gonna kill me, best do it now,' Nelson replied. 'I don't see a way out of this. You ain't going any further, and it looks like you can't go back.'

'No arguin' with your logic,' Christiansen said.

'So do it. Just fucking do it.'

Christiansen raised the gun and held it against Nelson's forehead.

'Is that what you want?' Christiansen said. 'You ready to die, are you? You had enough of this fuckin' bullshit too, have you?'

'I'm not goin' any further with you,' Nelson said. 'You make a run for it, sure, but you leave me here.'

'I say you get in the car, then you get in the fuckin' car.'

'I'm not getting in there. I'm done.'

Christiansen, enraged, swung sideways with the pistol and hit Nelson across the face. A lancing jolt of pain knocked him sideways to the ground. For a moment he was stunned, but then he was back up on his knees, his face mere inches from Christiansen's.

'This was always how it was gonna be,' Nelson said. 'You're dead or you're in Southern. I'm out of Southern now, never goin' back, and if we're both dead on this fucking highway then so be it. So do what you have to do, Mr Christiansen. Do whatever the fuck it is you're gonna do and stop kidding yourself that there's another end to this story.'

Christiansen gave a wry smile. 'Hell, I always thought you were just Frank Montgomery's little bitch, but you got some balls on you, boy. I gotta give it to you. You got a lot more spine that I gave you credit for.'

With the muzzle of the gun still pointed at Nelson's forehead, Christiansen looked up and through the rear window of the car.

The roadblock was, if anything, even wider. There was no way he would make it past. Behind them, the sound of the helicopter, growing ever louder, meant that there was no going back. Out there, endless highway in both directions, a landscape running to the horizon, he was as trapped as he had been in his cell at Southern.

'You know what my daddy used to tell me?' Christiansen asked. 'He used to say that you never heard the bullet that killed you. You think I'm a bad guy, you shoulda met him. He was worse than all o' Southern rolled up into one.'

Christiansen cocked the hammer on the pistol. That sound, ordinarily the faintest click, was deafening. It seemed to echo through Nelson's head. He knew this was it. He knew then that he would never see Hannah again, that he would never meet his own child, that no one but the Montgomerys would ever remember who he was, and even they, in time, would forget.

The pressure of the muzzle against his skin was the realest thing he had ever felt.

Christiansen, roaring out of some primeval impulse that impelled him to kill or be killed, was suddenly up on his feet. Nelson fell sideways, his head connecting with the rear wing of the car. The first and second gunshots were from Christiansen, firing blindly towards the roadblock. The third and fourth, so many after that, thudding into the car, the ground around them, came from the vehicles up ahead.

Nelson saw Christiansen go down. The gun flew from his hand and landed no more than six feet from where Nelson lay. Rolling over, his hands still cuffed, he managed to seize it.

Staying flat on his belly, his arms out ahead of him, he looked for Christiansen. He could hear him screaming, but the sound of the helicopter, now overhead, disorientated him.

A handful of seconds, no more, and Christiansen staggered back, dropped to one knee, and turned to look at Nelson. Blood covered his shoulder, the side of his neck, and all around the right side of his torso. The expression he wore was one of cruelty and defiance.

Nelson pulled the trigger. He pulled it again. He kept on pulling it until there was nothing but the sound of the hammer on spent shells.

78

Throughout the subsequent week Nelson was occupied with interviews. Try as he might to recount every detail of the events that led up to the killing of Jimmy Christiansen, it was as if his mind refused to reveal everything. Moments came back to him as he lay awake into the early hours, the sound of Hannah sleeping beside him. He would get up, make notes, and then find them indecipherable in the morning. He endured a sense of psychological pressure that was difficult to express. He was subdued, distant, and there were times that he could do nothing but look at Hannah with an expression that communicated his inability to explain what was going on.

Nelson needed to be alone, and most days he would take the car and disappear for three or four hours at a time. He would find diners or truckstops, and just sit there lost in his own thoughts with a cup of coffee growing ever colder before him.

By the second week, Nelson began to orient himself. He told Hannah that he was sorry for his absence, both physically and emotionally.

'Time doesn't heal,' she told him. 'I know that much. But it does give us a degree of separation. And I'm here for you, no matter what.'

*

A little after eleven on the morning of Wednesday, July 5, Hannah was standing near the stove in the kitchen. She was mid-sentence, something about needing soap powder. For a moment she felt faint, and then she turned to Nelson and said, 'We need to call the hospital.'

Nelson looked at her and frowned.

'Call them and tell them I think my waters broke.'

'That's a good thing, right?' Nelson said.

'Before I go into labor, not so good.'

'But—'

'Call them, Garrett. Tell them we're coming.'

Nelson got up.

'Oh, Jesus,' Hannah exhaled.

'What? What's happening?'

'Help me sit.'

Garrett held her under the arms and walked her to a chair.

'Make the call,' she said. 'And then get me into the car.'

Nelson, his hands shaking, his heart triphammering in his chest, tried to get through to Dr Clarke. Clarke was off duty. He spoke to a nurse who barraged him with questions that went by in a blur.

'Can you drive her, or do we need to send an ambulance?' the nurse finally asked.

'I don't know. Do we need an ambulance?'

The nurse, evidently all-too-experienced with panicking fathers, paused for a moment.

'Can you drive, Mr Nelson?'

'Yes.'

'Do you have a car and do you know the way?'

'Yes I do, and yes, I know the way.'

'Is your wife conscious, coherent, able to move?'

'Yes, she is.'

'Okay, good. Then help her to the car, Mr Nelson. Make sure

she is comfortable. Then drive over to the hospital. That will be faster than sending an ambulance.'

'Okay, okay... yes, I'll do that now.'

'Excellent. We'll see you soon.'

Nelson hung up, turned to Hannah.

'We have to go to the hospital,' he said.

Hannah smiled weakly. 'You don't say?'

The roads were clear. Nelson covered the forty miles to Fort Myers in less than thirty minutes.

Arriving at the hospital, he pulled up outside the main entrance, left the engine running, and ran into the building.

Moments later he returned to find Hannah lying on the back seat of the car, her eyes closed. She was breathing but it was fast and shallow.

'Hannah!'

Opening one eye, she looked at him, her expression pained.

'They're sending people out with a gurney. Can you get up?'

Hannah grimaced.

Nelson walked around the back of the car and opened the rear door nearest her head.

Reaching in, he put his hands beneath her arms and helped her into a sitting position. Edging her slowly backwards towards him, he had her ease her legs down until her feet were on the floor of the car. Her breathing quickened. She looked pale and distressed.

Before he could ask her what was happening, two orderlies and a nurse appeared.

Swiftly, saying nothing, the orderlies moved Nelson out of the way and maneuvered Hannah out of the back of the car and onto the gurney.

Starting towards the ramp at the side of the main steps,

Nelson walked beside her, holding her hand, watching her as she seemed to gasp for every breath.

Once inside the hospital, the orderlies hurried on. Nelson started to follow, but the nurse grabbed his arm and slowed him.

'Mr Nelson, yes?'

'Yes, that's right?'

'Okay,' the nurse said calmly. 'You need to stay here. You have to fill out some paperwork and then—'

'I need to go with her,' Nelson said. 'And where's Dr Clarke?'

'Dr Clarke will be here shortly. Meanwhile, you need to let us do our jobs, okay?'

'But—'

'I understand your concerns, Mr Nelson. I really do. You can't go into the delivery room or the operating theater or anywhere else—'

'Operating theater? Why would she need to go into theater?'

'Okay,' the nurse said. 'Come with me.'

With that, the nurse turned and started walking. Nelson followed without a word.

Out behind reception was a waiting area with rows of seats.

The nurse indicated for Nelson to take a seat. He did so. The nurse sat facing him.

'Right now, your wife is being examined by one of the resident Ob Gyns. As soon as Dr Clarke arrives, she will take over the supervision and monitoring of…'

'Hannah,' Nelson said.

'Well, Hannah is exactly where she needs to be and she's being looked after by the very best people.'

'She said something about her waters breaking before she went into labor. She said that might not be so good. What does that mean? Why isn't it good?'

'There's something called premature rupture of membranes.

All it means is that the fluid that has surrounded and protected your baby has been released a little prematurely.'

'And what does that mean?'

'There are numerous and varied complications that can occur when it comes to delivering a baby, Mr Nelson. Every single one of them is something with which we are extraordinarily experienced. The people taking care of your wife don't do anything but deliver babies. Dr Clarke is one of the most qualified Ob Gyns in the state. She'll be here very soon. What you need to do – and I know this is going to be really difficult for you – is to try your very best to have confidence in the hospital staff and facilities. Do you think you can do that for Hannah?'

'Y-yes,' Nelson said. 'And what happens if—'

'We are taking care of everything, Mr Nelson, and we're going to keep you informed as often as we can about what's going on, okay?'

'Okay, yes. I'm sorry. I'm just... you know, this is the first time for both of us.'

'Fathers-to-be are no better the second time or the third time, believe me. You're not experiencing anything that hasn't been experienced a million times before. Delivering a baby is the most natural thing on Earth, and I'm sure it's going to be fine.'

The nurse got up.

'Thank you,' Nelson said.

'There's phones there if you want to call anyone. You have any questions, speak to the girl at reception and she can page one of us. We might not be able to get to you immediately, but we'll do our very best.'

The nurse smiled one more time, and then she put her hand on Nelson's shoulder reassuringly.

'Okay, good,' she said. 'Now I'm going to go and help Hannah.'

Nelson watched her walk away. He sat back in the chair. His hands were clammy, his gut a swarm of butterflies, and when he tried to stand he felt a little dizzy. Trying a second time, he got to his feet and headed for the phones.

Nelson got through to Miriam at the Clewiston house and told her that he and Hannah were over at the hospital in Fort Myers.

Miriam nearly dropped the phone. She said she'd get hold of Frank and they'd be over as quickly as they could.

'Do you need me to bring anything, Garrett?' she asked. 'Maybe something to eat?'

'Thank you, but I'm not hungry, Miriam,' Nelson said. 'Last thing in the world I feel like doing is eating.'

'I'll bring something anyway,' Miriam replied. 'No idea how long she'll be in labor and we can't have you starving to death, now can we?'

Nelson didn't argue. He told Miriam he'd see her soon and hung up.

Walking back to the window, Nelson raised his hand and placed it against the glass. Closing his eyes, he took a deep breath. A wave of darkness seemed to cloud his mind. Anticipation and doubt fused seamlessly into a profound sense of fear. Nelson was haunted by his conscience. He thought of the man he'd killed outside of Sebring. He thought of CJ Whitman, the others that had died in the chair during his time at Southern. And then he thought of Jimmy Christiansen's body being pulverised by one bullet after another, of how the man was already helpless, of how there was no reason in the world for him to have done what he did. But he'd done it anyway. He didn't know if the feeling of guilt that now seemed an inherent part of him could ever be washed away.

More than anything, he was afraid that there was a price he yet had to pay for everything that had happened.

79

Frank and Miriam Montgomery arrived at one.

'So, how's she doing?' Frank asked.

'I think she's fine,' Nelson said.

'Think?'

'I don't know, Frank. They haven't really told me anything. I spoke to a nurse when we came in and she assured me that they knew exactly what they were doing and that everything was going to be okay.'

Frank's expression was that of a man dissatisfied. 'I'll go find out,' he said.

Frank left for reception. Miriam walked with Nelson to the chairs near the window. Once seated, she started to produce sandwiches, bottles of soda, a flask of coffee, cold cuts, pieces of chicken in Saran wrap.

'Eat,' she said.

'It's really appreciated, Miriam, but—'

Miriam smiled. 'Eat, Garrett, or I'll have them put you on a drip.'

Garrett accepted the offered sandwich. He took a bite, chewed, swallowed, couldn't have said what was in it.

'I've had five, Garrett,' Miriam said. 'Five children. All of them were complicated.' She smiled. 'And most of them have stayed that way. Ray was the toughest. It was like he didn't want to be born.'

Nelson turned at the sound of voices.

Frank came through from reception, and right behind him was Dr Clarke.

'Mr Nelson,' she said cheerfully. 'How are you?'

Nelson got up.

'Sit, sit, sit,' Dr Clarke said.

Nelson sat.

Frank stood behind Miriam. Dr Clarke pulled up a chair and sat beside Nelson.

'Right,' she said. 'First things first. Hannah is fine. I'm sorry I haven't come and spoken to you earlier but we've been somewhat preoccupied.'

'So what's happening?' Nelson asked.

'She's in labor now. We had to induce. You know what that means, right?'

'Yes, I do.'

'Nurse Whittaker told me that she'd explained the premature rupture, yes?'

'Yes, she did.'

'That may have sounded alarming, but we induced labor right away and it's going as it should. Of course, we don't really have any notion of how long it will last, but we are monitoring everything very closely. The only issue we're dealing with right now is that Hannah's contractions aren't very strong. They're frequent enough, but—'

'Is that bad?' Nelson asked.

'It's not bad, Mr Nelson. It's just something that sometimes happens. If the contractions aren't strong enough, then there's a possibility we'll have to do a Caesarean section. We're not there yet, but that may very well be the way we have to go. And that, as we discussed when we first met, is often the case when a woman is Hannah's age.'

'So everything is normal?'

'When it comes to delivering babies, there's no such thing as normal, Mr Nelson. Every delivery is as unique as the baby. There are commonalities and differences, of course, and we have contingencies and protocols for every single one of them. As I'm sure Nurse Whittaker said, you just need to try your best to stay calm and let us get on with this. It won't go on for ever, and, believe me, whatever stresses you might be experiencing will just evaporate into nothing once your baby is born.'

Dr Clarke reached forward and squeezed Nelson's hand. She got up, acknowledged both Frank and Miriam, and then walked back the way she'd come.

Half an hour later, Nelson's nerves on fire, Miriam said she was going to go outside for some air.

Once she was out of earshot, Nelson looked at Frank.

'Say it,' Frank said. 'Whatever it is that's eating away at you. Now's the time to say it.'

Nelson got up. He walked to the window, walked back again, started to the window once again.

'Garrett,' Frank said emphatically. 'Sit down for Christ's sake.'

Nelson did as he was told.

Frank took the chair facing him. He didn't speak. He looked at Nelson unflinchingly.

'It's crazy, Frank. It's nothing...'

'Well, it's one or the other, Garrett. Either it's crazy or it's nothing.'

'I can't stop asking myself whether... whether there is... Jesus, I don't even know what I'm saying.'

'You don't think we all have the same thoughts? You, me,

Don Trent, hell maybe even Max Sheehan. You don't think it haunts us, too?'

'What we've done…'

'What we've done can't be undone, Garrett. And who's to say it wasn't the right thing to do anyway, eh? That's what we've convinced ourselves, and there doesn't seem to be a great deal of point trying to contradict that when there's nothing you can do to change it.'

'It doesn't stop me asking myself the same question over and over, Frank.'

'And what would that be, Garrett? You gonna start talking about karma now? About some universal fucking balance that makes sure everyone gets what's comin' to them? Is that what we're doing?'

'That's what I've been thinking about, yes.'

'And whoever the hell might be out there, whoever's in charge, they're so concerned about you and your life that they're gonna smash it to pieces because you followed the law and did your job and you were there when some really fuckin' bad people got what was comin' to them? You ever think about it from that viewpoint? Maybe they were the ones who got some karma, and you were just a means of bringing it about? You ever consider that possibility?'

Nelson shook his head.

'And what about Hannah? What's she ever done that would warrant something terrible happenin' to her?'

'Nothing,' Nelson replied. 'She's done nothing.'

'So your argument doesn't hold up, Garrett, not that it ever did in the first place. This shit is random. There ain't no preordained plan. There ain't no one lookin' over your shoulder, watchin' everything you do, figurin' out what was good and what was bad, keepin' a tally, you know? That is just so much horseshit. Hannah is gonna be fine. The baby is gonna be fine. And, God help us, if they ain't then it has not a single fucking thing to do with what happened at Southern.'

'You really believe that?'

'I don't believe it, Garrett, I *know* it.'

'Did you worry? You know, when Miriam was…'

Frank laughed reflexively. 'Worry? Jesus, I was a wreck. Every single time, too. And it didn't get no easier.'

'But Miriam was so much younger than Hannah.'

'She was yes, but Danny was the last one and he was born over thirty years ago, and they sure as hell didn't have the facilities they got now.'

'Right.'

'Right,' Frank said. 'So let's have a cup of coffee and another fuckin' tuna mayo sandwich and talk about something else, okay?'

Nelson smiled. 'Okay.'

Dr Clarke appeared once again at half past four.

Her demeanor, that of reassuring confidence, was no different, but when she spoke she said that a Caesarean section was the only way forward.

'What we have is something called cephalopelvic disproportion,' she said. 'It sounds dramatic, but all it means it that the size of the baby's head and Hannah's pelvis are mismatched. Trying to deliver a baby in such a scenario would bring undue pressure and constriction. That, combined with the fact that Hannah's contractions are still insufficiently strong, means that we risk the possibility of the placenta tearing away from the uterine wall. That may then lead to haemorrhaging and other complications. It's not a risk we're prepared to take. I'm not here to alarm you, but just to inform you that that's what we're now going to be doing.'

'Are they okay?' Nelson asked.

'It's been a difficult few hours,' Dr Clarke said, 'for both of them, but yes, right now they're okay.'

'Right now?'

'Don't interpret what I'm saying in a negative light, Mr Nelson. I know it's easy for me to say that, but—'

'They're going to be okay aren't they, Dr Clarke?'

'I have undertaken hundreds of C-sections, Mr Nelson. I know what I'm doing.'

Dr Clarke got up. She looked at Frank and Miriam.

'Mr Montgomery, Mrs Montgomery.'

She looked back at Nelson.

Nelson opened his mouth to ask another question. It never came. He was still trying to find it as Dr Clarke vanished out of sight.

80

An hour and a half later, a little after 6 p.m., Hannah gave birth to a daughter. She weighed six pounds and thirteen ounces. They named her Grace.

Garrett Nelson held her in his arms and, perhaps for the first time in his life, believed there might indeed be a God.

One by one, the rest of the Montgomerys – Brian, Danny, Ray and Charlene, Earl and Mary – arrived to visit. They brought flowers, balloons, soft toys, but most of all they brought a wave of love that seemed to swallow the past and bury it whole.

Hannah, though exhausted, stayed awake until the last of them had left. After that it was only herself and Nelson, and they watched their sleeping daughter, Nelson holding Hannah's hand, and they didn't say a word.

At last, Hannah drifted away. It wasn't long before Nelson, his nerves finally settled, closed his eyes and went to sleep in the chair beside the bed.

81

Nelson had once seen his life like a map.

There was a route, carefully planned, and he'd been certain of his destination. He carried the map with him always, studying it carefully, ensuring that he was taking the right road. Folding and unfolding it time and again, the creases became pronounced, and then began to fade, and after a while he did not see that he had diverged from the road.

In time, the landscape behind him obscured the point of departure. He didn't know where he'd come from, and he didn't know where he was going. He was lost. Finally, the destination was forgotten.

Stumbling through unfamiliar country, he'd often wished he could return to the people and places he'd known. Though dark, there was comfort there. Better the devil you know.

Fatherhood changed Nelson. It changed the way he felt about himself, and it changed his perception of the world.

The wonder and magic of existence had been lost, and through the eyes of his daughter, discovering everything for the first time, it was if he'd been given a second lease of life.

After Southern, Nelson stayed home for a month. There was not a second he wanted to miss.

At last, knowing he couldn't stay home for ever, he took a job with a lumber company. It was hard work, but he enjoyed it. He would find another job, another direction to take, but that would come in time.

He and Hannah stayed in Port LaBelle. They spoke of moving, but there was no hurry. They were close to the Montgomerys, and Nelson valued their support and friendship. If anything, Grace bound them all inextricably together. They were bonded by blood, and the bond was strong.

Frank applied for early retirement and it was granted. He would be out of Southern before the end of the fall. Ray intended to stay on in General Population. He and Charlene seemed to spend more time at the Nelsons than their own home. Charlene was wearing Ray down, like water on a stone. Nelson didn't doubt she'd be pregnant soon enough.

The Federal investigation at Southern dragged on interminably. Nelson heard that Max Sheehan had somehow evaded prosecution. He guessed he'd given up William Cain for the killings of David Garvey and Jackson Forsyth. Nelson didn't know the details, and he didn't want to know. Southern was now behind him, a faded crease in the map.

There were nights when Nelson lay awake thinking of CJ Whitman. There were nights he dreamed he was lost in the glades. The nightmares he had – growing ever more infrequent with time – were populated by his father, by Jimmy Christiansen, others that he'd known at Southern, all of them twisted together into images and shapes and sounds and emotions that were hard to distinguish from one another.

There were moments when he imagined he could hear the sound of the bell from the tower, and it seemed as real as the last time he'd heard it.

But then he would look at his daughter, and she would look back at him with such trust and love, and everything else disappeared.

On Thursday morning in the third week of August, Miriam, Hannah and Grace were visiting with Earl and Mary for the day.

Nelson had taken a day off. The car needed work and it was long overdue.

Miriam arrived a little after nine. Grace was hungry, and then she needed changing. By the time they left, it was past ten.

'There's chicken in the fridge. Coleslaw, too,' Hannah said. 'And some of that potato salad you like.'

'I'll be fine,' Nelson said. 'Go.'

Hannah kissed him. Nelson kissed Grace. He stood in the doorway and watched them until the car was out of sight.

Closing the door behind him, he stood for a moment in the silence of the hallway.

For a fleeting moment, he thought of his father – whether, as a child, he himself had been loved in the same way that Nelson loved his daughter, and then the thought was gone.

Like so many things now, the past was behind him and could stay where it was.

Clearing breakfast things from the kitchen table, Nelson heard the phone in the hallway.

He dried his hands quickly, hoping to catch it before the caller hung up.

'Garrett Nelson,' he said.

At the other end of the line was silence, but he knew someone was there.

'Hello?'

'Mr Nelson,' a woman said. Her voice was gentle, subdued.

'Yes, this is Garrett Nelson. Who's this?'

'You don't know me,' she said. 'Or perhaps you do.'

There was a sound in the street. It seemed to come from a thousand miles away.

'My name is Sarah,' the woman said.

'Sarah,' Nelson repeated.

'You know who I am, don't you?'

'You're Sarah O'Brien.'

Another pause, another hiatus, and Nelson's thoughts tumbled backwards and over themselves in a riot of words and emotions and half-remembered conversations.

'I've had your number for a long time,' Sarah said. 'You gave it to my friend.'

The image of Caroline Southwell's face. The small flash of hope he'd seen so quickly extinguished.

'Yes,' Nelson said.

'I haven't talked about it,' Sarah said. 'Not to anyone. I haven't been able to. I haven't wanted to. But now…' Her voice trailed off.

Nelson could sense the emotion at the other end of the line.

'Were you with him, Mr Nelson? When he…'

'I was, yes,' Nelson replied.

Again a long silence, and into that void was crowded every second, every moment of that day in the bell tower. The tears on CJ's face, the words he uttered, the last goodbye that Nelson gave in return.

'I wanted to know if we could meet,' Sarah said.

'Meet?'

'I understand if you—'

'No. Yes. Of course. Yes, we can meet.'

'Okay.'

'Are you still in Georgia?' Nelson asked.

'That's where I live, but I'm not there now.'

'Where are you?'

'I'm in Sarasota,' Sarah replied. 'I have … well, why I'm here doesn't matter.'

'Tell me where you are exactly,' Nelson said. 'I'll come and see you.'

'Now?'

'Yes, I can come now. Unless—'

'No,' Sarah said. She hesitated. 'I've thought about this for a long time, Mr Nelson. I guess I'm afraid. But it's been difficult …'

'Tell me where we can meet, Sarah,' Nelson said.

'There's a diner. It's on the way to Sarasota. Are you coming north?'

'Yes, from Port LaBelle.'

'It's on 758 just outside Coral Cove. I'll give you the address.'

Nelson fetched a pen and paper. She told him and he wrote it down.

'Two hours,' Nelson said.

Silence.

'I'll be there in two hours,' Nelson repeated.

'Okay,' Sarah replied.

The line went dead.

82

Sarah O'Brien was not the person Nelson expected her to be.

Had he been asked, he would not have known how to answer, but he wouldn't have described the young woman who entered the diner, at once looking for him, uncertain, cautious, self-conscious.

Nelson knew it was her, however. He stood up. She caught his eye. He smiled and nodded. She walked towards him.

Of average height and build, her dark hair cut short, her dress that of a million other women in a thousand other cities, she yet possessed a presence. That was the only word Nelson could find. There was something about her that was both vulnerable and strong.

'Mr Nelson,' she said.

'Miss O'Brien.'

Sarah sat down.

For thirty seconds or more they said nothing. They merely looked at one another as if each hoped to understand something of the person before them. They were strangers, but they were connected, and connected through something that was founded in pain and loss and a shared history they perhaps both wished to forget.

But they were here to remember, and they knew that, too.

A waitress fussed. She took orders for coffee. She smiled, attempted a few moments of small talk, but it was as if she floated in some other world that was disconnected from whatever was happening at the table.

The coffee arrived. Still neither Nelson nor Sarah spoke.

At one moment, Sarah glanced to her left and out of the window.

'I have someone,' she said. 'In the car. A friend. They brought me here.'

'Okay,' Nelson said.

'I won't stay long,' Sarah said. 'I just wanted…' She smiled. 'To be honest, I don't know what I wanted, Mr Nelson.'

'I feel like I know you,' Nelson said. 'It's a foolish thought, but there it is.'

'So you were with—'

'CJ.'

Sarah smiled again. 'Clarence.'

'Clarence, yes. I was with him.'

'To the end.'

'Yes.'

Tears welled in Sarah's eyes. She took a handkerchief from her purse.

'He saved my life,' Sarah said.

'I know,' Nelson replied. 'Caroline told me about your husband.'

'No. That's not what I mean.'

Nelson frowned.

'He… he…' Sarah's breath hitched in her throat. She held the handkerchief to her face. Her chest rose and fell as she sobbed silently.

Nelson said nothing. He didn't move.

Looking up, her mascara streaked, her eyes wide, Sarah started to apologize.

'It's okay,' Nelson said. 'You can tell me.'

'It's not easy,' Sarah said. 'To say what happened. But I have to. I don't know that I can go on any longer without telling someone the truth.'

Nelson knew then. He sensed it.

'He didn't kill Garth, did he?'

Sarah looked up.

'But he said he did. For you.'

Sarah lowered her head. She didn't cry, but she breathed deeply – in out, in out – as if it was taking every ounce of her strength and will to hold back the grief.

'Not just for me,' she said.

She turned then, raised her hand.

Nelson saw movement to his right. The car door opened. A woman stepped out, someone Nelson had never seen before. She leaned down, stood up again, and then she came around the side of the car, passing out of Nelson's line of sight.

Moments later, the woman entered the diner.

Beside her, holding her hand, was a young boy. Nelson felt his heart stop in his chest.

Sarah turned. The boy came towards her, smiling.

Reaching them, she held out her hand and he took it. The boy looked at his mother, and then at Nelson.

'This is a friend of mine,' Sarah said to the boy. 'His name is Mr Nelson.'

The boy smiled but didn't speak.

Turning to Nelson, she said, 'This is my son, Charlie. Charles Jefferson O'Brien. He's going to be eight in August.' She paused, smiled. 'His friends call him CJ.'

They left a little while later. There was nothing left to say, and Nelson knew they would never speak again.

Perhaps, in some earlier life, he would have questioned his

conscience. He would have asked himself if it was right to let someone take a life and then go free. Now he had no such thought. Now he himself was a father, and he understood a language that only a parent could ever truly comprehend. His was a different life, and the person he'd once been now no longer existed.

Clarence Whitman had given his life for Sarah, for his own child – for love – and that, beyond all things, should never be tarnished with the burden of guilt.

Credits

RJ Ellory and Orion Fiction would like to thank everyone at Orion who worked on the publication of *The Bell Tower* in the UK.

Editorial
Celia Killen
Emad Akhtar
Sarah O'Hara
Millie Prestidge

Copyeditor
Clare Wallis

Proofreader
Linda Joyce

Audio
Paul Stark
Louise Richardson

Design
Tomás Almeida
Joanna Ridley

Contracts
Dan Herron
Ellie Bowker
Oliver Chacón

Editorial Management
Charlie Panayiotou
Jane Hughes
Bartley Shaw

Finance
Jasdip Nandra
Nick Gibson
Sue Baker

Publicity
Leanne Oliver
Jenna Petts

Marketing
Tom Noble
Javerya Iqbal
Hennah Sandhu

Production
Ameenah Khan

Operations
Jo Jacobs
Dan Stevens

Sales
Jen Wilson
Esther Waters
Victoria Laws
Toluwalope Ayo-Ajala
Karin Burnik
Frances Doyle
Rachael Hum
Ellie Kyrke-Smith
Sinead White
Georgina Cutler